Praise for *The Flatshare*

'The new Jojo Moyes . . . This has all the ingredients of *Me Before You*'
Cosmopolitan

'Deliciously funny and truly uplifting, this is a heartwarming story of
friendship, love and starting over'
Lucy Diamond

'Utterly charming . . . a Richard Curtis rom-com that also has its feet
firmly planted in real life . . . above all else, it's funny and winning'
Stylist

'It's funny and charming but there are moments of real poignancy,
too. Guaranteed to leave you with a smile on your face'
Good Housekeeping

'*The Flatshare* is a huge, heartwarming triumph'
Josie Silver

'Set to become the romcom of the year with its loveable characters,
comic situations and deeply satisfying love story – a *Sleepless In Seattle*
for the 21st century'
Sunday Express

'I loved the way various strands of Tiffy and Leon's lives were
crocheted together . . . A warm, colourful, unique story and a
thoroughly enjoyable read'
Sarah Haywood

'One of the most talked about books of 2019 . . . Fans of
Jojo Moyes's *Me Before You* will love this UpLit romcom'
Red Magazine

'Funny, emotional and uplifting . . . you'll devour
this well-written debut'
Sun

'There's no denying the sparky charm of this rather quirky love story'
Sunday Mirror

Beth O'Leary studied English at university before going into children's publishing. She lives as close to the courntryside as she can get while still being in reach of London, and wrote *The Flatshare* on her train journey to and from work. She is now writing novels full-time and if she's not at her desk, you'll usually find her curled up somewhere with a book, a cup of tea and several woolly jumpers (whatever the weather).

THE
FLAT
SHARE

BETH O'LEARY

Quercus

First published in Great Britain in 2019
This paperback edition published in 2020 by

Quercus Editions Ltd
Carmelite House
50 Victoria Embankment
London EC4Y 0DZ

An Hachette UK company

A CIP catalogue record for this book is available
from the British Library

PB ISBN 978 1 78747 441 3
EB ISBN 978 1 78747 439 0

12

Typeset by CC Book Production

Printed and bound in Great Britain by Clays Ltd, Elcograf S.p.A.

Papers used by Quercus are from well-managed forests and other responsible sources.

For Sam

FEBRUARY

1

Tiffy

You've got to say this for desperation: it makes you much more open-minded.

I really can see some positives in this flat. The technicolour mould on the kitchen wall will scrub off, at least in the short term. The filthy mattress can be replaced fairly cheaply. And you could definitely make the argument that the mushrooms growing behind the toilet are introducing a fresh, outdoorsy feel to the place.

Gerty and Mo, however, are not desperate, and they are not trying to be positive. I would describe their expressions as 'aghast'.

'You can't live here.'

That's Gerty. She's standing with her heeled boots together and her elbows tucked in tightly, as though occupying as little space as possible in protest at being here at all. Her hair is pulled back in a low bun, already pinned so she can easily slip on the barrister's wig she wears for court. Her expression would be comical if it weren't my actual life we are discussing here.

'There must be somewhere else within budget, Tiff,' Mo says worriedly, bobbing up from where he was examining the boiler cupboard. He looks even more dishevelled than usual, helped by the cobweb now hanging from his beard. 'This is even worse than the one we viewed last night.'

I look around for the estate agent; he's thankfully well out of ear-shot, smoking on the 'balcony' (the sagging roof of the neighbour's garage, definitely not designed for walking on).

'I'm not looking around another one of these hellholes,' Gerty says, glancing at her watch. It's 8 a.m. – she'll need to be at Southwark Crown Court for nine. 'There must be another option.'

'*Surely* we can fit her in at ours?' Mo suggests, for about the fifth time since Saturday.

'Honestly, would you stop with that?' Gerty snaps. 'That is not a long-term solution. And she'd have to sleep standing up to even fit anywhere.' She gives me an exasperated look. 'Couldn't you have been shorter? We could have put you under the dining table if you were less than five nine.'

I make an apologetic face, but really I'd prefer to stay here than on the floor of the tiny, eye-wateringly expensive flat Mo and Gerty jointly invested in last month. They've never lived together before, even when we were at university. I'm concerned that it may well be the death of their friendship. Mo is messy, absent-minded and has this uncanny ability to take up an enormous amount of room despite being relatively small. Gerty, on the other hand, has spent the last three years living in a preternaturally clean flat, so perfect that it looked computer-generated. I'm not sure how the two lifestyles will overlay without West London imploding.

The main problem, though, is if I'm crashing on someone's floor I can just as easily go back to Justin's place. And, as of 11 p.m. Thursday, I have officially decided that I cannot be allowed that option any longer. I need to move forward, and I need to commit to somewhere so I can't go back.

Mo rubs his forehead, sinking down into the grimy leather sofa. 'Tiff, I could lend you some . . .'

'I don't want you to lend me any money,' I say, more sharply than

I mean to. 'Look, I *really* need to get this sorted this week. It's this place or the flatshare.'

'The bedshare, you mean,' Gerty says. 'Can I ask why it has to be *now*? Not that I'm not delighted. Just that last I checked you were sitting tight in that flat waiting for the next time he-who-must-not-be-named deigned to drop by.'

I wince, surprised. Not at the sentiment – Mo and Gerty never liked Justin, and I know they hate that I'm still living at his place, even though he's hardly ever there. It's just unusual to hear Gerty bring him up directly. After the final peace-making dinner with the four of us ended in a furious row, I gave up on trying to make everyone get along and just stopped talking to Gerty and Mo about him altogether. Old habits die hard – even post break-up we've all dodged around discussing him.

'And why does it have to be *so* cheap?' Gerty goes on, ignoring the warning look from Mo. 'I know you're paid a pittance, but, really, Tiffy, four hundred a month is impossible in London. Have you actually thought about all this? Properly?'

I swallow. I can feel Mo watching me carefully. That's the trouble with having a counsellor as a friend: Mo is basically an accredited mind-reader, and he never seems to switch his superpowers off. 'Tiff?' he says gently.

Oh, bloody hell, I'll just have to show them. There's nothing else for it. Quickly and all at once, that's the best way – like pulling off a plaster, or getting into cold water, or telling my mother I broke something ornamental from the living-room dresser.

I reach for my phone and pull up the Facebook message.

Tiffy,

I'm really disappointed in how you acted last night. You were completely out of line. It's my flat, Tiffy – I can come by whenever I like, with whoever I like.

I would have expected you to be more grateful for me letting you stay. I know us breaking up has been hard on you – I know you're not ready to leave. But if you think that means you can start trying to 'lay down some rules' then it's time you paid me for the past three months of rent. And you're going to need to pay full rent going forwards too. Patricia says you're taking advantage of me, living in my place pretty much for free, and even though I've always stood up for you with her, after yesterday's performance I can't help thinking she might be right.

Justin xx

My stomach twists when I reread that line, *you're taking advantage of me*, because I never intended to do that. I just didn't know that when he left he really meant it this time.

Mo finishes reading first. 'He "popped in" again on Thursday? With Patricia?'

I look away. 'He has a point. He's been really good to let me stay there this long.'

'Funny,' Gerty says darkly, 'I've always had the distinct impression he likes keeping you there.'

She makes it sound weird, but I sort of feel the same way. When I'm still in Justin's flat, it isn't really over. I mean, all the other times, he's come back eventually. But . . . then I met Patricia on Thursday. The real-life, extremely attractive, actually quite lovely woman Justin has left me for. There's never been another woman before.

Mo reaches for my hand; Gerty takes the other. We stay like this, ignoring the estate agent smoking outside the window, and I let myself cry for a moment, just one fat tear down each cheek.

'So, anyway,' I say brightly, withdrawing my hands to wipe my eyes, 'I need to move out. Now. Even if I wanted to stay and risk him bringing Patricia back again, I can't afford the rent, and I owe Justin a ton of money, and I really don't want to borrow from anyone, I'm kind of sick of not paying for things myself, to be honest, so . . . yes. It's this or the flatshare.'

Mo and Gerty exchange a look. Gerty closes her eyes in pained resignation.

'Well, you clearly cannot live here.' She opens her eyes and holds out a hand. 'Show me that advert again.'

I hand her my phone, flicking from Justin's message to the Gumtree ad for the flatshare.

Double bedroom in sunny one-bed Stockwell flat, rent £350 per month including bills. Available immediately, for six months minimum.

Flat (and room/bed) is to share with twenty-seven-year-old palliative care nurse who works nights and is away weekends. Only ever in the flat 9 a.m. to 6 p.m. Monday to Friday. All yours the rest of the time! Perfect for someone with 9 to 5 job.

To view, contact L. Twomey – details below.

It's not just sharing a flat, Tiff, it's sharing a bed. Sharing a bed is *odd*,' Mo says worriedly.

'What if this L. Twomey is a man?' Gerty asks.

I'm prepared for this one. 'It doesn't matter,' I say calmly. 'It's not like we'd ever be in the bed at the same time – or the flat, even.'

This is uncomfortably close to what I said when justifying staying at Justin's place last month, but never mind.

'You'd be sleeping with him, Tiffany!' Gerty says. 'Everyone knows the first rule of flatsharing is don't sleep with your flatmate.'

'I don't think this sort of arrangement is what people are referring to,' I tell her wryly. 'You see, Gerty, sometimes when people say "sleeping together", what they really mean is—'

Gerty gives me a long, level look. 'Yes, thank you, Tiffany.'

Mo's sniggering stops abruptly when Gerty turns her glare on him. 'I'd say the first rule of flatsharing is to make sure you get on with the person before you move in,' he says, cannily redirecting the glare to me again. '*Especially* in these circumstances.'

'Obviously I'll meet this L. Twomey person first. If we don't get on, I won't take it.'

After a moment Mo gives me a nod and squeezes my shoulder. We all descend into the kind of silence that comes after you've talked about something difficult – half grateful for it being over, half relieved to have managed it at all.

'Fine,' Gerty says. 'Fine. Do what you need to do. It's got to be better than living in this kind of squalor.' She marches out of the flat, turning at the last moment to address the estate agent as he steps through from the balcony. 'And you,' she tells him loudly, 'are a curse upon society.'

He blinks as she slams the front door. There is a long, awkward pause.

He stubs out his cigarette. 'You interested, then?' he asks me.

I get to work early and sink down in my chair. My desk is the closest thing to home at the moment. It's a haven of half-crafted objects, things that have proven too heavy to take back on the bus, and pot plants arranged in such a way that I can see people approaching before they can tell whether I'm at my desk. My pot-plant wall is widely regarded among the other junior staff as an inspiring example of interior design. (Really it's just about choosing plants the same colour as your hair – in my case, red – and ducking/running away when you catch sight of anyone moving purposefully.)

My first job of the day is to meet Katherin, one of my favourite authors. Katherin writes books about knitting and crochet. It's a niche audience that buys them, but that's the story of Butterfingers Press – we love a niche audience. We specialise in crafting and DIY books. Tie-dye bedsheets, design your own dresses, crochet yourself a lampshade, make all your furniture out of ladders . . . That sort of thing.

I love working here. This is the only possible explanation for the fact that I have been Assistant Editor for three and a half years, earning below the London living wage, and have made no attempt to rectify the situation by, say, applying for a job at a publishing house that actually makes money. Gerty likes to tell me that I lack ambition, but it really isn't that. I just love this stuff. As a child, I spent my days reading, or tinkering with my toys until they suited me better: dip-dying Barbie's hair, pimping up my JCB truck. And now I read and craft for a living.

Well, not really a living, as such. But a bit of money. Just about enough to pay tax.

'I'm telling you, Tiffy, crochet is the next colouring books,' Katherin tells me, once she's settled herself down in our best meeting room and talked me through the plan for her next book. I examine the finger she's waggling in my direction. She has about fifty rings on each hand, but I've yet to discern whether any of them are wedding or engagement rings (I imagine that if Katherin has any, she'll have more than one).

Katherin is just on the acceptable side of eccentric: she has a straw-blonde plait, one of those tans that somehow ages well, and endless stories of breaking into places in the 1960s and peeing on things. She was a real rebel once. She refuses to wear a bra even to this day, when bras have become quite comfortable and women have mostly given up on fighting the power because Beyoncé is doing it for us.

'That'd be good,' I say. 'Maybe we could add a strapline with the word "mindful" in it. It *is* quite mindful, isn't it? Or mindless?'

Katherin laughs, tipping her head back. 'Ah, Tiffy. Your job's ridic-ulous.' She pats my hand affectionately and then reaches for her handbag. 'You see that Martin boy,' she says, 'you tell him I'll only do that cruise day class if I have a glamorous young assistant.'

I groan. I know where this is going. Katherin likes to drag me along to these things – for any class she needs a live model to show how to measure as you go when you're designing an outfit, apparently, and I once made the fatal error of offering myself up for the job when she couldn't find anyone. Now I am her go-to choice. PR is so desperate to get Katherin into these sorts of events that they've started begging me too.

'This is too far, Katherin. I'm not going on a cruise with you.'

'But it's free! People pay thousands for those, Tiffy!'

'You're only joining them for the Isle of Wight loop,' I remind her. Martin has already briefed me on this one. 'And it's on a weekend. I don't work weekends.'

'It's not work,' Katherin insists, gathering her notes and packing them into her handbag in an entirely random order. 'It's a lovely Saturday sailing trip with one of your friends.' She pauses. 'Me,' she clarifies. 'We're friends, aren't we?'

'I am your editor!' I say, bundling her out of the meeting room.

'Think about it, Tiffy!' she calls over her shoulder, unperturbed. She catches sight of Martin, who is already making a beeline for her from over by the printers. 'I'm not doing it unless she is, Martin, my boy! She's the one you need to talk to!'

And then she's gone, the grubby glass doors of our office swinging behind her.

Martin turns on me. 'I like your shoes,' he says, with a charming smile. I shudder. I can't stand Martin from PR. He says things like 'let's action that' in meetings, and clicks his fingers at Ruby, who is a Marketing Exec, but who Martin seems to think is his personal assistant. He's only twenty-three, but has decided it will further his merciless pursuit of seniority if he can seem older than he is, so he always puts on this awful jocular voice and tries to talk to our MD about golf.

The shoes *are* excellent, though. They're purple Doc Marten-style boots, with white lilies painted on them, and they took me most of

Saturday. My crafting and customising has really upped since Justin left me. 'Thanks, Martin,' I say, already attempting to sidle back to the security of my desk.

'Leela mentioned that you're looking for somewhere to live,' Martin says.

I hesitate. I'm not sure where this is going. I sense nowhere good.

'Me and Hana' – a woman in Marketing who always sneers at my fashion sense – 'have a spare room. You might have seen on Facebook, but I thought maybe I should bring it up, you know, IRL. It's a single bed, but, well, I guess that won't be a problem for you these days. As we're friends, Hana and I decided we could offer it for five hundred a month, plus bills.'

'That's so kind of you!' I say. 'But I've actually *just* found somewhere.' Well, I sort of have. Nearly. Oh, God, if L. Twomey won't have me, will I have to live with Martin and Hana? I mean, I already spend every working day with them, and frankly that is plenty of Martin-and-Hana time for me. I'm not sure my (already shaky) resolve to leave Justin's place can withstand the idea of Martin chasing me for rent payments and Hana seeing me in my porridge-stained *Adventure Time* pyjamas every morning.

'Oh. Right, well. We'll have to find someone else, then.' Martin's expression turns cunning. He has smelled guilt. 'You could make it up to me by going with Katherin to that—'

'No.'

He gives an exaggerated sigh. 'God, Tiffy. It's a free cruise! Don't you go on cruises all the time?'

I *used* to go on cruises all the time, when my wonderful and now ex-boyfriend used to take me on them. We'd sail from Caribbean island to Caribbean island in a sunny haze of romantic bliss. We'd explore European cities and then head back to the boat for incredible sex in our tiny little bunk. We'd stuff ourselves at the all-you-can-eat buffet and then lie out on the deck watching the gulls circle above us as we talked idly of our future children.

'Gone off them,' I say, reaching for the phone. 'Now, if you'll excuse me, I have to make a call.'

2

Leon

Phone rings as Doctor Patel is prescribing meds for Holly (little girl with leukaemia). Bad timing. Very bad timing. Doctor Patel not happy at interruption, and makes her feelings clear. Seems to have forgotten that I, too, as night nurse, should have gone home at 8 a.m., and yet am still here dealing with ill people and grouchy consultants like Doctor Patel.

Hang up when it rings, obviously. Make mental note to listen to voicemail and change ringtone to something less embarrassing (this one is called 'Jive' and is far too funky for hospice setting. Not that funk does not have role in place of sickness, just that is not *always* appropriate).

Holly: Why didn't you answer? Isn't that rude? What if it was your girlfriend with the short hair?

Dr Patel: What's rude is leaving your mobile on loud during a ward round. Though I'm surprised whoever-it-was even tried ringing him at this hour.

A glance at me, half irritable, half amused.

Dr Patel: You may have noticed that Leon is not a big talker, Holly.

Leans in, conspiratorial.

Dr Patel: One of the registrars has a theory. He says that Leon has a limited number of words to use each shift, and when it gets to this time of day, he's entirely run out.

Don't grace this with a response.

Speaking of girlfriend with short hair: haven't told Kay about the room thing yet. Not had time. Also, am avoiding inevitable conflict. But really must call her later this morning.

Tonight was good. Mr Prior's pain lessened enough that he could start telling me about the man he fell in love with in the trenches: a dark-haired charmer called Johnny White, with the chiselled jaw of a Hollywood star and a twinkle in his eye. They had one fraught, romantic, war-torn summer, then were split up. Johnny White was taken to hospital for shellshock. They never saw each other again. Mr Prior could've got in lots of trouble (homosexuality vexing to military sorts).

I was tired, coffee buzz dying, but stayed with Mr Prior after hand-over. The man never gets visitors and loves to talk when he can. Failed to escape conversation without a scarf (my fourteenth from Mr Prior). Can only say no a certain number of times, and Mr Prior knits so fast I wonder why anyone bothered with the Industrial Revolution. Pretty sure he's faster than a machine.

Listen to voicemail after eating dangerously reheated chicken stir-fry in front of last week's *Masterchef*.

Voicemail: Hi, is that L. Twomey? Oh, shite, you can't answer – I always do this on voicemails. OK, I'm just going to proceed on the assumption that you're L. Twomey. My name's Tiffy Moore and I'm ringing about the Gumtree ad, about a room? Look, my friends think it's weird that we'd be sharing a bed, even though it'd be at different times, but it doesn't bother me if it doesn't bother you, and to be honest I'd do pretty much anything for a central London flat I can move into right away at that price. [Pause] Oh, God, not anything. There's *loads* of things I wouldn't do. I'm not like . . . No, Martin, not *now*, can't you see I'm on the phone?

Who is Martin? A child? Does this rambly woman with Essex accent want to bring a child into my flat?

Voicemail continues: Sorry, that's my colleague, he wants me to go on a cruise with a middle-aged lady to talk to pensioners about crochet.

Not the explanation I was expecting. Better, definitely, but begs many questions.

Voicemail continues: Look, just call me back or text me if the room's still available? I'm super tidy, I'll keep right out of your way and I'm still in the habit of cooking double quantities of my dinner so if you like home-cooked food I can leave leftovers.

She reads out her number. Just in time, I remember to jot it down.

Woman is annoying, definitely. And is female, which may vex Kay. But only two other people have called: one asked if I had a problem with pet hedgehogs (answer: not unless they are living in my flat) and other was definitely a drug dealer (not being judgemental – was offered drugs during call). I need £350 extra a month if I'm going to keep paying Sal without Kay's help. This is the only available plan. Plus, will never actually see annoying woman. Will only ever be in when annoying woman is out.

I text her.

Hi there, Tiffy. Thanks for your voicemail. Would be great to meet you and talk about the arrangement for my flat. How is Saturday morning? Cheers, Leon Twomey.

Nice, normal-person message. Resist all urges to ask about Martin's cruise-ship plan, though find myself curious.

She replies almost instantly.

Hi! Sounds great. 10 a.m. at the flat itself, then? x

Let's make it 9 a.m., or I'll fall asleep! See you then. Address is on the ad.
Cheers, Leon.

There. Done. Easy: £350 a month, almost in the bag already.
Now to tell Kay.

3

Tiffy

So, naturally I get curious and google him. Leon Twomey is a pretty unusual name, and I find him on Facebook without having to employ the creepy stalker techniques I reserve for new writers I'm trying to poach from other publishing houses.

It's a relief to see that he's not my type at all, which will definitely simplify things – if Justin did ever meet Leon, for instance, I don't think he'd see him as a threat. He's got light-brown skin and thick, curly hair long enough to be pushed back behind his ears, and he's way too gangly for me. All elbows and neck, you know the type. He looks like a nice guy, though – in every photo he's doing this sweet lopsided smile that doesn't seem at all creepy or murderous, though actually if you look at a picture with that idea in mind everyone starts to look like an axe-wielding killer, so I try to put the thought out of my head. He looks friendly and unthreatening. These are good things.

However, I do now know unequivocally that he is a man.

Am I actually willing to share a bed with a man? Even sharing a bed with Justin was a bit horrible sometimes, and we were in a relationship. His side of the mattress sagged in the middle and he didn't always shower in between getting home from the gym and going to bed, so there was a sort of . . . sweaty smell to his bit of the duvet. I always had to make extra sure it was the same way up so I didn't get the sweaty side.

But still. £350 per month. And he would never actually *be* there.

'Tiffany!'

My head shoots up. Crap, that's Rachel, and I know what she wants. She wants the manuscript for this bloody *Make a Stir Bake and Make* book that I've been ignoring all day.

'Don't try sneaking off to the kitchen or pretending to be on the phone,' she says, from over my wall of pot plants. This is the trouble with having friends at work: you drunkenly tell them your tricks when the two of you go to the pub, and then you're defenceless.

'You've had your hair done!' I say. It's a desperate ploy to redirect the conversation early, but her hair *is* especially cool today. It's in braids, as always, but this time the tiny plaits have bright turquoise ribbon laced between them like corset strings. 'How do you braid it like that?'

'Don't try to distract me with my *Mastermind* specialist subject, Tiffany Moore,' Rachel says, tapping her perfectly polka-dotted nails. 'When am I getting that manuscript?'

'I just need . . . a *little* longer . . .' I put my hand over the papers in front of me so she can't see the page numbers, which are in the single digits.

She narrows her eyes. 'Thursday?'

I nod eagerly. Yeah, why not? I mean, that's totally unachievable at this point, but Friday sounds a lot better when you're saying it on Thursday, so I'll just tell her then.

'And go for a drink with me tomorrow night?'

I pause. I was meant to be good and not spend *any* money this week, on account of the looming debt, but nights out with Rachel are always brilliant, and frankly I could really do with having some fun. Besides, she won't be able to argue with me about this manuscript on Thursday if she's hungover.

'Done.'

•

Drunk Man No. 1 is the expressive kind. The sort of drunk who likes to throw his arms out wide regardless of what might be directly to his left or right (so far, that's included one large fake palm tree, one tray of sambuca shots, and one relatively famous Ukrainian model). Every movement is exaggerated, even the basic walking steps – you know, left foot out in front, right foot out, repeat. Drunk Man No. 1 makes walking look like the hokey-cokey.

Drunk Man No. 2 is the deceitful sort. He keeps his face very still when he's listening to you, as though the absence of expression will make it clear how very sober he is. He nods occasionally, and fairly convincingly, but doesn't quite blink enough. His attempts to stare at your boobs are much less subtle than he thinks they are.

I wonder what they think of me and Rachel. They headed straight for us, but that's not conclusively positive. Back when I was with Justin, if I was going out clubbing with Rachel he would always remind me that lots of men see 'quirky girl' and think 'desperate and easy'. He's right, as per usual. I actually wonder if it's easier to get laid as a quirky girl than a perky cheerleader type: you're more approachable, and nobody assumes you've already got a boyfriend. Which is probably another reason Justin wasn't a fan of my nights out with Rachel, on reflection.

'So, like, books about how to make cakes?' says Drunk Man No. 2, thus proving his listening skills and aforementioned sobriety. (Honestly. What's the point in having sambuca shots if you're just going to pretend you haven't been drinking all night?)

'Yeah!' Rachel says. 'Or build shelves or make clothes or . . . or . . . what do *you* like to do?'

She is drunk enough to find Drunk Man No. 2 attractive, but I suspect she's just trying to keep him busy to open the floor for me to jump Drunk Man No. 1. Of the two, Drunk Man No. 1 is clearly preferable – he is tall enough, for starters. This is the first challenge. I'm six foot, and though I have no problem with dating shorter men, it often seems to bother guys if I'm more than an inch or two taller than them. That's fine by me – I've no interest in the ones who care about that sort of thing. It's a useful filter.

'What do I like to do?' repeats Drunk Man No. 2. 'I like to dance with beautiful women at bars with bad names and overpriced drinks.' He flashes a sudden grin, which, though a little more sluggish and wonky than it's probably intended to be, is actually quite attractive.

I can see Rachel is thinking the same. She shoots me a calculating look – not so drunk as all that, then – and I can see her evaluating the situation between me and Drunk Man No. 1.

I look at Drunk Man No. 1 too, and do some evaluating of my own. He's tall, with nice broad shoulders and hair that's greying at the temples in a way that's actually quite sexy. He's probably mid-thirties – he could be a little 1990s Clooney-ish if you squinted a bit or dimmed the lights.

Do I fancy him? If I do, I could sleep with him. You can do that when you're single.

Weird.

I've not thought about sleeping with anyone since Justin. You get tons of time back when you're single and not having sex – not just the actual time doing it, but the time shaving legs, buying nice underwear, wondering whether all other women get bikini waxes, etc. It's a real plus. Of course, there's the overwhelming absence of one of the greatest aspects of your adult life, but you do get much more admin done.

Obviously I know that we broke up three months ago. I know that in theory I can have sex with other people. But . . . I can't help thinking about what Justin would say. How angry he'd be. I may be technically allowed, but I'm not . . . you know. *Allowed* allowed. Not in my head, not yet.

Rachel gets it. 'Sorry, mate,' she says, patting Drunk Man No. 2 on the arm. '*I* like to dance with my friend.' She scribbles her number on a napkin – God knows where she got that pen from, the woman's a magician – and then my hand is in hers and we're winding our way into the centre of the dance floor where the music hits my skull from both sides, sending my eardrums shivering.

'What kind of drunk are you?' Rachel asks, as we grind inappropriately to classic Destiny's Child.

'I'm a bit . . . *thoughtful*,' I shout at her. 'Too analytical to sleep with that nice man.'

She reaches for a drink from the tray of one of those shot ladies who wanders around asking you to overpay for things, and hands the woman some cash.

'"Not enough" sort of drunk, then,' she says, giving me the drink. 'You may be an editor, but no drunk girl trots out the word "analytical".'

'Assistant editor,' I remind her, and knock back the drink. Jägerbomb. It's strange how something so fundamentally disgusting, whose very aftertaste makes you want to vomit the next day, can taste delicious on a dance floor.

Rachel plies me with drink all night and flirts with every wingman in sight, chucking all attractive men in my direction. Whatever she says, I am plenty tipsy enough, so I don't think much of it – she's just being an excellent friend. The night spins by in a mass of dancers and brightly coloured drinks.

It is only when Mo and Gerty arrive that I start to wonder what this night out is all about.

Mo has the look of a man who was summoned on short notice. His beard is a little skewwhiff, like he slept on it funny, and he's in a worn-out T-shirt I think I remember from uni – though it's a little tighter on him now. Gerty looks haughtily beautiful, as usual, with no make-up on, and her hair yanked up in a ballerina topknot; it's hard to tell if she was planning to come because she never wears make-up, and dresses impeccably all the time anyway. She could well have just pulled on a slightly higher pair of heels to go with her skinny jeans last minute.

They're making their way across the dance floor. My suspicion that Mo was not planning to be here is confirmed – he's not dancing. Take Mo to a club and there will always be dancing. So why have they turned up on my random Wednesday night out with Rachel? They don't even know her that well – only through the odd birthday drinks or housewarming parties. In fact, Gerty and Rachel have a low-level alpha-wolf feud going on, and when we do all get together they usually end up bickering.

Is it my birthday? I drunkenly wonder. Do I have exciting surprise news?

I turn to Rachel. 'Wha—?'

'Table,' she says, pointing at the booths at the back of the club.

Gerty does a relatively good job of hiding her irritation at being redirected just when she's battled her way through to the centre of the dance floor.

I'm getting bad vibes. I'm just at the happiest point of drunk, though, so I'm willing to suspend worried thoughts in the hope that they're coming to tell me that I've won a four-week holiday to New Zealand or something.

But no.

'Tiffy, I didn't know how to tell you this,' Rachel is saying, 'so this was the best plan I could come up with. Get you happy drunk, remind you what flirting feels like, then call your support team.' She reaches to take both my hands. 'Tiffy. Justin is engaged.'

4

Leon

Conversation re flat not at all as predicted. Kay was unusually angry. Seemed upset at idea of someone else sleeping in my bed besides her? But she never comes round. Hates the dark-green walls and elderly neighbours – is part of her 'you spend too much time with old people' thing. We're always at hers (light-grey walls, cool young neighbours).

Argument ends at weary impasse. She wants me to pull down ad and cancel Essex woman; I'm not changing my mind. It's the best idea for getting easy cash every month that I've thought of, bar lottery winning, which cannot be factored in to financial planning. Do not want to go back to borrowing that £350. Kay was the one who said it: it wasn't good for our relationship.

She's come that far, so. She'll come around.

Slow night. Holly couldn't sleep; we played checkers. She lifts her fingers and dances them over the board like she's weaving a magic spell before she touches a counter. Apparently it's a mind game – makes the other player watch where you're going instead of planning their next move. Where did a seven-year-old learn mind games?

Ask the question.

Holly: You're quite naïve, Leon, aren't you?

Pronounces it 'knave'. Probably never said it out loud before, just read it in one of her books.

Me: I'm very worldly wise, thank you, Holly!

Gives me patronising look.

Holly: It's OK, Leon. You're just too nice. I bet people walk all over you like a doormat.

She picked that up from somewhere, definitely. Probably her father, who visits every other week in a sharp grey suit, bringing poorly chosen sweets and the sour smell of cigarette smoke.

Me: Being nice is a good thing. You can be strong and nice. You don't have to be one or the other.

The patronising look again.

Holly: Look. It's like how . . . Kay's strong, you're nice.

She spreads her hands, like, *it's the way of the world*. Am startled. Didn't know she knew Kay's name.

Richie rings just as I get in. Have to sprint to get to the landline – I know it'll be him, it only ever is – and hit head on low-hanging pendant light in kitchen. Least favourite thing about excellent flat.

Rub head. Close eyes. Listen closely to Richie's voice for tremors and clues to how he really is, and just for hearing a real, living, breathing, still-OK Richie.

Richie: Tell me a good story.

Close eyes tighter. It's not been a good weekend for him, then. Weekends are bad – they're banged up for longer. I can tell he's down from that accent, so peculiar to the two of us. Always part London, part County Cork, it's more Irish when he's sad.

I tell him about Holly. Her checkers skills. Her accusations of knavety. Richie listens, and then:

Richie: Is she going to die?

It's difficult. People struggle to see it's not about whether she's going to die – palliative care isn't just a place you go to slowly slip away. More people live and leave than die on our wards. Is about being comfortable for the duration of something necessary and painful. Making bad times easier.

Holly, though . . . she might die. She is very sick. Lovely, precocious, and very sick.

Me: Leukaemia statistics are pretty good for kids her age.

Richie: I don't want statistics, man. I want a good story.

I smile, reminded of when we were kids, acting out the plot of *Neighbours* in the month when the TV broke. Richie's always liked a good story.

Me: She'll be fine. She'll grow up to be a . . . coder. Professional coder. Using all her checkers skills to develop new digitally generated food that'll stop anyone going hungry and put Bono out of work around Christmas times.

Richie laughs. Not much of one, but enough to ease the worried knot in my stomach.

Silence for a while. Companionable, maybe, or just an absence of suitably expressive words.

Richie: It's hell in here, man.

The words hit like a punch in the gut. Too often this last year I've felt that connection in my stomach like a bunched fist. Always at times like this, when reality hits afresh after days of blocking it out.

Me: Appeal's not far off. We're getting there. Sal says—

Richie: Ey, Sal says he wants paying. I know the score, Lee. It can't be done.

Voice heavy, slow, almost slurred.

Me: What is this? What, have you lost faith in your big brother? You used to tell me I'd be a billionaire!

I hear a reluctant smile.

Richie: You've given enough.

Never. That's impossible. I will *never* give enough, not for this, though I've wished enough times that I could have swapped places to save him from it.

Me: I've got a scheme. A money-making scheme. You're going to love it.

Scuffle.

Richie: Hey, man, ah, give me one sec—

Muffled voices. My heart beats faster. When on the phone to him it's easy to think he is somewhere safe and quiet, with only his voice and mine. But there he is, in the yard, with a queue behind him, having made the choice between using this half hour out of his prison cell to make a phone call or to have his only shot at a shower.

Richie: Got to go, Lee. Love you.

Dial tone.

Half eight on Saturday. Even leaving now, I'll be late. And am not leaving now, evidently. Am changing dirty sheets on Dorsal Ward, according to Doctor Patel; according to the ward nurse on Coral Ward, I am taking blood from Mr Prior; according to Socha the junior doctor, I am helping her with the patient dying on Kelp Ward.

Socha wins. Call Kay as I run.

Kay, on picking up: You're stuck at work, aren't you?

Too out of breath for proper explanation. Wards too far apart for emergency situations. Hospice board of trustees should invest in shorter corridors.

Kay: It's OK. I'll meet that girl for you.

Stumble. Surprised. I'd planned to ask, obviously – that's why I called Kay and not Essex woman herself, to cancel. But . . . was very *easy*.

Kay: Look, I don't like this flatsharing plan, but I know you need the money, and I get it. However. If I'm going to feel OK about this, I think everything should go through me. I'll meet this Tiffy person, I'll handle the arrangements, and that way the random woman sleeping in your bed isn't someone that you actually interact with. Then I don't feel *quite* as weird about it, and you don't have to deal with it, which, let's be honest, you do not have time to do.

Pang of love. Could be stitch, of course, hard to be sure at this stage of relationship, but still.

Me: You . . . you sure?

Kay, firmly: Yes. This is the plan. And no working weekends. OK? Weekends are for me.

Seems fair.

Me: Thanks. Thank you. And – would you mind – tell her . . .

Kay: Yep, yep, tell her about the weird guy in Flat 5 and warn her about the foxes.

Definite love-pang.

Kay: I know you think I don't listen, but I actually do.

Still a good minute's running before I reach Kelp Ward. Have not paced self adequately. Rookie mistake. I'm thrown by the horrible *now*ness of this shift, with all its dying people and bed sores and tricksy dementia patients, and am forgetting basic rules of surviving in hospice setting. Jog, don't run. Always know the time. Never lose your pen.

Kay: Leon?

Forgot about talking out loud. Was just heavy breathing. Probably quite sinister.

Me: Thanks. Love you.

5

Tiffy

I consider wearing sunglasses, but decide that would make me look like a bit of a diva, given that it's February. Nobody wants a diva as a flatmate.

The question, of course, is whether they want a diva more or less than they want an emotional wreck of a woman who has clearly spent the last two days weeping.

I remind myself that this is not a flatmate situation. Leon and I don't need to get on – we're not going to be living together, not really, we're just going to be occupying the same space at different times. It's no bother to him if I happen to spend all my free time weeping, is it?

'Jacket,' Rachel commands, handing it over.

I have not yet reached the depths of needing someone else to dress me, but Rachel stayed over last night, and if Rachel's here she's probably going to take charge of the situation. Even if 'the situation' is me getting my clothes on in the morning.

Too broken to protest, I take the jacket and slip it on. I do love this jacket. I made it out of a giant ball dress I found in a charity shop – I just picked the whole thing apart and used the fabric from scratch, but left the beading wherever it fell, so now there's purple sequins and embroidery across the right shoulder, down the back and under my boobs. It looks a bit like a circus master's jacket, but fits perfectly, and oddly the under-boob beading is really flattering to the waistline.

'Didn't I give this to you?' I say, frowning. 'Last year sometime?'

'You, part with that jacket?' Rachel makes a face. 'I know you love me, but I'm pretty sure you don't love *anyone* that much.'

Right, of course. I'm such a mess I can hardly think straight. At least I actually care about what I'm wearing this morning, though. You know things are bad when I'll throw on whatever's top in the drawer. And it's not like other people won't notice it – my wardrobe is such that an insufficiently planned outfit will really show. Thursday's mustard yellow cords, cream frilled blouse and long green cardigan caused a bit of a stir at work – Hana in Marketing had a full-blown coughing fit when I walked into the kitchen as she was mid gulp of coffee. On top of that, nobody gets why I'm suddenly so upset. I can see them all thinking, *What's she crying about* now? *Didn't Justin leave months ago?*

They're right. I have no idea why this particular stage of Justin's new relationship bothers me so much. I'd already decided I was going to move out properly this time. And it's not like I wanted him to marry me or anything. I just thought . . . he'd come back. That's what's always happened before – he goes off, doors slam, he freezes me out, ignores my calls, but then he realises his mistake, and just when I think I'm ready to start getting over him, there he is again, holding out his hand and telling me to come with him on some kind of amazing adventure.

But this is it, isn't it? He's getting married. This is . . . This is . . .

Rachel wordlessly passes me the tissues.

'I'll have to redo my make-up again,' I say, once the worst of it is over.

'Reaaally not got time,' Rachel says, flashing me her phone screen.

Shit. Half past eight. I need to leave now or I'm going to be late, and that *will* look bad – if we're going to observe strict who's-in-the-flat-when rules, Leon's going to want me to be able to tell the time.

'Sunglasses?' I ask.

'Sunglasses.' Rachel hands them over.

I grab my bag and head for the door.

As the train rattles its way through the tunnels of the Northern Line I catch sight of my reflection in the window and straighten up a little. I look good. The blurry, scratched glass helps – sort of like an Instagram filter. But this is one of my favourite outfits, my hair is newly washed and coppery red, and though I may have cried away all my eyeliner, my lipstick is still intact.

Here I am. I can do this. I can manage just fine on my own.

It sticks for about as long as it takes to get to the entrance to Stockwell station. Then a guy in a car screams 'get your fanny out!' at me, and the shock is enough to set me spiralling back into shit-at-life post-break-up Tiffy again. I'm too upset even to point out the anatomical issues I'd have if I tried to comply with his request.

I reach the right block of flats in five minutes or so – it's a good distance to the station. At the prospect of actually finding my future home, I wipe my cheeks dry and take a proper look at the place. It's one of those squat, brick blocks, and out the front there's a small courtyard with a bit of sad-looking London-style grass that's more like well-mown hay. There are parking spaces for each flat's tenants, one of whom seems to be using their space to store a bewildering number of empty banana crates.

As I buzz for Flat 3, a movement catches my eye – it's a fox, strolling out from around where the bins seem to live. It gives me an insolent stare, pausing with one paw in the air. I've never actually been this close to a fox before – it's a lot mangier than they look in picture books. Foxes are nice, though, aren't they? They're so nice you're not allowed to shoot them for fun any more, even if you're an aristocrat with a horse.

The door buzzes and clicks out of the lock; I make my way inside.

It's very . . . brown. Brown carpet, biscuit-coloured walls. But that doesn't really matter – it's inside the flat that matters.

When I knock on the door of Flat 3 I find myself feeling genuinely nervous. No – borderline panicked. I'm really doing this, aren't I? Considering sleeping in some random stranger's bed? *Actually* leaving Justin's flat?

Oh, God. Maybe Gerty was right and this is all just a bit too much. For a vertiginous moment I imagine going back to Justin's, back to the comfort of that chrome-and-white flat, to the possibility of having him back. But the thought doesn't feel quite as good as I imagined it would. Somehow – perhaps around 11 p.m. the Thursday before last – that flat started to look a little different, and so did I.

I know, in a vague, don't-look-straight-at-it sort of way, that this is a good thing. I've got this far – I can't let myself go back now.

I need to like this place. It's my only option. So when someone answers the door who clearly isn't Leon, I'm so in the mood to be accommodating that I just go with it. I don't even act surprised.

'Hi!'

'Hello,' says the woman at the door. She's petite, with olive skin and one of those pixie haircuts that makes you look French if you've got a small enough head. I immediately feel enormous.

She does nothing to dispel this feeling. As I step into the flat, I can feel her looking me up and down. I try to take in the décor – ooh, dark-green wallpaper, looks genuine 1970s – but after a while the feel of her eyes on me starts to nag. I turn to meet her gaze head-on.

Oh. It's the girlfriend. And her expression could not be more obvious: it says, *I was worried you might be hot and try to steal my boyfriend from me while you make yourself at home in his bed, but now I've seen you and he'd never be attracted to you so yes! Come in!*

She's all smiles now. Fine, whatever – if this is what it takes to get this flat, no problem. She's not going to belittle me out of this one. She has no idea how desperate I am.

'I'm Kay,' she says, holding out a hand. Her grip is firm. 'Leon's girlfriend.'

'I figured.' I smile to take the edge off it. 'So nice to meet you. Is Leon in the . . .'

I lean my head into the bedroom. It's that or the living room, which has the kitchen in the corner – there's not really much more to the flat than this.

'. . . bathroom?' I try, on seeing the empty bedroom.

'Leon's stuck at work,' says Kay, ushering me through to the living area.

It's pretty minimalist and a little worn around the edges, but it's clean, and I do love that 1970s wallpaper everywhere. I bet someone would pay £80 a roll for that if Farrow & Ball started selling it. There's a low-hanging pendant light in the kitchen area that doesn't quite match the décor but is sort of fabulous; the sofa is battered leather, the TV isn't actually plugged in but looks relatively decent, and the carpet has been recently hoovered. This all looks promising.

Maybe this is going to be good. Maybe it's going to be *great*. I flip through a quick montage of myself here, lazing about on the sofa, rustling something up in the kitchen, and suddenly the idea of having all this space to myself makes me want to bounce on the spot. I rein myself in just in time. Kay does not strike me as the spontaneous dancing sort.

'So will I not . . . meet Leon?' I ask, remembering Mo's first rule of flatsharing with a wince.

'Well, I suppose you might do eventually,' Kay says. 'But it'll be me you speak to. I'm handling renting the place out for him. You'll never be in at the same time – the flat will be yours from six in the evening until eight in the morning in the week, and over the whole weekend. It's a six-month agreement for now. Is that OK with you?'

'Yeah, that's just what I need.' I pause. 'And . . . Leon won't ever pop in unexpectedly? Out of his hours, or anything?'

'Absolutely not,' Kay says, with the air of a woman who plans to make sure of it. 'From six p.m. until eight a.m., the flat is yours and yours alone.'

'Great.' I breathe out slowly, quieting the flutter of excitement in my stomach, and check the bathroom – you can always tell a place by its bathroom. All the appliances are a clean, bright white; there's a dark-blue shower curtain, a few tidy bottles of mysterious man-ly-looking creams and liquids, and a scuffed but serviceable mirror. Excellent. 'I'll take it. If you'll have me.'

I feel certain that she'll say yes, if it really is her decision to make. I knew it as soon as she gave me that look in the hallway: whatever Leon's criteria for a flatmate, Kay just has the one, and I've clearly ticked the 'suitably unattractive' box.

'Wonderful,' says Kay. 'I'll call Leon and let him know.'

6

Kay: She's ideal.

Am doing some slow blinking on the bus. Delicious slow blinks which are really just short naps.

Me: Really? Not annoying?

Kay, sounding irritated: Does that matter? She'll be clean and tidy and she can move in immediately. If you're really determined to do this then you can't expect much better than that.

Me: She wasn't bothered by the weird man living in Flat 5? Or the fox family?

Slight pause.

Kay: She didn't mention either being a problem.

Delicious slow blink. Really long one. Got to be careful – can't face waking up at the end of the bus route and having to come all the way back in again. Always a danger after a long week.

Me: What's she like, then?

Kay: She's . . . quirky. Larger than life. She was wearing these big horn-rimmed sunglasses even though it's basically still winter, and had painted flowers all over her boots. But the point is that she's skint and happy to find a room this cheap!

'Larger than life' is Kay-speak for overweight. Wish she wouldn't say things like that.

Kay: Look, you're on your way, aren't you? We can talk about it when you get here.

My plan for arrival was to greet Kay with customary kiss, remove work clothes, drink water, fall into Kay's bed, sleep for all eternity.

Me: Maybe tonight? When I've slept?

Silence. Deeply irritated silence. (I'm an expert at Kay silences.)

Kay: So you're just going straight to bed when you get in.

Bite tongue. Resist urge to give blow-by-blow account of my week.

Me: I can stay up if you want to talk.

Kay: No, no, you need your sleep.

I'm clearly staying up. Best make the most of these blink-naps until bus gets to Islington.

Frosty welcome from Kay. Make mistake of mentioning Richie, which turns temperature dial down even further. My fault, probably. Just can't talk to her about him without hearing The Argument, like she hits replay every time she says Richie's name. As she busies herself cooking brinner (combination of breakfast and dinner, suitable for both night and day dwellers), tell myself on repeat that I should remember how The Argument ended. That she said sorry.

Kay: So, are you going to ask me about weekends?

Stare at her, slow to answer. Sometimes find it hard to talk after a long night. Just opening my mouth to form comprehensible thoughts is like lifting a very heavy thing, or like one of those dreams where you need to run but your legs are moving through treacle.

Me: Ask you what?

Kay pauses, omelette pan in hand. She is very pretty against wintery sunlight through kitchen window.

Kay: The weekends. Where were you planning to stay, with Tiffy in your flat?

Oh. I see.

Me: Hoped I would stay here. As I'm here every weekend I'm not working anyway?

Kay smiles. Get that satisfying feeling of having said the right thing, followed quickly by a squeeze of anxiety.

Kay: I know you were planning on staying here, you know. I just wanted to hear you say it.

She sees my bemused expression.

Kay: Normally you're just here on weekends by *coincidence*, not because you've planned for it. Not because it's our life plan.

Word 'plan' is much less pleasant with 'life' in front of it. Suddenly very busy eating omelette. Kay squeezes my shoulder, runs her fingers up and down the back of my neck, tugs my hair.

Kay: Thank you.

I feel guilty, though I haven't exactly misled her – I *did* assume I'd be here every weekend, *did* factor that into plan with renting out room. Just didn't . . . think about it that way. The life-plan way.

Two in the morning. When I first joined the hospice nights team, nights coming off shift seemed useless – would sit awake, wishing for sunlight. But now this is my time, the muffled quiet, the rest of London sleeping or getting very drunk. I'm taking every locum night shift the hospice rota coordinator will give me – they're the highest paid, excluding weekend nights, which I've told Kay I won't take. Plus, it's the only way this flatshare plan will work. Not sure it'll even be worth recalibrating for weekends, now – will work five in seven nights. Might just stay nocturnal.

Generally use this 2 a.m. time to write to Richie. His phone calls are limited, but he can receive as many letters as I can send him.

It's been three months as of last Tuesday since he was sentenced. Hard to know how to mark an anniversary like that – raising a glass? Striking another tally on the wall? Richie took it well, considering, but when he went in Sal had told him he'd have him out of there by February, so this one was especially bad.

Sal. He's trying his best, presumably, but Richie is innocent and in prison, so can't help but feel a little resentful towards his lawyer. Sal isn't *bad*. Uses big words, carries a briefcase, never doubts himself – all seem classic reassuring lawyer things? But mistakes keep happening. Like unexpected guilty verdicts.

What are our options, though? No other lawyers sufficiently interested to take Richie on for reduced fee. No other lawyers familiar with his case, no other lawyers already all set up to speak to Richie in prison . . . no *time* to find someone new. Every day that goes by, Richie sinks further away.

Has to be me that deals with Sal all the time, too, never Mam, which means endless exhausting phone calls chasing him. But Mam is shouty and blamey. Sal is sensitive, easily put off from actually working on Richie's case, and completely indispensable.

This is doing me no good. Two a.m. is terrible time for dwelling on legal issues. Worst of all the times. If midnight is witching hour, 2 a.m. is dwelling hour.

Idly reaching for distraction, I find myself googling *Johnny White*. Mr Prior's Hollywood-jawed, long-lost love.

There are many Johnny Whites. One is a leading figure in Canadian dance music. Another is an American footballer. Both were definitely not around during World War Two, falling in love with charming English gentlemen.

Still. Internet was made for situations like this, no?

Try *Johnny White war casualties,* then hate myself a bit. Feels like betraying Mr Prior to assume Johnny's dead. But it's worth trying to eliminate those options first.

Find a website called Find War Dead. Am initially slightly horrified, but decide actually it's amazing – everyone's remembered here. Like digital, searchable tombstones. I can search by name, regiment, which war, dates of birth . . . I type in *Johnny White*, and specify *World War Two*, but don't have any more to give them.

Seventy-eight Johnny Whites died in armed forces in World War Two.

Sit back. Stare at the list of names. John K. White. James Dudley Jonathan White. John White. John George White. Jon R. L. White. Jonathan Reginald White. John—

All right. Feel suddenly overwhelmingly sure that Mr Prior's lovely Johnny White is dead, and wish there was a similar database for those who fought but did not die in the war. That would be nice. A survivors list. Struck, as one is at 2 a.m., by the horror of humanity and its inclination to terrible acts of mass murder.

Kay: Leon! Your bleep is going! *In my ear!*

Leave laptop on sofa after hitting print, and then open bedroom door to find Kay lying on side, duvet over head, one arm up in the air holding my bleep.

Grab bleep. Grab phone. I'm not working, of course, but the team wouldn't bleep me if it wasn't important.

Socha, Junior Doctor: Leon, it's Holly.

Am pulling on shoes.

Me: How bad?

Keys! Keys! Where are keys?

Socha: She's got an infection – obs are *not* looking good. She's asking for you. I don't know what to do, Leon, and Dr Patel isn't answering her bleep, and the reg is skiing and June couldn't get cover organised so there's nobody else to call . . .

Located keys in bottom of washing basket. Inspired place to keep them. Heading for the door, Socha talking white blood cell counts in my ear, shoelaces flapping—

Kay: Leon! You're still wearing your pyjamas!

Damn. Thought I'd managed to get to the door faster than usual.

7

Tiffy

OK, so the new flat's quite . . . full. Cosy.

'Cluttered,' Gerty confirms, standing in about the only unoccupied space in the bedroom. 'It's cluttered.'

'You know my style is eclectic!' I protest, straightening up the adorable tie-dyed bed throw I found at Brixton market last summer. I'm trying very hard to keep my positive face on. Packing up and leaving Justin's flat was awful, and the drive here took four times as long as Google said it would, and carrying everything up the stairs was torture. Then I had to hold a long conversation with Kay as she gave me the keys, when all I wanted to do was sit down somewhere and gently dab at my hairline until I stopped panting. It has not been a fun day.

'Did you discuss this with Leon?' Mo asks, perching on the edge of the bed. 'I mean, bringing all your stuff?'

I frown. Of course I would be bringing all my stuff! Did that need discussing? I'm moving in – that means my stuff has to live here with me. Where else would it live? This is my permanent abode.

However, I am now very aware that my bedroom is shared with another person, and that that person has their own stuff, which was, up until this weekend, occupying most of this room. It's been a bit of a squeeze getting everything in. I've solved a few problems by moving things into other parts of the house – lots of my candle holders are living on the edge of the bath now, for instance, and my amazing lava lamp has a great spot in the living area – but all the same, I could do with Leon having a bit of a clear-out. He should probably have done that beforehand, really – it was the decent thing, given that I was moving in.

Perhaps I should have taken *some* of my things to my parents' house. But most of this stuff lived in storage at Justin's and it had felt so good to dig it all out last night. Rachel joked that when I found the lava lamp it was like Andy being reunited with Woody in *Toy Story*, but to be honest it had been surprisingly emotional. I'd sat for a while in the hall, staring at the multi-coloured mess of my favourite things spilling out from the cupboard under the stairs, and felt for a weird moment that if the cushions could breathe again, so could I.

My phone rings; it's Katherin. She's the only writer I'd pick up the phone to on a Saturday, mainly because she's probably ringing me about something hilarious she's done, like tweeting a wildly inappropriate picture of herself from the 80s with a now-very-important politician, or dip-dying her elderly mother's hair.

'How's my favourite editor?' she asks when I pick up.

'All moved in to my new home!' I tell her, gesturing for Mo to put the kettle on. He looks mildly peeved but does so all the same.

'Perfect! Brilliant! What are you doing Wednesday?' Katherin asks.

'Just work,' I tell her, mentally scanning my diary. Actually, I have a tedious meeting on Wednesday with our Director of International Book Rights to talk about the new book I commissioned last summer from a debut bricklayer-turned-trendy-designer. It's her job to sell it abroad. When I acquired it I talked a *lot* (but really quite vaguely) about his international social media presence, which as it happens is rather a lot smaller than I made it out to be. She's always emailing me for 'more detail' and 'specific breakdowns of reach by territory'.

It's getting to the point where I can't avoid her any longer, even with my wall of stealthy pot plants.

'Great!' says Katherin, who is being suspiciously enthusiastic. 'I have some really good news for you.'

'Oh yes?' I'm hoping for early manuscript delivery, or a sudden change of heart about the chapter on hats and scarves. She's been threatening to remove it, which would be disastrous, as that's the only part that makes the book remotely sellable.

'The Sea Breeze Away people rescheduled my live *How to Crochet Your Own Clothes Fast* show to their Wednesday cruise last minute. So you can help me with the cruise after all.'

Hmm. This time it would be in work hours – and would put off that conversation with the rights director for at least another week. What would I prefer: getting dressed in homemade crochet waistcoats on a cruise ship with Katherin, or getting bollocked by the rights director in a meeting room with no windows?

'All right. I'll do it.'

'Honestly?'

'Honestly,' I say, accepting Mo's tea. 'I'm not doing any talking though. And you're not allowed to manhandle me as much as you did last time. I had bruises for days.'

'The trials and tribulations of life as a model, eh, Tiffy,' Katherin says, and I have a sneaking suspicion that she's laughing at me.

Everyone's gone. It's just me, in my flat.

Obviously I've been super chirpy all day and have made sure to give Mo, Gerty and Kay no indication that moving into Leon's flat is at all weird or emotional.

But it is a bit weird. And I feel like crying again. I look at my lovely tie-dyed blanket lying across the foot of the bed, and all I can think is that it really clashes with Leon's duvet cover, which has manly black and grey stripes, and that there's nothing I can do about that because this is as much Leon's bed as mine, whoever this Leon man is, and that his semi-naked or possibly fully naked body sleeps underneath that duvet. I hadn't really confronted the logistics of the bed situation until this moment, and now that I'm doing it, I am not enjoying the experience.

My phone buzzes. It's Kay.

I hope moving in all went smoothly. Help yourself to any food from the fridge (until you get fully settled and do your own shop). Leon has asked that you please sleep on the left side of the bed. Kay xx

That's it. I'm crying. This is really bloody weird. Who even is this Leon guy? Why have I not met him yet? I think about ringing him – I have his number from the advert – but it's pretty clear Kay wants to be the one handling things.

I sniff, wipe my eyes hard, and wander over to the fridge. It's actually surprisingly full for someone who works long hours. I help myself to raspberry jam and margarine, and locate the bread above the toaster. OK.

Hi Kay. I'm all moved in, thanks – the flat is feeling really cosy! Thanks for confirming re side of the bed.

It's a bit overly formal for discussing who sleeps on the left or right, but I sense Kay would prefer that we don't all get too friendly.

I type out a few queries about the flat – where's the light switch for the outside hall, can I plug in the TV, that sort of thing. Then, jam on toast in hand, I head back to the bedroom and contemplate whether it will look too passive-aggressive to remake the bed with my own sheets. Surely Leon would have put freshly laundered ones on in the circumstances. But . . . what if he hasn't? Oh, God, now the thought is there – I'm going to have to change them. I yank up his mattress cover with my eyes screwed shut like I'm afraid of seeing something I don't want to.

Right. The probably-already-clean sheets are in the washing machine, my lovely definitely-clean ones are on the bed, and I'm slightly breathless with all the activity. On second look, the room does feel more me than it did when I got here. Yes, the duvet cover is still wrong (I felt changing that *would* look a little bit pointed) and there are weird books on the shelves (*none* about making your own clothes! I'll soon fix that), but with my bits and bobs around the place, and my dresses in the wardrobe, and ... yes, I'll just pull the blanket all the way up to cover the duvet, just for now. Much better.

As I'm rearranging the blanket I notice a black plastic sack sticking out from under the bed, with something woollen flopping out of it on to the floor. I must have left one bin bag unpacked; I drag it out to check the contents.

It's full of scarves. Amazing woollen scarves. They're not mine, but the craftsmanship is beautiful – it takes real talent to knit and crochet like this. They *should* be mine. I'd pay money that I do not have for these scarves.

Belatedly I realise I'm rummaging through what must be Leon's stuff – and something he's keeping under the bed, too, so probably doesn't want everyone looking at. I let myself linger over the weave for a second or two longer before I push the bag back to where it came from, careful to leave it how it was. I wonder what the significance of all those scarves is. You don't keep that many handmade scarves for no reason.

It occurs to me that Leon could actually be any kind of weird. Keeping scarves isn't in itself weird, but it could be the tip of the iceberg. Plus there was quite a large number of scarves in there – at least ten. What if he stole them? Shit. What if they are trophies of the women he murdered?

Maybe he's a serial killer. A winter-based killer who only strikes in scarf weather.

I need to call someone. Being alone with the scarves is making me feel genuinely a bit scared, and, as a consequence, a bit mad.

'What's up?' Rachel says when she answers.

'I am worried Leon might be a serial killer,' I announce.

'Why? Has he tried to kill you or something?'

Rachel sounds a bit distracted. I am concerned that she's not taking this seriously enough.

'No, no, I've not met him yet.'

'You've met his girlfriend, though, right?'

'Yeah, why?'

'Well, do you think she knows?'

'What?'

'About the murdering.'

'Umm. No? I suppose not?' Kay *does* seem very normal.

'She's a pretty unobservant sort of woman, then. You managed to spot the signs in just one evening alone in his flat. Think how much time she must have spent there, and seen the very same signs, and not followed them through to their only logical conclusion!'

There is a pause. Rachel's point is deceptively simple but very well made.

'You are an excellent friend,' I tell her eventually.

'I know. You're welcome. I should go, though, I'm on a date.'

'Oh, God, sorry!'

'Nah, no worries, he doesn't mind, do you, Reggie? He says he doesn't mind.'

There is a muffled noise at the other end. I suddenly can't help wondering if Rachel currently has Reggie tied to something.

'I'll leave you to it,' I say. 'Love you.'

'Love you too, babe. No, not you, Reggie, pipe down.'

8

Leon

Hollow-cheeked, tired-eyed Holly looks up at me from bed. Seems littler. In all dimensions, too – wrists, tufty growing-back hair . . . everything but the eyes.

She grins at me weakly.

Holly: You were here last weekend.

Me: In and out. They needed my help. Short-staffed.

Holly: Is it because I asked for you?

Me: Absolutely not. You know you're my least favourite patient.

Bigger grin.

Holly: Were you having a nice weekend with your girlfriend with the short hair?

Me: Yes, actually.

Looks decidedly mischievous. Don't want to get hopes up but she is visibly better – that smile was nowhere to be seen last weekend.

Holly: And you had to leave her behind because of me!

Me: Short-staffing, Holly. Had to leave h— come in to work because of short-staffing.

Holly: I bet she was annoyed that you like me better than her.

Socha, the junior doctor, leans in past the curtain to get my attention.

Socha: Leon.

Me, to Holly: Back in a sec, homewrecker.

Me, to Socha: And?

She breaks into a big, tired smile.

Socha: Bloods just in. The antibiotics are finally having an effect. Just got off the phone with the GOSH med reg, he said as she's improving she doesn't need to go back into hospital. Social services are on board with that as well.

Me: Antibiotics are working?

Socha: Yep. CRP and white cell count both falling, no more fevers, lactate normal. Obs all stable.

The relief is instant. Nothing quite like that feeling of someone getting better.

Good-mood glow resulting from Holly's bloods buoys me all the way home. Teens smoking joint on street corner seem positively cherubic. Smelly man on bus removing socks to scratch his feet evokes only genuine sympathy. Even a Londoner's true enemy, the slow-moving tourist, just makes me smile indulgently.

Already planning excellent 9 a.m. dinner as I let myself into the flat. The first thing I notice is the smell. It smells . . . womanly. Like spicy incense and flower stalls.

The next thing I notice is the sheer quantity of crap in my living room. Enormous heap of books up against breakfast bar. Cow-shaped cushion on sofa. Lava lamp – lava lamp! – on coffee table. What is this? Is Essex woman holding a jumble sale in our flat?

In a slight daze, I go to drop my keys in their usual spot (when not opting for bottom of laundry basket) and find it has been occupied by a moneybox shaped like Spot the Dog. This is unbelievable. It's like a terrible episode of *Changing Rooms*. Flat has been redecorated to look immeasurably worse. Can only conclude that she was doing it on purpose – nobody could be this tasteless accidentally.

Wrack brains to remember what Kay actually told me about this woman. She's a . . . book editor? Sounds like profession of reasonable person with taste? Feel fairly certain that Kay made no mention of Essex woman being a bizarre-object collector. And yet.

I sink into a nearby beanbag and sit for a while. Think of the three hundred and fifty pounds I would otherwise not have been able to give to Sal this month. Decide this is not so bad – beanbag is excellent, for instance: it's patterned with paisley and remarkably comfortable. And lava lamp has comedic value. Who has a lava lamp these days?

Notice my sheets hanging off the clothes horse in the corner of the room – she's washed them. Irritating, as I went to great lengths to wash those and was late for shift as a result. But must remember that annoying Essex woman does not actually know me. Would not know that I would obviously clean sheets before inviting stranger to sleep in them.

Eh. What's the bedroom going to look like?

Venture in, intrepid. Let out a strangled wail. It looks like someone vomited rainbows and calico in here, covering every surface in colours that do not belong together in nature. Horrific, moth-eaten blanket over bed. Enormous beige sewing machine taking up most of desk. And clothes . . . clothes *everywhere*.

This woman owns more clothes than a respectably sized shop would stock. Has clearly not been able to manage with the half of wardrobe I freed up for her, so has hung up dresses on back of door, all along wall – from old picture rail, actually quite resourceful – and over back of now-almost-invisible chair under window.

Consider ringing her and Putting Foot Down for approximately three seconds before reaching inevitable conclusion that that would be awkward, and, in a few days, I will have stopped caring. Probably stopped noticing, actually. Still. Right now, opinion of Essex woman has reached new low. I'm about to head back to spot on very inviting beanbag when I notice the bin bag of the scarves Mr Prior knitted me, poking out from under bed.

Forgot about those. Essex woman may think I'm odd if she finds bag of fourteen hand-knitted scarves stashed under bed. Have been meaning to take them to the charity shop for ever, but of course Essex woman won't know that. Haven't actually met her; don't want her to think I'm, you know. A scarf collector or something.

Grab pen and paper and scrawl FOR CHARITY SHOP on a Post-it note, then stick it to bag. There. Just to remind myself, in case I forget.

Now to the beanbag for dinner, and bed. So tired that even the horrible tie-dyed bed blanket is beginning to look attractive.

9

Tiffy

So, here I am. On the freezing cold dock. In 'neutral clothing I can work with' according to Katherin, who is beaming cheekily at me, the wind whipping her straw-blonde hair against her cheeks as we wait for the cruise ship to batten down the hatch, or turn three sails to the wind, or whatever it is these ships do in order to let people on board.

'You have the perfect proportions for this sort of thing,' Katherin is telling me. 'You're my favourite model, Tiffy. Really. This is going to be an absolute scream.'

I raise an eyebrow, looking out to sea. I don't see a vast selection of other models for Katherin to choose from. I have also, over the years, got a bit tired of people lauding my 'proportions'. The thing is, I'm like Gerty and Mo's flat in reverse – just about twenty per cent bigger than the average woman, in all directions. My mother likes to declare that I am 'big-boned' because my father was a lumberjack in his youth (was he? I know he's old, but didn't lumberjacks only exist in fairy tales?). I can barely walk into a room without someone helpfully informing me that I am very tall for a woman.

Sometimes it annoys people, like I'm purposefully taking up more room than I'm allowed, and sometimes it intimidates them, especially when they're used to looking down at women they're talking to, but mostly it just makes them compliment me on my 'proportions' a lot.

I think what they're really saying is, 'Gosh, you're big, but without being particularly fat!' or, 'Well done on being tall but not lanky!' Or perhaps, 'You are confusing my gender norms by being very woman-shaped despite the fact that you are the height and width of an average male!'

'You're the sort of woman the Soviets liked,' Katherin goes on, oblivious to my raised eyebrow. 'You know, on their posters about women working the land while the men were out fighting, that sort of thing.'

'Wear a lot of crochet, did they, the Soviet women?' I ask rather tetchily. It's drizzling, and the sea looks very different from a busy dock like this – it's a lot less glamorous than when you're on the beach. It's basically just a big cold salty bath, really. I wonder how warm the rights director is now, in her meeting about the international reach of our spring season titles.

'Possibly, possibly,' Katherin muses. 'Good idea, Tiffy! What do you think – a chapter on the history of crochet in the next book?'

'No,' I tell her firmly. 'That won't be popular with your readers.'

You have to nip ideas in the bud fast with Katherin. And I'm definitely right on this one. Nobody wants history – they just want an idea for a new crochet item they can give their grandson to drool on.

'But—'

'I'm just conveying the brutality of the market to you, Katherin,' I say. That's one of my favourite lines. Good old market, always there to be blamed. 'The people don't want history in their crochet books. They want cute pictures and easy instructions.'

Once all our documents have been checked, we file on board. You can't really tell where the dock ends and the boat begins – it's just like walking into a building and developing very slight light-headedness, as though the floor is shifting a little beneath you. I thought we might get a different, more exciting welcome for being special guests who've been invited here, but we're just traipsing on with the rest of the riff-raff. All of whom are at least twenty times richer than me, obviously, and much better dressed.

It's actually pretty small for a cruise ship – so only the size of, say, Portsmouth, rather than London. We're shuffled politely into a corner of the 'entertainment area' to wait for our cue. We're to set up after the guests have had lunch.

Nobody brings *us* lunch. Katherin, of course, has brought her own sandwiches. They're sardine. She cheerfully offers me half, which is actually very sweet of her, and eventually my stomach-rumbling gets so bad that I concede defeat and accept one. I'm twitchy. The last time I was on a cruise it was through the Greek islands with Justin, and I was positively glowing with love and post-sex hormones. Now, huddled in a corner with three Aldi bags of knitting needles, crochet hooks and wool, accompanied by an ex-hippy and a sardine sandwich, I can no longer deny the fact that my life has taken a turn for the worse.

'So what's the plan, then?' I ask Katherin, nibbling the crusts off the sandwich. The fishiness isn't so bad at the edges. 'What do I need to do?'

'I'll demonstrate how to take measurements from you first,' Katherin says. 'Then I'll talk through the basic stitches for any beginners, then I'll use my pre-prepared bits to show them the tricks of compiling yourself a perfectly fitted outfit! And of course, I'll show them my five top tips for measuring as you go.'

'Measuring as you go' is one of Katherin's catchphrases. It has yet to catch on.

In the end, when it's finally time for us to kick off, we gather quite a crowd. Katherin knows how to do that – she probably practised at rallies and things, back in days of yore. It's largely a crowd of old ladies and their husbands, but there are a few younger women in their twenties and thirties, and even a couple of guys. I'm quite encouraged. Maybe Katherin's right that crochet is on the up.

'A big hand for my glamorous assistant!' Katherin is saying, as though we're putting on a magic show. Actually, the magician in the other corner of the entertainment area is looking pretty miffed.

Everyone claps me dutifully. I try to look cheerful and crochet-ish, but I'm still chilly, and I feel drab in my neutral clothing – white jeans, pale grey T-shirt, and a lovely warm pink cardigan that I thought I'd sold sometime last year but rediscovered in my wardrobe this morning. It's the only colourful element to this outfit, and I can tell Katherin is about to . . .

'Cardigan off!' she says, already undressing me. This is so undignified. And cold. 'Are you all paying close attention? Phones away, please! We managed without checking Facebook every five minutes in the Cold War, didn't we? Hmm? That's right, a bit of perspective for you all! Phones away, that's it!'

I try not to laugh. That's trademark Katherin – she always says bringing up the Cold War startles people into submission.

She starts measuring me – neck, shoulders, bust, waist, hips – and it occurs to me that my measurements are now being read out to a really quite large group of people, which makes my urge to laugh even more powerful. It's the classic, isn't it – you're not allowed to laugh, and suddenly that's what you want to do more than anything.

Katherin shoots me a warning look as she measures my hips, chatting away about pleating to create sufficient 'room for the buttocks', and no doubt feeling how my body is beginning to shake with supressed laughter. I know I need to be professional. I know I can't just burst out laughing right now – it'll totally undermine her. But . . .

Look at me. That old lady over there just wrote down my inner thigh measurement in her notebook. And that guy at the back looks—

That guy at the back . . . That . . .

That's Justin.

He moves away when I clock it's him, slipping off into the crowd. But first, before he goes, he holds my gaze. It sends a shock right through me, because it's not your ordinary eye contact. It's a very distinct sort of eye contact. The sort you get locked into in the moment just before you toss a twenty on the table and scramble out of the pub to make out in a cab home, or in the moment when you put down the wine glass and head upstairs to bed.

It's *sex* eye contact. His eyes say, *I'm undressing you in my head.* The man who left me months ago, who hasn't picked up one of my calls since, whose fiancée is probably on this very cruise with him . . . He's giving me that look. And in that moment I am more exposed than any number of elderly ladies with notebooks could make me feel. I feel completely naked.

10

Leon

Me: You could have found each other again. Love finds a way, Mr Prior! Love finds a way!

Mr Prior is unconvinced.

Mr Prior: No offence, lad, but you weren't there – that's not how it worked. Of course, there were lovely stories, girls who thought their lads were long dead, then came home to find them traipsing up the path in their uniform, fresh as a daisy . . . but for every one, there were hundreds of stories of lovers who never came back. Johnny's probably dead, and if he's not, he's long since married to some gentleman or lady somewhere, and I'm forgotten.

Me: But you said he wasn't on that list.

I'm waving a hand at the list of war dead I printed, unsure why I'm pushing this point so hard. Mr Prior hasn't asked to find Johnny; he was just pining. Reminiscing.

But I see a lot of elderly people here. I'm used to reminiscing; I'm used to pining. Felt this was different. I felt Mr Prior had unfinished business.

Mr Prior: I don't think so, no. But then, I'm a forgetful old man, and your computer system is a new-fangled thing, so either of us could be wrong, couldn't we?

He gives me a gentle smile, like I'm doing this for me, not him.

Look closer at him. Think of all the nights when I've arrived to chatter about visitors from other patients, and have seen Mr Prior sitting quietly in the corner, hands in his lap, face folded in neat wrinkles like he's trying hard not to look sad.

Me: Humour me. Tell me the facts. Regiment? Birthplace? Distinctive features? Family members?

Mr Prior's little, beady eyes look up at me. He shrugs. Smiles. It folds his papery, age-spotted face, shifting the tan lines like ink on his neck, left there from decades of shirt collars of precisely the same width.

He gives a slight shake of the head, like he'll tell someone later how barmy these modern nurses are, but starts talking all the same.

Thursday morning. Ring Mam for short, difficult conversation on bus.

Mam, bleary: Is there news?

This has been customary greeting for months.

Leon: Sorry, Mam.

Mam: Shall I call Sal?

Leon: No, no. I'm dealing with it.

Long, miserable silence. We wallow in it. Then,

Mam, with effort: Sorry, sweetheart, how are you?

Return home afterwards to find pleasant surprise: home-baked flapjack on sideboard. It's filled with colourful dried fruit and seeds, like Essex woman cannot resist clashing colours even in food, but this seems less objectionable when I see the note beside the tray.

Help yourself! Hope you had a good ~~day~~ night. Tiffy x

An excellent development. Will definitely endure high levels of clutter and novelty lamps for three hundred and fifty pounds per month *and* free food. Help myself to large slice and settle down with it to write to Richie, filling him in on Holly's condition. She's 'Knave

Girl' in my letters to him, and a bit of a caricature of herself – sharper, snarkier, cuter. I reach for more flapjack without looking, filling page two with descriptions of the stranger Essex-woman items, some of which are so ridiculous I think Richie won't believe me. An iron in the shape of Iron Man. Actual clown shoes, hung on the wall like a work of art. Cowboy boots with spurs, which I can only conclude she wears regularly, looking at how worn they are.

Notice absently, as I fiddle with the stamp, that I have eaten four slices of flapjack. Hope she really meant 'help yourself'. While biro is in hand, scribble on back of her note.

Thanks. So delicious I accidentally ate most of it.

Pause before finishing the note. Feel I need to repay her in something. There is really hardly any flapjack remaining in tray.

Thanks. So delicious I accidentally ate most of it. Leftover mushroom stroganoff in fridge if you need dinner (on account of having hardly any flapjack left). Leon

Better make mushroom stroganoff now.

That was not the only note left for me this morning. There's this one on the bathroom door.

Hi Leon,
Would you mind putting the toilet seat down please?
I'm afraid I was unable to write this note in a way that didn't sound passive-aggressive – seriously, it's something about the note form, you pick up a pen and a Post-it note and you immediately become a bitch – so I'm just styling it out. I might put some smiley faces to really hammer the thing home.
Tiffy x

There are smiley faces all along the bottom of the note.

I snort with laughter. One of the smiley faces has a body and is pissing towards the corner of the Post-it note. Wasn't expecting that. Not sure why – I don't know this woman – but hadn't imagined she had much of a sense of humour. Maybe because all her books are about DIY.

11

Tiffy

'That is ridiculous.'

'I know,' I say.

'That was *it*?' Rachel yells. I flinch. Last night I drank a bottle of wine, panic-baked flapjack, and barely slept; I'm a little fragile for shouting.

We're sitting in the 'creative space' at work – it's like the other two Butterfingers Press meeting rooms, except annoyingly it doesn't have a proper door (to convey a sense of openness), and there are whiteboards on the walls. Somebody used them once; now the notes from their creative session are ingrained in dried-out whiteboard marker, totally incomprehensible. Rachel has printed out the layouts we're meeting to discuss, and they're spread out across the table between us. It's the bloody Make a Stir baking book, and you can really tell I was hungover and in a rush when I edited this the first-time around.

'You're telling me that you see Justin on a *cruise ship* and then he gives you an *I want to fuck you* stare and then you go on about your business and *don't see him again*?'

'I know,' I say again, positively miserable.

'Ridiculous! Why didn't you go looking for him?'

'I was busy with Katherin! Who, by the way, gave me an actual injury,' I tell her, yanking my poncho out of the way to show her the angry red mark where Katherin pretty much stabbed my arm mid-demonstration.

Rachel gives it a cursory look. 'I hope you brought her manuscript delivery date forward for that,' she says. 'Are you sure it was Justin? Not some other white guy with brown hair? I mean, I imagine a cruise ship is—'

'Rachel, I know what Justin looks like.'

'Right, well,' she says, throwing her arms out wide and sending layouts sliding across the table. 'I can't believe this. It's *such* an anti-climax. I really thought your story was going to end with sex in a cabin bunk! Or on the deck! Or, or, or in the middle of the ocean, on a dinghy!'

What actually happened was that I spent the rest of the session in paralysed, panicky suspense, desperately trying to look like I was listening to Katherin's instructions – 'Arms up, Tiffy!' 'Watch your hair, Tiffy!' – and simultaneously keep my eyes on the back of the crowd. I did start to wonder if I'd imagined it. What the hell were the chances? I mean, I know the man likes a cruise, but this is a very large country. There are many cruise ships floating around the edge of it.

'Tell me again,' Rachel says, 'about the look.'

'Ughh, I can't explain it,' I tell her, laying my forehead down on the pages in front of me. 'I just . . . I know that look from when we were together.' My stomach twists. 'It was *so* inappropriate. I mean – God – his girlfriend – I mean, his fiancée . . .'

'He saw you across a crowded room, semi-unclothed, being gloriously you-like and pissing about with a middle-aged eccentric author . . . and he remembered why he used to fancy the pants off you,' Rachel concludes. 'That's what happened.'

'That's not . . .' But what *did* happen? Something, definitely. That look wasn't nothing. I feel a little flutter of anxiety at the base of my ribs. Even after a whole night of thinking about this, I still can't work out how I feel. One minute Justin appearing on a cruise ship and catching my eye seems like the most romantic, fateful moment, and then the next I find myself feeling a bit shivery and sick. I was all jittery on the journey home from the docks, too – it's been a while since I've travelled outside London on my own to anywhere other than my parents'. Justin had a real thing about how I always ended up on the wrong train, and he was sweet about taking journeys with me just in case; as I waited alone in the darkness of Southampton station I felt categorically certain I'd end up taking a train to the Outer Hebrides or something.

I reach to check my phone – this 'meeting' with Rachel is only in the diary for half an hour, and then I really do need to edit Katherin's first three chapters.

I have one new message.

So good to see you yesterday. I was there for work, and when I saw 'Katherin Rosen and assistant' on the programme, I thought, hey, that's got to be Tiffy.

Only you could laugh your way through someone reading out your measurements – most girls would hate that. But I guess that's what makes you special. J xx

Hands shaking, I stretch the phone out to show Rachel. She gasps, hands to mouth.

'He loves you! That man is still in love with you!'

'Calm down, Rachel,' I tell her, though my heart is currently making an attempt at a getaway via my throat. I feel as if I'm choking and breathing too much all at the same time.

'Can you text back and tell him that comments like that are the reason womankind cares so much about their measurements? And that by declaring that "most girls would hate that", he is perpetuating the female body image problem, and setting women up against one another, which is one of the greatest problems feminism faces to this day?'

I narrow my eyes at her, and she flashes me a big grin. 'Or you could just say, "Thanks, come over and show me how special I am all night long"?'

'Ugh. I don't know why I talk to you.'

'It's me or Martin,' she points out, gathering up the layouts. 'I'll take in these changes. You go get your man back, all right?'

'No,' Gerty says immediately. 'Do *not* text him that. He is scum of the earth who treated you like shit, tried to isolate you from your friends, and almost certainly cheated on you. He does not deserve a text of this niceness.'

There is a pause.

'What made you want to reply with that message, Tiffy?' Mo asks, as if he's translating for Gerty.

'I just ... wanted to talk to him.' My voice is very small. The tiredness is starting to eat away at me; I'm curled up on my beanbag with a hot chocolate, and Mo and Gerty are staring down at me from the sofa, their faces a picture of concern (actually, Gerty's isn't – she just looks angry).

Gerty reads my draft message out again. '*Hi Justin. So good to hear from you. I'm just sorry we didn't get to catch up properly, despite being on the same cruise ship!* And then two kisses.'

'He did two kisses,' I say a little defensively.

'The kisses are last on my list of things to change about that message,' Gerty says.

'Are you sure you want to start up contact with Justin again at all, Tiffy? You seem a lot better in yourself since you've moved out of his flat,' Mo says. 'I wonder if that might not be a coincidence.' He sighs when I don't say anything. 'I know you find it hard to think badly of him, Tiffy, but whatever excuses you can give him for everything else, even you can't ignore the fact that he left you for another woman.'

I flinch.

'Sorry. But he did, and even if he's left her, which we don't have any evidence he has, he still went off with her. You can't reason that away or convince yourself you've imagined it, because you've met Patricia. Look back at that Facebook message. Remember how it felt when he turned up with her at the flat.'

Ugh. Why do people keep saying things I don't want to hear? I miss Rachel.

'What do you think he's *doing*, Tiffy?' Mo asks. He's pushing so hard all of a sudden – it's making me squirm.

'Being friendly. Trying to get in touch again.'

'He's not asked to meet up,' Mo points out.

'And the look he gave you was more than friendly, by the sounds of it,' Gerty says.

'I . . .' It's true. It wasn't a *hey, I've missed you so much, I wish we could talk again* look. But it was . . . something. It's true I can't ignore the fiancée, but I can't ignore that look either. What did it mean? If he wanted to – if he wanted to get back together . . .

'Would you?' Gerty asks.

'Would I what?' I ask, buying myself time.

She doesn't answer. She knows my game.

I think about how miserable I've been these last few months, how bleak it was to say goodbye to his flat. How many times I've looked Patricia up on Facebook and cried on to my laptop keyboard until I got a bit worried about electrocution.

I was so lucky to have him. Justin was always so . . . fun. Everything was a whirlwind; we'd be flying from country to country, trying everything, staying up until four in the morning and climbing on to the roof to watch the sunrise. Yes, we fought a lot and I made a lot of mistakes in that relationship, but mostly I'd just felt so lucky to be with him. Without him I feel . . . lost.

'I don't know,' I say. 'But a big part of me wants to.'

'Don't worry,' Gerty says, standing up smartly and patting me on the head, 'we won't let you.'

12

Leon

Hi Leon,

All right, fine – the truth is, I panic-bake. When I'm sad or things are difficult, baking is my go-to. And what of it? I turn my negativity into delicious, calorific goodness. As long as you can't taste traces of my misery in the cake mix, I don't think you should be questioning why I have been baking every night this week.

Which, as it happens, is because my ex-boyfriend turned up on my cruise ship* and gave me the eye and then buggered off. So now I'm all muddled. He sent me this sweet text about how special I was, but I didn't text back. I wanted to, but my friends talked me out of it. They're annoying, and usually right about stuff.

Anyway, that's why you've had so much cake.

Tiffy x

*Not my cruise ship. No offence, but I wouldn't be sharing a bedroom with you if I was the sort of person who owned a cruise ship. I'd be living in a Scottish castle with technicolour turrets.

Hi Tiffy,

Sorry to hear about your ex. Guessing from your friends' reactions that they don't think he's good for you – is that what you think?

I'm Team Ex if it means cake.

Leon

Hi Leon,

I don't know – I've not really thought about it like that, actually. My kneejerk reaction is yeah, he's good for me. But then, I don't know. We were very up and down, one of those couples everyone's always talking about (we've broken up and got back together a few times before). It's easy to remember the happy times – and there were tons of them, and they were awesome – but I guess since we broke up I've only remembered those. So I know that being with him was fun. But was it good for me? Ugh. I don't know.

Hence the Victoria sandwich with homemade jam.

Tiffy x

On a large ring-bound printout of a book, titled *Built: My Amazing Journey from Bricklayer to High-End Interior Designer*:

Be honest – picked this up off table as thought it sounded hilariously rubbish. Couldn't put it down. Didn't get to sleep until noon. Is this man your ex? If not, can I marry him?

Leon

Hey Leon,

I'm so glad you enjoyed the book! My beautiful bricklayer-turned-designer is not in fact my ex, and yes, he is much more likely to want to marry you than me. I imagine Kay would have opinions on the subject, though.

Tiffy x

Kay says am not allowed to marry beautiful bricklayer-turned-designer. Shame. She says hi.

Good to catch her yesterday! She says I'm making you fat with all the cake. She made me promise to channel my emotional turmoil into healthier

*options from now on, so I made us carob and date brownies. Sorry, they're
totally disgusting.*

I'm moving this Post-it note on to Wuthering Heights *now as I need
to take* Built *back to the office! x*

On cupboard above kitchen bin:

When is our bin day again?
    Leon

*Is this a joke? I've lived here for five weeks! You've lived here for years!
How can you be asking me when bin day is?!*
    . . . but yes, it was yesterday, and we forgot. x

*Oh, thought so . . . Can never remember if it's Tuesday or Thursday. It's
a days-beginning-with-T thing. Difficult.*

*Any news from the ex? You've stopped baking. It's OK, freezer stockpile
will get me through for a while, but am keen for you to have another
crisis in, say, mid-May.*
    Leon

Hey,
*Total radio silence. He's not even been updating his Twitter or Facebook so
I can't stalk him – so he is probably still with his fiancée (I mean, why
wouldn't he be, all he did was look at me a bit funny), and I probably
completely misread the cruise-ship moment, and he's probably a despicable
human being like my friend Gerty says he is. Anyway, I've paid him back
all the money I owe him. I now owe the bank a terrifying amount instead.*

*Thanks for the risotto, it was delicious – you're a really good cook for
someone who only ever eats meals at the wrong times of the day!*
    Tiffy x

Beside baking tray:

Jesus. Didn't know about the fiancée. Or the money.
Does millionaire shortbread mean you got news?

Beside baking tray, now full of crumbs:

Nothing. He's not even sent a message to say he received the payment.
This is totally tragic but I found myself wishing yesterday that I'd just
kept paying a few hundred a month – then in a way we'd still be in touch.
And I wouldn't be quite so deep into my overdraft.
Basically, in summary, he hasn't said a word to me since the cruise-ship
text. I'm officially an idiot x

Eh. Love makes us all idiots – first time I met Kay I told her I was a jazz
musician (saxophone). Thought she'd like it.
Chilli on hob for you.
Leon x

APRIL

13

Tiffy

'I think I'm having palpitations.'

'Nobody has had palpitations since the olden days finished,' Rachel informs me, taking an unacceptably large sip of the latte the head of Editorial bought me (every so often he feels guilty for Butterfingers not paying me enough, and splashes out £2.20 on a coffee to assuage his conscience).

'This book. Is. Killing me,' I say.

'The saturated fat in your lunch is killing you.' Rachel prods the banana bread I'm currently munching my way through. 'Your baking is getting worse. By which I mean better, obviously. Why aren't you getting fatter?'

'I am, but I'm just bigger than you, so you don't notice the difference as much. I stash my new cake weight in bits you won't spot. Like the upper arm, for instance. Or the cheek. I'm getting rounder cheeks, don't you think?'

'Edit, woman!' Rachel says, slapping a hand on the layouts between us. Our weekly catch-ups about Katherin's book soon became daily catch-ups as March slipped by; now, faced with the terrifying realisation that it is *April* and our print date is only a couple of months away, they have become daily catch-ups and daily lunches. 'And when are you getting me the photos of the hats and scarves?' Rachel adds.

Oh, God. The hats and scarves. I wake up in the middle of the night thinking about hats and scarves. There is no agency free to take on making them at such short notice, and Katherin *really* doesn't have time. Contractually she doesn't have to make all the samples herself – this is a mistake I will never make again at negotiation stage – so I have no ammunition to make her do it. I tried actual begging, but she told me, not unkindly, that I was embarrassing myself.

I gaze mournfully at my banana bread. 'There is no solution,' I say. 'The end is nigh. The book is going to go to print with no pictures in the hats and scarves chapter.'

'No it bloody well isn't,' Rachel says. 'For starters, you've not got enough words to fill the space. Edit! And then think of something! And do it fast!'

Ugh. Why do I like her again?

When I get home I put the kettle on straight away – it's a cup-of-tea sort of evening. There's an old note from Leon stuck on the underside of the kettle. They get everywhere, these Post-it notes.

Leon's mug is still by the sink, half full of milky coffee. He always drinks it that way, from the same chipped white mug with a cartoon rabbit on the side. Every night that mug will either be on this side of the sink, half drunk, which I guess means he was pushed for time, or washed up on the draining board, which I assume means he managed to get up with the alarm.

The flat is pretty homely now. I had to let Leon reclaim some of the space in the living area – sometime last month he removed half of my cushions and put them in a pile in the hall with a label reading 'I Am Finally Putting My Foot Down (sorry)' – but he may have been right that there were a few too many. It was getting quite hard to sit on the sofa.

The bed is still the strangest part of this whole flatsharing thing. For the first month or so I put my own sheets on and took them off again every morning, and I'd lie on the furthest edge of my left-hand side, my pillow pulled away from his. But now I don't bother alternating the sheets – I only lie on my side anyway. It's really all quite normal. Of course, I still haven't actually met my flatmate, which I acknowledge is technically a bit weird, but we've started leaving each other notes more and more often now – sometimes I forget we haven't had these conversations in person.

I chuck my bag down and collapse on the beanbag while the tea brews. If I'm honest with myself, I'm waiting. I've been waiting for months now, ever since I saw Justin.

Surely he's going to get in touch with me. OK, so I never replied to his text – something I still intermittently hate Gerty and Mo for not letting me do – but he gave me that look on the cruise ship. Obviously it's now been so long that I've almost entirely forgotten the look itself, and it's just a compilation of different expressions I remember on Justin's face (or, maybe more realistically, remember from all his Facebook photos) . . . but still. At the time it felt very . . . OK, I still don't know what it felt. Very *something*.

As more time passes I've found myself thinking about how *weird* it was that Justin was on that very cruise ship on the one day that Katherin and I were doing the *How to Crochet Your Own Clothes Fast* show. As much as the thought appeals, it can't have been because he came specially to see me – we were rescheduled at the last minute, so he wouldn't have known I was going to be there. Plus his text said he was there for work, which is perfectly plausible – he works for an entertainment company that arranges shows for things like cruises and tourist tours of London. (I was always a bit hazy on the details, to be honest. It all seemed very logistical and stressful.)

So if he didn't come on purpose, then doesn't it feel a bit like fate?

I grab my tea and wander into the bedroom, at a loose end. I don't even *want* to get back together with Justin, do I? This is the longest we've ever been broken up, and it does feel different from the other times. Maybe because he left me for a woman he then promptly proposed to. It's probably that.

In fact, I shouldn't even care whether he's going to get in touch with me. What does that say about me, that I'm waiting for a man who most likely cheated on me to give me a call?

'It says that you're loyal and trusting,' Mo says, when I ring him and ask this very question. 'The exact qualities that mean Justin is likely to try and get in touch again.'

'You think he will too?' I realise I'm twitchy, jumpy, hungry for reassurance, which annoys me even more. I start tidying my *Gilmore Girls* DVDs into the correct order, too jittery to stand still. There's another note jammed between series one and two; I yank it loose and skim over it. I'd been trying to persuade Leon to try actually using our television, offering him my very high-quality DVD collection as a place to start. He was not convinced.

'Almost certainly,' Mo says. 'That seems to be Justin's way. But . . . are you sure you want him to?'

'I'd like him to talk to me. Or at least acknowledge me. I don't know where his head is at. He seemed so mad at me about the flat, but then that message after I saw him on the cruise ship was really sweet, so . . . I don't know. I want him to call. Ugh.' I clench my eyes shut. 'Why *is* that?'

'Maybe you spent a lot of time being told you couldn't manage without him,' Mo says gently. 'That would explain why you want him back, even when you don't *want* him.'

I flounder around looking for a change of subject. The latest episode of *Sherlock*? The new assistant at work? But I find I don't even have the energy to be diverting.

Mo waits quietly. 'It's true, though, isn't it?' he says. 'I mean, have you thought about dating anyone else?'

'I could date someone else,' I protest.

'Hmm.' He sighs. 'How did that look on the cruise ship really make you feel, Tiffy?'

'I don't know. It was ages ago now. I guess ... it was kind of ... sexy? And nice to be wanted?'

'You weren't afraid?'

'What?'

'Did you feel afraid? Did the look make you feel smaller?'

I frown. 'Mo, give it a rest. It was just a look. He definitely wasn't trying to *scare* me – besides, I rang you to talk about whether he'll ever call me, and thanks, you made me feel a bit better about that, so let's draw the line there.'

For a long while there's silence at the other end of the phone. I'm a little shaken despite myself.

'That relationship took its toll on you, Tiffy,' Mo says gently. 'He made you miserable.'

I shake my head. I mean, I know me and Justin argued, but we always made up, and things only got more romantic after a fight, so it didn't really count. It wasn't like when other couples argued – it was all just part of the beautiful, crazy rollercoaster that was our relationship.

'It'll all sink in eventually, Tiff,' Mo says. 'When it does, you just get on the phone to me, OK?'

I nod, not really sure what I'm agreeing to. From my vantage point I've just spotted the perfect distraction from how I'm feeling right now: the bag of scarves under Leon's bed. The one I found on my first night here, which convinced me that Leon was probably some kind of serial killer. There's a note on them which I'm sure wasn't there when I looked at them before – it says FOR CHARITY SHOP.

'Thanks, Mo,' I say into the phone. 'See you Sunday for coffee.' I hang up, already looking around for a pen.

Hey,

OK, sorry for snooping under (y)our bed. I get that that's definitely unacceptable. But these scarves are INCREDIBLE. As in, designer incredible. And I know we've never talked about this or anything, but I'm guessing that if you're letting a random stranger (me) sleep in your bed then you're doing it because you're short of cash, not because you're a really nice man who feels bad about how hard it is to get a cheap flat in London.

So while I am ALL FOR giving old clothes to charity shops (after all, I buy most of my possessions from charity shops – people like me need people like you), I think you should consider selling these scarves. You'd probably get around £200 a pop.

If you feel like giving one 90% off to your lovely flatmate, I won't object.

Tiffy x

PS Where did you get them all from, by the way? If you don't mind me asking.

14

Leon

Arms out wide, legs akimbo. A stern-looking prison guard frisks me *very* enthusiastically. Suspect I fit her profile of person who may bring drugs or weapons into visiting hall. Imagine her flicking through her mental checklist. Gender: Male. Race: Indeterminate, but a bit browner than would be preferable. Age: Young enough not to know better. Appearance: Scruffy.

Try to smile in a non-threatening, good-citizen sort of way. Probably comes across as cocky, on reflection. Begin to feel slightly queasy, the reality of this place seeping in despite the efforts I have made to pointedly ignore rolls of barbed wire on top of thick steel fences, windowless buildings, aggressive signs about consequences of smuggling drugs into prisons. Despite having done this at least once a month since November.

The walk from security to the visiting hall is perhaps the worst part. It involves a maze of concrete and barbed wire, and all the way you are ferried by different prison guards, taking their key chains from their hips for gates and doors that need locking behind you before you can even take a step towards the next one. It's a beautiful spring day; the sky is just visible above the wires, tauntingly blue.

Visiting hall is better. Kids toddle between tables, or get lifted overhead, squealing, by muscly dads. Prisoners wear bright-coloured bibs to differentiate them from the rest of us. Men in high-viz orange inch closer to visiting girlfriends than they're strictly allowed to be, fingers wound tight. There's more emotion here than at an airport arrivals lounge. *Love Actually* was missing a trick.

Sit at assigned table. Wait. When they bring Richie in, my stomach does a peculiar lurch, like it's trying to turn inside out. He looks tired and unwashed, cheeks hollow, head hastily shaved. He's in his only pair of jeans – won't have wanted me to see him in the prison-issue joggers – but they're too loose around the waist now. Hate it, hate it, hate it.

I get up and smile, stretching my arms out for a hug. Wait for him to come to me; can't leave allocated area. Prison guards line the walls, watching closely, expressionless.

Richie, slapping me on the back: All right, brother, you're looking good!

Me: You too.

Richie: Liar. I look like shit warmed up. Water's been knocked out after some scene on E Wing – no idea when it'll come back on, but until then, I wouldn't recommend trying to use the toilets.

Me: Noted. How're you doing?

Richie: Peachy. Have you heard anything from Sal?

Thought I could avoid that topic for at least one minute.

Me: Yeah. He's sorry about those papers holding up the appeal, Richie. He's working on it.

Richie's face closes up.

Richie: I can't keep waiting, Lee.

Me: You want me to try and find someone new, I'll do it.

Glum silence. Richie knows as well as I do that this'll probably slow things down even further.

Richie: Did he get the footage from the Aldi camera?

Did he even *request* the footage from the Aldi camera is the question. Am starting to doubt it, even though he told me he did. Rub back of neck, look down at shoes, wish harder than ever that Richie and I were anywhere but here.

Me: Not yet.

Richie: That's the key, man, I'm telling you. That camera in Aldi will show them. They'll see it's not me.

Wish this was true. How high-res is this footage, though? How likely is it that it'll be clear enough to counteract the witness identification?

We talk about the appeal case for almost the full hour. Just can't get him off the topic. Forensics, overlooked evidence, always the CCTV. Hope, hope, hope.

Leave with shaking knees, take a cab to the station. Need sugar. Have some tiffin Tiffy made in bag; eat about three thousand calories of it as the train rolls through the countryside, flat field after flat field, taking me away from my brother and back to the place where everyone's forgotten him.

Find bin-bag of scarves in centre of bedroom when I get home, with Tiffy's note pasted on its side.

Mr Prior makes two-hundred-pound scarves? Doesn't even take him very long! Ahhh. Think of all the times I turned down his offer of new scarf, hat, glove, or tea cosy. Could have been a billionaire by now.

On bedroom door:

> Hi Tiffy,
>
> THANK YOU for telling me about the scarves. Yes, need the money. Will sell – can you recommend where/how?
>
> Gentleman at work knits them. He's basically giving them away to anyone/everyone who will take them (or else I'd feel bad taking the money . . .)
>
> Leon

Hey,

Oh, definitely – you should sell these through Etsy or Preloved. They'll have tons of customers who would love these scarves.

Umm. Odd question, but might this gentleman at your work be interested in crocheting for commission?

Tiffy x

No idea what that means. Btw, take your fave scarf – will put rest on interweb tonight.

Leon

Fallen on floor by bedroom door (quite hard to track down):

Morning,

As in, I'm working on a book called Crochet Your Way (I know – it's one of my best titles, I have to say) and we need someone to make us four scarves and eight hats very, very fast so we can photograph them to include in the book. He'd have to follow my author's brief (on colour and stitch etc). I can pay him, but not a lot. Can you give me his contact details? I'm really desperate and he's obviously crazily talented.

Oh my God, I'm going to be wearing this scarf all the time (I don't care if it's technically spring time). I love it. Thank you!

Tiffy x

Back to bedroom door again:

Eh. Can't see why this wouldn't work, though might need to run it by Matron. Write me a letter and will give it to her, then to gentleman knitter if she gives the OK.

If you're wearing that scarf all the time, can you dispose of the five hundred scarves currently occupying your side of wardrobe?

Other news: first scarf just sold for £235! Mad. It's not even nice!

Leon

On kitchen breakfast bar, beside unsealed envelope:

Hey,

My side is the key part of that sentence, Leon. My side, and I want to fill it with scarves.

The letter is here – let me know if you think it needs changing at all. At some point we may need to do a bit of a tidy of our notes to one another, by the way. The flat is starting to look like a scene from A Beautiful Mind.

Tiffy x

I pass Tiffy's letter to Matron, who gives me the all-clear to offer Mr Prior the opportunity to knit for Tiffy's book. Or crochet. Am extremely unclear on the difference. No doubt Tiffy will write me a long note at some point with detailed explanation, unprompted. She loves a lengthy explanation. Why use one clause when you could use five? Strange, ridiculous, hilarious woman.

One night later and Mr Prior's got two hats done already – they look hat-like and woolly, so I'm assuming all is as it should be.

Only downside to this arrangement is now Mr Prior is fascinated with Tiffy.

Mr Prior: So she's a book editor.

Me: Yes.

Mr Prior: What an interesting profession.

A pause.

Mr Prior: And she lives with you?

Me: Mm.

Mr Prior: How interesting.

Look at him sideways while writing his notes. He blinks back at me, beady-eyed and innocent.

Mr Prior: I just didn't imagine you'd like living with another person. You like your independence so much. Isn't that why you didn't want to move in with Kay?

Must stop talking to patients about personal life.

Me: It's different. I don't have to see Tiffy. We just leave each other notes, really.

Mr Prior nods thoughtfully.

Mr Prior: The art of letter writing. A profoundly . . . *intimate* thing, a letter, isn't it?

I stare at him suspiciously. Not sure what he's getting at here.

Me: It's Post-it notes on the fridge, Mr Prior, not hand-delivered letters on scented paper.

Mr Prior: Oh, yes, I'm sure you're right. Absolutely. Post-it notes. No art in that, I'm sure.

Next night, and even Holly has heard about Tiffy. Amazing how uninteresting news travels so fast between wards when significant proportion of people in building are bedbound.

Holly: Is she pretty?

Me: I don't know, Holly. Does it matter?

Holly pauses. Thoughtful.

Holly: Is she nice?

Me, after a moment's thought: Yes, she's nice. Bit nosy and strange, but nice.

Holly: What does it mean, that she's your 'flatmate'?

Me: Flatmate means she shares my flat. We live there together.

Holly, eyes widened: Like boyfriend and girlfriend?

Me: No, no. She's not my girlfriend. She's a friend.

Holly: So you sleep in different rooms?

Get bleeped before I have to answer that one, thankfully.

MAY

15

Tiffy

As I peel the Post-it notes and taped scraps of paper off cupboard doors, tables, walls and (in one case) the bin lid, I find myself grinning. It was a weird way to get to know Leon, writing all these notes over the last few months, and it sort of happened without me noticing – one minute I was scribbling him a quick note about leftovers, the next I was in a full-on, day-to-day correspondence.

Though, as I follow the trail of heart-to-hearts along the back of the sofa, I can't help noticing that I generally write about five times as many words as Leon does. And that my Post-it notes are a lot more personal and revealing than his. It's kind of strange reading it all back – you can see how dodgy my memory is, for starters. Like in one of the notes, I mentioned how super awkward it was that I'd forgotten to pass on Rachel's birthday-party invite to Justin last year, but I remember now – I *did* invite him. We ended up having a huge fight about whether I could go. Justin always said my memory was terrible; it's very annoying to find written evidence that he's right.

It's half five now. I finished work early because everyone's out of the office for a goodbye party that I can't afford to go to, so I made an executive decision to go home in the absence of any actual executives to make the decision for me. I'm sure it's what they would have wanted.

I thought I might actually catch Leon tonight, as I got back at around 5 p.m. It felt a bit strange. I'm not really allowed to come home early and bump into him, according to the official terms of our agreement. I knew when I signed up for this that we wouldn't be in the flat at the same time – that was why it was such a good idea. But I didn't realise that we would *literally* never meet. Like, ever, at all, for four whole months.

I did think about spending this hour at the coffee place around the corner, but then I thought . . . it is starting to get a bit weird, being friends but not having actually met. And it does feel like that, like we're friends – I don't think it could be otherwise, the way we're in each other's space all the time. I know exactly how he likes his eggs fried, though I've never actually seen him eat one (there's always tons of runny yolk left over on the plate). I could describe his dress sense pretty accurately, even though I've never seen him *in* any of the clothes drying on the clothes horse in the living room. And, weirdest of all, I know what he smells like.

I don't see any reason why we shouldn't meet – it wouldn't change the terms of how we live here. It would just mean I would actually recognise my flatmate if I saw him walking down the street.

The phone rings, which is odd, because I wasn't aware we had a phone. At first I go for my mobile, but my ringtone is a jingly happy tune from right down the list of those available from Samsung, not the retro *ring ring* that's currently singing out from somewhere invisible in the living room.

I eventually track down a landline on the kitchen counter, under one of Mr Prior's scarves and a string of notes about whether or not Leon used up all the butter (he totally did).

A landline! Who knew! I thought landlines were just relics you paid for in order to get broadband.

'Hello?' I try tentatively.

'Oh, hey,' says the guy at the other end. He sounds surprised (presumably I am more female than he had expected) and has a weird accent – kind of half Irish, half Londoner.

'It's Tiffy,' I offer. 'Leon's flatmate.'

'Ey! Hi!' He seems to have been greatly cheered by this fact. 'And don't you mean bedmate?'

'We prefer flatmate,' I say, wincing.

'Fair play,' he says, and somehow I can sort of hear that he's grinning. 'Well, nice to meet you, Tiffy. I'm Richie. Leon's brother.'

'Pleased to meet you too, Richie.' I didn't know Leon had a brother. But then I suppose there are probably an enormous number of things I don't know about Leon, even if I do know what he's reading before bed at the moment (*The Bell Jar*, very slowly). 'You just missed Leon, I guess. I got in half an hour ago and he was already gone.'

'The man works too hard,' Richie says. 'I didn't realise it was half five already. What's your tap-in-tap-out time?'

'Six, usually, but I got out of work early,' I say. 'You could try him on his mobile?'

'Ah, now you see, Tiffy, I can't do that,' Richie says.

I frown. 'You can't call his mobile?'

'To be honest with you, it's a bit of a long story.' Richie pauses. 'Short version is, I'm in a high-security prison, and the only phone number I've managed to get set up for me to call is Leon's home line. Mobiles cost twice as much to call, too, and I earn about fourteen pounds a week in my job cleaning the wing, which by the way I had to pay someone to get me . . . so that doesn't get me very far.'

I feel a little shell-shocked. 'Shit!' I say. 'That's awful. Are you all right?'

It just comes out. It's almost certainly not the right thing to say in the circumstance, but there we are – that's what I'm thinking, and that's what comes out of my mouth.

To my surprise – and maybe to his too – Richie starts laughing.

'I'm all right,' he says, after a moment. 'Cheers, though. It's been seven months now. I guess I'm . . . what is it Leon calls it? *Acclimatising*. Learning how to live, as well as just get through each minute.'

I nod. 'Well, that's something, at least. How is it? On the scale of, you know, Alcatraz to the Hilton?'

He laughs again. 'Definitely somewhere on that scale, yeah. Where-abouts depends on how I'm feeling day to day. But I'm pretty lucky compared to lots of people, let me tell you that. I have my own cell now, and I can see visitors twice a month.'

It doesn't seem like he's lucky from where I'm standing. 'I don't want to keep you on the phone if it's costing you. Did you have a message for Leon?'

There's a rattling sort of silence at the other end, just the sound of echoing background noise.

'Aren't you going to ask what I'm in for, Tiffy?'

'No,' I say, taken aback. 'Do you want to tell me?'

'Yeah, a bit. But normally people ask.'

I shrug. 'It's not my place to judge – you're Leon's brother, and you rang to talk to him. And anyway, we were talking about how horrible prison is, and that's true regardless of what you did. Everyone knows prison doesn't work. Right?'

'Right – I mean, do they?'

'Oh, sure.'

More silence.

'I'm in for armed robbery. But I didn't do it.'

'God. I'm sorry. This is really shit, then.'

'Pretty much, yeah,' Richie says. He waits. And then he asks, 'Do you believe me?'

'I don't even know you. Why does it matter?'

'I don't know. It just . . . does.'

'Well, I need some of the facts before I say I believe you. It wouldn't mean much otherwise, would it?'

'That's my message for Leon then. Tell him I'd like him to give you the facts, so you can tell me if you believe me.'

'Hang on.' I reach for a pad of Post-it notes and a pen. '*Hi Leon*,' I say, reading as I write. '*This is a message from Richie. He says . . .*'

'I'd like Tiffy to know what happened to me. I want her to believe I didn't do it. She seems like a very nice lady, and I bet she's pretty to boot, you can just tell man, she's got that kind of voice – deep and sexy, you know the—'

I'm laughing. 'I'm not writing that!'

'How far did you get?'

'"Sexy",' I admit, and Richie laughs.

'All right. You can sign the note off now. But leave that last bit, if you don't mind – it'll make Leon smile.'

I shake my head, but I'm smiling too. 'Fine. I'll leave it. It was good to meet you, Richie.'

'You too, Tiffy. You look after my brother for me, all right?'

I pause, surprised at the request. For starters, it seems like Richie's the one who needs looking after, and for seconds, I'm really not best placed for looking after any of the Twomey family, given that I've never met a single one of them. But by the time I open my mouth to respond, Richie's hung up the phone, and all I can hear is the dial tone.

16

Leon

Can't help laughing. This is typical. He's trying to charm his way into the affections of my flatmate even from a prison yard.

Kay leans over my shoulder, reading the note.

Kay: Richie is still his old self, I see.

I stiffen. She feels it and tenses too, but doesn't backtrack or say sorry.

Me: He's trying to keep things light. Keep everyone laughing. It's Richie's way.

Kay: Well, is Tiffy on the market?

Me: She's a human, not a cow, Kay.

Kay: You're so *principled*, Leon! It was an expression, 'on the market'. You know I'm not actually trying to sell the poor girl to Richie.

There's something else wrong with that sentence, but am too tired to trace it.

Me: She's single, but in love with her ex still.

Kay, interested now: Really?

Can't fathom why she'd care – whenever I mention Tiffy she switches off or gets grumpy. This is first time we've been in my flat for months, actually. Kay has the morning off work so came to see me for brinner before bed. She got a bit prickly about the notes stuck everywhere, for some reason.

Me: Ex seems average. Far inferior to bricklayer-turned—

Kay rolls eyes.

Kay: Will you *stop* talking about that bloody bricklayer book!

She wouldn't be so judgemental if she'd read it.

A few weeks on and it's the sort of sunny day that normally only happens abroad. England is unaccustomed to such warmth, especially when it strikes so suddenly. It's only June, barely summer yet. Commuters hurry around corners, heads still down as if it's raining, backs of pale-blue shirts stained dark with Vs of sweat. Teenage boys whip off T-shirts until there are stark white limbs and chests and gawky sticking-out elbows all over the place. Can barely move without being confronted with sunburnt skin and/or unpleasant body heat emanating from man in suit.

Am on my way back from visit to Imperial War Museum Research Room, following a final lead on the hunt for Johnny White. In my backpack, I have a list of eight names and addresses. Addresses were gathered through endless record-office riffling, contacting relatives, and online stalking, so not exactly foolproof, but it's a start – or rather, eight starts. Mr Prior gave me plenty to bulk out my research in the end. Get the man talking and he remembers a lot more than he claims to.

Every man on list is called Johnny White. Unsure where to start. Pick favourite Johnny? Nearest Johnny?

Get out phone and text Tiffy. Filled her in on the search for Mr Prior's Johnny White last month. Was after a lengthy letter from her about ups and downs of book about crochet; I was obviously in a sharing sort of mood. It's peculiar. Like Tiffy's compulsive oversharing is contagious. Always feel slightly embarrassed when I get to the hospice and remember whatever I ended up revealing in that evening's scribbled note written with coffee before heading to the door.

> Hi. Got eight Johnnies (sing. Johnny) to choose from. How to pick where to start? Leon

Response comes five minutes or so later. She's working on the crazy crochet author's book full-time, and it appears her concentration is low. I'm not surprised. Crochet is weird and boring. Even tried reading some of the manuscript when she left it on the coffee table, to check was not like bricklayer book, but no. It's just a book of detailed crochet instructions, with end results that look very difficult to achieve.

> That's easy. Eenie meenie mini emo, catch a tiger by its toe . . . xx

And then, two seconds later,

> Eenie meenie MINIE MO. Autocorrect. I don't think you'd gain much by getting any small emos involved xx

Peculiar woman. Nonetheless, dutifully pause in patch of shade under bus stop to get out list of names and do eenie meenie. Land on Johnny White (obviously). It's the one who lives up near Birmingham.

> Good choice. Can visit this one when next visiting Richie – he's in Birmingham area. Thanks. Leon.

A few minutes of silence. Walk through busy, sweaty London as it basks in the heat, sunglasses turned up to the sky. I'm knackered. Should have been in bed hours ago. But I spend so little actual daylight time out here in the open air these days, and miss the feel of sun on skin. Consider idly whether I might be vitamin D deficient, then thoughts shift, and I'm wondering how much open-air time Richie got this week. According to government, he should be let outside for thirty minutes a day. That rarely happens. Prison guards are low on numbers; time unlocked is even more limited than usual.

> Did you get my note about Richie, by the way? And telling me what
> happened to him? I don't want to push but it was over a month ago now,
> and I just want you to know I would like to hear it, if you want to tell it. xx

I stare down at her text, sun bleaching my screen until the words are almost invisible. I shade it with one hand and reread. It's odd, how it came like that, just as I was thinking of Richie.

Wasn't sure what to make of Richie's note about telling Tiffy. As soon as I knew they'd spoken I found myself wondering if Tiffy thinks he's innocent, even though she doesn't know him and doesn't know a thing about the case. Ridiculous. Even if she knew everything, it shouldn't matter if she believes him. Haven't even met her. But it's always like this – a constant nagging that you feel with everybody, no matter who they are. You're conversing perfectly normally, and then, next moment, you're thinking, 'Would you believe my brother is innocent?'

Can't ask people, though. Is a horrible conversation to have and a horrible thing to be asked on the spot, as Kay will testify.

Reply via note when I get home. Don't really text Tiffy much; feels a bit weird. Like emailing Mam. Notes are just . . . how we talk.

On wardrobe (latest note trail stops here):

I'll ask Richie to write to you, if that's OK. He can tell it best.

Also, a thought: could your crochet author come to St Marks (where I work) sometime? We're looking to put on more entertainment for patients. Strikes me that crochet, though dull, may interest ill elderly people. x

Hey Leon,

Of course. Whenever Richie's ready.

And yes! Please! PR are always looking for opportunities like that. Can I just say, though, you've timed this very well, because Katherin has just become A CELEBRITY. Check out this tweet she did.

Printed-out screenshot from Twitter, pasted below note:

Katherin Rosen @KnittingKatherin

One of the fantastic scarves you can make from my upcoming book, Crochet Your Way. Take time out for mindfulness, and create something beautiful!

117 comments, 8k retweets, 23k likes.

New Post-it note below that:

Yeah. EIGHT THOUSAND RETWEETS. (For one of Mr Prior's scarves, too – be sure to tell him!)

Next Post-it note:

I'm assuming you don't know much about Twitter because your laptop hasn't even moved for several months, let alone been charged, but that is a lot of retweets, Leon. A LOT. And it all happened because this amazing DIY Youtuber called Tasha Chai-Latte retweeted it and said this:

Printed-out screenshot from Twitter (now so low down the wardrobe door I have to crouch to read it):

Tasha Chai-Latte @ChaiLatteDIY

Crochet is totally the new colouring-in! So much awe for @KnittingKatherin for her amazing designs. #bemindful #crochetyourway

69 comments, 32k retweets, 67k likes.

Another two Post-it notes beneath:

She has 15 million followers. The marketing and PR teams are basically peeing themselves with excitement. Unfortunately this means I've had to explain YouTube to Katherin, and she's even worse than you with technology (she has one of those old Nokias that only drug dealers use), plus odious Martin from PR 'live tweets' from all Katherin's events now, but still. It's exciting! My lovely oddball Katherin might actually be in with a shot at a bestsellers list! Not the *bestsellers list, obviously, but one of the niche ones on Amazon. Like, you know, number one in crafts and origami, or something. xx*

. . . Will wait until I've slept before attempting to reply to this one.

JULY

17

Tiffy

It's still light when I get home. I *love* summer. Leon's trainers are missing, so I guess he walked to work today – I'm so jealous he can do that. The tube is even more gross when it's hot.

I scan the flat for new notes. They're not always that easy to spot these days – there's usually Post-it notes on pretty much everything, unless one of us has got around to doing a clear-up.

I spot it on the kitchen counter eventually: an envelope, with Richie's name and prisoner number on one side and our address on the other. There's a short note in Leon's handwriting next to the address.

The letter from Richie is here.

And then, inside:

Dear Tiffy,
Twas a dark and stormy night . . .
   All right, OK, no it wasn't. It was a dark and grotty night at Daffie's Nightclub in Clapham. I was already plastered when I got there – we were coming from a friend's housewarming.
   I danced with a few girls that night. You'll get why I'm telling you

that later. It was a really mixed crowd, lots of young guys out of uni, lots of those creepy types who hang around the edges of the dance floor waiting for girls to get too drunk so they can make their move. But right at the back, at one of the tables, there were a few guys who looked like they belonged somewhere else.

It's hard to explain. They looked like they were there for a different reason from everyone else. They didn't want to pull, they didn't want to get drunk, they didn't want to dance.

So I know now they wanted to do business. They're known as the Bloods, apparently. I only found that out much later, when I was inside and telling guys here my story, so I'm guessing you've never heard of them either. If you're a pretty much middle-class person who just happens to live in London and goes about their business going to work and everything, you'll probably never know gangs like this exist.

But they're important. I think even then I could tell that, looking at them. But I was also very drunk.

One of the guys came to the bar with his girl. There were only two women with the group, and this one looked bored out of her mind, you could just see it. She caught my eye down the bar and started to look a lot more interested.

I looked back. If she's bored of her bloke, that's his problem, not mine. I'm not going to miss the chance to make eyes with a pretty lady just because the guy standing next to her looks tougher than the average bloke in Daffie's, let me tell you that.

He found me later, in the bathroom. Pushed me up against the wall.

'Keep your hands off, you hear me?'

You know the drill. He was shouting right in my face, a vein pulsing in his forehead.

'I have no idea what you're talking about,' I said. Calm as a cucumber.

He shouted a lot more. Pushed me a bit. I stood firm, but I didn't push back or hit him. He said he'd seen me dancing with her, which wasn't true. I know she wasn't one of the girls I'd danced with earlier in the night, I would have remembered her.

Still, he'd wound me up, and when she turned up later, just before the club closed, I was probably more inclined to chat to her than I would have been, just to piss him off.

We flirted. I bought her a drink. The Bloods, out there at the back, talked business and didn't seem to notice. I kissed her. She kissed me back. I remember I was so drunk I felt dizzy when I closed my eyes, so I kissed her with my eyes open.

And then that was it. She just sort of faded back into the club somewhere – it's all hazy, I really was plastered. I couldn't tell you exactly when she left, or I left, or whatever.

From this point on, I can't verify everything. If I could, obviously I wouldn't be writing this to you from here, I'd be chilling on your famous beanbag with a cup of Leon's milky coffee and this would probably just be a funny anecdote I'd tell at the pub.

But anyway. Here's what I think happened.

They followed me and my mates when we left. The others got night buses, but I didn't live far, so I walked it. I went into the off-licence on Clapham Road that stays open all night and bought cigarettes and a six-pack of beers. I didn't even want them – I definitely didn't need them. It was nearly four in the morning and I was probably not even walking straight. But I went in, paid cash, went home. I didn't even see them, but they can't have been far away when I got out of there, because according to the camera in the store 'I came back in' two minutes later with my hoody pulled up and a balaclava on.

When you watch the footage, the guy does have a similar build to me. But as I pointed out in court – whoever it is, they're doing a better job of walking properly than I did. I was way too drunk to be able to dodge the bargain bins and get the knife out of the back of my jeans all at the same time.

I had no idea any of this had happened until two days later when I was arrested at work.

They got the kid at the till to unlock the safe. There was four thousand five hundred pounds in there. They were smart, or maybe just experienced – they didn't speak any more than they had to, and so when the kid gave evidence she hardly had anything to recount. Other than the knife pointed in her face, obviously.

I was on CCTV. I had a previous criminal record. They pulled me in.

Once I'd been charged they wouldn't grant me bail. My lawyer took me on because he was interested, and he felt confident in the only witness, the girl at the till, but they got to her as well in the end. We were expecting her to stand up there and say the guy who came in the second time couldn't have been me. That she'd seen me in the off-licence before and I'd been perfectly nice and not tried to nick anything.

But she pointed at me across the courtroom. Said it was me for sure. It was like a living nightmare, I can't even tell you. I could just see it playing out, and watch how the jury members' faces changed, but I couldn't do anything. I tried to get up and speak and the judge just shouted at me – you're not allowed to talk out of turn. My turn never seemed to come, though. By the time they got to questioning me, everyone's mind was made up.

Sal asked me bullshit stupid questions, and I didn't get the chance to say anything good, my head was all over the place, I just hadn't thought it would come to that. The prosecution played on my dodgy record from a few years back – I'd got in a couple of fights on nights out when I was nineteen, when I was at my lowest (that's another story, and I swear it isn't as bad as it sounds). They made out like I was violent. They even dredged up a guy I used to work with in a café who properly hated me – we'd fallen out over some girl he'd liked in college, who I'd ended up taking to the prom or some other crap like that. It was kind of amazing, watching them spin it. I can see why the jury believed I was guilty. Those lawyers were really fucking good at making it sound true.

They sentenced me to eight years for armed robbery.

So here I am. I can't even tell you. Every time I write it out or tell it to someone I can't believe it even more, if that makes sense. All I get is angrier.

It wasn't a complicated case. We all thought Sal would sort it on appeal. (Sal's the lawyer, by the way.) But he hasn't fucking got to the appeal yet. I was sentenced last November and there's no appeal even in sight. I know Leon is trying to sort it, and I love that man for it, but the fact is nobody gives a shit about getting me out of here except him. And Mam, I guess.

I'll be honest with you, Tiffy, I'm shaking now. I want to scream. These times are the worst – there's nowhere to go. Press-ups are your friend, but sometimes you need to run, and when you've got three steps between your bed and your toilet, there's not a lot of room for that.

Anyway. This is a very long letter, and I know it took me a while to write it – you've maybe forgotten about the whole conversation we had by now. You don't have to reply, but if you want to, Leon can send it with his next letter maybe – if you do write, please send stamps and envelopes too.

I hope you believe me, even more than I usually do. Maybe it's because you're important to my brother, and my brother is like the only person who is properly important to me.

Yours,

Richie xx

The next morning I reread the letter in bed, the duvet pulled up around me like a nest. I'm all cold in my stomach, and my skin has gone kind of prickly. I want to cry for this man. I don't know why this is hitting me so hard, but whatever it is, this letter has woken me up at half five on a Saturday morning. That is how much I cannot bear it. It's so *unfair*.

I'm reaching for my phone before I've really thought about what I'm doing.

'Gerty, you know your job?'

'I'm familiar with it, yes. Primarily as the reason that I am awoken at six a.m. almost every morning, bar Saturday mornings.'

I look at the clock. Six a.m.

'Sorry. But – what kind of law do you do again?'

'Criminal law, Tiffy. I do criminal law.'

'Right, right. What does that *mean* though?'

'I'm going to give you the benefit of the doubt and assume that this is urgent,' Gerty says. She is audibly gritting her teeth. 'We deal with crimes that are against people and their property.'

'Like armed robbery?'

'Yes. That is a good example, well done.'

'You hate me, don't you? I'm top of your hate list right now.'

'It's my one lie-in and you've ruined it, so yes, you have climbed past Donald Trump and that Uber driver I sometimes get who hums for the whole journey.'

Shit. Things are not going well.

'You know the special cases you do for free, or for less money, or whatever?'

Gerty pauses. 'Where's this going, Tiffy?'

'Just hear me out. If I give you a letter from a guy convicted of armed robbery will you just take a look at it? You don't have to do anything. You don't have to take him on or whatever, obviously, I know you have tons more important cases. But will you just read it, and maybe write a list of questions?'

'Where did you get this letter from?'

'It's a long story, and it doesn't matter. Just know I wouldn't ask you if it wasn't important.'

There is a long, sleepy sort of silence at the other end of the phone.

'Of course I'll read it. Come over for lunch and bring the letter.'

'I love you.'

'I hate you.'

'I know. I'll bring you a latte from Moll's, though. Donald Trump would never bring you a latte from Moll's.'

'Fine. I'll make my decision on your relative placement on the hate list when I've tasted how hot the coffee is. Do not ring me again before ten.' She hangs up.

Gerty and Mo's flat has been completely Gerty-fied. You almost can't tell Mo lives here. His room at his last place was a tip of washed and unwashed clothes (no system) and paperwork that was probably confidential, but here, every object has a purpose. The flat is tiny, but I don't notice it nearly as much as I did the first time I saw the place – somehow Gerty's drawn attention away from the low ceilings and towards the enormous windows, which fill the kitchen-diner with soft summer sunlight. And it's so *clean*. I have new respect for Gerty and what she can achieve through sheer willpower, or possibly bullying.

I hand her the coffee. She gives it a sip, then nods in approval. I do a little fist pump, officially becoming a less odious human being than the man who wants to build a wall between Mexico and the US.

'Letter,' she says, stretching out her free hand.

Not one for small talk, Gerty. I rifle through my bag and pass it over, and she immediately heads off to read, picking up her glasses from the side table by the front door where, unbelievably, she never seems to forget to put them.

I fidget. I pace a bit. I mess up the order of the pile of books on the end of their dining table, just for the thrill of it.

'Go away,' she says, not even raising her voice. 'You are distracting me. Mo is at the coffee place on the corner that does inferior coffee. He will entertain you.'

'Right. Fine. So . . . you're reading it though? What do you think?'

She doesn't answer. I roll my eyes, and then scarper in case she noticed.

I've not even made it to the coffee shop before my phone rings. It's Gerty.

'You might as well come back,' she says.

'Oh?'

'The trial transcript will take forty-eight hours to get to me even with the express service. I can't tell you anything useful until I've read that.'

I'm smiling. 'You're applying for the trial transcript?'

'Men often have very convincing stories of their innocence, Tiffy, and I would recommend against believing their summaries of their court cases. They are, obviously, extremely biased, and also do not tend to be well versed in the intricacies of the law.'

I'm still smiling. 'You're applying for the trial transcript, though.'

'Don't get anyone's hopes up,' Gerty says, and her voice is serious now. 'I mean it, Tiffy. I'm just going to read up on it. Don't tell this man anything, please. It would be cruel to give him unfounded hope.'

'I know,' I say, smile dropping. 'I won't. And thanks.'

'You're welcome. The coffee was excellent. Now get back here – if I must be up this early on a Saturday, I would at least like to be entertained.'

18

Leon

On the way to meet Johnny White the First. It's very early – four-hour journey there, then three buses to get from Johnny White the First's place to HMP Groundsworth, where I have a 3 p.m. visit with Richie. Legs stiff from train seats with limited leg room; back sweaty from carriages without air conditioning. As I roll up shirt sleeves further, discover old Post-it note from Tiffy stuck in the cuff. Something from last month about what the strange man in Flat 5 does at 7 a.m. Hmm. Embarrassing. Must check clothes for notes before leaving the flat.

Greeton, home of Johnny White, is a surprisingly pretty little town, stretched out flat on the matt green fields of the Midlands. Walk from bus station to JW's address. Have emailed him a couple of times, but am not sure what to expect in person.

When I arrive, a very large and intimidating Johnny White barks at me to come in; I find myself immediately obeying and following him through to sparsely furnished living room. Only distinctive feature is piano in corner. It's uncovered and looks well treated.

Me: You play?

JW the First: I was a concert pianist in my day. I don't play so much now, but I keep the old girl in here. It doesn't feel like home without her.

I'm delighted. It's perfect. Concert pianist! World's coolest profession! And no pictures anywhere of wife or children – excellent.

JW the First offers me tea; what appears is a thick, chipped mug of builder's brew. It reminds me of tea at Mam's. A strange moment of homesickness follows – must go and see her more.

JW the First and I settle on sofa and armchair, opposite one another. Suddenly realising this is a potentially difficult subject to broach. Did you have a love affair with a man in World War Two? Is perhaps not something this man wants to talk about with stranger from London.

JW the First: So, what was it you were after, exactly?

Me: I was wondering. Umm.

Clear throat.

Me: You served in the army in World War Two, yes?

JW the First: Two years, with a short break for them to dig a bullet out of my stomach.

Find myself staring at his stomach. JW the First flashes surprisingly dynamic grin at me.

JW the First: You're thinking they must have had a job finding it, aren't you?

Me: No! I was thinking there are lots of vital organs in the stomach area.

JW the First, chuckling: German buggers missed those, lucky for me. Anyway, I was more worried about my hands than my stomach. You can play the piano without a spleen, but you can't play the piano if frostbite's eaten your fingers off.

Gaze at JW the First in awe and horror. He chuckles again.

JW the First: Ah, you don't want my old war horror stories. Did you say you're looking into your family history?

Me: Not mine. A friend's. Robert Prior. He served in the same regiment as you, though I'm not sure it was exactly at the same time. Do you happen to remember him?

JW the First thinks hard. Scrunches up nose. Tilts head.

JW the First: No. Doesn't ring any bells. Sorry.

Eh, was long shot. One down, though, still seven on list to go.

Me: Thanks, Mr White. I won't take more of your time. Just one question – have you ever married?

JW the First, gruffer than ever: No. My Sally died in an air raid back in forty-one, and that was that for me. I never found anyone like my Sally.

I almost get teary at that. Richie would laugh at me – he always calls me a hopeless romantic. Or ruder things to that effect.

Kay, on other end of phone: Honestly, Leon. I think if you had your way, all of your friends would be over the age of eighty.

Me: He was an interesting man, is all. I enjoyed speaking to him. And – concert pianist! World's coolest profession, no?

Amused silence from Kay.

Me: Still seven to go, though.

Kay: Seven what?

Me: Seven Johnny Whites.

Kay: Oh, yeah.

She pauses.

Kay: Are you going to be spending all your weekends traipsing across Britain trying to find an old man's boyfriend, Leon?

I pause this time. Had sort of planned on doing that, yes. When else am I going to find Mr Prior's Johnny? Can't do it during working week.

Me, tentatively: . . . No?

Kay: Good. Because I see you rarely enough as it is, with all your visits and your shifts. You do see that, don't you?

Me: Yes. Sorry. I'm—

Kay: Yep, yep, I know, you care about your job, Richie needs you. I do know all that. I'm not trying to be difficult, Leon. I just feel like . . . it should bother you more. As much as it bothers me. The not seeing each other.

Me: It bothers me! But I saw you this morning?

Kay: For about half an hour, for a very rushed breakfast.

Flash of irritation. Gave up half an hour of three-hour power nap to allow for breakfast with Kay. Deep breath. Notice where we are out of window.

Me: Got to go. I'm pulling into the prison.

Kay: Fine. Let's talk later. Will you text me what train you get?

I don't like this – the checking-up, the texting about trains, always knowing where the other person will be. But . . . it's unreasonable of me. Can't object. Kay already thinks I'm a commitment-phobe. It's a favourite term of hers at the moment.

Me: Will do.

But I don't, in the end. Mean to, but don't. It's the worst argument we've had in ages.

19

'It's the perfect venue for you, Katherin,' Martin gushes, spreading the photos out on the table.

I smile encouragingly. Though initially I thought the whole enormous-venue thing was ridiculous, I'm starting to come around to it. Twenty different YouTube videos have been made by various Internet celebrities sporting outfits they claimed to have crocheted themselves from Katherin's instructions. After a tense unscheduled meeting with the MD in which the head of PR did a quite convincing job of pretending to know what this book was, let alone have budget allocated for it, the whole Butterfingers office is now up to speed and abuzz with excitement. Everyone seems to have forgotten that last week they didn't give a crap about crochet; yesterday I heard the sales director declare she'd 'always suspected this book would be a winner'.

Katherin is perplexed by all of this, particularly the Tasha Chai-Latte thing. At first she reacted as literally everyone does when they see some random person making tons of money on YouTube ('I could do that!' she announced. I told her to start by investing in a smartphone. Baby steps.) Now she's just irritated at Martin having taken control of her Twitter account ('She can't be trusted with this! We need to *maintain control*!' Martin was yelling at Ruby this morning).

'So, what *is* a proper book launch?' Katherin asks. 'I mean, normally

I just potter around drinking the wine and chatting to any old lady who bothers to turn up. But how do you do it when there are all these people?' She gestures to the photo of a gigantic Islington hall.

'Ah, now, Katherin,' Martin says, 'I'm glad you asked. Tiffy and I are going to take you along to one of our other big book launches in two weeks' time. Just so you can see how these things are done.'

'Are there free drinks?' Katherin asks, perking up.

'Oh, absolutely, tons of free drinks,' Martin says, having previously told me that there won't be any at all.

I glance at my watch as Martin returns to the task of selling the enormous venue to Katherin. Katherin is very worried about the people at the back not being able to see. I, on the other hand, am very worried about getting to Leon's hospice on time.

It's the evening of our visit. Leon will be there, which means tonight, after five and a half months of living together, he and I will finally meet.

I'm oddly nervous. I changed my clothes three times this morning, which is unusual – normally I can't imagine the day looking any other way once I've got an outfit on. Now I'm not sure I've got it right. I've toned down the lemon-yellow pouf dress with a denim jacket, leggings, and my lily boots, but I'm still dressed in something a sixteen-year-old girl would wear to prom. There's just something fundamentally try-hard about tulle.

'Don't you think we should be heading over now?' I say, interrupting Martin mid bullshit. I want to get to the hospice in time to find Leon and say thanks before we start. I'd rather he didn't walk in Justin-style, just as Katherin's sticking pins into me.

Martin glares at me, turning his head so Katherin won't see quite how vicious a look he is shooting in my direction. She of course spots it anyway, and cheers up at the sight, chuckling into her coffee cup. She was grumpy with me when I got here because I'd (clearly) ignored her instruction to wear 'neutral clothing' again. My excuse that wearing beige sucks the life out of me did not fly. 'We all have to make sacrifices for our art, Tiffy!' she said, waggling a finger. I did point out that this isn't actually *my* art, it's hers, but she looked so wounded I gave up and said I'd compromise by taking out the poufy underskirt.

It's good to see our mutual dislike of Martin has united us again.

I'm not sure why I think I know what a hospice will look like – I've never been to one before. This one ticks a few of my boxes, even so: lino floors in halls, medical equipment spouting wires and tubes, poor quality art in wonky frames on the walls. But there's a friendlier atmosphere than I expected. Everyone seems to know each other: doctors make sardonic comments as they cross paths in the corridor, patients chuckle wheezily to their ward-mates, and at one point I hear a nurse arguing quite passionately with an elderly Yorkshireman about which flavour of rice pudding is best on tonight's dinner menu.

The receptionist leads us down the bewildering maze of corridors to a sort of living area. There's a rickety plastic table where we're to set up, plus lots of uncomfortable-looking seating and a television like the one in my parents' house – it's blocky and enormous at the back, like they're stashing all the extra shopping channels in there.

We dump the bags of wool and crochet hooks. A few of the more mobile patients drift into the room. Evidently word of our crochet show has spread, probably via the nurses and doctors, who seem to be running in totally random directions at all times, like pinballs. It's fifteen minutes until we start, though – plenty of time for me to track Leon down and say hello.

'Excuse me,' I say to a nurse whose pinball path has briefly crossed the living area, 'is Leon here yet?'

'Leon?' she asks, looking at me distractedly. 'Yeah. He's here. You need him?'

'Oh, no, don't worry,' I say. 'It's not, you know, medical. I was just going to say hi and thanks for letting us do this.' I wave an arm in the direction of Martin and Katherin, who are untangling wool with varying degrees of enthusiasm.

The nurse perks up and focuses on me properly. 'Are you Tiffy?'

'Umm. Yes?'

'Oh! Hi. Wow, hello. If you want to see him, he'll be in Dorsal Ward, I think – follow the signs.'

'Thanks so much,' I say as she scurries off again.

Dorsal Ward. OK. I check the sign fixed to the wall: left, apparently. Then right. Then left, left, right, left, right, right – bloody hell. This place goes on for ever.

'Excuse me,' I ask, snagging a passing person in scrubs, 'am I on track to get to Dorsal Ward?'

'Sure are,' he says, without slowing. Hmm. I'm not sure how much he engaged with that question. I guess if you work here you get really sick of visitors asking for directions. I stare at the next sign: Dorsal Ward has now disappeared altogether.

The guy in scrubs pops up beside me, having backtracked down the corridor again. I jump.

'Sorry, you're not Tiffy, are you?' he says.

'Yes? Hi?'

'Really! Damn.' He looks me up and down quite blatantly, and then realises what he's doing and pulls a face. 'God, sorry, it's just none of us quite believed it. Leon will be on Kelp Ward – take the next left.'

'Believed what?' I call after him, but he's already gone, leaving a set of double doors swinging behind him.

This is . . . weird.

As I turn back I spot a male nurse with light-brown skin and dark hair, whose navy-blue scrubs look threadbare even from here – I've noticed how worn Leon's scrubs are when they're drying on the clothes horse. We make eye contact for a split second, but then he turns his head, checking the pager on his hip, and jogs off down the opposite corridor. He's tall. It might have been him? We were too far apart to tell for sure. I walk more quickly to follow him, get slightly out of breath, then feel a bit stalkerish, and slow down again. Crap. I think I missed the turning to Kelp Ward.

I take stock in the middle of the corridor. Without the tulle skirt my dress has deflated, clinging to the fabric of my leggings; I'm hot and flustered, and, let's be honest, completely lost.

The sign says next left for the Leisure Room, which is where I started. I sigh, checking the time. Only five minutes until our show should begin – I'd better get back in there. I'll track Leon down afterwards, hopefully without encountering any more slightly freaky strangers who know my name.

There's a sizeable crowd when I head back into the room; Katherin spots me with relief and kicks off the show right away. I dutifully follow her instructions, and, while Katherin enthusiastically extols the virtues of the closed stitch, I scan the room. The patients are a mix of elderly ladies and gentlemen, about two thirds of whom are in wheelchairs, and a few middle-aged ladies who look quite poorly but much more interested in what Katherin's saying than anybody else is. There are three kids, too. One is a little girl whose hair is just growing back after chemo, I'm guessing. Her eyes are enormous and I notice them because she's not staring at Katherin like everybody else is, she's watching me, and beaming.

I give her a little wave. Katherin slaps my hand.

'You're a dreadful mannequin today!' she scolds, and I'm brought back to the moment on the cruise ship in February, the last time Katherin was manhandling me into various uncomfortable positions in the name of crochet. For an instant, I can recall Justin's expression exactly as it was when our eyes locked – not the way it looks in my memory, faded and changed with time, but as it actually was. A shiver goes through me.

Katherin casts me a curious look, and I snap out of the memory with an effort, managing a reassuring smile. As I look up I see a tall, dark-haired man in scrubs push through a door into one of the other wards, and my heart jumps. But it's not Leon. I'm almost glad. I'm unsettled, off-kilter – it's somehow not the moment I want to meet him.

'Arms up, Tiffy!' Katherin trills in my ear, and, with a shake of my head, I go back to doing as I'm told.

20

Leon

Letter is crumpled in trouser pocket. Tiffy asked me to read it before I send it on to Richie. But haven't, yet. It's painful. Feel suddenly sure that she won't understand. That she'll say he's a calculating criminal, just like the judge did. Say his excuses don't add up, that given his character and his past he's exactly what we should all have expected.

I'm stressed, shoulders tense. Barely caught a glimpse, and yet can't shake the feeling that red-headed woman at the other end of the corridor to Dorsal Ward might have been her. If it was, hope she didn't think I ran off. Obviously, did run off. But still. Would rather she didn't know it.

Just . . . don't want to face her before I've read the letter.

So. Clearly, must read letter. In the meantime, might hide out on Kelp Ward to avoid unplanned mid-corridor encounters.

Pass through reception en route and am accosted by June, who's at the desk.

June: Your *friend* has arrived!

Only told a couple of people that this crochet event was organised by my flatmate. It has proven to be incredibly interesting gossip. Everyone seems insultingly surprised that I have a flatmate; apparently I look like a man who lives alone.

Me: Thanks, June.

June: She's in the Leisure Room!

Me: Thanks, June.

June: She's ever so pretty.

Blink. Haven't given Tiffy's appearance much thought, aside from wondering whether she wears five dresses at once (would explain sheer quantity hanging in our wardrobe). Am briefly tempted to ask if she has red hair, but think better of it.

June: Lovely girl. Really lovely. I'm *so* glad you've found such a lovely girl to live with.

I stare suspiciously at June. She beams back at me. Wonder who she's been talking to – Holly? That girl has become obsessed with Tiffy.

Do odd jobs on Kelp Ward. Take unprecedented coffee break. Can't put this off any longer. Not even any seriously unwell patients to keep me busy – I've got nothing to do but read this letter.

Unfold it. Look away, heart twisting. This is ridiculous. Why does it even matter?

Right. Looking at letter. Confronting letter, like adult faced with opinion of another adult who has asked them to read something and whose opinion shouldn't even matter.

Does matter, though. Should be honest with myself: I like having Tiffy's notes to come home to, and I'll be sad to lose her if she is cruel to Richie. Not that she will be. But . . . that's what I've thought before. Never know how people will react until you see it.

Dear Richie,

Thanks so much for your letter. It made me cry, which puts you in the same category as Me Before You, my ex-boyfriend, and onions. So that's kind of impressive. (What I'm saying is, I'm not a willy-nilly crier – it takes some serious emotional turmoil or weird vegetable enzymes to get me weepy.)

I can't believe how shit this is. I mean, you know things like this happen, but I guess it's hard to relate to until you hear the full story from someone's own mouth/pen. You didn't tell me anything about what it felt like being in that courtroom, what prison has been like for you . . . so I can imagine the parts you've left out would make me cry even more.

But it's no use me just telling you how shit this is (you already know that) and how sorry I am (you probably get that a lot from people). I was thinking that before I wrote this letter, and feeling pretty useless. I can't just write to you and say 'sorry, this is shit for you', I thought. So I rang my best friend Gerty.

Gerty is a superb human being in the least obvious way. She's mean to pretty much everyone, totally obsessive about her work, and if you cross her she'll cut you out of her life completely. But she is deeply principled in her way, and very good to her friends, and values honesty above all else.

She also happens to be a barrister. And, if her ridiculously successful career is anything to go by, a bloody good one.

I'll be honest: she looked at the letter as a favour to me. But she read the transcript of your trial for her own interest, and – I think – for you, too. She's not saying she's taking on your case (you'll see that from her note, enclosed), but she has a few questions she'd like answered. Feel free to totally ignore this – you probably have an awesome lawyer who has already looked into this stuff. I mean, maybe getting Gerty involved was more about me than you, because I wanted to feel like I was doing something. So feel free to tell me to piss off.

But if you do want to write back to Gerty, send something in your next letter to Leon, and we'll get it over to her. And maybe . . . don't mention it to your lawyer. I don't know how lawyers feel about you talking to other lawyers – is it like adultery?

Tons of stamps enclosed (another victim of the 'wanting to help' impulse I'm struggling with here).

Yours,

Tiffy

*

Dear Mr Twomey,

My name is Gertrude Constantine. I suspect Tiffany will have given me some sort of grandiose introduction in her letter, so I shall skip the pleasantries.

Please let me be clear: this is not an offer of representation. This is an informal letter, not a legal consultation. If I offer advice, it is as a friend of Tiffany's.

- It appears from the trial transcript that the friends with whom you visited Daffie's, the nightclub in Clapham, were not called as witnesses by either prosecution or defence. Please confirm.

- 'The Bloods' are not mentioned by you or any other person in the trial transcript. I presume from your letter that you only became aware of this gang's chosen name while in prison. Can you confirm which information led you to believe that the group you saw at the nightclub, and the man who assaulted you in the toilets, were members of this gang?

- Did you report the assault in the nightclub toilets?

- The bouncers at the nightclub gave evidence that the gang (as we shall refer to them) left the club soon after you did. They were not questioned further. From where they stood, might they have been able to indicate whether you and the gang were travelling in the same or a similar direction?

- It appears that the jury made their decision on the basis of only one segment of CCTV footage, filmed from within the establishment. Was CCTV from Clapham Road, Aldi car park and the adjacent launderette requested by your legal representative?

Yours faithfully,

Gertrude Constantine

21

Tiffy

When it comes to the part where we take crochet hooks and wool out to the crowd, I head towards the little girl who was staring at me earlier. She grins as I approach, all big front teeth and cheekiness.

'Hello,' she says. 'Are you Tiffy?'

I stare at her, and then duck down to the level of her wheelchair, because looming feels weird. 'Yeah! People keep asking me that today. How did you guess?'

'You *are* pretty!' she says gleefully. 'Are you nice as well?'

'Oh, I'm horrible, actually,' I tell her. 'Why did you think I might be Tiffy? And' – as an afterthought – 'pretty?'

'They said your name at the beginning,' she points out. Oh, right, of course. Though that doesn't explain all the creepy nurses. 'You're not really horrible. I think you're nice. It was nice of you to let that lady measure your legs.'

'It was, wasn't it?' I say. 'I think that particular act of niceness has gone quite underappreciated up until this point, actually, so thank you. Do you want to learn how to crochet?'

'No,' she says.

I laugh. At least she's honest, unlike the man behind her, who is valiantly having a go at making a slip knot under Katherin's super-vision. 'What do you want to do, then?'

'I want to talk to you about Leon,' she says.

'Ah! You know Leon!'

'I'm his favourite patient.'

I smile. 'I bet. So he's mentioned me, has he?'

'Not very much,' she says.

'Oh. Right. Well—'

'But I told him I'd find out if you were pretty.'

'Did you now! Did he ask you to do that?'

She thinks about it. 'No. But I think he wanted to know.'

'I don't think he does . . .' I realise I don't know her name.

'Holly,' she says. 'Like the Christmas plant.'

'Well, Holly, me and Leon are just friends. Friends don't need to know if friends are pretty.'

Suddenly Martin is right at my shoulder. 'Can you pose with her?' he mutters in my ear. God, that man knows how to creep up on you. He should wear a bell, like cats that eat birds.

'Pose? With Holly?'

'The leukaemia girl, yeah,' Martin says. 'For the press release.'

'I can hear you, you know,' Holly declares loudly.

Martin has just enough decency to look embarrassed. 'Hello,' he says in a stilted sort of way. 'I'm Martin.'

Holly shrugs. 'All right, *Martin*. My mum hasn't given permission for you to take my photo. I don't want my photo taken. People always feel sorry for me because I don't have very much hair and I look sick.'

I can see Martin thinking that that was pretty much the idea. I am overcome by a sudden but not unprecedented urge to punch him, or at least kick him in the shins. Maybe I could stumble over Holly's wheelchair and make it look like an accident.

'Fine,' Martin mutters, already off in Katherin's direction, no doubt hoping that she's located a similarly cute patient with fewer qualms about being plastered all over the Internet in order to further Martin's career.

'*He's* horrible,' Holly says matter-of-factly.

'Yes,' I say, without really thinking. 'He is, isn't he?' I check my watch; we finish up in ten minutes.

'Do you want to go and find Leon?' Holly asks, looking at me rather cannily.

I glance over at Katherin and Martin. I mean, my work as a model is done, and I'm not even any good at crocheting, let alone teaching other people to do it. It'll take them ages to get all this wool cleared up, and it would be quite nice not to be here for that bit.

I tap out a quick text to Katherin. *I'm just heading off to find my flatmate to say thanks for organising. I'll be back in time to tidy up xx* (I definitely won't.)

'That way,' Holly says, and then, when I totally fail to push her wheelchair, she laughs and points to the brake. '*Everyone* knows you have to take the brake off.'

'I just thought you were really heavy,' I tell her.

Holly giggles. 'Leon will be in Coral Ward. Don't follow the signs, they take you the long way. Turn left!'

I do as I'm told. 'You really know your way around this place, don't you?' I say, after being directed down a dozen corridors and, at one point, through an actual closet.

'I've been here seven months,' Holly says. 'And I'm friends with Mr Robbie Prior. He's on Coral Ward and he was very important in one of the wars.'

'Mr Prior! Does he knit?'

'*All* the time,' Holly says.

Excellent! I'm on my way to meet my life-saving knitter *and* my note-writing flatmate. I wonder if Leon will talk the way he writes, all short sentences and no pronouns.

'Hey, Doctor Patel!' Holly yells suddenly at a passing doctor. 'This is Tiffy!'

Dr Patel pauses, lowers her glasses down her nose, then flashes me a smile. 'Well I never,' is all she says, before disappearing into the nearest patient's room.

'OK, Miss Holly,' I say, spinning the wheelchair so we're facing each other. 'What is going on? Why does everyone here know my name? And why do they seem so surprised to see me?'

Holly looks mischievous. 'Nobody believes you're real,' she says. 'I *told* everyone Leon is living with a girl and he writes her notes and she makes him laugh and *nobody* believed me. They all said Leon couldn't . . .' she scrunches up her nose '. . . *tolerate* a flatmate. I think that means he wouldn't want one because he's so quiet. They don't know, though, that *actually* he saves all his talking up for the really good people, like me and you.'

'Seriously?' I shake my head, grinning, and set off down the corridor again. It's funny hearing about Leon from someone else. So far my only point of reference has been Kay, who hardly ever pops around these days.

With Holly's instructions, we finally reach Coral Ward. She looks around, bracing herself on the arms of her chair to get a better look. 'Where's Mr Prior?' she calls.

An elderly gentleman in a chair over by the window turns and smiles at Holly, his face a mass of deep wrinkles. 'Hello, Holly.'

'Mr Prior! This is Tiffy. She's pretty, isn't she?'

'Ah, Ms Moore,' Mr Prior says, attempting to stand and holding out his hand. 'What a pleasure.'

I scuttle over, desperate for him to sit down in his chair again. It looks like unfolding himself out of that position would not be wise. 'It's such an honour to meet you, Mr Prior! I have to tell you, I *adore* your work – and I can't thank you enough for crocheting all those scarves and hats for Katherin's book.'

'Oh, I enjoyed it very much. I would have come to your demonstration, but' – he pats his chest absently – 'I wasn't feeling quite up to it, I'm afraid.'

'Oh, that's all right,' I say. 'It's not like you need the lesson.' I pause. 'I don't suppose you've seen . . .'

Mr Prior smiles. 'Leon?'

'Well, yeah. I just wanted to track him down to say hi.'

'Mmm,' Mr Prior says. 'You'll find our Leon is somewhat tricky to pin down. In fact, he just slipped out. I think someone tipped him off that you were coming.'

'Oh.' I look down, embarrassed. I didn't mean to hound him around the hospital. Justin always said I never knew when to let something drop. 'If he doesn't want to see me, I should probably . . .'

Mr Prior waves a hand. 'You mistake me, my dear,' he says. 'It isn't that at all. I'd say Leon is rather nervous about meeting you.'

'Why would he be nervous?' I ask, as if I've not been nervous all day.

'I couldn't say for sure,' Mr Prior says, 'but Leon doesn't like things . . . changing. I'd say he very much enjoys living with you, Ms Moore, and I do wonder if he doesn't want to ruin it.' He pauses. 'I would suggest that if you want to introduce a change into Leon's routine, you're better off doing it very quickly, and all at once, so he has no means of dodging it.'

'Like a surprise,' Holly says solemnly.

'Right,' I say. 'Well. Anyway, it was great to meet you, Mr Prior.'

'One more thing, Ms Moore,' Mr Prior says. 'Leon was looking a little emotional. And holding a letter. I don't suppose you'd know anything about that, would you?'

'Oh, God, I hope I didn't say the wrong thing,' I say, desperately trying to remember what I'd put in that letter to Richie.

'No, no, he wasn't upset. Just in a spin.' Mr Prior takes his glasses off and rubs them against his shirt with shaky, gnarled fingers. 'I would say, at a guess, that he was rather . . .' the glasses go back on his nose '. . . surprised.'

22

Leon

It's too much. I'm shaking. This is the most hope I have felt in months, and I've forgotten how to handle this emotion – insides have gone wobbly and skin has turned all cold and hot at same time. Heartrate has been raised for a good hour now. Can't slow down.

I should go and thank Tiffy in person. She's trying to find me and I keep hiding which is clearly childish and ridiculous. Am just feeling very odd about this. Like if we meet, everything will be different, and there will be no going back to how it was. And I like how it was. Is.

Me: June, where's Tiffy?

June: Your lovely flatmate?

Me, patiently: Yes. Tiffy.

June: Leon, it's almost one in the morning. She left after the show.

Me: Oh. Did she . . . leave a note? Or anything?

June: Sorry, love. She was trying to find you, though, if that's any consolation.

It isn't. And no note, either. Feel like a fool. I've missed the chance to say thank you; probably upset her, too. Don't like that thought. But – still buzzing about the letter, and it buoys me through the rest of the night with only the occasional crushing memory of dodging down corridors to avoid social interaction (extreme antisocialness, even for me. Wince at the thought of what Richie will say).

At the end of my shift I leave at a jog and head for the bus stop. Call Kay as soon as I'm out the door. Cannot wait to tell her about the letter, the criminal lawyer friend, the list of questions.

Kay is unusually quiet.

Me: This is amazing, no?

Kay: This lawyer's not actually done anything, Leon. She's not taking on the case – or even saying she believes Richie is innocent, really.

Almost stumble, like someone has physically put out hand to stop me.

Me: It's *something*, though. There's not been something for so long.

Kay: And I thought you weren't ever going to meet Tiffy. That was the first rule we set when I agreed to this flatshare.

Me: What . . . ever? Can't meet her *ever*? She's my flatmate.

Kay: Don't make out like I'm being unreasonable.

Me: Didn't realise you meant . . . Eh, this is silly. I didn't meet her, anyway. I called to tell you Richie news.

Another long silence. I frown, walking slower now.

Kay: I wish you'd come to terms with Richie's situation, Leon. It's draining so much of your energy, all of this – it's changed you these last few months. I think the healthiest thing – if I'm honest – is to reach acceptance. And I'm sure you will, it's just . . . it's been a while. And it's really putting a strain on you. On us.

Don't understand. Did she not hear? It's not like I'm saying same old things, hanging on to same old hopes – I'm saying, there is new hope. There are new things.

Me: What are you suggesting? We just give up? But there's new evidence to get, now that we know what to look for!

Kay: You're not a lawyer, Leon. And Sal is a lawyer, and you've said yourself that he did his best, and I personally think it's not right for this woman to be interfering and giving you and Richie hope when the case was so open and shut. The jury all thought he was guilty, Leon.

Coldness growing low down in stomach. Heartrate ups again, and for all the wrong reasons this time. I'm getting angry. That feeling again, the trapped hateful rage at hearing someone you try so hard to love saying the worst things.

Me: What is this, Kay? I can't figure out what you want from me.

Kay: I want you back.

Me: What?

Kay: I want you *back*, Leon. Present. In your life. With me. It's like . . . you've stopped seeing me. You drift in and out and spend your spare time here, but you're not really with me. You're always with Richie. You always care about Richie – more than you care about me.

Me: Of course I care more about Richie.

The pause is like silence after a gunshot. I slap hand to mouth. Didn't mean to say it; don't know where it came from.

Me: I don't mean it like that. I don't mean that. Just . . . Richie needs more of my . . . care right now. He has nobody.

Kay: Do you have any of your *care* left for anyone else? For you?

She means, *for me*?

Kay: Please. Actually think about it. Actually think about you and me.

She's crying now. I feel wretched, but that roaring hot–cold sensation deep in my stomach is still burning.

Me: You still think he's guilty, don't you?

Kay: Damn it, Leon, I'm trying to talk about us, not about your brother.

Me: I need to know.

Kay: Can't you just listen to me? I'm saying this is the only way you can heal. You can carry on believing he didn't do it if you like, but you need to accept that he is in prison and will be for a good few years. You can't keep *fighting*. It's pulling your life apart. All you do is work and write to Richie and fixate on things, whether it's some old guy's boyfriend or the latest detail in Richie's appeal. You used to *do* stuff. Go out. Spend time with me.

Me: I've never had much spare time, Kay. What I have has always been for you.

Kay: You go to see him every other weekend these days.

Is she really angry at me for visiting my brother in prison?

Kay: I know I can't be mad at you for that. I know that. But I just . . . What I mean is, you have so little time, and now I feel I get an even smaller fraction of it, and . . .

Me: Do you still think Richie is guilty?

There is silence. I think I'm crying now too; there's a hot wetness on my cheeks as yet another bus speeds by, and I can't bear to get on.

Kay: Why does it always come back to this? Why does it matter? Our relationship shouldn't have this much of your brother in it.

Me: Richie is part of me. We're family.

Kay: Well, we're partners. Doesn't that mean anything?

Me: You know I love you.

Kay: Funny. I'm not sure I do know that.

Silence stretches on. Traffic speeds by. Scuff my feet, looking down at the sun-scorched pavement, feeling unreal.

Me: Just say it.

She waits. I wait. Another bus waits, then drives on.

Kay: I think Richie did it, Leon. It's what the jury decided, and they had all the information. It's the sort of thing he'd do.

Close my eyes slowly. It doesn't feel like I expected it to – it's strange, but it's almost a relief. Have been hearing her say it in silence for months, ever since The Argument. This is an end to the endless twisting in the gut, the endless waiting on the edges of conversations, the endless knowing but trying not to know.

Kay is sobbing. I listen, eyes still closed, and it's like I'm floating.

Kay: This is it, isn't it?

It's obvious, all at once. This is it. Can't do this any more. Can't have this eating away at my love for Richie, can't be with a person who doesn't love him too.

Me: Yes. This is it.

23

Tiffy

The day after my visit to the hospice, I come home to the longest and most incoherent note I've ever had from Leon, laid on the kitchen counter beside an uneaten plate of spaghetti.

Hi Tiffy,
Am a bit all over the place but thank you so much for note for Richie. Can't thank you enough. Definitely need all help we can get. He will be thrilled.
    Sorry I didn't find you at work. Was my fault completely – left it too late to come and find you, wanted to read your letter to Richie first like you'd asked but took me ages, then just messed up and left it too late, always takes me a while to process things – sorry, am just going to go to bed, if that's all right, see you later x

I stare at it for a while. Well, at least he didn't avoid me all night because he didn't want to see me. But . . . uneaten dinner? All these long sentences? What does it mean?

I lay a Post-it note beside his note, sticking it carefully to the countertop.

Hey Leon,
Are you all right?! I'll make tiffin, just in case.
    Tiffy xx

The unusual wordiness of Leon's letter is very much a one-off. For the next two weeks his notes are even more monosyllabic and lacking in personal pronouns than usual. I don't want to push it, but something has clearly upset him. Are he and Kay fighting? She's not been around, and he hasn't mentioned her for weeks. I don't know how to help when he won't tell me, though, so I just bake a bit too much and don't complain that he's not been cleaning the flat properly. Yesterday his coffee mug wasn't on the left of the sink *or* the right – it was still in the cupboard, and he must have gone to work without any caffeine at all.

In a flash of inspiration I leave Leon the next manuscript from my bricklayer-turned-designer, the one who wrote *Built*. Book two – *Skyscraping* – is maybe even better, and I'm hoping it'll cheer him up.

I come home to this note on top of the ring-bound manuscript:

This man. What a guy!
Thanks, Tiffy. Sorry the flat's a bit of a mess. Will clean soon, promise.
   Leon x

I'm counting that exclamation mark as a major sign of improvement.

It's the day of our trial book launch, the one we're taking Katherin to so PR can persuade her that a huge launch is exactly what she's always wanted.

'No tights,' Rachel says decisively. 'It's August, for God's sake.'

We're getting ready together in the office loos. Every so often someone comes in to pee and lets out a little yelp as they see that the room has been transformed into a dressing room. Both our make-up bags are emptied across the sinks; the air is clouded with perfume and hairspray. We each have three outfit choices hung up along the mirrors, plus the ones we're now wearing (our final choices: Rachel is in a lime green silk wraparound dress, and I'm in a tea dress covered in enormous prints of Alice in Wonderland – I found the fabric in a Stockwell charity shop and bribed one of my most obliging free-lancers to make it into a dress for me).

I wriggle around and whip my tights off. Rachel nods in approval. 'Better. More leg is good.'

'You'd have me dressed in a bikini if you had your way.'

She grins cheekily at me in the mirror as she dabs at her lipstick. 'Well, you might meet a handsome young Nordic man,' she says.

Tonight is all about *Forestry for the Ordinary Man*, our woodwork editor's latest acquisition. The author is a Norwegian hermit. It's quite a big deal that he's left his treehouse for long enough to come to London. Rachel and I are hoping that he has a complete meltdown and turns on Martin, who is organising this event, and really should have taken the author's hermit lifestyle as a sign that he probably doesn't want to give a speech to a room full of woodwork fanatics.

'I'm not sure I'm ready for handsome young Nordic men. I don't know.' I find myself thinking back to what Mo said to me about Justin a few months ago, when I'd rung him in a state about whether Justin would ever get in touch with me. 'I'm struggling with being . . . ready to date. Even though Justin left *ages* ago.'

Rachel pauses mid dab to stare at me with concern. 'Are you all right?'

'I think so,' I say. 'Yeah, I think I'm fine.'

'So it's because of Justin?'

'No, no, I don't mean that. Maybe I just don't need that in my life right now.' I know that's not true, but I say it anyway because Rachel is looking at me as if I'm ill.

'You do,' Rachel tells me. 'You've just not had sex for too long. You've forgotten how exceptional it is.'

'I don't think I've forgotten what sex is, Rachel. Isn't it like, you know. Riding a bike?'

'Similar,' Rachel concedes, 'but you've not been with a man since Justin, which ended, what, November last year? So that means it's been more than . . .' She counts on her fingers. 'Nine months.'

'*Nine months?*' Wow. That is a very long time. You can grow a whole baby in that time. Not that I am, obviously, because otherwise this tea dress would *not* fit.

Unsettled, I apply blusher a bit too vigorously and end up looking sunburnt. Ugh. I'll have to start again.

Martin from PR may be a pain in the arse, but the man can put on a woodwork-themed party. We're in a pub in Shoreditch with exposed beams looming low above us; there are piles of logs as centrepieces on every table, and the bar is decorated with pine branches.

I look around, ostensibly trying to find Katherin, but really trying to locate the Norwegian author who hasn't seen a human being in six months. I check the corners, where I suspect he will be cowering.

Rachel drags me to the bar to find out once and for all if the drinks are free. They are for the first hour, apparently – we curse ourselves for arriving twenty minutes late and order gin and tonics. Rachel befriends the bartender by talking about football, which actually works a surprising amount of the time, despite being the most un-original topic to assume a man would be interested in.

We obviously drink very quickly, that being the only reasonable reaction to a one-hour window for free drinks, so when Katherin arrives I give her an especially effusive hug. She looks pleased.

'This is a bit decadent,' she says. 'Will this man's book pay for this?' She is no doubt thinking of her previous royalty cheques.

'Oh, no,' Rachel says airily, gesturing for a top-up from her new best friend and now fellow Arsenal fan (Rachel supports West Ham). 'Not likely. But you have to do this sort of thing occasionally otherwise everyone will just self-publish.'

'Shhh,' I hiss. I don't want Katherin getting any ideas.

Several gin and tonics later, Rachel and the bartender are more than friendly, and other people are really having trouble getting served. To my surprise, Katherin is in her element. Right now she's laughing at something our head of PR has said, which I know is an act, because the head of PR is literally never funny.

These events are perfect for people-watching. I swivel on my bar stool to get a better view of the room. There are indeed quite a lot of handsome Nordic men about. I consider the possibility of taking myself out into the room until someone obligingly introduces me to one of them, but I just can't bring myself to do it.

'Kind of like watching ants, isn't it?' says someone from beside me. I turn; there's a smartly dressed business type leaning against the bar to my left. He smiles ruefully at me. His light-brown hair is buzzed short, the same length as his stubble, and his eyes are a cute blue-grey with crinkles at the edges. 'That sounded a lot worse out loud than in my head.'

I look back at the crowd. 'I know what you mean,' I say. 'They all look so . . . busy. And purposeful.'

'Except him,' the man says, nodding to a guy in the opposite corner, who has just been abandoned by the young woman he was talking to.

'He's a lost ant,' I agree. 'What do you reckon – is he our Norwegian hermit?'

'Oh, I don't know,' the man says, giving him an appraising look. 'Not good-looking enough, I don't think.'

'Why, have you seen the author photo?' I ask.

'Yep. Handsome guy. Dashing, some might say.'

I narrow my eyes at him. 'It's you, isn't it? You're the author.'

He smiles, and the crinkles in the corners of his eyes lengthen into tiny crow's feet. 'Guilty.'

'You're very well dressed for a hermit,' I say, a little accusingly. I feel misled. He doesn't even have a Norwegian accent, damn it.

'If you'd read this,' he says, waving one of the samplers that was available on our way in, 'then you'd know that before I chose to live alone in Nordmarka, I was an investment banker in Oslo. I last wore this suit on the day I resigned.'

'Really? What made you do it?'

He opens the sampler and begins to read. '*Tired of the corporate toil, Ken had a revelation after a weekend spent hiking with an old school friend who now made his living in woodwork. Ken had always loved to use his hands*' – and now the look he gives me is *definitely* flirtatious – '*and when he went back to his old friend's workshop, he felt suddenly at home. It was clear within moments that he was an extraordinarily skilled woodworker.*'

'If only we always had a pre-written biography for meeting new people,' I say, raising an eyebrow. 'Makes it so much easier to brag.'

'Give me yours, then,' he says, snapping the sampler closed with a smile.

'My bio? Hmm. Let me see. *Tiffy Moore escaped the smallness of her village upbringing for the great adventure that is London as soon as she could. There, she found the life she had always wanted: overpriced coffee, squalid accommodation, and an extraordinary lack of graduate jobs that didn't involve spreadsheets.*'

Ken laughs. 'You're good. Are you in PR too?'

'Editorial,' I tell him. 'If I was in PR, I'd have to be out there with the ants.'

'Well, I'm glad you're not,' he says. 'I prefer to be away from the crowd, but I don't think I could have resisted saying hello to the beautiful woman in the Lewis Carroll dress.'

He gives me a look. A very intense look. My stomach flutters. But . . . I can do this. Why not?

'Do you want to get some air?' I find myself saying. He nods, and I grab my jacket off the chair and head for the door to the pub garden.

It's a perfect summer evening. The air is still tinged with warmth even though the sun set hours ago; the pub has hung up strings of lightbulbs between the trees, and they cast a soft yellow glow across the garden. There are a few people out here, mainly smokers – they have that hunched look that smokers get, like the world is against them. Ken and I take a seat on a picnic bench.

'So, when you say "hermit" . . .' I begin.

'Which I haven't,' Ken points out.

'Right. But what exactly does that involve?'

'Living alone, somewhere secluded. Very few people.'

'Very few?'

'The odd friend, the grocery delivery woman.' He shrugs. 'It's not as quiet as people make it out to be.'

'The grocery delivery woman, eh?' I give him a look this time.

He laughs. 'I'll admit, that's one downside of solitude.'

'Oh, please. You don't need to live alone in a treehouse to not have any sex.'

I press my lips together. I'm not entirely sure where that came from – possibly from the last gin and tonic – but Ken just smiles, a slow, really quite sexy smile, and then leans down to kiss me.

As I close my eyes and lean in, I feel giddy on possibility. There's nothing to stop me going home with this man, and it's a sunlight-through-the-clouds moment – like something's lifted. I can do whatever I want now. I'm free.

And then, as the kiss deepens, with disorientating suddenness I remember something.

Justin. I'm crying. We've just had a fight and it was all my fault. Justin has gone cold, his back turned on me in our enormous white bed with all its trendy brushed cotton and endless pillows.

I am deeply miserable. More miserable than I have remembered being before, and yet it doesn't feel at all unfamiliar. Justin turns towards me, and suddenly, giddily, his hands are on me and we're kissing. I'm muddled, lost. I'm so grateful he's not angry with me any more. He knows just where to touch me. The misery hasn't gone, it's still there, but he wants me now, and the relief makes everything else seem small.

Back here, in the garden in Shoreditch, Ken pulls back from the kiss. He's smiling. I don't think he can even tell that my skin has gone clammy and my heart is racing for all the wrong reasons.

Fuck. *Fuck.* What the hell was that?

AUGUST

24

Leon

Richie: How are you feeling, man?

How am I feeling? Untethered. Like something's got dislodged somewhere in my chest and my body doesn't function quite right any more. Like I'm alone.

Me: Sad.

Richie: You've not been in love with Kay for months, I'm telling you. I'm so glad you're out of that relationship, man – it was about habit, not about love.

Wonder why the fact that Richie's right doesn't lessen the pain in any meaningful way. Miss Kay almost constantly. Like a nagging ache. It worsens every time I pick up the phone to call her, and then have nobody to call.

Me: Anyway. Any news from Tiffy's lawyer friend?

Richie: Not yet. I can't stop thinking about it. You know every single thing in her letter just made me go, 'Oh, yeah, shit, why didn't we think of that?'

Me: Same.

Richie: You did pass on my reply? You made sure she got it?

Me: Tiffy gave it to her.

Richie: You're sure?

Me: I'm sure.

Richie: OK. All right. Sorry. I'm just . . .

Me: I know. Me too.

For the last two weekends, have Airbnb'ed my way around UK on quest for Mr Prior's boyfriend. It was an excellent distraction. Met two radically different Johnny Whites – one bitter, furious and alarmingly right wing, and the other living in a caravan and smoking weed out of the window as we discussed his life since the war. Has at least provided amusement for Tiffy – notes about Johnny Whites always get good response. Got this after describing trip to meet Johnny White the Third:

If you're not careful I'll commission you to write a book about this. Obviously in order for it to fit with my publishing list I'd have to introduce some element of DIY – could you learn a different craft from each Johnny, or something? You know, like, Johnny White the First spontaneously teaches you how to make a bookcase, and then there you are with Johnny White the Second and he's making royal icing and you just happen to join in . . . Oh my God, is this the best idea I've ever had? Or maybe the worst? I absolutely cannot tell. xx

Often think it must be very tiring, being Tiffy. Even in note form she seems to expend so much energy. Quite cheering to come home to, though.

This weekend's visit to Richie was cancelled – not enough prison staff. Will have been five weeks between visits. That's too long for him, and, I'm realising, for me also. With Kay gone and Richie able to ring even less than usual – too few prison staff means more time banged up, less access to phones – I'm finding that even I can suffer from not talking enough. It's not like there aren't friends I can call. But they're not . . . the people I can talk to.

Had booked Airbnb up near Birmingham for Richie visit, but have cancelled that now, and am forced to confront the fact that this coming weekend, I will need somewhere to stay. I was clearly too complacent about the state of my relationship when arranging this living situation. Am now homeless at weekends.

Wrack brains for options. Nothing for it. Am on way to work; check time on phone. It's about the only window of the day when I can ring my mother. I get off the bus a stop early and call her as I walk.

Mam, on answering: You don't call me enough, Lee.

Close eyes. Deep breath.

Me: Hi, Mam.

Mam: Richie calls me more than you. From *prison*.

Me: Sorry, Mam.

Mam: Do you know how hard this is for me? My boys never talking to me?

Me: I'm calling now, Mam. I've got a few minutes before work – I want to talk to you about something.

Mam, suddenly alert: Is it the appeal? Has Sal called you?

I haven't told Mam about Tiffy's lawyer friend. Don't want to get her hopes up.

Me: No. It's about me.

Mam, suspicious: About you?

Me: Kay and I broke up.

Mam melts. Suddenly all sympathy. This is what she needs: a son to call her and ask for help with something she can handle. My mother is good at dealing with romantic heartbreak. Has had lots of personal practice.

Mam: Oh, sweetheart. Why did she end it?

Mildly insulted.

Me: I ended it.

Mam: Oh! You did? What for?

Me: I . . .

Oh. It's surprisingly difficult, even with Mam.

Me: She couldn't handle my hours. Didn't like me how I was – wanted me to be more sociable. And . . . she didn't believe Richie's innocent.

Mam: She *what*?

Wait. Silence. Gut twists; it feels terrible dobbing Kay in, even now.

Mam: That cow. She always did look down on us.

Me: Mam!

Mam: Well, I'm not sorry. Good riddance to her.

It's like speaking ill of the dead, somehow. I'm desperate to veer off subject.

Me: Can I come stay this weekend?

Mam: Stay? Here? At mine?

Me: Yeah. I used to stay at Kay's every weekend. It's part of . . . the living arrangement. With Tiffy.

Mam: You want to come home?

Me: Yeah. Just for . . .

Bite tongue. It's not just for this weekend. It's until I find solution. But it's automatic to put a firm endpoint on these things; that's the only way to feel able to escape. When I get home, Mam will have me, and will not let me go.

Mam: You can stay as long as you need, and whenever you need, all right?

Me: Thanks.

Moment of quiet. I can hear how pleased she is; gut twists again. Should visit more.

Me: Can I check . . . Do you . . . Is there anyone else? Living there?

Mam, awkwardly: Nobody else, sweetie. I've been on my own for a few months now.

That's good. Unusual, and good. Mam always has a man, and he always seems to be living with her, whoever he is. Almost always someone who Richie despises and I would rather not have to see. Mam has unequivocally bad taste. She's always been a woman led astray by a bad man, a hundred times over.

Me: I'll see you Saturday night.

Mam: Can't wait. I'll get us Chinese, all right?

Silence. That's what we would do when Richie came home: Saturday night Chinese from Happy Duck down Mam's road.

Mam: Or let's get Indian. I feel like a change, don't you?

25

Tiffy

'Are you all right?' Ken asks.

I'm pretty much frozen. My heart is pounding.

'Yes. Sorry, yes, I'm fine.' I try a smile.

'Do you want to get out of here?' he says tentatively. 'I mean, the party's nearly over . . .'

Do I? I did, about one minute ago. Now, even with the buzz of that kiss still warm on my lips, I want to run away. I'm not really thinking thoughts – my brain is just producing this extremely unhelpful one-tone note of panic, like a loud long *uuuhhhh* rattling back and forth between my ears.

Someone calls my name. I recognise the voice, but I don't connect the dots until I turn and see Justin.

He's standing in the doorway between the garden and the pub, dressed in an open-necked shirt with his old leather satchel slung over his shoulder. He looks painfully familiar, but things are different too: his hair is longer than he ever wore it when we were together, and he's got new city-corporate shoes. I feel as if I've conjured him up by thinking about him – how else could he possibly be here?

His eyes flick to Ken for a moment, and then they're back to me. He crosses the grass between us. I am glued to the spot, shoulders tensed, crouched over on the bench with Ken beside me.

'You look beautiful.'

This, unbelievably, is the first thing he says.

'Justin.' This is about all I can manage. I look back at Ken, and no doubt my face is a picture of misery.

'Let me guess,' says Ken lightly. 'Boyfriend?'

'Ex,' I say. 'Ex! I would never – I . . .'

Ken smiles an easy, sexy smile at me, and then turns an equally good-natured one on Justin. 'Hi,' he says, holding out his hand for Justin to shake. 'Ken.'

Justin barely looks at him; he shakes his hand for approximately half a second before turning back to me. 'Can I talk to you?'

I look between him and Ken. I can't believe I was even thinking about going home with Ken. I can't do that.

'I'm sorry,' I begin. 'I really . . .'

'Hey, don't worry about it,' Ken says, standing up. 'You have my contact details if you fancy getting in touch while I'm still in London.' He waves the sampler, still in his hand. 'Nice to meet you,' he says, extremely politely, in Justin's direction.

'Yeah,' is all Justin says.

As Ken walks away, the *uuuhhhh* quietens and I feel as if I'm waking up a little, coming out of some sort of trance. I stand, knees shaking, and face Justin.

'What. The hell. Are you doing here?'

Justin doesn't react to the venom in my voice. Instead he puts his hand on my back and starts leading me towards the side gate. I move mechanically, unthinking, and then shrug him off sharply as soon as I clock what's happening.

'Hey, whoa.' He looks at me as we pause in the gateway. The evening air is warm, almost stifling. 'Are you OK? Sorry if I surprised you.'

'And ruined my evening.'

He smiles. 'Come on, Tiffy. You needed rescuing. You'd never go home with a guy like that.'

I open my mouth to speak, and then close it again. I was going to say he doesn't know me any more, but somehow it doesn't come out. 'What are you doing here?' I manage instead.

'I was just coming in for a drink. I come to this place a fair bit.'

I mean, this is just ridiculous. I cannot believe this. The cruise ship might have been a coincidence – a very weird one, but just about plausible – but this?

'Do you not think this is odd?'

He's confused. He tilts his head, like *huh*? My stomach flips – I used to love that little head-tilt.

'We've bumped into each other twice in six months. Once, *on a cruise ship.*'

I need an explanation for this that isn't 'Justin appears when you think bad thoughts about him', which is currently all my half-frozen brain can believe. I'm scaring myself a little.

He smiles indulgently. 'Tiffy. Come on. What are you suggesting? That I got on that cruise to see you? That I turned up tonight just to see you? If I wanted to do that, why wouldn't I just call you? Or turn up at your office?'

Oh. I . . . I guess that makes sense. My cheeks flush; I'm suddenly embarrassed.

He squeezes my shoulder. 'It is great to see you, though. And yeah, it's a pretty crazy coincidence. Fate, maybe? I did wonder why I suddenly wanted a pint this evening, of all evenings.' He does an exaggerated mysterious face, and I can't help smiling. I'd forgotten how cute he is when he clowns around.

No. Not smiling. Not cute. I think of what Gerty and Mo would say, and gather my resolve.

'What did you want to talk to me about?'

'I am glad I bumped into you,' he says. 'I really . . . I have been meaning to call. But it's so hard to know where to start.'

'Hit the phone icon, I'd suggest, then search your contacts by name?' I say. My voice is shaking a little, and I hope he doesn't hear it.

He laughs. 'I forgot how funny you are when you're angry. No, I mean, I didn't want to tell you this on the phone.'

'Tell me what? Let me guess. That you've broken up with the woman you left me for?'

I've caught him off guard. There's a little thrill when I see his perfect confident smile waver, and then a wash of something else – more like anxiety. I don't want to piss him off. I take a deep breath. 'I don't *want* to see you, Justin. This doesn't change anything. You still left me for her, you still – you still . . .'

'I never cheated on you,' he says immediately. We've begun walking, I'm not sure where; he stops me again and puts his hands on my shoulders, turning me so I have to look him in the face. 'I would never do that to you, Tiffy. You know how crazy I am about you.'

'Was.'

'What?'

'How crazy I *was* about you, is what you meant to say.' Already I wish I'd taken the chance to tell him that the reason I don't want to see him is actually nothing to do with Patricia. Although I'm not sure what it *is* about. It's about . . . all the other stuff, whatever that was. I feel very muddled all of a sudden. Justin's presence always does this to me – makes me all confused until I lose my train of thought. That was part of the romance, I guess, but right now it doesn't feel nice at all.

'Don't tell me what I mean and don't mean.' He looks away for a moment. 'Look, I'm here now. Can't we just go get a drink somewhere and talk about it? Come on. We can go to that champagne bar around the corner where they serve your drinks in paint cans. Or we can go to the top of the Shard, remember when I took you there as a treat? What do you say?'

I stare at him. His big, brown eyes, always so earnest, always sparkling with that crazy excitement that caught me up every time. His perfect jawline. His confident smile. I try very hard not to think about the awful memory that came when I kissed Ken, but it seems to be in my system now, worse than ever with Justin here. My skin's crawling with it.

'Why didn't you call me?'

'I told you,' he says, impatient now, 'I didn't know how to tell you about this.'

'And why are you here?'

'Tiffy,' he says sharply, 'just come for a drink.'

I flinch, and then take another deep breath. 'You want to talk to me, you call ahead and we arrange a time. Not now.'

'When, then?' he asks, frowning, his hands still heavy on my shoulders.

'Just ... I need time.' My head feels cloudy. 'I don't want to talk to you right now.'

'Time like a couple of hours?'

'Time like a couple of months,' I say before I've thought about it, and then I bite my lip, because now I've given us a deadline.

'I want to see you *now*,' he says, and suddenly the hands that are on my shoulders have moved to touch my hair, my upper arm.

That flashback plays behind my eyes. I shrug him off. 'Try delayed gratification, Justin. It's the only kind you're going to get, and I have a feeling it'll be good for you.'

And with that, I turn before I can change my mind, and stumble back into the bar.

26

Leon

Holly has almost a full head of hair now. She's like a female Harry Potter – hair sticking up all over the place no matter how much her mum tries to smooth it flat.

Her face has changed too, got fuller, livelier. Eyes look less out of proportion with the rest of her these days.

She grins up at me.

Holly: Have you come to say goodbye?

Me: I've come to check your bloods.

Holly: For one last time?

Me: Depends what they say.

Holly: You're being grumpy. You don't want me to leave.

Me: Of course I do. I want you to be well.

Holly: No you don't. You don't like stuff changing. You want me to stay here.

Don't say anything. It's annoying, being so completely understood by one so very small.

Holly: I'll miss you too. Will you visit me at home?

I glance at her mum, who's wearing a tired but very happy smile.

Me: You'll be too busy at school and all your after-school clubs. You won't want visitors.

Holly: Yes I will.

Holly's Mum: I'd love to have you round for dinner. Really – and Holly would too. Just to say thank you.

Sheer euphoria surrounding Holly's mother like a cloud of perfume.

Me: Well, maybe. Thanks.

Holly's mum is welling up. I never cope well with these situations. Start to feel slightly panicked; edge towards door.

She hugs me before I can escape. Feel suddenly very wobbly. I'm not sure if it's Holly or Kay I want to cry about, but someone hugging me is doing something involving my tear glands.

Wipe eyes and hope Holly doesn't notice. Ruffle her messy brown hair.

Me: Be good.

Holly grins. Get the impression she has other plans.

I get out of work in time to see the last traces of a truly glorious sunrise behind London's skyscrapers and reflected in the steel grey of the Thames, turning it blue-pink. Seem to have so much time now Kay is gone. Makes me wonder if I really did give her as little time as she always claimed – if that's true, where have all these hours come from?

Decide to stop somewhere for a tea, then walk home – only takes an hour and a half, and it's the sort of morning you want to be out in. People are buzzing in all directions, on their way to work, coffees clutched close. I let them all stream by. Walk up through the back roads as much as I can; they're a little sleepier than the main roads.

I find myself on Clapham Road without really noticing. Go cold when I see the off-licence. But make myself stop. Seems respectful, like taking your hat off when a hearse goes by.

Can't help noticing that the Aldi security cameras really do point in every possible direction, including this one. Something wishful grips me. I remember the whole point of why Kay and I broke up. I've been too sad to remember that there is hope for Richie.

Maybe Gerty will have written back to Richie by now. I walk on, faster now, keen to get home. He might try to call, expecting me to be back at usual time. Feel sure he has; am furious with myself for missing him.

Deep breaths. I fumble with the key in the door, but oddly it's not double-locked – Tiffy has never forgotten before. I give a cursory look around the room when I get in to make sure we've not been burgled, but TV and laptop are still there, so head straight for landline and check for missed calls or voicemails.

Nothing. Breathe out. Am sweaty from power-walking in the morning sunshine; chuck keys in customary space (they now live under the Spot the Dog moneybox) and yank off T-shirt as I head to bathroom. Shove the row of multi-coloured candles off the edge of the bath so I can actually shower. Then turn the hot water on and stand there, washing off yet another week.

27

Tiffy

Oh, God.

I think this is the worst I've ever felt. It's worse than the hangover I had after Rachel's twenty-fifth. It's worse than the time at uni when I drank two bottles of wine and vomited outside the faculty office. It's worse than swine flu.

I'm still wearing the Alice in Wonderland dress. I have slept on top of the duvet, under just my Brixton blanket. I at least had the foresight to take my shoes off and leave them at the door.

Oh, God.

The line-of-sight from where I am to the shoes intersects with the alarm clock. It is saying a time that cannot possibly be correct. It is saying 08:59.

I should be at work in one minute.

How has this happened? I scramble up, my stomach lurching and my head spinning, and as I fumble about looking for my purse – oh good, at least I didn't lose that, and ah yes, aspirin – I remember how this all started.

I'd gone back inside after walking away from Justin, and dragged Rachel off the bartender's face in order to weep at her for a while. She was not the best person to speak to – she's the only person left who's Team Justin. (I didn't mention that weird kiss flashback. And

I do not want to think about it now, either.) At first Rachel told me to go back out there and hear what he had to say, but then she came around to my delayed gratification strategy, which Katherin also approved of – oh, God, I told Katherin . . .

I neck some aspirin and try not to gag. Was I sick last night? I have vague and unpleasant memories of being way too close to a toilet seat in that bar's bathroom.

I type a quick apology text to the head of Editorial, panic rising. I'm never this late for work, and everyone will know it's because I'm hungover. If they don't, I'm sure Martin will be happy to enlighten them.

I can't go to work like this, I realise, in my first moment of clarity of the morning. I need to wash and change. I unzip the dress and kick it off, already reaching for my towel on the back of the door.

I don't hear the running water. There is a constant buzzing in my ears that sort of already sounds like a shower turned on, and I am in such a panic I don't think I would notice if my stuffed elephant came alive on the armchair and started telling me I need to detox.

I only realise Leon is in the shower when I see him there. Our shower curtain is *mostly* opaque, but you can definitely see a bit. I mean, outlines.

He does the natural thing: panics and throws the curtain back to see who's there. We stare at each other. The shower keeps running.

He comes to his senses faster than I do and pulls the curtain again.

'Ahhh,' he says. It's more of a gargled noise than a word.

I am in my extremely small, lacy going-out underwear. I haven't even wrapped my towel around myself – it's thrown over my arm. Somehow that feels a lot worse than not having any means of covering myself up at all – I was so close to not exposing myself, and yet so far.

'Oh, God,' I squeak. 'I'm so – I'm so sorry.'

He flips the shower off. He probably can't hear me over the noise.

He turns his back on me; the fact that I notice this makes me realise that I should really stop looking at the outline behind the shower curtain. I turn my back on him too.

'Ahhh,' he says again.

'I know,' I say. 'Oh, God. This is not . . . how I imagined meeting you.'

I wince. That sounded a bit keen.

'Did you . . .' he begins.

'I didn't see anything,' I lie quickly.

'Good. OK. Me neither,' he says.

'I should . . . I'm *so* late for work.'

'Oh, you need the shower?'

'Well, I . . .'

'I'm finished,' he says. We still have our backs to one another. I slip the towel off my arm and now – about five minutes too late – wrap it around myself.

'Well, if you're sure,' I say.

'Umm. Need my towel,' he says.

'Oh, of course,' I say, grabbing it off the rail and turning.

'*Eyes closed*,' he yells.

I freeze and close my eyes. 'They're closed! They're closed!'

I feel him take the towel from my hand.

'OK. You can open them again.'

He steps out of the shower. I mean, he's decent now, but he's still not wearing a lot. I can see all of his chest, for instance. And quite a lot of his stomach.

He's a couple of inches taller than me. Wet, his thick curly hair still doesn't sit flat; it's smoothed back behind his ears and dripping on to his shoulders. His face is fine-boned and his eyes are deep brown, a few tones darker than his skin; he has laughter lines, and his ears stick out a little, as if they've learnt the habit from always keeping his hair back from his face.

He turns to sidestep past me. He's doing his best, but there's really not room for two of us, and as he slides by me the warm skin of his back brushes against my chest. I inhale, hangover forgotten. Despite the lace bra and the towel between us, my skin has gone prickly and something has started fizzing hotly at the base of my stomach, where all the best feelings tend to sit.

He glances over his shoulder at me, an intense, half-nervous, half-curious look that only makes me feel warmer. I can't help it. As he turns towards the door I glance down.

Is he . . . That looks like . . .

It can't have been. It must have been some bunched-up towel.

He closes the door behind him and I collapse backwards against the basin for a moment. The reality of the last two minutes is so painfully embarrassing that I find myself saying 'oh, God' out loud and pressing the heels of my hands into my eyes. This does not help with my hangover, which has come rushing back now that the naked man has left the bathroom.

God. I'm flushed with heat, all flustered and skin-prickly and breathless – no, I'm *turned on*. I didn't see that coming. Surely this situation was far too awkward for that to even be possible? I'm a grown woman! Can't I handle seeing a man naked? It's probably just because I haven't had sex for so long. It's some sort of biological thing, like how the smell of bacon gets you salivating, or how holding other people's babies makes you want to end your career and immediately start procreating.

In a sudden panic I swivel to look at myself in the mirror, wiping the condensation from its surface to reveal my pale, gaunt face. My lipstick has ingrained itself into the dry skin of my lips, and my eyeshadow and eyeliner have blurred into a black mess around each eye. I look like a toddler who's attempted to use its mother's make-up.

I groan. This is a disaster. This could not have gone worse. I look *terrible*, and he looked really quite astonishingly good. I think back to the day when I checked him out on Facebook – I don't remember him being attractive. How did I not notice? Oh, God, why does it even matter? It's Leon. Flatmate Leon. Leon-with-a-girlfriend Leon.

Right, I've *got* to shower and go to work. I'll deal with my hormones and incredibly awkward living situation tomorrow.

Oh, God. I am *so* late.

28

Leon

Ahhh.

Ahhh.

Lie on back in bed, immobilised by pounding shame. Cannot think in words. *Ahhh* is only sound adequate to express sufficient horror.

Didn't Kay say Tiffy was unattractive? I'd just assumed! Or . . . or . . . I'd not even thought about it, actually. But, Jesus. She's like . . . Ahhh.

Can't spring a scantily clad lady on a man in the shower. Can't do that. It's not fair.

Can't connect that woman in the bathroom in the red underwear with the woman I write notes to and clean up after. Had just never . . .

Landline rings. Freeze. Landline is in kitchen. Chance of bumping into Tiffy again: high.

Unfreeze and shake self. Obviously have to answer phone – will be Richie. Dart out of bedroom, clutching towel at waist, and locate phone under pile of Mr Prior's hats on kitchen sideboard; answer while dashing back to bedroom.

Me: Hey.

Richie: Are you all right?

Make groaning noise.

Richie, alert: What is it? What's happened?

Me: No, no, nothing bad. Just . . . met Tiffy.

Richie, cheered: Oh! Is she hot?

Repeat groaning noise.

Richie: She is! I *knew* it.

Me: She wasn't meant to be. I assumed Kay made sure she wasn't!

Richie: Did she look anything like Kay?

Me: Eh?

Richie: Kay wouldn't think anyone's hot unless they look like Kay.

Wince, but sort of know what he means. Can't get image of Tiffy out of head. Ruffled red hair all over the place, like she's just got out of bed. Light-brown freckles across pale skin, dusting her arms and dappled across her chest. Red lace bra. Ridiculously perfect breasts. Ahhh.

Richie: Where is she now?

Me: Shower.

Richie: And where are you?

Me: Hiding in the bedroom.

Pause.

Richie: You realise she's going to come there next, yeah?

Me: Shit!

Sit bolt upright. Flounder around looking for clothes. Can only find hers. See her dress, thrown on the floor unzipped.

Me: Hang on. Need to dress.

Richie: Wait, what?

Put him down on the bed as I pull on boxers and tracksuit bottoms. Horribly aware of my bum pointing towards door as I do so, but is better option than facing the other way. Find old vest within reach and throw it on, then breathe.

Me: OK. Right. I think it's safest to . . . go to the kitchen? She won't pass on the way from the bathroom to the bedroom. Then I can hide in the bathroom until she leaves.

Richie: What the hell happened? Why aren't you wearing any clothes? Have you shagged her, man?

Me: *No!*

Richie: All right. It was a reasonable question.

Make my way across living room to kitchen. Skulk as far as possible behind fridge, so I can't be seen en route from bathroom to bedroom.

Me: We bumped into each other in the shower.

Richie gives a proper belly laugh that makes me smile a little despite myself.

Richie: She was naked?

Groan.

Me: Nearly. I was, though.

Richie's laugh scales up a notch.

Richie: Ah, man, this has made my day. So she was in, what, a towel?

Me: Underwear.

Richie groans too this time.

Richie: Good?

Me: I'm not talking about this!

Richie: Good point. Can she hear you?

Pause. Listen. Ahhh.

Me, in a hiss: Shower has stopped!

Richie: Don't you want to be there when she comes out in a towel? Why don't you just go back to the bedroom? It won't look like you did it on purpose. I mean, you did nearly do it accidentally. Throw you together one more time, you never—

Me: I'm not going to *lie in wait* for the poor woman, Richie! I already exposed myself to her, didn't I? She's probably traumatised.

Richie: Did she look traumatised?

Think back. She looked . . . Ahhh. So much skin. And big blue eyes, freckles across her nose, that little intake of breath as I moved past her to the door, way too close for comfort.

Richie: You're going to need to speak to her.

Sound of bathroom door unlocking.

Me: Shit!

Hide further behind fridge, then, when no noise follows, peek out.

She doesn't look my way. Her towel is wrapped tightly under her arms and her long hair is darker now and dripping down her back. She disappears into the bedroom.

And breathe.

Me: She's in the bedroom. I'm going to the bathroom.

Richie: Why don't you just leave the flat if you're that worried, man?

Me: I can't talk to you, then! I cannot handle this alone, Richie!

I hear Richie grin.

Richie: There's something you're not telling me, isn't there? No, let me guess . . . did you get a bit excited . . . ?

I make my loudest, most humiliated groan yet. Richie roars with laughter.

Me: She came from nowhere! I was not prepared! I have not had sex for weeks!

Richie, laughing hysterically: Ah, Lee! Do you think she noticed?

Me: No. Definitely not. No.

Richie: So maybe, then.

Me: No. She can't have. Too awkward to think about.

Lock bathroom door behind me and pull toilet seat down to sit. Stare down at my legs, heart pounding.

Richie: I have to go.

Me: No! You can't leave! What do I do now?

Richie: What do you want to do now?

Me: Run away!

Richie: Come on, now, Lee! Calm yourself down.

Me: This is terrible. We *live together*. I can't be walking around with an erection in front of my flatmate! It's . . . it's . . . it's obscene! It's probably a crime!

Richie: If it is, then I definitely do belong in here. Come on, man.

Don't freak out about it. Like you say, you and Kay have been broken up a few weeks and not sleeping together for a fair while before that –

Me: How did you know that?

Richie: Come on. It was obvious.

Me: You haven't seen us together for months!

Richie: The point is, it's not a big deal. You saw a naked chick and you started thinking with your – hang on, man, give me . . .

He sighs.

Richie: Got to go. But chill out. She didn't see anything, it doesn't mean anything, just relax.

He hangs up.

29

Tiffy

Rachel is positively vibrating with excitement.

'You are joking! You are joking!' she says, bouncing in her seat. 'I cannot believe he had a hard-on!'

I groan and rub my temples, which I've sometimes seen tired people do on television so am hoping will make me feel better. It doesn't work. How is Rachel so bloody perky? I was sure she drank nearly as much as me.

'It's not funny,' I tell her. 'And I said he *might* have done. I'm not saying he definitely did.'

'Oh, please,' she says. 'You're not so out of action that you've forgotten what that looks like. Three men in one night! You are literally living the dream.'

I ignore her. The head of Editorial luckily found it funny that I was late, but I still have a huge pile of work to get done today, and it hasn't helped my to-do list that I arrived over an hour late.

'Stop pretending to check those proofs,' Rachel says. 'We need a plan of action!'

'For what?'

'Well, what now? Are you calling Ken the hermit? Going for a drink with Justin? Or jumping in the shower with Leon?'

'I'm going back to my desk,' I tell her, grabbing the stack of proofs. 'This has not been a productive session.'

She sings 'Maneater' at me as I walk away.

Rachel is right about the plan of action, though. I need to work out what the hell I'm going to do about the Leon situation. If we don't speak soon, there's a serious risk this morning will ruin everything – no more notes, no more leftovers, just silent, painful awkwardness. Humiliation is like mould: ignore it and the whole place will get smelly and green.

I've got to . . . I've got to text him.

No. I've got to call him, I decide. It needs to be drastic. I check the clock. Well, he'll be asleep now – it's two in the afternoon – so I've got a glorious four hours or so in which I can't do anything about this situation. I suppose I should probably use that time to go through the proofs of Katherin's book, especially now there's a real danger that quite a lot of people might actually buy it, what with all this social media buzz about crochet.

Instead, after a long night and morning of trying very hard not to, I think about Justin.

And then, because I am not good at thinking on my own, I ring Mo to talk about Justin. He sounds a little groggy when he answers the phone, as if he's just woken up.

'Where are you?' I ask.

'At home. Why?'

'You sound weird. Isn't it Gerty's day off?'

'Yes, she's here too.'

'Oh.' It's odd to think of the two of them just hanging out together without me. It just . . . doesn't work as a combination. From freshers' week of uni it was Gerty and me, inseparable; we took Mo under our collective wing at the end of first year, after seeing him solo dancing very enthusiastically to 'Drop it Like it's Hot' and deciding anyone with those moves needed to be involved in all our nights out. After that we did everything as a three, and if a rare pairing did come about it was always me plus Gerty or me plus Mo. 'Put loudspeaker on?' I say, trying not to sound petulant.

'Hang on. Hey, you're all set.'

'Let me guess,' Gerty says, 'you've fallen in love with Leon's brother.'

I pause. 'Normally your radar is pretty good, but you're way off.'

'Damn. Leon, then?'

'Can't I just call you for a chat?'

'This isn't a chat,' Gerty says. 'You don't call at two in the afternoon for chats. You WhatsApp for that.'

'This,' I tell her, 'is why I rang Mo.'

'So? What's the drama?' Gerty asks.

'Justin,' I say, too tired to argue with her.

'Ooh! An oldie but a goodie.'

I roll my eyes. 'Can you let Mo chime in with something supportive, at least *occasionally*?'

'What happened, Tiffy?' Mo says.

I fill them in on my evening. Or at least, an abridged version of it – I don't mention the dreadful kiss incident. It's just a lot of drama to fit in one phone call, especially when you're trying to check page numbers while you're talking.

Also, as well as that, there's the whole I-desperately-don't-want-to-think-about-it thing.

'This all sounds like pretty typical Justin behaviour, Tiffy,' Mo says.

'*Well done* for saying no,' Gerty says, with surprising fervour. 'It's fucking creepy that he was at the cruise, and now this? I wish you could see how—' There's a muffled noise and Gerty stops talking. I get the sense that Mo may have poked her.

'I didn't quite say no,' I point out, staring down at my feet. 'I said "in a couple of months".'

'That's still a hell of a lot better than dropping everything and running off with him again,' Gerty says.

There's a long silence. My throat feels tight. I need to talk about that kiss, I know I need to, but I can't seem to get there. 'Gerty,' I say eventually. 'Would you mind if I just spoke to Mo? For a moment?'

There's another muffled sort of silence.

'Fine, sure,' Gerty says. She is audibly trying not to sound miffed.

'Just me now,' Mo says.

I swallow. I don't want to talk about this here – I head for the office doors, down the stairs and out of the building. Outside everyone is moving a little more slowly than usual, as if the heat has calmed London down.

'You told me once that my – that me and Justin . . . took its toll on me.'

Mo doesn't say anything, he just waits.

'You said that would sink in eventually. And you said to call you when it does.'

More silence, but it's Mo-style silence, which means it is somehow incredibly reassuring. Like an audio hug. He doesn't need words, Mo – his arts are beyond them.

'Something weird happened last night. I was – that Ken guy and I kissed, and then we . . . well, I, I remembered . . .'

Why can't I say it?

'I remembered sleeping with Justin after a fight. I was so unhappy.' I'm tearing up; I sniff, trying very hard not to cry.

'How did you feel?' Mo asks. 'When the thought came to you, I mean.'

'Scared,' I admit. 'I don't remember our relationship being like that. But now I think I might have just sort of – airbrushed it? Forgotten those bits? I don't know, is that even possible?'

'Your brain can do amazing stuff to protect itself from pain,' Mo tells me. 'But it'll struggle to keep secrets from the rest of you for long. Has this feeling of remembering things differently happened a lot since you left Justin?'

'Not a lot.' But, you know, a *bit*. Like there was that note I wrote about not inviting Justin to Rachel's party, even though I know I did. It sounds crazy but I think Justin might've made me believe I'd not invited him, because that way he could be mad about me going? And lately I keep finding things – clothes, shoes, jewellery – that I remember Justin telling me I'd sold or given away. I'd usually put it down to my bad memory, but I've had a nagging sense of wrongness for months now, not helped by Mo's relentless, annoyingly supportive nudging every time we talk about Justin. I am very good at not thinking about things, though, so I've just . . . resolutely not thought about it.

Mo talks about gaslighting and triggers. I squirm uncomfortably, and finally a tear creeps from my bottom lashes down my cheek. I'm officially crying.

'I should go,' I say, wiping my nose.

'Just think about what I've said, OK, Tiffy? And remember how well you stood up to him last night – you've come a million miles already. Give yourself credit for that.'

I head back inside, suddenly drained. This last day has been too much. Up and down and up and down . . . Ugh. And the hangover is crushing.

By the time I finally finish checking the proofs of Katherin's book, I've filed the nasty Justin thoughts back into their usual box, and I'm feeling a lot calmer. I've also had three packets of Wotsits, which Rachel suggested as the ultimate hangover cure, and which do appear to have taken me from full-on zombie to semi-sentient. So once I've dumped *Crochet Your Way* on Rachel's desk, I scuttle back to mine to do what I've been itching to do since last night: go back on Leon's Facebook page.

There he is. He's smiling at the camera, his arm slung around someone at what looks like a Christmas party – there are twinkly fairy lights hung up behind them, and a room full of heads. I flick through his profile pictures and remember looking at these before. I'd not thought he looked at all attractive – and it's true that he's too gangly and long-haired to be my usual type. But clearly he is just one of those people who suddenly becomes fanciable in person.

Maybe it was just the initial shock, and the nakedness. Maybe second time around it'll all be nice and platonic, and I can forget about it and call Ken the sexy Norwegian hermit. Although I can't face that, not after the way Justin humiliated me in front of him. Ugh, no, don't think about Justin—

'Who's that?' Martin says from behind me. I jump, spilling coffee across my scattering of very urgent Post-it notes.

'Why do you always creep up on me?' I ask, snapping the window closed and dabbing at the coffee with a tissue.

'You're just jumpy. So who was that?'

'My friend Leon.'

'*Friend?*'

I roll my eyes. 'Since when have you been even slightly interested in my life, Martin?'

He gives me an oddly smug look, as if he knows something I don't, or perhaps is just having some intestinal issues.

'What do you need?' I ask, through gritted teeth.

'Oh, nothing, Tiffy. Don't let me interrupt you.' And he walks off.

I sit back in my chair and take a deep breath. Rachel pops her head up over her computer and mouths 'Still can't believe it! Hard-on!' at me, then does a double thumbs-up. I sink further in my seat, hangover resettling, and decide that I will absolutely definitely never drink again.

30

Leon

Mam at least provides distraction from painfully awkward memory of this morning.

She's making astonishing effort. And it seems she was telling the truth about being single – no telltale signs of man about house (Richie and I got to be very good at identifying them in childhood) and she's not changed her hair and clothes since last time I saw her, which means she's not trying to fit to someone else.

I talk to her about Kay. Feels surprisingly good. She nods in the right places and pats my hand, welling up occasionally, then makes me oven chips with nuggets, which all make me feel ten years old again. Not unpleasant, though. Nice to be looked after.

The strangest part is going back to the bedroom Richie and I shared when we moved to London in our early teens. I've only been back here once since the trial. Came to stay for a week after that; didn't think Mam could cope alone. Wasn't needed for long, though – she met Mike, who was keen to have the place to themselves, so I moved back to the flat.

The room is unchanged. Has the feeling of a shell missing its sea creature. It's full of holes where things should be: Blu-Tack marks on walls for posters long-since taken down, books tipping at diagonals without enough there to hold them up. Richie's stuff still boxed up from when his old housemates dropped it around.

It takes enormous mental effort not to riffle through it. Would be unnecessarily upsetting, and he'd hate me doing it.

I lie down on the bed and find my mind drifting back to image of Tiffy – first in that red underwear, then padding into the bedroom wrapped in a towel. Second image feels even more unacceptable, as she didn't even know I was watching. Fidget, uncomfortable. It's wrong to be so attracted to her. It's probably a reaction to Kay break-up.

Phone rings. Rising panic. Check screen: Tiffy.

Don't want to answer. Phone rings and rings – seems to go on for ever.

She hangs up without leaving a message. I feel oddly guilty. Richie told me I had to talk to her. But I prefer option of total radio silence going forward, or, at most, the odd note left on kettle or back of door.

Lie back down. Reflect on this. Wonder if it's true.

Phone buzzes. A text.

Hey. So. Hmm. I feel like we should chat about this morning? Tiffy x

The memory hits me afresh, and I find myself groaning again. Should definitely reply. Put phone down. Stare at ceiling.

Phone buzzes again.

I should totally have started with an apology. It was me who shouldn't have been there, according to our flatsharing rules. And then I went and accosted you in the shower. So yes, I am very, very sorry! xx

Oddly, I feel a lot better after seeing this text. It doesn't sound like she was traumatised, and also sounds familiarly Tiffy-ish, so is easier to imagine this text coming from the Tiffy I had in my head before I met the real one. That one was sort of . . . not irrelevant, exactly, but in the 'safe space' in my head. Person for talking to, without pressure or implication. Easy and undemanding.

Now Tiffy is definitely not in safe headspace.
I muster the courage to start a reply.

Don't apologise. We were bound to bump into each other eventually! No
need to worry – it's already forgotten.

Delete this last part. Clearly this is not true.

Don't apologise. We were bound to bump into each other eventually! No
need to worry – am happy to put it behind us if you are. Leon x

Send, then regret the kiss. Do I normally put a kiss? Have no re-
collection. Scroll back up thread of last few messages and find that
I am entirely inconsistent, which is probably best outcome. I settle
back on the bed and wait.

And wait.

What is she doing? She normally replies fast. Check the time –
eleven at night. Could she have fallen asleep? Did seem like she was
out late last night. Finally, though:

Let's forget all about it! I promise it won't happen again (the barging in OR
the sleeping in, that is). I hope Kay didn't totally flip out about me breaking
the flatshare rules . . .? And, you know, accosting her boyfriend in the
shower . . . xx

Deep breath.

Kay and I broke up a couple of weeks ago. X

Reply is almost instant.

Oh, shit, I'm so sorry. I did think something might be wrong – you were all

quiet in your notes (more so than usual, I mean!) How are you holding
up?

Think about it. How am I holding up? Am lying in bed in my
mother's flat, fantasising about naked flatmate, all thoughts of ex-girl-
friend briefly but genuinely forgotten. Is probably not *entirely* healthy,
but . . . better than yesterday? I go for:

Getting there. x

There's a long pause after this one. Wonder if I should have said
a bit more. Not that that's ever put Tiffy off before.

Well, this might cheer you up: in my hungover state I walked into the printer
at work today.

I snort. A beat later, an image of printer appears. It's enormous.
Could probably fit four Tiffys inside it.

Did you not . . . spot it?

I think I just lost the ability to stop walking at the necessary moment. I had
just come off a call with my gorgeous bricklayer-turned-designer though,
so . . .

Ah. You must've still been weak at the knees.

Probably! It's been that sort of day xx

Stare at this one until phone screen times out. *That sort of day.* What sort of day? Weak-kneed sort of day? But why – because she . . .

No, no, won't be because of me. That's ridiculous. Except . . . what *did* she mean, then?

Hope this isn't going to be how I am whenever communicating with Tiffy now. Is absolutely exhausting.

31

My dad likes to say, 'Life is never simple'. This is one of his favourite aphorisms.

I actually think it's incorrect. Life is often simple, but you don't notice how simple it was until it gets incredibly complicated, like how you never feel grateful for being well until you're ill, or how you never appreciate your tights drawer until you rip a pair and have no spares.

Katherin has just done a guest vlog on Tasha Chai-Latte's page about crocheting your own bikini. The Internet has gone mental. I can't keep track of all the influential people who have retweeted her – and because Katherin hates Martin, every time she freaks out or needs help with something, she calls me. I, who know nothing about PR, then have to go to Martin and feed back to Katherin. If this was a divorce and I was their child, social services would be called.

Gerty rings me as I'm leaving work.

'You've only just left? Have you asked for a rise yet?' she asks. I check my watch – it's half seven. How have I been at work for almost twelve hours, and yet achieved so little?

'No time,' I tell her. 'And they don't do rises. They'd probably fire me for asking.'

'Ridiculous.'

'What's up, anyway?'

'Oh, I just thought you might want to know I've got Richie's appeal moved forward by three months,' Gerty says airily.

I stop dead in my tracks. Someone behind me walks into me and swears (stopping abruptly in central London is a heinous crime, and immediately gives the people around you permission to kick you).

'You took his case?'

'His previous barrister was appalling,' Gerty says. 'Really. I've half a mind to report him to the bar standards board. We'll have to find Richie a new solicitor, too, especially since I've gone over this one's head and royally pissed him off, but—'

'You *took his case*?'

'Keep up, Tiffy.'

'Thank you. So much. God, I . . .' I can't stop smiling. 'Has Richie told Leon?'

'Richie probably doesn't know yet,' Gerty says. 'I only wrote to him yesterday.'

'Can I tell Leon?'

'That'd save me a job,' Gerty says, 'so go for it.'

My phone buzzes almost as soon as I hang up. It's a text from Leon; my heart does a funny little twisty spasm thing. He's not messaged me or left me a note since we texted at the weekend.

Heads up: enormous bunch of flowers for you in foyer from your ex. Not sure whether to ruin surprise (good or bad surprise?) but if it was me, would want to be pre-warned x

I stop dead in my tracks again; this time a businessman on a scooter runs over my foot.

I've not heard from Justin since Thursday. No call, no text, nothing. I had just about convinced myself that he'd taken what I'd said seriously and wasn't going to contact me, but I should have known better – that would have been entirely out of character. This, though – this is much more like it.

I don't *want* a big bunch of flowers from Justin. I just want him gone – it's so hard to get on with getting better when he keeps popping up all over the place. As I march up to our building, I press my lips together and prepare myself.

It really is an enormous bunch of flowers. I'd forgotten how rich he is, and how inclined to spend money on ridiculous things. For my birthday dinner last year he bought me an insanely pricey designer gown, all silver silk and sequins; wearing it felt like going out in costume as somebody else.

Stuck in amongst the flowers is a note that reads, *To Tiffy – we'll speak in October. Love, Justin.* I lift the bouquet and check underneath it for a proper note, but no. A note would be far too straightforward – a giant, expensive gesture is much more Justin's style.

This has really annoyed me, for some reason. Perhaps because I've never told Justin where I live. Or maybe because it's so flagrantly disregarding what I asked of him on Thursday, and because he's made my 'I need a couple of months' into a 'I will speak to you in two months' time'.

I stuff the flowers into the ornamental plant pot I usually keep my spare wool in. I was waiting for Justin to do this – to turn up with his explanations and his expensive gestures and sweep me off my feet again. But that Facebook message, the engagement . . . He tipped me over the edge, and now I am in a very different place from the last time he tried to get me back.

I slump down on the sofa and stare at the flowers. I think about what Mo said, and how despite myself I've been remembering things. The way Justin used to tell me off for forgetting stuff, how confused it made me feel. The half-excitement, half-anxiety every day when he came home. The reality of how my stomach lurched when he put

his hand on my shoulder and snapped at me to go for a drink with
him at the pub on Thursday.

That flashback.

God. I don't want to go back to all that. I'm happier now – I like living
here, safely hidden away in this flat which I've made my own. In two
weeks' time I'll be at the end of my lease here – Leon's not mentioned
it, so I've not brought it up either, because I don't *want* to move out. I've
got money, for once, even if most of it is paying off my overdraft. I've
got a flatmate who I can talk to – who cares if it's not face-to-face? And
I've got a home that actually feels like it's exactly fifty per cent *mine*.

I reach for my phone and reply to Leon.

Bad surprise. Thanks for the heads-up. We now have a lot of flowers in the
flat xx

He replies almost instantly, which is unusual.

Glad to hear it x

And then, a minute or so later:

About the flowers in the flat, not the surprise, obviously x

I smile.

I have some good news for you xx

Perfect timing – on coffee break. Hit me. x

He doesn't get it – he thinks this is small good news, like I cooked
a crumble or something. I pause, fingers hovering over the keys. This

is the perfect thing to cheer me up – and what's more important, the ins and outs of my old relationship, or the reality of Richie's case right now?

Can I call you? As in, if I call you, can you pick up? xx

The reply comes more slowly this time.

Sure. x

I'm hit with a very abrupt and intense wave of nerves, and a flashback to Leon, naked, dripping wet, his hair pushed back from his face. I press the call button because there is now no other option but to do it, or to come up with a very weird and elaborate excuse.

'Hey,' he says, his voice a little low, as if he's somewhere he has to be quiet.

'Hi,' I say. We wait. I think about him naked, and then try very hard not to. 'How's the shift?'

'Quiet. Hence the coffee break.'

His accent is almost exactly like Richie's, and completely unlike anyone else's. It's like South London had a fling with Irish. I sit back on the sofa, pulling my knees up and hugging them close.

'So, uh . . .' he begins.

'Sorry,' I say, almost at the same time. We wait again, and then I find myself doing a stupid little awkward laugh I'm sure I've never done before. What an excellent time to wheel out a brand-new awkward laugh.

'You go,' he says.

'Let's just . . . I didn't call to talk about the other day,' I begin, 'so let's just pretend that whole shower situation was a strange shared dream for the duration of this conversation so I can tell you my good news without us both feeling incredibly awkward?'

I think I hear him smile. 'Deal.'

'Gerty took Richie's case.'

All I hear is a sharp intake of breath, and then silence. I wait until it has been a painfully long time, but I have a feeling Leon is the kind of person who needs time to absorb stuff the same way Mo does, so I resist the urge to say anything else until he's ready.

'Gerty took Richie's case,' Leon repeats, in a wondering sort of way.

'Yeah. She took it. And that's not even the good news!' I find I'm bouncing slightly on the sofa cushions.

'What's . . . the good news?' he asks, sounding slightly faint.

'She's got his appeal moved forward by three months. You were looking at January next year, right? So now we're talking, what . . .'

'October. October. That's . . .'

'Soon! Really soon!'

'That's *two months* away! We're not ready!' Leon says, suddenly sounding panicked. 'What if— Does she—'

'Leon. Breathe.'

More silence. I can hear the distant sound of Leon taking deep, slow breaths. My cheeks are starting to hurt from supressing an enormous grin.

'She's an amazing lawyer,' I tell him. 'And she wouldn't take the case if she didn't think Richie stood a chance. Really.'

'Don't do this to me if she's going to – to pull out, or . . .' His voice comes out strangled, and my stomach twists in sympathy.

'I'm not telling you she's definitely going to get him out of there, but I think there's reason to hope again. I wouldn't say that if I didn't mean it.'

He lets out a long, slow breath, half-laughing. 'Does Richie know?'

'Not yet, I don't think. She wrote to him yesterday – how long do letters take to get there?'

'Depends – they tend to get held up at prison before they get to him. It means I get to tell him myself, though, when he next calls.'

'Gerty will want to talk to you about the case soon too,' I say.

'A lawyer who wants to talk about Richie's case,' Leon says. 'Lawyer. Who. Wants. To . . .'

'Yeah,' I interrupt, laughing.

'Tiffy,' he says, suddenly serious. 'I cannot thank you enough.'

'No, *shh*,' I begin.

'Really. It's . . . I cannot tell you how much this means to – to Richie. And to me.'

'I just passed on Richie's letter.'

'That was more than anyone else has done off their own back for my brother.'

I fidget. 'Well, you tell Richie he owes me a letter.'

'He'll write. I should go. But – thank you. Tiffy. I'm so glad it was you, and not the drug-dealer or the man with the hedgehog.'

'Pardon?'

'Don't worry,' he says quickly. 'See you later.'

32

Leon

New string of notes (Tiffy always uses several. Never has enough room):

> *Leon, can I ask . . . What's the deal with the neighbours?! I've only ever seen the strange man in Flat 5 (do you think he knows about the hole in those trackies, by the way? He lives alone, maybe nobody has told him!). I think Flat 1 is those two old ladies who hang out at the bus stop on the corner reading gory true crime novels. But what about Flat 4 and 2? xx*

> *Flat 4 is nice middle-aged man with unfortunate crack habit. Always assumed Flat 2 belongs to the foxes. x*

Written on back of draft manuscript on coffee table:

> *Ah, yes! The foxes. Well, I hope they're paying rent. Did you notice Fatima Fox has had three little cubs?!*

Below:

> *. . . Fatima Fox?*

And, speaking of rent. Have an alert in my phone saying we've hit six months since you moved in. Technically end of your lease I think? You want to stay?

Then, added that evening, post-sleep:

As in, hope you want to stay. Don't need the money so badly any more what with scarf sales and new, unbelievably excellent free lawyer. But not sure what flat would look like without you in it now. Could not survive without beanbag, for starters. x

Beneath this, Tiffy has sketched a group of foxes on a sofa, with heading *Flat 2*. Each fox is carefully labelled.

Fatima Fox! She's the mama fox. The chief vixen, if you will.

Florentina Fox. The cheeky second-in-command. Her usual haunt is the smelly corner by the bins.

Fliss Fox. The whimsical young chancer. Generally found attempting to enter the building via a window.

Fabio Fox. The resident dog fox. (This is actually what male foxes are called but I do also imagine he's a bit of a dog.)

The new babies, as yet unnamed by me. Would you like to do the honours?

Below this:

Yes, please, the beanbag and I would love to stay a while longer. Shall we say another six months? xx

Another six months. Perfect. Done x

New note, beside empty tiffin tray:

I'm sorry, WHAT? Noggle, Stanley and Archibald?
They don't even begin with F!

Same note, now left beside large plate of shepherd's pie:

What can I say. Fabio Fox liked Noggle. The other two were Fatima's idea.
Also, sorry, couldn't help noticing recycling bin contents when putting it out today. Are you OK? x

Shepherd's pie all gone. New note:

Yeah, don't worry, I'm actually really good. A purge of ex-related memorabilia was long overdue, and it has also freed up a lot more under-bed space for storing scarves. (In case you were wondering, we're really not Team Ex any more.) xx

Ah, no? Must say I'd become less keen on Ex anyway. Well, more scarf space is certainly welcome. Got my foot caught in one yesterday – it was lying on bedroom floor waiting to snag the unwary. x

Oops, sorry, sorry, I know I must stop leaving clothes on the bedroom floor! Also, apologies if this is way too personal but have you bought, like, ENTIRELY new boxers? Suddenly all the old ones with amusing cartoon characters are never on the clothes horses, and the flat has become an homage to Mr Klein whenever you do laundry.
And while we're on the subject of exes . . . Have you heard anything from Kay? xx

New double Post-it note. Very occasionally, I run out of room. Also, thought quite hard about what to say in this one.

Saw her last weekend, at an old friend's wedding. Was weird. Nice. Chatted as friends, and felt good. Richie was right: relationship had ended long before it ended.

Eh. Yes, did a general clothes overhaul. Realised I hadn't bought new clothes in approx. five years. Also, became suddenly aware that a woman lives in this flat and sees my laundry.

Seems you've been shopping too. I like the blue and white dress on the back of the door. Looks like the sort one of the Famous Five might wear for going on adventures. x

Thanks ☺ It feels like the perfect time for an adventure dress. It's summer, I'm single, the foxes are frolicking across the tarmac, the pigeons are singing from the drainpipes . . . Life. Is. Good. xx

33

Tiffy

I'm sitting on the balcony crying like a toddler who's dropped their ice cream. Full on, stuttering, mouth-pulled-wide crying.

The sudden rememberings are striking at entirely random times now, just bobbing up out of nowhere and sending me absolutely reeling. This one was particularly nasty: I was minding my own business heating up some soup, and then BAM, up it popped – the night Justin came around in February, before the Facebook message, and brought Patricia. He'd looked at me with total disgust, barely saying a word to me. Then, when Patricia was out in the hallway, he'd kissed me goodbye on the lips, one hand on the back of my neck. Like I was his. For a moment, as I was remembering it, I felt with absolute horror that I still was.

So. Despite me being technically much happier, this remembering thing keeps happening and ruining it. It is clear that I have some problems to confront here, and my diversionary tactics are no longer serving me. I have to think about this.

Thinking time means I need Mo and Gerty. They arrive together, an hour or so after I text them. As Gerty pours out glasses of white wine, I realise I'm nervous. I don't want to talk. But then once I start I can't really stop, and it all comes out in this big garbled mess: the memories, the old stuff from the very start, all of it right through to the flowers he sent me last week.

Eventually I trail off, exhausted. I down the rest of the glass of wine.

'Let's not beat around the bush,' says Gerty, who has literally never beaten around a single bush in her whole life. 'You've got a crazy ex-boyfriend, and he knows where you live.'

My pulse starts to quicken; it feels as if there's something trapped in my chest.

Mo shoots Gerty the sort of look that usually only Gerty is allowed to give people. 'I'll talk,' he says, 'and you can be in charge of the wine. OK?'

Gerty looks as if someone's just slapped her in the face. But then, curiously, she turns her head away from him, and from where I'm sitting I can see she's smiling.

Weird.

'I wish I hadn't said I'd go for a drink with him in October,' I say, faced with Mo's listening face. 'Why did I *say* that?'

'I'm not sure you did say that, did you? I think he chose to take it that way,' Mo says. 'But you don't have to see him. You don't owe him anything.'

'Do you two remember all of this?' I ask abruptly. 'I'm not im-agining it?'

Mo pauses for a moment, but Gerty doesn't miss a beat.

'Of course we do. I remember every bloody minute of it. He was vile to you. He'd tell you where to be and how to get there, and then he'd walk you there because you wouldn't be able to find your way on your own. He'd make every argument your fault, and he wouldn't give up until you were sorry. He'd ditch you and then pick you up again at a moment's notice. He told you you were overweight and weird and nobody else would want you, even though you are clearly a goddess of a woman and he ought to have felt lucky to have you. It was terrible. We *hated* him. And if you hadn't banned me from talking about him, I would have told you that every bloody day.'

'Oh,' I say, in a small voice.

'Is that how it felt to you?' Mo asks, with the air of a handyman with limited tools trying to patch up the damage done by a bomb going off.

'I . . . I remember being really happy with him,' I say. 'As well as being, you know, really bloody miserable.'

'He wasn't horrible to you *all* the time,' Gerty begins.

'He wouldn't have been able to keep you with him if he was,' Mo goes on. 'He knew that. He's a smart guy, Tiffy. He knew how to . . .'

'. . . play you,' Gerty finishes.

Mo winces at her choice of words.

'But I think we were happy together once.' I don't know why this feels important. I don't like the thought of everyone seeing me in that relationship and thinking I was an idiot for being with someone who treated me that way.

'Sure,' Mo says, nodding. 'Especially at the start.'

'Right,' I say. 'At the start.'

We sip our wine in silence for a while. I feel very odd. Like I ought to be crying, and I sort of want to be crying, but there's a strange tightness in my eyes that's making tears impossible.

'Well. Thanks. You know, for trying. And sorry for . . . making you stop talking about him,' I say, looking down at my feet.

'It's all right. At least that meant you would still see us,' Mo says. 'You had to come to this on your own, Tiff. As tempting as it was to bulldoze in and whisk you away from him, you would have just gone back.'

I muster the courage to glance up at Gerty. She holds my gaze; her expression is fierce. I can't imagine how hard she found it sticking to her word and not mentioning Justin.

I wonder how on earth Mo persuaded her to leave me to do this on my own. He was right, though – I would have just pushed them away if they'd told me to leave Justin. The thought is faintly nauseating.

'You're doing great, Tiff,' Mo says, topping up my wine. 'Just hold on to what you're figuring out. It might be hard to remember it all the time, but it's important. So do your best.'

Somehow, when Mo says something, it seems to make it true.

It is so hard to remember. One week with no sudden memories or random Justin appearances, and I waver. I wobble. I almost topple altogether and decide I made the whole thing up.

Thankfully Mo is there to talk to. We go through incidents as I remember them – shouted arguments, subtle jabs, the even subtler ways my independence was eroded. I can't believe how not-OK my relationship with Justin was, but even more than that, I can't believe I hadn't *noticed*. I think that will take a while to sink in in itself.

Thank God for friends and flatmates. Leon has no idea this is all going on, of course, but seems to have clocked that I need some distraction – he's cooking more, and if we don't speak for a while he'll start a new thread of notes. It used to always be me that did that – I get the feeling that initiating conversation is not something Leon is particularly keen on doing, as a rule.

This one is on the fridge when I get home from work with Rachel, who's come around so I can cook her dinner (she says I owe her indefinite free meals because I've ruined her life by commissioning *Crochet Your Way*):

Hunt for Johnny White is going poorly. Got drunk under the table by Johnny White the Fourth at very grimy pub near Ipswich. Nearly had a repeat of our memorable bathroom collision: slept in and was extremely late x

Rachel raises her eyebrows at me, reading it over my shoulder. 'Memorable, eh?'

'Oh, shut up. You know what he means.'

'I believe I do,' she says. 'He means: I keep thinking about you in your underwear. Do you think about me naked?'

I chuck an onion at her. 'Dice that and make yourself useful,' I say, but I can't help smiling.

SEPTEMBER

34

Leon

Already September. Summer starting to cool. Never thought it possible that time could pass quickly when Richie was in prison, but he says the same – his days move like they should, instead of dragging and trailing and forcing him to feel every minute.

It's all because of Gerty. I've only met her a few times, but we speak on the phone every few days; often the solicitor joins the call too. Barely ever spoke to last solicitor. This one seems to be endlessly doing things. Amazing.

Gerty is brusque beyond the point of rudeness, but I like her – she does not seem to have the capacity for bullshitting (opposite of Sal?). She's often in the flat, and has taken to joining Tiffy in writing me notes. Thankfully, though, it's very easy to tell them apart. These two are side by side on breakfast bar:

Hey! I'm sorry to hear about that two-day hangover – I feel your pain, and recommend Wotsits. However . . . no WAY does your hair get curlier on hangover days! That just can't be a thing, because there is no upside to a hangover. And, from my limited knowledge of what you look like, I'm betting the curlier your hair is the cooler you look. xx

Leon – tell Richie to call me. He has not supplied me with the answers to the ten-page list of enquiries I sent him last week. Please remind him that I am an extremely impatient person who is usually paid a lot for reviewing things. G

On way back from the last Richie visit, I popped in to see a Johnny White. He lives in a care home north of London, and, within moments, I felt sure he was not our guy. Wife and seven children was strong sign (though, obviously, not conclusive), but then, after a very difficult conversation, I discovered he only served in the army for three weeks before being shipped home with a gangrenous leg.

This resulted in a long conversation about gangrene. Felt a lot like being at work, except much more awkward.

The following week Mr Prior is unwell. Find myself surprisingly distressed. Mr Prior is a very old man – it's entirely to be expected. My job is to make him comfortable. Has been from the first day I met him. But I always thought I'd find him the love of his life before he had to go, and none of my five Johnny Whites has been any use at all. Three to go, but still.

I was naïve. Pretty sure Kay said so at the time.

On the boiler:

So, if you've reached this point, you've probably figured out that the boiler is broken. But don't worry, Leon, I have excellent news for you! I've already called a plumber and she is going to come tomorrow evening to sort it. Until then you'll have to shower in ICE-COLD WATER but actually if you've come to look at the boiler you may well have already done that, in which case, the worst is over. I recommend curling up in the beanbag with a hot cup of spiced apple tea (yes, I bought a new fruit tea; no, we don't already have too many in the cupboard) and our lovely Brixton blanket. That's what I did, and it worked a treat xx

Not sure how I feel about it being *our* Brixton blanket, assuming she means the ratty multi-coloured thing I'm always having to throw off the bed. Is definitely one of the worst objects in the flat.

Settle down on beanbag with latest variety of fruit tea and think about Tiffy, here, in this spot, just a few hours before me. Wet hair, bare shoulders. Wrapped in just a towel and this blanket.

Blanket isn't *so* bad. It's . . . characterful. Quirky. Maybe I'm coming round to it.

35

Tiffy

This is my first session with Someone Other Than Mo.

Mo himself suggested it. He said it would benefit me to do proper counselling and talk to a person who didn't already know me. And then Rachel told me that, unbelievably, our employee benefits actually include up to fifteen sessions of counselling, paid for by Butterfingers. I have no idea why they're willing to provide that but not pay above minimum wage – maybe they're sick of employees leaving on stress.

So here I am. It is very weird. Someone Other Than Mo is called Lucie and is wearing a gigantic cricket jumper as a dress, which obviously immediately makes me like her and ask her where she shops. We talked about vintage stores in South London for a while, and then she got me a water, and now here we are, in her office, facing one another in matching armchairs. I'm extremely nervous, though I haven't got a clue why.

'So Tiffy, what was it that made you want to come and see me today?' Lucie asks.

I open my mouth and close it again. God, there's so much to explain. Where do I even begin?

'Just start with that,' Lucie says. She has Mo's mindreading skills, clearly – they must teach them that when they're accredited. 'The thing that made you want to pick up the phone and make an appointment.'

'I want to fix whatever the hell it was my ex-boyfriend did to me,' I say, and then pause, startled. How have I managed to say that outright to a complete stranger within five minutes of meeting her? How embarrassing.

But Lucie doesn't even blink. 'Sure,' she says. 'Would you like to tell me a bit more about that?'

'Are you healed?' Rachel asks me, plonking a coffee down on my desk.

Ah, coffee, elixir of the overworked. Recently it has overtaken tea in my affections – a sign of how little I'm sleeping. I blow Rachel a kiss as she makes her way over to her screen. As per usual, we continue the conversation on instant messenger.

Tiffany [09:07]: It was really weird. I literally told her the most embarrassing stuff about me within like ten minutes of meeting her.

Rachel [09:08]: Did you tell her about when you vomited in your hair on the night bus?

Tiffany [09:10]: Well, that didn't actually come up.

Rachel [09:11]: How about the time you broke that guy's penis at university?

Tiffany [09:12]: Didn't come up either.

Rachel [09:12]: That's what he said.

Tiffany [09:13]: Does that joke work?

Rachel [09:15]: Well, anyway, I am now reassured that I know more of your embarrassing secrets than this new imposter into your affections. OK. Go on.

Tiffany [09:18]: She didn't really *say* much. Even less than Mo does. I thought she'd tell me what was wrong with me. But instead I kind of figured some stuff out all on my own . . . which I totally couldn't have done without her sitting there. So weird.

Rachel [09:18]: What kind of stuff?

Tiffany [09:19]: Like . . . Justin was cruel sometimes. And controlling. And other bad stuff.

Rachel [09:22]: Can I just say, I officially stand corrected on the Justin issue. Gerty is right. He's scum of the earth.

Tiffany [09:23]: You realise you just typed 'Gerty is right'?

Rachel [09:23]: I forbid you to tell her.

Tiffany [09:23]: Screenshot already sent.

Rachel [09:24]: Bitch. All right, so you'll go again?

Tiffany [09:24]: Three sessions this week.

Rachel [09:24]: Blimey.

Tiffany [09:25]: I have this fear that because the first flashback happened when that Ken guy kissed me . . .

Rachel [09:26]: Yes?

Tiffany [09:26]: What if that's what happens now? What if Justin has, like, reprogrammed me, and I WILL NEVER BE ABLE TO KISS A MAN AGAIN?!

Rachel [09:29]: I mean, that is fucking terrifying.

Tiffany [09:30]: Thanks Rachel.

Rachel [09:31]: You should see someone about that.

Tiffany [09:33]: [glaring emoji] Thank you, Rachel.

Rachel [09:34]: Oh, come on. I know that made you laugh. As in, I literally just watched you laugh and then try and turn it into a cough when you realised the head of Editorial was walking past.

Tiffany [09:36]: Did it work, do you think?

'Tiffy? Do you have a minute?' calls the head of Editorial.

Shit. 'Do you have a minute' is always bad. If it was urgent but non-problematic, he'd just shout it across the room or send me an email with one of those passive-aggressive red exclamation marks on it. No, 'do you have a minute' means it's confidential, and that almost certainly means it's worse than just sniggering at my desk because I'm messaging Rachel about kissing.

What's Katherin done? Has she uploaded a picture of her vagina on Twitter, as she threatens to do literally every time I ask her to do another interview at Martin's request?

Or is it one of the many, many books that I have completely ignored in the madness that has been *Crochet Your Way*? I can't even remember their titles any more. I've shifted pub dates like I've been playing Bananagrams, and I definitely haven't run the changes by the head of Editorial. It'll be that, won't it? I've ignored someone's book for so long that it's actually gone to print without any words in it.

'Sure,' I say, pushing away from my desk in what I hope is a brisk and professional manner.

I follow him into his office. He closes the door behind me.

'Tiffy,' he begins, perching on the edge of his desk. 'I know it's been a busy few months for you.'

I swallow. 'Oh, it's been fine,' I say. 'Thanks, though!'

He gives me a slightly odd look at this point, which is entirely understandable.

'You've done a fantastic job with Katherin's book,' he says. 'It really is a stellar piece of publishing. You spotted that trend – no, you shaped it. Really, top notch.'

I blink, bewildered. I neither spotted that trend nor shaped it – I've been publishing crochet books ever since I started at Butterfingers.

'Thanks?' I say, feeling a bit guilty.

'We're so impressed with your recent work, Tiffy, that we'd like to promote you to editor,' he says.

It takes a good few seconds for the words to sink in, and when they do, I make a very peculiar choking noise.

'Are you all right?' he asks, frowning.

I clear my throat. 'Fine! Thanks!' I squeak. 'I mean, I just didn't expect . . .'

. . . ever to get promoted. Literally, ever. I had entirely given up hope.

'It's extremely well deserved,' he says, smiling benevolently.

I manage to smile back. I don't really know what to do with myself. What I *want* to do is ask how much more money I'll be getting, but there's no dignified way to ask that question.

'Thanks so much,' I gush instead, and then I feel a bit pathetic, because let's be honest they should have promoted me two years ago, and it's undignified to grovel. I draw myself up to my full height and give him a more purposeful smile. 'I'd better get back to work,' I say. Senior people always like to hear you say that.

'Absolutely,' he says. 'HR will send over details of the salary increase et cetera.'

I like the sound of that et cetera.

Congratulations on the promotion! Better late than never? Made you mushroom stroganoff to celebrate. x

I smile. The note is stuck on the fridge, which is already one layer deep in Post-it notes. My current favourite is a doodle Leon did, depicting the man in Flat 5 sitting on an enormous heap of bananas. (We still don't know why he keeps so many banana crates in his parking space.)

I rest my forehead against the fridge door for a moment, then run my fingers across the layers of paper scraps and Post-it notes. There's so much here. Jokes, secrets, stories, the slow unfolding of two people whose lives have been changing in parallel – or, I don't know, in synch. Different times, same place.

I reach for a pen.

Thank you ☺ I've been doing a lot of celebratory dancing around the flat, just so you know. Like, seriously uncool, trying-to-moonwalk dancing. I can't imagine that's something you ever partake in, somehow . . .

Can I ask what you're up to this weekend? I'm guessing you'll be

staying at your mum's again? I just wondered if you wanted to maybe
go out for a drink or something to celebrate with me. xx

Waiting for the reply makes me wish, for the very first time, that
Leon and I communicated via WhatsApp like normal people. I'd kill
for a little double blue tick right now. Then, when I get home, pasted
carefully below my note on the fridge:

Am partial to the occasional moonwalk from kitchen to living room.
    Can't come for a drink unfortunately as I'm off hunting Johnny Whites.
This one is in Brighton.

Then, just below, but in a different coloured pen:

Might be ridiculous idea but if you fancy a trip to the seaside you could
come too?

I'm standing in the kitchen, facing the fridge, absolutely beaming.

I'd love to come! I totally love the seaside. It legitimises wearing a sunhat,
for starters, or carrying a parasol, which are both wonderful things that
I do NOT get to do enough. Where do you want to meet? xx

The response takes two days to come. I wonder if Leon is losing
his nerve, but then, eventually, scribbled fast in blue ink:

Victoria station at half ten on Saturday. It's a date! X

36

Leon

It's a date? It's a date?!

What has happened to me? Should have written *see you there.* Instead, I said *it's a date.* Which it's not. Probably. Also, am not a person who says things like *it's a date,* even when it is.

Rub eyes and fidget on the spot. I'm under the departure boards at London Victoria station, along with a hundred or so other people, but while they're all staring up at the boards, I'm keeping my eyes on the exit from the underground. Wonder if Tiffy will recognise me when I've got clothes on. On that point: it's a freakishly warm day for September. Should not have worn jeans.

Check directions from Brighton station are loaded up on my phone. Check time. Check train platform. Fidget some more.

When she finally appears, there's no danger of missing her. She's in a canary yellow jacket and tight trousers; her orange-red hair is thrown over her shoulders and bounces as she walks. She's also taller than most of the people streaming all around her, and is wearing yellow sandals with a heel, giving her an extra few inches on the general population.

She seems entirely oblivious of how many eyes she catches as she walks by, which only makes the whole effect more attractive.

Smile and wave as she spots me. Proceed to stand awkwardly

smiling as she approaches, then, at this extremely late moment, am struck by question of whether we should hug hello. Could have spent last ten minutes of waiting time debating this. Instead, have left it until she is right in front of me, eye to eye, her cheeks flushed from the stuffy heat hanging in the station air.

She hangs back; too late for a hug.

Tiffy: Hey.

Me: Hi.

And then, simultaneously:

Tiffy: Sorry I'm late—

Me: Not seen those yellow shoes before—

Tiffy: Sorry, you go.

Me: Don't worry, you're hardly late.

Thank God she spoke over me. Why would I draw attention to the fact I am familiar with most of her shoes? Sounds extremely creepy.

We walk to the platform side by side. I keep glancing at her; can't get over how tall she is, for some reason. Didn't imagine her tall.

Tiffy looks sideways at me, catches my eye, and smiles.

Tiffy: Not what you expected?

Me: Sorry?

Tiffy: Me. Am I what you expected?

Me: Oh, I—

Tiffy quirks an eyebrow.

Tiffy: As in, before you saw me last month.

Me: Well, didn't expect you to be so . . .

Tiffy: Big?

Me: I was going to say naked. But also tall, yes.

Tiffy laughs.

Tiffy: I wasn't as naked as you were.

Me, wincing: Don't remind me. I'm so sorry for—

Ahhh. How to finish that sentence? It might be my imagination, but her cheeks seem to be flushed a little pinker.

Tiffy: Seriously, it was my fault. You were just innocently showering.

Me: Not your fault. Everyone oversleeps.

Tiffy: Especially when they've drunk pretty much a whole bottle of gin.

We're on the train now, so conversation stops as we move down the aisle. She chooses us a table seat; in a split second, I decide it's less awkward to sit facing one another rather than side by side, but as I slide into the seat, realise my mistake. This way is very eye-contacty.

She slips off her jacket; underneath she's wearing a blouse covered in enormous green flowers. Her arms are bare, and the blouse drops to a low V across her chest. My inner teenager attempts to take control of my gaze and I just about catch myself in time.

Me: So – whole bottle of gin?

Tiffy: Oh yeah. Well, I was at this book launch, then Justin turned up, and – anyway, lots of gin was involved in the aftermath.

Frown.

Me: The ex? That's . . . weird?

Tiffy shakes her hair out and looks a little uneasy.

Tiffy: I thought that too at first, and wondered if he'd tracked me down or something, but if he wanted to see me he could have just come to my work – or, apparently, my flat, judging by that bunch of flowers. I'm clearly just paranoid.

Me: Did he say that? That you were paranoid?

Tiffy, after a pause: No, he never said that exactly.

Me, catching up: Wait. You didn't tell him where you live?

Tiffy: No. I'm not sure how he found me. Facebook or something, probably.

She rolls eyes like it's a minor irritation, but I'm still frowning. This doesn't sound right. Have nasty suspicion I know men like this from my mother's life. Men who tell you you're crazy for getting suspicious of their behaviour, who know where you live when you don't expect them to.

Me: Were you together long?

Tiffy: A couple of years. It was all very intense, though. Lots of breaking up and shouting and crying and things.

She looks slightly surprised at herself, opens her mouth as though to correct that, then thinks better of it.

Tiffy: Yeah. It was about two years in all.

Me: And your friends don't like him?

Tiffy: They never did, actually. Not even at the start. Gerty said she got 'bad vibes' even when she only saw him from far away.

Am liking Gerty more and more.

Tiffy: Anyway, so he turned up and tried to whisk me off somewhere for a drink to explain everything away, as per.

Me: You said no?

Tiffy nods.

Tiffy: I said he has to wait a while to ask me out for a drink. A couple of months, at least.

Tiffy looks out of the window, eyes flicking as she watches London slide away around us.

Tiffy, quietly: I just didn't feel like I could say no. Justin's like that. He makes you want what he wants. He's very . . . I don't know. He owns a room straight away, you know? He's forceful.

Try to ignore warning sirens in my head. I'm not liking this situation at all. Hadn't got this sense of things from the notes – but maybe Tiffy herself hadn't got this sense of things until recently. It can take people time to notice and process emotional abuse.

Tiffy: Anyway! Sorry. God. Weird.

She smiles.

Tiffy: This is a very deep conversation to have with someone you've only just met.

Me: We've not just met.

Tiffy: True. There was the memorable bathroom collision.

Another eyebrow quirk.

Me: I meant, it feels like we've known each other ages.

Tiffy smiles at that.

Tiffy: It does, doesn't it? I guess that's why it's so easy to talk.

Yes. It's true: it is easy to talk, which is even more surprising to me than to her, probably, because there are about three people in the world I find it easy to talk to.

37

Tiffy

I don't understand what compelled me to go on about Justin like that. I've not mentioned anything about the counselling or the flash-backs in my notes to Leon – those Post-it notes make me warm and fuzzy, I'm not ruining them with Justin crap – but suddenly now I'm face-to-face with him it feels natural to talk to him about the things occupying my thoughts. He just has one of those non-judgemental faces that make you want to, you know . . . share.

We slip into silence as the train speeds through open countryside. I get the sense that Leon likes silence; it doesn't feel as awkward as I would expect it to, more like this is his natural state. It's strange, because when he talks, he's really engaging, albeit in a quiet, intense sort of way.

He's looking out of the window, squinting against the sunlight, so I sneak a chance to look at him. He's a little scruffy, in a worn grey T-shirt with a cord necklace around his neck that has the look of something he hardly ever takes off. I wonder what its significance is. Leon doesn't strike me as the type to wear accessories for anything other than sentimental reasons.

He catches me looking and meets my gaze. My stomach flutters. Suddenly the silence feels different.

'How's Mr Prior?' I blurt.

Leon looks startled. 'Mr Prior?'

'Yeah. My life-saving knitter. The last time I spoke to him was at the hospice.' I give him a wry smile. 'When you were busy avoiding me.'

'Ah.' He rubs the back of his neck, looking down, then shoots me a little lopsided grin. It's so quick I almost miss it. 'Wasn't my finest moment.'

'Mmm.' I pull a mock stern face. 'Do I scare you, is that it?'

'A bit.'

'A bit! Why?'

He swallows, Adam's apple bobbing, and pushes his hair back from his face. I think he's nervous-fidgeting. It's absolutely adorable.

'You're very . . .' He waves a hand.

'Loud? Brash? Larger than life?'

He winces. '*No*,' he says. 'No, not that.'

I wait.

'Look,' he says, 'have you ever looked forward to reading a book so much you can't actually start it?'

'Oh, totally. All the time – if I had a grain of self-restraint I never would've been able to read the last Harry Potter book. The anticipation was *painful*. You know, like, what if it doesn't live up to the last ones? What if it's not what I hope it'll be?'

'Right, well.' He waves a hand at me. 'I think it might have been . . . like that.'

'But with me?'

'Yeah. With you.'

I look down at my hands in my lap, trying very hard not to smile.

'As for Mr Prior . . .' Leon's talking out of the window now. 'I'm sorry. Can't really talk about a patient.'

'Oh, of course. Well, I hope we find his Johnny White. Mr Prior is *lovely*. He deserves a happy ending.'

As we rumble on, slipping in and out of comfortable conversation, I sneak more discreet little looks at Leon across the table. At one point our eyes meet in the window's glass, and we both look away fast, like we've seen something we shouldn't have.

I'm just about feeling that all awkwardness has departed when we arrive at Brighton, but then he gets up to grab his rucksack from the overhead space and he's suddenly standing, with his T-shirt riding up to show the dark band of his Calvin Klein boxers above his jeans, and I'm back to not knowing what to do with myself. I attempt to find the table very interesting.

When we reach Brighton there's a weak September sun shining; it's not quite autumn yet. From outside the station I can see streets of white town houses stretching out ahead of us, dotted with the sorts of pubs and cafés that everyone in London would overpay to have on their street corner.

Leon has arranged to meet Mr White on the pier. When we reach the seafront I let out an involuntary squeal of excitement. The pier stretches out into the grey-blue sea like this is a painting of one of those old seaside resorts where Victorians used to hang out in ridiculous knee-length swimwear. It's perfect. I reach into my bag and get out my big, floppy, 1950s sunhat, yanking it on to my head.

Leon looks at me with amusement.

'What a hat,' he says.

'What a day,' I counter, spreading my arms out wide. 'No other headwear would do it justice.'

He grins. 'To the pier?'

My hat bobs as I nod. 'To the pier!'

38

Leon

We spot Johnny White without any difficulty. Very old man sitting on end of pier. Literally, right on the end, sitting on the railings with feet dangling over – I'm surprised nobody has had him moved. It looks pretty dangerous.

Tiffy, on the other hand, is not worried. She bounces, sunhat flapping.

Tiffy: Look! A Johnny White of my very own! I bet he's the real deal. I can just tell.

Me: Impossible. You can't win on first go.

But have to admit, Brighton-dweller is a better bet than weed-smoking Midlander was.

Tiffy is over there before I've had time to collect my thoughts or consider the safest means of approaching; she climbs on to the railings to join him.

Tiffy, to JW the Sixth: Hello, are you Mr White?

The old man turns. He's beaming.

JW the Sixth: I am indeed. Are you Leon?

Me: I'm Leon. Pleased to meet you, sir.

JW the Sixth's beam widens.

JW the Sixth: The pleasure's all mine! Will you join me? It's my favourite spot.

Me: Is it . . . safe?

Tiffy has already swung her feet over.

Me: Don't people worry? About you jumping, or falling in?

JW the Sixth: Oh, everyone here knows me.

He gives a cheerful wave in the direction of the man running the candyfloss stall, who equally cheerfully flips him the bird. JW the Sixth chuckles.

JW the Sixth: So what's this family project, then? Are you my long-lost grandson, young man?

Me: Unlikely. Though not impossible.

Tiffy gives me a curious look. Doesn't feel like the time to fill her in on the many gaps in my family history. I shift, uncomfortably warm; the heat is stronger here with the sun on the water, and I can feel sweat prickling on my hairline.

Tiffy: We're here for a friend. A . . . a Mr Prior?

A seagull caws behind us, and Johnny White the Sixth gives a little start.

JW the Sixth: You're going to need to give me more than that, I'm afraid.

Me: Robert Prior. Think he served in the same regiment as you during the—

JW the Sixth's smile drops. He holds up a hand to stop me.

JW the Sixth: If you don't mind, I would prefer you stopped there. That's not . . . my favourite topic of conversation.

Tiffy, smoothly: Hey Mr White, how about we go somewhere to cool off? I've not got the complexion for this sort of sunshine.

She holds out her arms to show him. His smile returns slowly.

JW the Sixth: An English rose! And what a beautiful one.

He turns to me.

JW the Sixth: You're a lucky man, finding a woman like that. They don't make 'em that way any more.

Me: Oh, she's not—

Tiffy: I'm not—

Me: We're actually just . . .

Tiffy: Flatmates.

JW the Sixth: Oh!

Looks between the two of us. Does not seem convinced.

JW the Sixth: Anyhow. The best way to cool off around here is to go for a dip.

He gestures towards the beach.

Me: I didn't bring trunks.

But, at the same time, Tiffy is saying . . .

Tiffy: I will if you will, Mr White!

I stare at her. Tiffy is full of surprises. It's rather disorientating. Not sure I like this idea.

JW the Sixth, on the other hand, seems delighted at Tiffy's proposal. She is already helping him back over the railings. I rush to help her, what with this being a very elderly man, very near a sudden drop.

Walking down pier past rides and packed arcades gives me plenty of time to bottle it.

Me: One of us had better look after our stuff.

JW the Sixth: Don't you worry about that. We'll leave them with Radley.

Radley turns out to be man with multi-coloured turban running old-school Punch and Judy stand. Tiffy shoots me a delighted look as we introduce ourselves and dump our bags. *Isn't this brilliant?* she mouths at me. Can't help smiling. This Johnny White is fast becoming my favourite, I have to admit.

I follow Tiffy and Johnny as they weave their way between sunbathers and deckchairs on their way to the shoreline. Stop for a moment to kick off my shoes, the pebbles cool beneath my feet. Sun blazes low across the water and wet shingle shines silver. Tiffy's hair burns red. Johnny White is wrestling off his shirt as he goes.

And now . . . Ahhh. Tiffy is too.

39

Tiffy

I haven't felt like this in way too long. In fact, if you'd asked me a few months ago, I'd have told you I could only feel this way with Justin. This rush of doing something ridiculously spontaneous – the total *alive*ness of whirling yourself off-plan and shutting up all the bits of your brain that tell you why this isn't a sensible idea . . . God, I've missed this. Laughing, tripping, my hair in my face, I wriggle out of my jeans and duck as Mr White chucks his shorts in the direction of our impromptu clothing pile.

Leon is behind us; I glance back and he's grinning too, so that's good enough for me. Mr White is down to his briefs.

'Ready?' I yell at him. It's breezy out here; my hair whips my cheeks and the wind tickles the bare skin of my stomach.

Mr White doesn't need telling twice. He's wading into the sea already – he can move *very* quickly for a man who must be at least ninety. I look back at Leon, who is still dressed, and looking at me in an unreadably muddled sort of way.

'Come on!' I shout at him, running backwards into the water. I feel giddy, almost drunk.

'This is ridiculous!' he calls.

I hold my arms out wide. 'What's stopping you?'

It might be my imagination, and he's pretty far away to tell, but his eyes don't seem to be spending all their time on my face. I supress a smile.

'Come on!' Johnny White shouts from the sea, where he's already doing breaststroke. 'It's lovely!'

'I don't have swimming trunks!' Leon says, hovering in the shallows.

'What's the difference?' I yell, gesturing to my underwear, which – plain black, no lace this time – is pretty indistinguishable from the bikinis other people out here are wearing. I'm in up to my hips now, and I bite my lip against the cold of the water.

'Maybe nothing if you're a woman, but it's a little different if—'

Presumably Leon finishes his sentence, but I don't hear the rest of it. Suddenly I'm underwater, and all I can think about is a searing pain in my ankle.

I shriek and swallow a gulp of seawater so salty it burns the back of my throat; my hands flail, and for a moment my good foot connects with the ground, but then my other foot tries to find purchase too, and the pain sends me falling again. I'm twisted, spinning; everything is flashes of water and sky. I must have twisted my ankle, some distant corner of my brain registers. *Don't panic*, it tries to tell me, but it's too late, I'm coughing up water and my eyes and throat are burning, I can't turn, I can't find my footing, my ankle roars with pain every time I move it as I try to swim—

Someone's trying to grab me. I can feel strong hands scrabbling to get a grip on my body; something knocks my bad ankle and I try to cry out, but it's as if my throat's closed up. It's Leon, and he's hauling me up out of the water, pulling me close; I reach for him and he stumbles, almost tumbling in with me, but he kicks out until he's swimming, arms tight around my waist, and drags me closer to shore until he can find his footing.

I'm so dizzy everything is sliding back and forth. I can't breathe. I grip his sodden T-shirt, retching and coughing as he lays me down on the pebbles of the beach. I'm so tired – the kind of tired you get when you've been up all night because you're sick, where your eyes just can't bear to stay open.

'Tiffy,' Leon is saying.

I can't stop coughing. There's so much water lodged in my throat – I vomit great spurts of it on to the wet shingle, my vision still spinning, my head so heavy I can hardly keep it lifted. Distant, almost forgotten, my ankle throbs.

I'm gasping. There can't possibly be any more water inside me. Leon has smoothed my hair away from my face and is pressing his fingers gently into the skin of my neck as though checking for something, and now he's wrapping me in my jacket, rubbing my arms with the fabric; it hurts my skin and I try to roll away from him, but he holds me tightly.

'You're OK,' he says. Above me, his face slides back and forth. 'Think you've sprained your ankle, Tiffy, and you swallowed a lot of water, but you're going to be OK. Try to breathe more slowly if you can.'

I do my best. Behind him appears the worried face of Johnny White the Sixth. He is struggling back into his jumper, trousers already back on.

'Is there somewhere warm nearby where we can take her?' Leon asks him.

'The Bunny Hop Inn, just up there,' Mr White says. I vomit again and rest my forehead on the pebbles. 'I know the manager. She'll give us a room, no problem.'

'Grand.' Leon sounds perfectly calm. 'I'm going to lift you, Tiffy. Is that OK?'

Slowly, my head pounding, I nod. Leon picks me up and carries me in both arms. My breathing slowing, I let my head fall against his chest. The beach passes in a blur around me; faces are turned our way, shocked pink and brown splodges against the multi-coloured backdrop of towels and sunshades. I close my eyes – keeping them open makes me feel sicker.

Leon swears under his breath. 'Where are the steps?'

'This way,' Johnny White says, somewhere off to my left.

I hear the screech of brakes and the rush of traffic as we cross the road. Leon is breathing hard, his chest rising and falling against my cheek. In contrast, my breathing is getting easier – that tightness in my throat and the weird heaviness in my lungs has lifted a little.

'Babs! Babs!' Johnny White the Sixth is shouting. We're inside, and the sudden warmth makes me realise how much I'm shivering.

'Thank you,' Leon says. There's commotion all around me. For a moment I'm embarrassed, and try to shift out of Leon's arms to walk, but then my head lurches and I cling back on to his T-shirt again as he stumbles. 'Easy there,' he says.

I cry out. He's knocked my ankle into the bannister. He swears, pulling me closer so my head lolls back against his chest.

'Sorry, sorry,' he says, backing up the stairs. I can see pale pink walls covered with paintings in ostentatious frames, all gilt and swirly bits, then a door, then Leon's laying me down on a gloriously soft bed. Unfamiliar faces shift in and out of view. There's someone dressed in a lifeguard's kit; I blearily wonder if she's been here this whole time.

Leon is pulling the pillows up behind me, supporting my weight with one forearm.

'Can you sit up?' he asks quietly.

'I . . .' I try to talk, and start coughing, rolling on to my side.

'Careful.' He shifts my sodden hair back behind my shoulders. 'Are there any extra blankets in here?'

Someone is spreading thick, scratchy blankets over me. Leon is still tugging me up, trying to get me into a sitting position.

'I'll feel better if you're upright,' he says. His face is close to mine; I can see the start of stubble on his cheeks. He looks me right in the eyes. His are a soft dark brown that makes me think of Lindt chocolate. 'Can you do that for me?'

I shift myself higher against the pillows and grab ineffectually at the blankets with freezing fingers.

'How about a tea to warm you up?' he says, already looking around for someone to fetch one. One of the strangers slips out of the door. There's no sign of Johnny White any more – I hope he's gone to get himself some warm clothes – but there are still about a million people here. I cough again and turn my face away from all the staring faces.

'Let's give her some space. Can we have everyone out, please? Yes, don't worry,' Leon says, getting up to usher people from the room. 'Just let me do an examination with a bit of peace and quiet.'

A lot of people say things about what to do if we need anything. They file out one by one.

'I'm so sorry,' I say, as the door closes behind everyone. I cough; it's still hard to talk.

'None of that,' Leon says. 'How are you feeling now?'

'Cold and a bit achy.'

'I didn't see you go down. Do you remember if you banged your head on a rock or anything?'

He kicks off his shoes and pulls his feet up to sit cross-legged on the end of the bed. I notice, finally, that he's soaking wet and shivering too.

'Shit, you're drenched!'

'Just reassure me you've not got brain fluid seeping out from anywhere. Then I'll go get changed, OK?'

I smile a little. 'Sorry. No, I don't think I banged my head. Just twisted my ankle.'

'That's good. And can you tell me where we are?'

'Brighton.' I look around. 'Hey, and the only place I've ever been with nearly as much floral wallpaper as my mother's house.' The full sentence makes me cough, but it's worth it to see Leon's frown loosen a little, and his lopsided grin return.

'I'll take that as a correct answer. Can you tell me your full name?'

'Tiffany Rose Moore.'

'Didn't know the middle name. Rose – it suits you.'

'Shouldn't you be asking me questions you know the answers to?'

'I think I liked you better when you were all drowned and dopey.' Leon leans forward, one hand raised, and lifts his palm to my cheek. It's very intense and a little out of nowhere. I blink as he stares into my eyes, checking for something, I guess. 'Are you feeling at all sleepy?' he asks.

'Umm. Not really. I'm tired, but not in a sleepy way.'

He nods and then, a little belatedly, drops his hand from my cheek. 'I'm going to give my colleague a ring. She's a doctor, and she's just come off her rotation in Accident and Emergency, so she'll know the drill with an ankle exam. Is that OK? Pretty sure it's just a sprain from your history and what I've seen of how you're moving, but we'd better check.'

'Umm. Sure.'

It's strange being in the room for a conversation between Leon and one of the doctors he works with. He's no different – just as quiet and measured as when he speaks to me, with just the same lilting touch of an Irish accent – but he seems more . . . grown up.

'OK, it's a pretty simple exam,' Leon says, turning back to me once he's hung up. His forehead is furrowed in a frown, and he perches on the bed again, shifting the blankets so he can reach my ankle. 'Are you happy for me to give it a go? See if you need to go to A&E?'

I swallow, suddenly a little nervous. 'OK.'

He pauses, looking at me for a moment as if he's wondering whether I'll change my mind, and my cheeks get hot. Then he slowly presses his fingers to the skin of my ankle, gently feeling for different points until I wince with pain.

'Sorry,' he says, laying a cool hand on my leg. My skin goes goose-pimply almost instantaneously, and I pull the blanket up, a little embarrassed. Leon twists my foot very gently from side to side, eyes moving from my ankle to my face as he tries to gauge my reaction.

'How painful is that, out of ten?' he asks.

'I don't know, like, six?' I'm really thinking *eight eight eight* but I don't want to seem pathetic.

The corner of Leon's mouth lifts a little and I get the impression he knows exactly what I'm doing. As he continues examining me, I watch his hands move over my skin, and I wonder why I've never realised how peculiarly intimate medical stuff like this is, how much of it's about touch. I guess generally you're in a GP's surgery, not scantily clad and in a big double bed.

'Right.' Leon sets my foot down gently. 'I'd say you have officially sprained your ankle. You probably don't need to bother with five hours in A&E, to be honest. But we can go if you'd like?'

I shake my head. I feel like I'm in safe hands right here.

Someone knocks at the door, and then a middle-aged lady appears with two steaming mugs and a pile of clothes.

'Oh, perfect. Thank you.' Leon grabs the mugs from her and passes one to me. It's hot chocolate, and it smells amazing.

'I took the liberty of making yours an Irish one,' the woman says, giving me a wink. 'I'm Babs. How're you holding up?'

I take a deep, shuddering breath. 'A lot better now I'm here. Thank you so much.'

'Could you just stay with her while I change?' Leon asks Babs.

'I don't need . . .' I start coughing again.

'Watch her like a hawk,' Leon says warningly, and then he's slipped off to the bathroom.

40

Lean back on bathroom door, eyes closed. No concussion and a sprained ankle. Could have been much, much worse.

Got time to think about how cold I am now; shrug off my wet clothes and turn the shower on to hot. I tap out a quick thank you text to Socha. Phone is thankfully still functional, if a little damp – it was in my trouser pocket.

I get in the shower and make myself stand until I stop shivering. Remind myself that Babs is with her. Still, dress faster than I have ever dressed before, and don't even bother with belt to keep up ridiculously oversized trousers that Babs has found for me; will just wear them low, 90s-style.

When I head back into the bedroom, Tiffy has scraped her hair up into a bun. There's a touch of pink in her lips and cheeks again. She smiles up at me and I feel something shift in my chest. Hard to describe. Maybe like a lock clicking into place.

Me: How's that hot chocolate going down?

Tiffy pushes the other mug along the bedside table towards me.

Tiffy: Try yours and see.

Someone knocks at the door; I take the hot chocolate with me as I go to answer it. It's Johnny White the Sixth, looking very worried and also wearing comically large trousers.

JW the Sixth: How's our girl?

I have a feeling Tiffy becomes 'our girl' easily – she's the sort of person distant relatives and absent neighbours still like to claim some credit for.

Tiffy: I'm fine, Mr White! Don't you worry about me.

She lapses into an ill-timed fit of wet coughing. JW the Sixth fidgets in the doorway, looking miserable.

JW the Sixth: I'm so sorry. I feel responsible – it was my idea to go swimming. I should have checked you could both swim!

Tiffy, once recovered: I can swim, Mr White. I just lost my footing and got a little panicked, that's all. Blame the rock that knackered my ankle if you feel the need to blame something.

JW the Sixth looks a little less anxious now.

Babs: Well, you two are staying here tonight. No arguments. It's on the house.

Both Tiffy and I try to protest, but again Tiffy descends into spluttery half coughing, half retching, taking some of the sting out of our argument that she doesn't need to stay in bed.

Me: I should at least go – you don't need me now that—

Babs: Nonsense. It's no extra bother to me, is it? Besides, Tiffy needs looking after, and my medical knowledge doesn't extend much further than what a glass of whisky can do. John, do you want a lift home?

JW the Sixth tries to argue his way out of this favour also, but Babs is one of those formidably nice people who will not take no for an answer. It's a good five minutes before they agree and head out the door. When they're gone the click of the door makes me breathe out in relief. Hadn't realised how much I want quiet.

Tiffy: Are you all right?

Me: Fine. Just not a fan of . . .

Tiffy: Commotion?

I nod.

Tiffy smiles, pulling her blankets up closer.

Tiffy: You're a nurse – how can you avoid it?

Me: Work is different. But it still drains me. I need quiet afterwards.

Tiffy: You're an introvert.

Make a face. I'm not a fan of those Myers–Briggs type things that tell you your personality type, like horoscopes for businesspeople.

Me: Guess so.

Tiffy: I'm the opposite. I can't process anything without calling Gerty, or Mo, or Rachel.

Me: You want to call someone now?

Tiffy: Oh, shit, my phone was in my . . .

She spots the pile of her clothes, brought up from the shoreline by one of the hundred helpful strangers who followed us up the beach in procession. Tiffy claps hands in glee.

Tiffy: Would you pass my trousers?

I hand them over and watch as she rummages in the pockets for her phone.

Me: I'll go get us some lunch. How long do you need?

Tiffy pushes a few stray strands of hair back from her face, looking up at me, phone in hand. That clicked-in lock hums in my chest again.

Tiffy: Half an hour?

Me: Got it.

41

Tiffy

'Are you all right?' is Mo's first question. 'Have you been to A&E?'

Gerty, on the other hand, is focused on the real issue. 'Why didn't you tell us about the bathroom incident before? Are you in love with this man you're sharing a bed with, and hiding it because you're going to end up sleeping with him and I *explicitly* told you that the first rule of flatsharing is that you don't sleep with your flatmate?'

'Yes, I'm fine, and no, but Leon examined my ankle with some help from a friend of his who's a doctor. I just need lots of rest, apparently. And whisky, depending on whose medical opinion you're asking.'

'My question now,' Gerty says.

'No, I'm not in love with him,' I tell her, shifting my weight on the bed and wincing as my ankle throbs. 'And I'm not going to sleep with him. He's my friend.'

'Is he single?'

'Well, yes, actually. But—'

'Sorry, but just to check, Tiffy, has anyone examined you for—'

'Oh shut up, Mo,' Gerty interrupts. 'She's with a trained nurse. The woman is fine. Tiffy, are you sure you're not suffering from Stockholm Syndrome?'

'Pardon?'

'An A&E nurse is very different from a palliative care nurse—'

'Stockholm Syndrome?'

'Yes,' Gerty says. 'This man gave you a home when you were homeless. You are forced to sleep in his bed, and now you think you are in love with him.'

'I *don't* think I'm in love with him,' I remind her patiently. 'I told you, he's my friend.'

'But this was a date,' Gerty says.

'Tiffy, you do seem fine, but I just want to double-check – I'm on NHS Choices now – can you weight-bear on that ankle?'

'You with Google is not better than a nurse with a doctor on the phone,' Gerty tells Mo.

'It wasn't a date,' I say, even though I'm pretty sure it was. I wish Mo and Gerty hadn't got into this new habit of answering the phone together whenever they're both home. I called Mo because I wanted to talk to Mo. It's not that I don't like talking to Gerty, it's just that that is a very different experience, and not necessarily one you want after nearly drowning.

'You're going to need to explain this whole Johnny White thing to me again,' Gerty says.

I check the time on my phone screen. Only five minutes until Leon gets back with lunch.

'Listen, I have to go,' I say. 'But Mo, I'm fine. And Gerty, calm your protective instincts, please. He's not trying to sleep with me or entrap me or lock me away in his basement, OK? In fact, I have very little reason to think that he's at all interested in me.'

'But you are interested in him?' Gerty insists.

'Goodbye, Gerty!'

'Look after yourself, Tiffy,' Mo manages to say before Gerty hangs up (she's not big on goodbyes).

I dial Rachel's number without pause.

*

'So the key point here,' Rachel says, 'is that you are yet to have an interaction with Leon that doesn't involve you stripping down to your underwear.'

'Umm.' I'm grinning.

'You better keep your clothes on from now on. He'll think you're a – what's it called when you're one of those men who likes exposing themselves in the park?'

'Hey!' I protest. 'I do not—'

'I'm just saying what everybody's thinking, my friend. You're definitely not about to kick the bucket?'

'I feel fine really. Just achy and exhausted.'

'All right then. In that case, make the most of your free hotel stay, and call me if you find yourself accidentally whipping your bra off during dinner.'

There's a knock at the door.

'Shit. Got to go, bye!' I hiss into the phone. 'Come in,' I call. I managed to put on the jumper Babs left me while Leon was out, so I'm now decent from the waist up, at least.

Leon smiles at me and holds up a very full bag of what smells like fish and chips. I gasp in delight.

'Proper seaside food!'

'And . . .' He reaches into the bag and pulls out another one, handing it to me. I look inside: red velvet cupcakes with cream-cheese icing.

'Cake! The best kind of cake!'

'Doctor's orders.' He pauses. 'Well, Socha said, "get her some food". The fried fish and cupcakes were a bit of artistic licence.'

His hair is nearly dry; the salt has turned it even curlier, and it keeps springing from behind his ears. He catches me watching him try and smooth it back and grins ruefully.

'You're not meant to see me looking like this,' he says.

'Oh, and this is exactly how you're meant to see me,' I say, gesturing in the vague direction of my enormous baggy jumper, pale face and crazy matted hair. '"Drowned rat" is a favourite look of mine.'

'Mermaid-like?' Leon suggests.

'Funny you should mention that. I do actually have a fin under here,' I say, patting the blanket over my legs.

Leon smiles at that, spreading out the fish and chips on the bed between us. He kicks off his shoes and sits, careful to avoid my swollen ankle.

The food is amazing. It's just what I need, though I wouldn't have known it until I smelled it. Leon got pretty much every add-on to fish and chips you can imagine – mushy peas, onion rings, curry sauce, pickled onions, even one of those plastic-looking sausages they always have behind the glass – and we eat our way through it all. When it comes to the cupcake, finishing the last mouthfuls requires serious mental effort.

'Nearly dying is exhausting,' I declare, suddenly overcome by sleepiness.

'Nap,' Leon tells me.

'You're not worried about me falling asleep and never waking up again?' I ask, eyelids already drooping. Being warm and full is amazing. I'll never take being warm and full for granted ever again.

'I'll just wake you every five minutes to check you're not suffering from brain trauma,' he says.

My eyes fly open. 'Every five minutes?'

He chuckles, already gathering up his stuff and heading for the door. 'See you in a few hours.'

'Oh. Nurses shouldn't make jokes,' I call after him, but I don't think he hears me. Maybe I only think of saying it. I'm slipping off to sleep even as I hear the door close behind him.

I wake with a jolt that sends a shock of pain through my ankle. Crying out, I look around me. Floral wallpaper. Am I at home? Who's that man in the chair by the door, reading . . .

'*Twilight?*'

Leon blinks at me, putting the book down in his lap. 'You went from unconscious to judgemental very quickly there.'

'I did think this was a weird dream for a second,' I say. 'But my dream version of you would have much better book taste.'

'It's all Babs had to offer. How're you feeling?'

I give the question some thought. My ankle is throbbing and my throat feels horribly sore and salty, but the ache in my head has disappeared. I can feel that my stomach muscles are going to be painful from all the coughing, though.

'Much better, actually.'

He smiles at that. He is *very* cute when he smiles. When he's serious his face is a little severe – fine-boned brow, cheekbones, jaw – but when he's smiling, it's all soft lips and dark eyes and white teeth.

I check the time on my phone, more to break eye contact than anything – I'm suddenly very aware that I'm lying in bed, hair mussed and bare legs only half hidden under the blankets.

'Half *six*?'

'You were sleepy.'

'What have you been doing this whole time?' I ask him. He shows me his bookmark – he's nearly read the whole of *Twilight*.

'This Bella Swan is a very popular lady, for one who declares herself to be so unattractive,' he tells me. 'Seems every single man in the book who isn't her father is in love with her.'

I nod solemnly. 'It's *very* hard being Bella.'

'Sparkly boyfriends can't be easy,' Leon agrees. 'You want to try walking on that ankle of yours?'

'Can't I just stay in bed for ever?'

'Dinner and more whisky if you can get downstairs.'

I shoot him a look. He looks back, perfectly placid, and I realise what an excellent nurse he must be.

'Fine. But you need to look away first, so I can put my trousers on.'

He doesn't say anything about the fact that he's already seen way too much for turning around to be necessary; he just swivels in the armchair and reopens *Twilight*.

42

Leon

Definitely don't get drunk. Am telling myself this on repeat, but still can't stop sipping my drink. It's a whisky on the rocks. Horrible. Or it would be if Babs hadn't said it was on the house, which instantly made it much more appetising.

We're at a rickety wooden table with a sea view and a teapot with a big fat candle stuck in it. Tiffy is delighted with teapot candle holder. Cue animated conversation with waiting staff about interior design (or 'interiors', as they call it).

Tiffy has her foot up and resting on a cushion, as per Socha's orders. The other foot is now up too – she's basically horizontal at the table, hair thrown back and blazing against the sunset over the sea. She's like a Renaissance painting. Whisky has painted the colour back in her cheeks and brought a slight flush to the skin of her chest, which I can't stop looking at whenever her attention is elsewhere.

Have barely thought about anything but her all day, even before all the drowning started. Mr Prior's search for Johnny White has shifted into the background – last week that project was what Kay would call my 'fixation'. Now it feels like something I want because I've shared it with Tiffy.

She's telling me about her parents. Every so often she tips her head back, throws her hair further over the back of her chair, half closes her eyes.

Tiffy: Aromatherapy is the only one that's stuck. Mum did candle-making for a while, but there's no money in that, and after a while she just sort of snapped and declared that she was buying the ones from Poundland again and nobody was allowed to tell her they told her so. Then she went through a really weird phase where she got into seances.

That snaps me out of staring at her.

Me: Seances?

Tiffy: Yeah, you know, when you sit around a table and try to talk to dead people?

Waiter appears at Tiffy's foot's chair. Looks at it, mildly puzzled, but doesn't comment. You get the impression they're used to all sorts here, including bedraggled people with their feet up as they eat.

Waiter: Would you like a pudding?

Tiffy: Oh, no, I'm stuffed, thanks.

Waiter: Babs says it's on the house.

Tiffy, without pause: Sticky toffee pudding, please.

Me: Same here.

Tiffy: All this free stuff. It's like a dream come true. I should drown more often.

Me: Please don't.

She lifts her head to look at me properly, her eyes a little sleepy, and holds my gaze for a few seconds longer than is strictly necessary.

Clear throat. Swallow. Flounder for subject.

Me: Your mum did seances?

Tiffy: Oh, yeah. So for a couple of years while I was at secondary school I'd come home to find all the curtains drawn and a bunch of people saying, 'Please make yourself known', and 'Knock once for yes, twice for no'. I reckon at least sixty per cent of the visitations were actually just me getting home and chucking my bag in the cupboard under the stairs.

Me: So what was after seances?

Tiffy thinks about it. Sticky toffee pudding arrives; it's enormous and drenched in toffee sauce. Tiffy makes an excited noise which makes my stomach clench. Ridiculous. Can't be getting turned on by a woman moaning about pudding. Must pull self together. Sip more whisky.

Tiffy, mouth full of pudding: She made curtains for a bit. But the upfront costs were massive, so that turned into making doilies. And then it was aromatherapy.

Me: Is that why we have so many scented candles?

Tiffy smiles.

Tiffy: Yeah – the ones in the bathroom are all carefully chosen with scents that help you relax.

Me: They have the opposite effect on me. Have to move them every time I want to shower.

Tiffy gives me a cheeky look over her spoon.

Tiffy: Some people are beyond aromatherapeutic help. You know, my mum chose my perfume too. It 'reflects and enhances my personality', apparently.

I think of that first day when I walked into the flat and smelled her perfume – cut flowers and spice markets – and how odd it felt, having someone else's scent in my flat. It's never strange now. Would be odd to come home to anything else.

Me: What's that then?

Tiffy, promptly: Top note rose, then musk, then clove. Which means, according to my mum . . .

Crinkles her nose a little in thought.

Tiffy: 'Hope, fire, strength.'

Looks amused.

Tiffy: That's me, apparently.

Me: Sounds about right.

She rolls her eyes at that, having none of it.

Tiffy: 'Skint, mouthy, stubborn' would be better – probably what she meant anyway.

Me, definitely tipsy now: What would I be, then?

Tiffy tilts her head. She looks right at me again, with an intensity that makes me half want to look away, half want to lean across the table and kiss her over the candle teapot.

Tiffy: Well there's hope in there, definitely. Your brother's relying on it.

That catches me by surprise. There are so few people who really know about Richie; even fewer who'll bring him up unprompted. She's watching me, testing for my reaction, like she'll pull away if it hurts. I smile. Feels good to talk about him like this. Like it's normal.

Me: So I get rose smell in my aftershave?

Tiffy makes a face.

Tiffy: There's probably a whole different set of smells if you're a man. I am only versed in the art of perfumery for women, I'm afraid.

I want to push her for the other words – want to hear what she thinks of me – but it's conceited to ask. So we sit in silence instead, candle flame darting back and forth between us in its teapot, and I sip more whisky.

43

Tiffy

I'm not drunk, but I'm not exactly sober, either. People always say swimming in the sea makes you hungry – well, nearly drowning in it makes you a lightweight.

Plus, whisky on the rocks is really very strong.

I can't stop giggling. Leon is definitely tipsy too; he's loosened up at the shoulders, and that lopsided smile is almost a permanent fixture now. Plus he's stopped trying to smooth his hair down, so every so often a new curl breaks free and bobs up to stick out sideways.

He's telling me about when he was a kid, living in Cork, and the elaborate man-traps he and Richie would come up with to piss off their mum's boyfriend (which is why I'm giggling).

'So, hang on, you'd string wire across the hall? Didn't everyone else trip up too?'

Leon shakes his head. 'We'd sneak out and set up after Mam had put us to bed. Whizz always stayed late at the pub. It was a real education in swearwords, hearing him trip over.'

I laugh. 'His name was *Whizz*?'

'Mmhmm. Though, I would guess, not by birth.' His expression sobers. 'He was one of the worst for Mam, actually. Awful to her, always telling her how stupid she was. And yet she always stuck with him. Always let him back in every time she kicked him out. She was doing this adult learning course when they got together, but he soon had her dropping out.'

I scowl. The man-trap story suddenly isn't so funny any more. 'Seriously? What an absolute fucking prick!'

Leon looks a little startled.

'Did I say the wrong thing?' I ask.

'No.' He smiles. 'No, just surprising. Again. You'd give Whizz a run for his money in a swearing contest.'

I incline my head. 'Why, thank you,' I say. 'What about your and Richie's dad? Was he not in the picture?'

Leon is almost as horizontal as I am now – he's sharing my foot chair, his feet crossed at the ankles – and he's dangling his whisky glass between his fingers, spinning it back and forth in the candle-light. There's hardly anyone else left here; the waiting staff are discreetly clearing tables over on the other side of the room.

'He left when Richie was born, moved to the US. I was two. I don't remember him, or . . . just the odd shape and sort of . . .' He waves a hand. 'The odd feeling. Mam almost never talks about him – all I know is he was a plumber from Dublin.'

I widen my eyes. I can't imagine not knowing any more than that about my father, but Leon says it like it's nothing. He clocks my expression and shrugs.

'It's just never been a thing for me. Finding out more about him. It bothered Richie in his teens, but don't know where he got with it – we don't talk about it.'

It feels like there's more to be said there, but I don't want to push him and ruin the evening. I reach across and lay my hand on his wrist for a moment; he shoots me another surprised, curious look. The waiter drifts closer, perhaps sensing that our aimless conversation is unlikely to move anywhere else if he doesn't do something to nudge things along. He starts clearing the last bits and pieces from our table; I belatedly take my hand from Leon's wrist.

'We should go to bed, shouldn't we?' I say.

'Probably,' Leon says. 'Is Babs still about?' he asks the waiter.

He shakes his head. 'She went home.'

'Ah. Did she say which room was mine? She said Tiffy and I could stay over.'

The waiter looks at me, then Leon, then me again.

'Err,' he says. 'I think . . . she assumed . . . you were . . .'

It takes Leon a while to clock the issue. When he realises, he groans and facepalms.

'It's all right,' I say, getting the giggles again, 'we're used to sharing a bed.'

'Right,' says the waiter, looking between us again, more puzzled than ever. 'Well. That's good then?'

'Not at the *same time*,' Leon tells him. 'We share a bed at *different times*.'

'Right,' the waiter repeats. 'Well, err, shall I . . .? Do you need me to do something?'

Leon waves a hand good-naturedly. 'No, you go home,' he says. 'I'll just sleep on the floor.'

'It's a big bed,' I tell him. 'It's fine – we can just share.'

I let out a yelp – I'd been way too ambitious with trying to put weight on my sprained ankle as I get up from the table. Leon is at my side in an instant. He has very fast reactions for a man who has consumed quite a lot of whisky.

'I'm OK,' I tell him, but I let him put his arm around me to help support me as I hop-walk. After a certain amount of that, when we get to the stairs, he says, 'Feck it,' and picks me up again to carry me.

I shriek in surprise and then burst out laughing. I don't tell him to put me down – I don't want him to. Again I see the polished bannister and quirky pictures in their curly gilt frames sliding by as he jogs me up the stairs; again he opens the door to my room – our room – with his elbow and carries me through the doorway, kicking the door shut again behind him.

He lays me on the bed. The room is almost dark, the light from the streetlamp outside the window casting soft yellow triangles across the duvet and running gold through Leon's hair. His big, brown eyes stare down at me, his face only inches from mine as he gently takes his arm from underneath me to settle my head on the pillows.

He doesn't move. We stare at one another, our gazes locked, just a breath or two between us. The moment hangs taut, charged with possibility. A little flicker of panic sparks somewhere in the back of my mind – what if I can't do this without freaking out? – but I'm aching for him to kiss me, and the panic flickers out again, blissfully forgotten. I can feel Leon's breath on my lips, see his eyelashes in the half-light.

Then he closes his eyes and pulls back, turning his head aside with a quick sigh as if he was holding his breath.

Oof. I pull back too, suddenly uncertain, and that taut silence between us breaks. Did I . . . misread that whole gazes-locked, staring-at-each-other, lips-almost-touching thing?

My skin's hot, my pulse fluttering. He glances back at me; there's still heat in his eyes and a little frown between his eyebrows. I'm *sure* he was thinking about kissing me. Maybe I did something wrong – I'm a little out of practice with all this, after all. Or maybe the Justin curse has stretched to ruining kisses before they even begin.

Leon lies back on the bed; he's looking miserably awkward, and as he fidgets with his shirt I wonder if I should take the lead and kiss him, just press myself up beside him and turn his face towards mine. But what if I've misunderstood the situation and this is one of those times when I should just let things drop?

I lie down carefully beside him. 'We should probably go to sleep?' I say.

'Yeah.' His voice is low and quiet.

I clear my throat. Well, I guess that's that then.

He shifts a little. His arm brushes mine; my skin turns goosebumpy. I hear him breathe in as we touch, just a quiet huff of startlement, and then he's up, heading for the bathroom, and I'm left here with my goosebumps and my heart fluttering, staring at the ceiling.

44

Leon

Her breathing slows. Risk a sideways glance at her; can just make out the soft fluttering of her eyelids as she dreams. She's asleep, then. I breathe out slowly, trying to relax.

Really, really hope I have not messed this up.

It was very out of character for me, picking her up like that, lying her down on the bed. It just seemed like . . . I don't know. Tiffy is so impulsive it's contagious. But then, of course, am still me, so impulsiveness ran out at potentially crucial moment, to be replaced by familiar, panicked indecision. She's drunk and injured – you don't kiss drunk injured women. Do you? Maybe you do. Maybe she wanted that?

Richie gets the reputation for being the romantic, but it's always been me. He used to call me a pussy when we were teenagers, him chasing anything that'd give him so much as a look, me pining after the girl I'd fancied since primary school and been too scared to talk to. I've always been the one who thinks before they fall – though both of us fall just as hard.

I swallow. Think of the feeling of Tiffy's arm pressed against mine, how the hairs on my forearm stood on end at the merest brush of her skin. Stare at the ceiling. Realise belatedly that curtains are still open, streetlight streaming in to light our room in ribbons.

As I lie there, thinking, watching the light move across the floor, it comes to me slowly that I haven't been in love with Kay for a very long time. Loved her, felt close to her, liked her being part of my life. That was safe and easy. But I had forgotten the blazing can't-think-of-anything-else madness of these early days of meeting someone. There wasn't even a spark of that left with Kay for the last . . . year, maybe, even?

I look across at Tiffy again, her eyelashes casting shadows on her cheeks, and think back to what she's told me about Justin. Notes made me feel he wasn't especially good to her – why did she have to pay back that money all of a sudden? But nothing as alarming as what she'd said on the train. But then, as much as they were significant to me, they were just notes. Easier to lie to yourself in writing and for nobody to spot it.

Head is too full of panic, regret and whisky buzz for me to sleep. Stare up at the ceiling. Listen to Tiffy's breath. Play out all the ways it could have gone: if we'd kissed and she'd stopped me, if we'd kissed and she hadn't . . .

Best not to pursue that one. Thoughts becoming inappropriate.

Tiffy turns over, dragging the duvet with her. Half of my body is now exposed to night-time air. Can't really begrudge her, though. Important that she gets warm after near-drowning.

She turns over again. More duvet. Now only my right arm has coverage. Absolutely cannot sleep like this.

I'll have to just pull it back. Try it gently at first, but it's like playing tug-of-war. The woman has the duvet in a vice-like grip. How can she be this strong when unconscious?

Going to have to opt for an assertive yank. Maybe she won't wake up. Maybe she'll just—

Tiffy: Oww!

She came with the duvet, rolling over, and I seem to have migrated towards the middle too, and now we're face to face in the darkness, tantalisingly close.

My breath quickens. Her cheeks are flushed, her eyes heavy with sleep.

I belatedly clock that she just said *oww*. The movement must have jerked her ankle.

Me: Sorry! Sorry!

Tiffy, confused: Did you try and pull the duvet off me?

Me: No! I was trying to get it back.

Tiffy blinks. I really want to kiss her. Could I kiss her now? She's probably sobered up? But then she winces at the pain in her ankle and I feel like the world's worst human being.

Tiffy: Get it back from where?

Me: Well, you sort of . . . stole it all.

Tiffy: Oh! Sorry. Next time, just wake me up and tell me. I'll go right back to sleep.

Me: Oh, OK. Sure. Sorry.

Tiffy shoots me a half-amused, half-asleep look as she rolls back over, pulling the duvet up to her chin. I turn my head into the pillow. Don't want her to see that I'm smiling like a love-struck teenager because she just said 'next time'.

45

Tiffy

I wake to the daylight, which is much less pleasant than people make it sound. We didn't close the curtains last night. I turn my face away from the window instinctively, rolling over and realising the right-hand side of the bed is empty.

At first it feels totally normal: I wake up every day in Leon's bed without him there, after all. My sleepy brain goes, *oh, of course – no, hang on, wait . . .*

There's a note on his pillow.

Gone out in search of breakfast. Back soon, bearing pastries x

I smile, and roll back the other way to check the time on my phone on the bedside table.

Shit. Twenty-seven missed calls, all from an unknown number.

What the—

I scramble out of bed, heart thumping, then yelp with pain as I knock my ankle. Fuck. I dial voicemail, a bad feeling blooming in the base of my stomach. It's like . . . yesterday was too good to be true. Something terrible has happened – I knew I shouldn't have—

'Tiffy, are you all right? I saw Rachel's status on Facebook. Did you nearly drown?'

It's Justin. I go very still as the message rolls on.

'Look, I know you're in a mood with me at the moment. But I need to know you're OK. Call me back.'

There are more like this. Twelve more, to be precise. I'd deleted his number after a particularly girl-power-inducing counselling session, so that'd be why the calls came from an unknown number. I think I knew who it was going to be, though. Nobody else has ever called me that many times before, but Justin has – usually after a fight, or a break-up.

'Tiffy. This is ridiculous. If I knew where you were I'd come out there. Call me, all right?'

I shiver. This feels . . . I feel awful. Like yesterday with Leon should never have happened. Imagine if Justin knew where I'd been, and what I'd been doing?

I shake myself. I can feel that that doesn't make sense even as I think it. I'm scaring myself again.

I tap out a text.

I'm fine, I lightly sprained my ankle. Please don't call me any more.

Within moments, he replies.

Oh, thank God! What are you like without me there to look after you, hey?
You made me so worried. I'll be good and stick to your rules, no contact until
October. Just know I'll be thinking of you xx

I stare at the message for a while. *What are you like*. As if I'm *such* a klutz. Yesterday Leon pulled me out of the sea, and yet this is the first time all weekend I've felt like the girl who needs rescuing.

Fuck this. I hit *block* and delete all the voicemails from my phone.

I hop to the bathroom. It's not the most dignified method of travel – the chintzy lamps on the walls are vibrating a little as I go – but something about the general stompiness is quite therapeutic. *Stomp, stomp, stomp. Stupid, bloody, Justin.* I slam the bathroom door with satisfying force.

Thank God Leon went out for breakfast, both because he avoided witnessing this mess of a morning and because he will hopefully return with something highly calorific to make me feel better.

Once I've showered and redressed in yesterday's clothes – which, because they're covered in grainy, shingly grit, also ticks exfoliating off my to-do list – I hop back to the bed and launch myself on to it with a thud, burying my face in the pillow. Ugh. Yesterday was so lovely, and now I feel all horrible and mucky, like the voicemails left a taint on me. Still, I blocked him, something I would never have been able to bring myself to do a few months ago. Maybe I should be glad of all those voicemails for pushing me to do it.

I sit up on my elbows and reach for the note Leon wrote me. It's on hotel stationery; *The Bunny Hop Inn* is traced in jaunty letters across the bottom of the paper. The handwriting is just the same as ever, though – Leon's neat, tiny, rounded letters. In a moment of embarrassing sentimentality, I fold the paper in half and reach to slip it into my handbag.

There's a quiet knock on the door.

'Come in,' I call.

He's dressed in a giant T-shirt with a picture of three sticks of rock on the front, and BRIGHTON ROCKS in big letters underneath. My mood immediately improves about tenfold. There's nothing like a man in a novelty T-shirt to brighten up your morning – especially when he's holding a very promising paper bag with *Patisserie Valerie* written on the side.

'One of Babs's finest?' I say, pointing at the T-shirt.

'My new personal stylist,' Leon says.

He passes me the bag of pastries and sits down on the end of the bed, smoothing his hair back. He's nervous again. Why do I find his nervous fidgeting so adorable?

'You made it to the shower OK?' he asks eventually, nodding towards my wet hair. 'With your foot, I mean?'

'I showered flamingo style.' I curl one knee up. He smiles. Getting one of those lopsided grins from him feels like winning at a game I wasn't aware I was playing. 'The door doesn't lock, though. I thought you might walk in on me, but it seems Karma was busy elsewhere this morning.'

He makes a strangled sort of *mmhmm* sound and busies himself eating his croissant. I suppress a smile. An unfortunate side effect of finding his nervous fidgeting adorable is that I seem unable to resist saying things I know will make him fidget.

'But anyway, you've basically seen me naked,' I go on. 'Twice. Already. So you wouldn't have been in for any huge surprises.'

He looks up at me this time. 'Basically,' he says emphatically, 'is not the same as actually. Some key differences, in fact.'

My stomach flips. Whatever that awkwardness was last night, I definitely wasn't imagining the sexual tension. The air is heavy with it.

'It should be me worrying about the lack of surprises,' he says. 'You've *actually* seen me naked.'

'I did wonder . . . when I walked in on you in the shower, did you . . .'

He disappears in the direction of the bathroom so fast I barely hear the excuse he makes as he goes. As he closes the door behind him and turns the shower on, I smile. I guess there's my answer. Rachel will be delighted.

46

Leon

Have never thought this hard about the notes before. Was *much* easier when I was just scribbling random thoughts to friend who I had not met. Now am carefully crafting messages to woman who has taken up residence in most of my waking thoughts.

It's terrible. Sit down with pen and Post-it note and suddenly forget all the words. Her messages are cheeky, flirty, noisily her. This was the first after the weekend in Brighton, fixed to the bedroom door with Blu-Tack:

So, hey, roomie. How's the transition back to nocturnal life gone today? I see that Fatima and family went through the bins again while we were away – little minxes.

I wanted to write and say thanks again for whisking me out of the sea. Just make sure you fall in a large body of water at some point so I can return the favour, you know, in the name of equality. Also because I feel like you'd really own the whole Mr Darcy just-out-of-the-lake look. xx

Mine are stilted and overthought. Write them when I get in from work, then rewrite them before I walk out the door, then regret them all night in the hospice. Until I get home to a reply and feel instantly better again. Thus the cycle repeats.

Eventually, on Wednesday, I muster the courage to leave this one on the kitchen counter:

Weekend plans? x

Was paralysed by self-doubt as soon as I'd left the building and got far enough away for going back to be inconceivable. In retrospect, was a very short note. Perhaps too short for meaning to be clear? Perhaps insultingly short? Why is this so difficult?

Now, though, I'm feeling better.

Well I'll be home alone this weekend. Do you fancy coming over and cooking me your mushroom stroganoff? I've only ever had it reheated, and I bet it's even better fresh out the oven. xx

I reach for a Post-it note and scribble my reply.

Tiffin for dessert? x

Richie: You're nervous, aren't you?

Me: No! No, no.

Richie snorts. He's in good mood – he's generally in a good mood now. He calls Gerty at least every other day to catch up on appeal case progress. So much to talk about, calls every other day are apparently essential. Evidence re-examined. Witnesses coming forward. And, at last, CCTV obtained.

Me: OK. A bit nervous.

Richie: You'll be great, man. You know she's into you. What's the plan? Is tonight the night?

Me: Of course not. Far too soon.

Richie: Have you shaved your legs just in case?

Don't deign to respond to this. Richie chuckles.

Richie: I like her, man. You've got a good one.

Me: Not sure I've 'got' her yet.

Richie: What? You think – the ex?

Me: She doesn't love him any more. But it's complicated. I'm a bit worried about her.

Richie: Was he a prick?

Me: Mm.

Richie: He hurt her?

Gut twists at the thought.

Me: To some degree, I think. She doesn't really talk about it with me but . . . got a bad feeling about him.

Richie: Shit, man. Are we dealing with some kind of post-trauma situation here?

Me: You think so?

Richie: You're speaking to the king of the night sweats. I dunno, I haven't met her, but if she is still processing some shit she had to deal with, all you can do is be there and let her decide when she's ready for whatever.

The trauma of the trial and first month in prison hit Richie about six weeks into his sentence. Shaking hands, sudden terrors, intrusive flashbacks, jumping at the slightest noises. The last part always annoyed him the most – he seemed to think that particular brand of PTSD should be reserved for people whose trauma had actually involved loud noises, like soldiers.

Richie: And don't try and make the decision for her. Don't assume she can't be feeling better yet. That's her call.

Me: You're a good man, Richard Twomey.

Richie: Hold that thought and tell it to the judges in three weeks' time, bro.

Arrive at the flat at five-ish; Tiffy's with Mo and Gerty for the day. Weird, being here at a weekend. It's her flat now.

Stop short of shaving legs, but do spend inordinately long time getting ready. Can't stop thinking about where we're each going to sleep tonight. Will I go back to Mam's, or sleep here? We've already shared a bed in Brighton . . .

I consider messaging to say I'll stay at Mam's tonight, to show good-will. But decide that's putting nail in coffin earlier than necessary, and is an example of making decisions for her, as advised against by Richie, so I leave it be.

Key in door. I try to spring up from the beanbag, but that would be impossible even for a person with thighs of steel, so Tiffy walks in to find me in a half squat, attempting to extricate myself.

Tiffy, laughing: It's like quicksand, isn't it?

She looks beautiful. Tight blue top and a long floaty grey skirt with bright pink shoes that she proceeds to balance on her good leg to remove.

I move to give her a hand but she waves me off, hiking herself up to sit on kitchen counter and make the job easier. Her ankle looks more mobile, though – good sign. Seems to be healing well.

She raises her eyebrows at me.

Tiffy: Checking out my ankles?

Me: Purely medical interest.

Tiffy grins at me, sliding down from the counter and limping over to examine the pot on the hob.

Tiffy: Smells amazing.

Me: Something told me you'd like mushroom stroganoff.

She smiles over her shoulder, and I want to move behind her, put my arms around her waist and kiss her neck. Resist the urge, on account of it being very presumptuous and inappropriate.

Tiffy: That was in your cubby hole downstairs, by the way.

She points to small white envelope on the kitchen counter, addressed to me. I open it. It's an invite, handwritten in careful, slightly wobbly joined-up letters.

Dear Leon,

I am having a birthday party on Sunday because I am going to be eight.
Please come!!! Bring your friend Tiffy who likes nitting. Sorry that this
is late Mum says your proper invitasion got lost at St Marks by one of
the nurses who is rubbish and then they said we couldn't have you're
address but they said they will send this for us so I hope they got it rite
anyway please come!!

Holly xoxoxoxoxox

Smile and show it to Tiffy.

Me: Maybe not what you had planned for tomorrow?

Tiffy, looking delighted: She remembers me!

Me: She was obsessed with you. We don't have to go, though.

Tiffy: Are you joking? We're totally going. Please. You only turn
eight once, Leon.

47

Tiffy

I really didn't think chocolate-tiffin eating could be so sexually charged. We're sitting on the sofa in front of our television (which is basically just a novelty ornament shelf) with wine glasses in our hands and our legs touching. I'm not far off sitting in his lap, really. That's definitely where I *want* to be sitting.

'Go on,' I say, nudging him with my knee. 'Tell me the truth.'

He looks shifty. I narrow my eyes at him, sliding nearer, my gaze flicking to his lips. He's doing the same – that eyes-lips-eyes thing that seems to tug you closer, and we hover in the moment as if we're at the top of a rope swing, waiting for gravity to kick in, feeling the tug but not quite going. No doubts this time: I *know* he's thinking about kissing me.

'Tell me,' I say.

He tilts his head, but at the last moment I pull back just a little, and he lets out a quiet huff, half amused, half frustrated at the teasing.

'Much shorter,' he says reluctantly, pulling back too and reaching for another square of tiffin. I watch him lick chocolate from his fingers. Amazing, really – I've always found it weird how in films people think licking things like that is sexy, but here Leon is, proving me wrong.

'Shorter? That's it? You told me that already.'

'And . . . dumpier.'

'Dumpier!' I crow. This was the stuff I was after. 'You thought I'd be dumpy?'

'I just – assumed!' Leon says, shifting in and pulling me closer again so I'm almost bundled up against his chest.

I lean into him, relishing the feeling. 'Short and dumpy. And what else?'

'I thought you would dress weirdly.'

'Well, I do,' I point out, gesturing to the laundry drying in the corner, which includes my bright red pantaloons and the rainbow knitted jumper Mo got me for my birthday last year (though even I would draw the line at wearing those two items simultaneously).

'You make it look good, though,' he says. 'Like you do it on purpose. It makes you look like you.'

I laugh. 'Well, thanks.'

'And you?' he asks, shifting his hold on me to take another sip of his wine.

'And me what?'

'What did you think I'd look like?'

'I cheated and looked you up on Facebook,' I admit.

Leon looks shocked, wine halfway to his mouth. 'I didn't even think of that!'

'Of course you didn't. I mean, I would want to know what someone looked like if they were moving in and sleeping in my bed, but you don't care about appearances much, do you?'

He pauses to think about it. 'I cared about yours once I'd seen it. But otherwise, why would it make a difference? The first rule of the flatshare was that we wouldn't meet.'

I laugh despite myself. 'We broke *that* one, then.'

'That one?'

'Don't worry.' I wave him off. I don't fancy explaining Gerty's 'first rule', or quite how much time I've spent thinking about breaking it.

'Ahhh,' Leon says suddenly, catching sight of the time on my Peter Pan clock on top of the fridge. Half midnight. 'It's late.' He looks at me worriedly. 'Lost track of time.'

I shrug. 'That's OK?'

'Can't get back to Mam's now – last train was at ten past twelve.' He looks pained. 'I'll just . . . sleep on the sofa? If that's all right?'

'On the sofa? Why?'

'So you can have the bed?'

'This sofa is tiny. You'd have to curl up in the foetal position.' My heart's thumping. 'You have your side, I have mine. We've stuck to the left and right rule all year so far. Why should we change it now?'

He watches me, his eyes flicking back and forth across my face as if he's trying to read me.

'It's just a bed,' I say, moving closer again. 'We've shared a bed before.'

'Not sure . . . this will be quite as straightforward,' Leon says, in a slightly strangled voice.

On impulse, I lean forwards and press my lips lightly to his cheek, then again, and again, until I've kissed a path from his cheekbone to the very edge of his lips.

I sit back and meet his eyes. My skin is already buzzing, but the look he gives me sends a jolt through me, and now it's as if eighty per cent of my body has suddenly become heartbeat. I swallow. We're as close as two humans can possibly be without kissing. There's no flicker of panic this time, just blissful, fiery wanting.

So, at last, I kiss him.

When I kissed him on the cheek I'd planned to make our first proper kiss soft and slow, the kind of kiss you feel in your toes, but when I actually get there it's clear there's been way too much waiting and sexy tiffin-eating for that. This is a proper kiss, the kind that promises very imminent undressing, the kind that generally happens while in the process of stumbling towards a bed. I'm not surprised, then, to find that when we surface for air, I'm straddling him, my hair hanging down on either side of us, my long skirt ruched to my thighs, his hands on my back pulling me as close as I can possibly be.

We don't pause for long. I twist to dump my wine glass unceremoniously on the coffee table and shift a little to ease the angle on my ankle, and then we're kissing again, hungry, and my body is responding with a heat I genuinely don't think I've felt before. One of his hands shifts to the back of my neck, grazing the side of my breast en route, and I pretty much yelp as the sensation hits. Everywhere and everything seems to be in overdrive.

I have no idea what will happen next. I actually can't even consider the question. I'm incredibly grateful for that – all thought of flashbacks and exes has evaporated altogether. Leon's body is hard and warm and all I can think about is getting all of these clothes out of the way so I can be as close to it as possible. This time when I move to unbutton his shirt, he drops his grip on my waist to help me, shrugging it off and chucking it over the back of the sofa, where it hangs like a flag from the lamp. I run my hands over Leon's chest, marvelling at the strangeness of being able to touch him like this. I break away from him for just long enough to wriggle out of my top.

He breathes in sharply, and as I lean back in to kiss him again, he stops me, hands on my upper arms, eyes on my body. I'm wearing a thin chemise under the top, its neckline following the line of my bra, dipping to a low V.

'God,' he says, his voice hoarse. 'Look at you.'

'Nothing you've not seen before,' I remind him, already ducking in impatiently to get another kiss. He holds me back again, still staring. I let out a little frustrated noise, but then he moves to press his lips against my collarbone, then lower, kissing across the top of my breasts, and I stop objecting.

It's becoming impossible to form thoughts for longer than about two seconds. They just evaporate. I can feel great sections of my brain rededicating themselves to thinking about sex. The part of my brain that deals with pain, for instance, has entirely forgotten about my ankle and is now much more interested in what exactly Leon's lips are doing as his kisses dip lower and lower to the edge of my bra. The section that usually busies itself wondering if I look fat in things seems to have died off altogether. I've resorted to moaning because my brain's speech centre is clearly out of action too.

Leon's hands dip under the waistline of my skirt, touching the silk of my underwear. I wore nice underwear, obviously. I may not have planned for this, but I hadn't *not* planned for it.

I pull away and yank off the chemise – it's only getting in the way now. I'm going to have to stop straddling him in order for either of us to remove any more clothes, but I really don't want to. My brain makes a real effort at some long-term thinking, but that's no use, obviously, so I abandon the problem and hope Leon has some sort of solution.

'Bed?' Leon says, his lips back up on my neck.

I nod, but when he shifts underneath me I mumble an objection, dipping my head to kiss him again. I can feel his smile against my lips.

'Can't get to bed without you moving,' he reminds me, trying to shift again.

I make another incoherent objection. He chuckles, lips still pressed against mine.

'Sofa?' he suggests instead.

Better. I knew Leon would have a solution. Reluctant, I slide off his lap so he can move. His hands tug at the fabric of my skirt, fingers searching for a zip or button.

'It's got a hidden zip,' I say, twisting to find the zip tucked in the seam along my hip.

'Devilish women clothes,' Leon declares, helping me pull the skirt off once it's undone. Like before, I move to press myself against him again, but he stops me so he can look at me properly. The look in his eyes makes my cheeks glow. I undo his belt and he breathes in sharply, his gaze back on my face as I unbutton his jeans.

'A little help?' I say, eyebrow raised, as I fumble around with the buttons.

'Leaving that part to you,' he says. 'Take as long as you need.'

I grin, and he tugs off his jeans, then pulls me to lie down beside him on the sofa. We're a mess of limbs and cushions and skin. We completely don't fit. There's no space. We're laughing now, but only in between kisses, and wherever his body touches mine it's like someone's reprogrammed my nerves to feel five times as much as usual.

'Whose idea was the sofa?' Leon asks. His head is level with my chest; he kisses his way along the bottom of my bra now, and I moan. I'm incredibly uncomfortable, but discomfort is a small price to pay, as far as I'm concerned.

It's only when he elbows me in the stomach in an effort to sit up enough to kiss me that I call time. 'Bed,' I say firmly.

'Sensible woman.'

It takes us another ten minutes or so actually to get moving. He gets up first, then, as I shift to stand, bends to pick me up again and carry me.

'I can walk fine,' I protest.

'It's our thing. Plus, it's faster.' He's right – he's laid me out on the bed in seconds, and then he's on top of me, his lips hot on mine, his hand on my breast. No laughing now. I can hardly breathe, I'm so turned on. It's absurd. I can't possibly wait any longer.

And then the doorbell rings.

48

Leon

We both freeze. I lift my head to look at her. Her cheeks are flushed red, her lips swollen from kissing, and her hair lies in a tangle of orange against the white pillows. Impossibly sexy.

Me: For you?

Tiffy: What? No!

Me: But nobody I know thinks I'm here at weekends!

Tiffy groans.

Tiffy: Don't ask me complicated questions. I can't . . . do thinking right now.

I press my lips against hers again, but the doorbell rings for a second time. Curse. Roll to side; try to calm down.

Tiffy rolls with me so she's on top of me.

Tiffy: They'll go away.

This suddenly seems like by far the best suggestion. Her body is incredible. Can't stop myself from touching – I know I'm being way too scattergun, hands all over her, but don't want to miss anything. I should have at least ten more hands, ideally.

Doorbell rings again. And again. Five-second intervals. Tiffy throws herself back to her side of the bed with a growl.

Tiffy: Who the fuck is it?

Me: We should answer.

She reaches out and runs a finger from my bellybutton to my boxers. Mind goes entirely blank. Want her. Want her. Want her. Want—

Doorbell doorbell doorbell doorbell.

Tiffy: Fuck! I'll go.

Me: No, I'll go. I can wear a towel and pretend I was in the shower.

Tiffy looks at me.

Tiffy: How the hell can you think of something like that right now? My brain has stopped functioning. You are clearly much more distracting than I am.

She's lying there, topless, just a scrap of silk underwear between now and naked. It's taking enormous inner strength and an insistent loud buzzing sound to hold me back.

Me: Trust me. You are very distracting.

Tiffy kisses me. Doorbell now buzzing non-stop – is not even pausing. Person has their finger held against buzzer.

Whoever they are, I hate them.

Pull myself away from Tiffy, swear again, and reach for towel on radiator as I stumble through from bedroom to hall. Need to pull self together. Will just answer door, punch person who has interrupted us, then head back to bed. A good, solid plan.

I press the button to let them up, then throw open the front door and wait. It occurs to me, belatedly, that as my hair is dry it will not actually look like I've just got out of shower.

The man who appears in the doorway is nobody I've met before. He's also not the sort of man I would back myself to punch. He's tall, built in the way that suggests he spends a lot of time in the gym. Brown hair, perfectly trimmed beard, expensive shirt. Angry eyes.

Suddenly have a bad feeling about this. Wish I was wearing more than towel.

Me: Can I help you?

He looks confused.

Angry-eyed man: Isn't this Tiffy's place?

Me: Yes. I'm her flatmate.

Angry-eyed man does not look at all happy at this information.

Angry-eyed man: Well, is she in?

Me: Sorry, I didn't catch your name?

Gives me long, angry stare.

Angry-eyed man: I'm Justin.

Ah.

Me: No, she's not in.

Justin: I thought she had this place at weekends.

Me: Did she tell you that?

Justin looks shifty for a moment. Covers well, though.

Justin: Yeah, she mentioned it when I saw her last. Your arrangement. The whole bed-sharing thing.

She definitely wouldn't have told Justin about that. Pretty clear she'd know he wouldn't like it. Extremely hostile body language suggests that he does indeed not like it.

Me: Room sharing. But yes. She normally has the place on weekends, but she's away.

Justin: Where?

Shrug. Look bored. Simultaneously stand that little bit taller, just so he clocks we're the same height. It's a bit caveman-ish of me, but feels good all the same.

Me: How should I know?

Justin, suddenly: Can I see the flat?

Me: What?

Justin: Can I see the place? Just have a look around.

He's already moving towards me like he's coming in. Suppose this is how he always gets his way: asking unreasonable things and then going ahead and taking them.

I don't move. Eventually he has to stop walking, because I am directly in his way.

Me: No. Sorry. You can't.

He senses my hostility now. He's riled. He was already angry when he got here; he's like dog on leash, snapping for a fight.

Justin: Why not?

Me: Because it's my flat.

Justin: And Tiffy's. She's my . . .

Me: Your what?

Justin doesn't finish the lie. He knows, perhaps, that I will at least know whether Tiffy is single or in relationship.

Justin: It's complicated. But we're very close. I can promise you she wouldn't mind me looking around the place, checking it's up to standard for her. I presume you have a sub-letting agreement, the two of you? All signed off by the property owner?

Do not want to get into this with this man. Also, do not have sub-letting agreement. Landlord hasn't spoken to me in years, so just haven't . . . brought Tiffy up.

Me: You can't come in.

Justin squares up to me. I'm wearing nothing but a towel around waist; we're eye to eye. Really don't think Tiffy would enjoy it coming to a fight.

Me: I've got a girl in there, man.

Justin jerks his head back. He wasn't expecting that.

Justin: You have?

Me: Yeah. So I'd appreciate it if you . . .

His eyes narrow.

Justin: Who is it?

Oh, for fuck's sake.

Me: What does it matter to you?

Justin: It's not Tiffy, then?

Me: Why would you think it was Tiffy? I just told you—

Justin: Yeah. She's away this weekend. Except I know she's not with her parents, and Tiffy doesn't leave London on her own for anything except a visit home. So—

He tries to push past me, but I'm ready for it. I put my weight into him, knocking him off balance.

Me: Get out of here. Now. I don't know what your problem is, but as soon as you entered my flat you broke the law, so if you don't want me to call the police – if the woman in my bedroom hasn't done it already – then get the fuck out of here.

I can see his nostrils flaring. He wants to fight; it's taking all his energy not to. Not a pleasant sort of man. Though I notice that I'm ready for a fight too. I'm almost hoping he'll punch me.

He doesn't, though. His eyes flick to bedroom door, and then take in the sight of my jeans spread out on the floor. My shirt, hanging off Tiffy's ridiculous monkey lamp. Thank God Tiffy's clothes aren't visible – he'd recognise them, I imagine. What an unpleasant thought.

Justin: I'll be back to see Tiffy.

He backs out.

Me: Maybe call ahead next time to check she's in. And wants to see you.

Slam the door behind him.

49

I mean, nobody would say it's nice, having your ex-boyfriend turn up as you're getting with the new guy. Nobody would wish for something like that to happen, except perhaps for weird sexual reasons.

But surely nobody else would be quite this upset.

I am shaking – not just my hands, but my legs too, all the way up past my knees. I try to dress as quietly as I can, paralysed with the thought of Justin coming in here and seeing me in just my knickers, but I only get halfway before the fear of being heard overrules that impulse, and I sink back on to the bed in just my underwear and a giant jumper with Santa on it (it was the closest thing in the wardrobe).

When the door to the flat slams, I jump as though someone's pulled a trigger. It's ridiculous. My face is wet with tears and I am really, truly scared.

Leon knocks gently on the bedroom door.

'It's just me,' he calls. 'Can I come in?'

I take a deep, wobbly breath and wipe the tears from my cheeks. 'Yeah, come in.'

He takes one look at me and does what I did – heads for the wardrobe and pulls out the nearest thing. Once he's dressed, he comes and sits on the far end of the bed. I'm grateful. Suddenly I don't want to be near anybody naked.

'Is he definitely gone?' I ask him.

'I waited until I heard the building door close too,' Leon tells me. 'He's gone.'

'He'll be back, though. And I cannot face the idea of ever seeing him again. I can't ... I hate him.' I take another deep, juddering breath, feeling tears leaking out again. 'Why was he so *angry*? Was he always like that, and I've just forgotten?'

I stretch out a hand towards Leon; I want to be held. He shifts across the bed and pulls me in against him, laying me down so he's behind me, my body tucked into his.

'He can feel he's losing his grip on you,' Leon says quietly. 'He's scared.'

'Well, I'm not going back this time.'

Leon kisses my shoulder. 'You want me to call Mo? Or Gerty?'

'Will you just stay with me?'

'Of course.'

'I just want to go to sleep.'

'Then sleep it is.' He reaches around for the Brixton blanket, pulling it over the two of us, and then leans to flick off the lamp. 'Wake me if you need me.'

I don't know how, but I sleep all the way through, only waking to the sound of the guy upstairs doing whatever it is he always does at 7 a.m. (it sounds like some kind of energetic aerobics involving lots of hopping; I'd be angry, but it is much better than my alarm for waking me up for work).

Leon is gone. I sit up, bleary-eyed from falling asleep after crying, and try to get a handle on reality again. Just as I'm working my way through yesterday – sadly finishing up with the good sofa bit, and remembering Justin's arrival – Leon pokes his head in.

'Tea?'

'Did you make it?'

'No, I got the house elf to do it.'

I smile at that.

'Don't worry. I told him to make yours especially strong,' he says. 'Can I come in?'

'Of course you can. It's your bedroom too.'

'Not when you're here.' He hands me a suitably strong cup of tea. This is the first cup of tea he's ever made me, but – just like I know how milky he likes his – he must've figured out how I drink mine. It's weird how easily you can get to know someone from the traces they leave behind.

'I'm so sorry about last night,' I begin.

Leon shakes his head. 'Please don't. It's not your fault, is it?'

'Well. I did date him. Voluntarily.'

My tone's light, but Leon frowns. 'Relationships like that stop being about "voluntarily" very quickly. There's lots of ways someone can make you stay with them, or think you want to.'

I tilt my head, looking at him as he sits on the edge of the bed, forearms on his knees, both hands around his mug of tea. He's talking to me half over his shoulder, and every time he meets my eyes I want to smile. He's redone his hair – it's the neatest I've ever seen it, smoothed behind his ears and flicking into curls at the base of his neck.

'You seem very well informed,' I say carefully.

He's not looking at me now. 'Mam,' he says by way of explanation. 'She spent a lot of her time with men who abused her.'

The word makes me flinch. Leon clocks it.

'Sorry,' he says.

'Justin never hit me or anything,' I say quickly, my cheeks flushing. Here's me, making a fuss about a boyfriend who bosses me about a bit, when Leon's mum has been through—

'That's not the sort of abuse I meant,' Leon says. 'I meant emotional.'

'Oh.' Was that what it was, with Justin?

Yes, I think immediately, before I have time to second guess myself. Of course it bloody was. Lucie and Mo and Gerty have all been saying as much without saying it for months, haven't they? I swallow a gulp of tea, hiding behind my mug.

'It was hard to watch,' Leon says, staring down at his tea. 'She's on the mend now. Lots of counselling. Good friends. Getting to the root of the problem.'

'Mmm. I'm trying that . . . counselling thing, too.'

He nods. 'That's good. That'll help.'

'It is already, I think. It was Mo's idea, and he's literally always right about things.'

I could do with one of Mo's audio hugs right now, actually. As I look around for my phone, Leon points to where it lies on the bedside table.

'I'll give you a minute. And don't worry about Holly's birthday. Bet it's probably the last thing you . . .'

He trails off at my outraged expression.

'You think I'm missing Holly's birthday because of last night?'

'Well, I just thought it must've taken it out of you, and . . .'

I'm shaking my head. 'Absolutely not. The last thing I want to do is let this . . . Justin stuff get in the way of the important things.'

He smiles, his eyes lingering on my face. 'Well, OK. Thanks.'

'We need to leave early enough to buy a present!' I call after him as he leaves.

'I gave her the gift of good health!' he calls back through the door.

'That won't cut it – it needs to be something from Claire's Accessories!'

50

Leon

Holly's mum's home is a poky, crumbling town house in Southwark. Paint peels everywhere and pictures lean on walls, unhung, but it feels friendly. Just a little tired.

Streams of children are darting in and out of the front door when we arrive. Feel slightly overwhelmed. I'm still processing last night, still buzzing with adrenaline from the altercation with Justin. We reported the incident to the police, but I want to do more. She should get a restraining order. Can't suggest it, though. Her choice. I'm helpless.

We step inside the house. There are many party hats and a few crying babies, possibly baited into tears by boisterous eight-year-olds.

Me: Can you see Holly?

Tiffy stands on one tiptoe (her good foot).

Tiffy: Is that her? In the Star Wars outfit?

Me: Star Trek. And no. Maybe over there by the kitchen?

Tiffy: Pretty sure that's a boy. Did you tell me this was fancy dress?

Me: You read the invite too!

Tiffy ignores this, picks up abandoned cowboy hat and plants it on my head.

I turn to the hall mirror to admire the effect. The hat perches on top of my hair precariously. Pull it off and put it on Tiffy instead.

Much better. A sort of sexy cowgirl thing. Very clichéd, of course, but sexy nonetheless.

Tiffy checks her reflection and yanks the hat down further.

Tiffy: Fine. You're a wizard then.

She pulls a moon-covered cape off the back of a chair and reaches up to drape it over my shoulders, fixing it with a bow at my throat. Just the feel of her fingers makes me think of last night. It's a highly inappropriate location for these sorts of thoughts, so I try to ward them off, but she is not helping. She trails her hands down my chest in a gesture familiar from time on sofa.

Grab her hand.

Me: Can't be doing that.

Tiffy quirks an eyebrow, mischievous.

Tiffy: Doing what?

At least if she's planning on torturing me in this fashion it must mean she's feeling a little better.

Eventually locate Holly sitting on stairs and realise why she was so hard to spot. She looks completely transformed. Bright eyes. Hair thicker and healthier, falling forward to be blown back impatiently as she talks. She's actually looking a little chubby.

Holly: LEON!

She skids downstairs then stops short at bottom. She's dressed as Elsa from *Frozen*, much like every girl hosting a birthday party in the Western hemisphere since 2013. She's a little old for it, but then, she missed out on most of her time being little, so.

Holly: Where's Tiffy?

Me: She's here too. She's just gone to the bathroom.

Holly looks placated. Links her arm through mine and drags me off to the living room to try and feed me small sausage rolls that have been fingered by many unclean children.

Holly: Are you dating Tiffy yet?

I stare down at her, plastic cup of tropical juice halfway to mouth.

Holly does her classic eye roll, thus convincing me that she is still the same person, not chubbier lookalike.

Holly: Come *on*. You two are Meant to Be!

I look around nervously, hoping Tiffy is not within hearing. But I'm smiling too, it seems. Think fleetingly of my reaction to similar comments made about me and Kay – generally was the sort of response that made Kay call me a commitment-phobe. Admittedly those comments rarely came from the mouth of a small, precocious child wearing a fake plait around her neck (guess it fell off her head a while ago).

Me: As it happens . . .

Holly: Yes! I knew it! Have you told her you love her?

Me: It's a bit soon for that.

Holly: Not if you've been in love with her for ages.

Pause.

Holly: Which you have. By the way.

Me, gently: I'm not sure about that, Holly. We've been friends.

Holly: Friends who love each other.

Me: Holly—

Holly: Well, have you told her you like her?

Me: She definitely knows.

Holly narrows eyes.

Holly: *Does* she, Leon?

I feel slightly discomposed. Yes? She does? The kissing is a clear clue, no?

Holly: You're terrible at telling people how you really feel about them. You hardly ever told me how you liked me better than all the other patients. But I know you did.

She stretches out her hands, like *case in point*. I try not to grin.

Me: Well, I'll make sure she knows.

Holly: It doesn't matter. I'll tell her anyway.

And she's off, darting through the crowd. Shit.

Me: Holly! Holly! Don't say any—

I eventually find them together in the kitchen. Burst in at the end of what is clearly an intervention on Holly's part. Tiffy is leaning down to hear her, smiling, hair shining red-gold under the over-bright kitchen lights.

Holly: I just want you to know he's nice, *and* you're nice.

She stands on tiptoe, and adds, in a stage whisper:

Holly: So that means there isn't a doormat.

Tiffy looks up at me, enquiring.

Press lips together as something warm and melting settles in my chest. I step in and pull Tiffy towards me, reaching over to ruffle Holly's hair. Weird, clairvoyant child.

51

Tiffy

Mo and Gerty come around in the afternoon, once Leon's headed off to his mum's place, and I fill them in on the night's dramas over a much-needed bottle of wine. Mo does his best empathetic nod; Gerty, on the other hand, just keeps swearing. She has some really inventively nasty names for Justin. I think she's been saving them up for some time.

'Do you want to stay at ours tonight?' Mo says. 'You can have my bed.'

'Thanks, but no, I'm fine,' I say. 'I don't want to run away. I know he doesn't want to hurt me or anything.'

Mo doesn't look too sure about that. 'If you're certain,' he says.

'Call us anytime and we'll order a taxi to collect you,' Gerty tells me, finishing off her wine. 'And give me a ring in the morning. You need to tell me about having sex with Leon.'

I stare at her. 'What!'

'I knew it! I could just tell,' she says, looking pleased with herself.

'Well, actually, we haven't,' I tell her, sticking my tongue out. 'So your radar is off – again.'

She narrows her eyes. 'There was nudity though. And . . . touching.'

'On that very sofa.'

She jumps up as if she's been stung. Mo and I snigger.

'Well,' Gerty says to me, brushing down her skinny jeans with distaste, 'we're seeing Leon on Tuesday. So we will make sure to grill him and check his intentions with you are all as they should be.'

'Hang on, you're what?'

'I'm talking him through where we're at with the case.'

'And Mo is going along because . . .' I look at Mo.

'Because I want to meet Leon,' he says, unabashed. 'What? Everyone else has met him.'

'Yes, but . . . but . . .' I narrow my eyes. 'He's *my* flatmate.'

'And *my* client,' Gerty points out, grabbing her handbag off the counter. 'Look, meeting Leon may have been a huge rigmarole for you, but we can just drop him a text and meet for brunch like normal people.'

Annoyingly, there's not much I can say to that. And I can't exactly fault them for being overprotective friends in the circumstances – without that, without them, I'd still probably be crying myself to sleep in Justin's flat. Still, I'm not sure I'm ready to be at meeting-the-friends stage with Leon, and the meddling is irritating.

All's forgiven when I get home from work on Tuesday, though, and find this note on the coffee table.

BAD THINGS REALLY DID HAPPEN. (Mo asked me to remind you.)

But you got through said bad things, and now you are stronger for it.

(Gerty told me to pass on . . . though her version had more swear-words.)

You're lovely, and I will never hurt you how he hurt you.

(That part was me.)

Leon xx

'You are going to love me,' Rachel says, standing on tiptoes to talk to me over my wall of pot plants.

I rub my eyes. I've just got off the phone to Martin, who has taken to calling me rather than walking down the corridor. I suspect he thinks it makes him seem like he's busy and important – far too busy and important for getting up off his bum and coming to talk to me. Still, I now have the power to screen his calls, and if I really do have to talk to him then I can make faces at Rachel at the same time, so there are upsides.

'Why? What have you done? Have you bought me a castle?'

She stares at me. 'It is *so weird* you just said that.'

I stare back at her. 'Why? Have you actually bought me a castle?'

'Obviously not,' she says, recovering, 'because if I could afford a castle I'd buy one for myself first, no offence – but this does *involve* a castle.'

I reach for my mug and swing my legs out from under the desk. This conversation requires tea. We take our usual route to the kitchen: doubling back past the colour room to avoid the head of Editorial and MD's desks, ducking behind the pillar by the photocopier so Hana won't spot us, hitting the kitchen from an angle that ensures we can see if any senior members of staff are lurking in there.

'Go! Go! Talk!' I tell Rachel as we step into the safety of the kitchen.

'Well. You know that illustrator I commissioned for our bricklayer-turned-designer's second book, who's a Lord Somebody?'

'Sure. Lordy Lord Illustrator,' I say. This is how Rachel and I refer to him.

'Well, Lordy Lord has come up with literally the perfect solution for Katherin's photoshoot.'

Marketing now want to showcase the products from Katherin's book. The mainstream media have been reluctant to come on board – they still don't quite get how YouTubers like Tasha Chai-Latte's words translate into sales – so we're going to fund the shoot and 'seed it across social'. Tasha has promised to share on her blog, and, with just over one week to go until pub date, Marketing and PR are having periodic meltdowns about getting the shoot organised.

'He *owns a Welsh castle*,' Rachel finishes. 'In Wales. That we can use.'

'You're serious? For free?'

'Absolutely. This weekend. And, because it's so far to drive, he's said he'll put us up for Saturday night! *In the castle!* And the best part is, Martin can't drop me because I'm just the designer . . . because Lordy Lord Illustrator is insisting that I bring Katherin!' She claps her hands with glee. 'And you'll be coming, obviously, because Katherin won't do anything unless you're there to shield her from the horrors that are Martin and Hana. Welsh castle weekend! Welsh castle weekend!'

I shush her. She has started singing really quite loudly and doing some sort of castle dance (which is quite hip-shaky), and though we have ascertained that there are no senior members of staff in the kitchen, you never know when they'll show up. It's like that thing people say about rats – there's always one six feet away from you at all times.

'Now we just need to find models willing to work for free in two days' time,' Rachel says. 'I almost don't want to tell Martin. I don't want him to start liking me or something. It'll throw off the whole balance of the office.'

'Tell him!' I say. 'This is a great idea.'

And it is. But Rachel's right. Katherin won't go without me, and that means a whole weekend away from home. I'd really hoped that I could spend some of the weekend with Leon. You know. Naked.

Rachel quirks an eyebrow, clocking my expression. 'Ah,' she says.

'No, no, this is great.' I try to rally. 'A weekend away with you and Katherin is going to be hilarious. Plus – it's a free castle visit! I'm going to pretend I'm scouting out my future home.'

Rachel leans back against the fridge, waiting for our teas to brew and watching me carefully. 'You really like this boy, don't you?'

I busy myself removing teabags. I *do* really like him, actually. It's kind of scary. Nice-scary, on the whole, but also a bit scary-scary.

'Well, bring him, then, so you don't miss out on seeing him.'

I look up. '*Bring* him? How am I swinging that one with the Powers That Be in Charge of Transport Costs?'

'Remind me what this stud looks like?' Rachel says, shifting so I can get the milk from the fridge. 'Tall, dark, handsome, with mysterious sexy smile?'

Only Rachel could say 'stud' without irony.

'Reckon he'd model for free?'

I nearly spit out my first mouthful of tea. Rachel grins and passes me a paper towel to help with lipstick damage.

'Leon? Model?'

'Why not?'

'Well . . . Because . . .' He'd hate it, surely. Or . . . maybe not actually – he cares so little about what other people think, someone taking photos of him and putting them on the Internet probably wouldn't bother him.

But if he did agree to it that would mean inviting him for a proper weekend away together – if a slightly unconventional one. And that definitely seems . . . *serious*. Relationship-ish. That thought makes my throat feel tight and starts a little flutter of panic in my stomach. I swallow the feeling away, irritated with myself.

'Go on. Ask,' Rachel insists. 'I'm betting he'll say yes if it means more time with you. And I'll sort it with Martin. Once I give him this castle, he'll be kissing my arse for days.'

It's very tricky to know exactly how to broach this conversation. I initially thought it would come up naturally on the call, but oddly enough castles and/or modelling don't come up at all, and now it's seven forty and I've only got five minutes before I know Leon has to head in to work.

I'm not copping out of asking, though. Since the night when Justin turned up things with Leon have shifted; this is more than sexual tension and flirty Post-it notes now, and for some reason I'm finding that slightly terrifying. When I think about him I get this rush of unstoppable smiley joy chased with a sort of claustrophobic panic. But I suspect that's probably a Justin hang-up, and frankly I'm done letting those hold me back.

'So,' I begin, pulling my cardigan closer around me. I'm on the balcony; it's become my favourite spot for evening phone calls. 'You're free this weekend, right?'

'Mmhmm,' he says. He's eating his brinner at the hospice while talking to me, so is even less chatty than usual, but I feel that will actually work to my advantage here. I think this proposal needs to be heard in full before it can be discussed.

'So, I have to go to a Welsh castle for the weekend to take photos of knitwear with Katherin, because I am her personal carer and despite the fact that I am paid a pittance, it is assumed that I will work weekends when told to, and that's just how it is.'

A moment's silence. 'Mmkay?' Leon says. He doesn't sound annoyed. Which, now I think about it, he wouldn't be – it's not like I'm blowing him off, I have to work. And if anyone understands that, Leon does.

I relax a bit. 'But I really want to see you,' I say, before I can second-guess myself. 'And Rachel has come up with a potentially terrible idea which could actually be really fun.'

'Mm?' Leon says, sounding a little nervous. He's heard enough about Rachel to know that her ideas often involve large amounts of alcohol and indiscretion.

'How would you feel about a free weekend in a Welsh castle with me . . . in exchange for modelling some knitwear while you're there, to go on the Butterfingers' social media?'

There is a loud choking noise at the other end of the phone.

'You hate the idea,' I say, feeling my cheeks go pink. There's a long silence. I should never have suggested this – Leon is all about quiet nights in with wine and good conversation, not parading himself around in front of cameras.

'I don't hate the idea,' Leon says. 'Just . . . absorbing it.'

I wait, giving him some time. The pause is excruciating, and then, just when I think I know exactly how this whole embarrassing conversation is going to end:

'All right then,' Leon says.

I blink. Beneath the balcony, Fabio Fox roams by, and then a police car goes screaming past, sirens shrieking.

'All right then?' I say, when it's quiet enough for him to hear me. 'You'll do it?'

'Sounds like a relatively small price to pay for a weekend away with you. Plus, the only person who'd likely mock me for it would be Richie, and he doesn't have Internet access.'

'You're serious?'

'Are you modelling too?'

'Oh, Martin probably thinks I'm too big,' I say, waving an arm. 'I'll just be there to Kathperone.'

'Will I meet this Martin we like so much? And you'll be there to what?'

'Kathperone. Sorry, that's Rachel's word for all the Katherin-chaperoning I have to do. And yeah, Martin will be coordinating the whole thing. He'll be especially insufferable, because he'll be in charge.'

'Excellent,' Leon says. 'I can spend my posing time plotting his downfall.'

OCTOBER

52

Leon

So. I'm standing in between two suits of armour, wearing a woolly jumper, staring into the middle distance.

My life has got stranger with Tiffy in it. Have never been afraid of a strange life, but lately have grown rather . . . comfortable. Set in my ways, as Kay used to say.

Can't stay that way for long with Tiffy around.

She's helping Katherin style us models. The other two are waif-like teens; Martin is staring at them as if they're edible. They're nice, but conversation dried up after we caught up on this year's *Bake Off*, and I'm now just counting down the minutes until Tiffy next gets to come over and adjust my woolly jumper in indiscernible ways that (I'm pretty sure) are just excuses to touch me.

Lordy Lord Illustrator flits around set. He is a pleasant posh gentleman; his castle is a little ramshackle, but it has rooms and suitably epic views, so everyone seems happy.

Except Martin. I joked with Tiffy about plotting his downfall, but when he's not salivating over the other models, he looks as if he's trying to work out the easiest way to push me off the battlements. Can't figure it out. Nobody here knows about Tiffy and me – we thought that was simplest. But am wondering if he's worked it out. If he does know, though, why would he care enough to glare at me so much?

Ah, well. I do as I'm told and stare in slightly different direction. Am just grateful to get away from the flat this weekend; had a bad feeling Justin would appear. He will eventually. Clearly wasn't finished when he left last Saturday. And yet he's been quiet since. No flowers, no texts, no turning up wherever Tiffy is despite having no way of knowing where she might happen to be. Suspicious. I'm worried he is biding his time for something. Men like that don't go away after a little scare.

Try not to yawn (have been awake for many, many hours, with only small naps). I let my gaze drift in Tiffy's direction. She's in wellies and blue tie-dyed jeans, lounging sideways on an enormous *Game of Thrones*-style chair that stands in the corner of the armoury and probably isn't intended for sitting on. Catch a glimpse of smooth skin as she shifts, her cardigan falling open. Swallow. Return gaze to particular bit of middle distance insisted upon by photographer.

Martin: All right, let's take a twenty-minute break!

I make a run for it before he can commandeer me into doing something other than talking to Tiffy (so far, have had to spend my breaks moving ancient weaponry, hoovering up errant straw, and checking tiny graze on finger of one of the waif-like models).

Me, on approaching Tiffy's throne chair: What is that man's problem with me?

Tiffy shakes her head and swings her legs around to get up.

Tiffy: Really, I have no idea. He's even more of a dick to you than the rest of us, though, isn't he?

Rachel, in a hiss, from behind me: Run! Flee! Incoming!

Tiffy doesn't need telling twice. She grabs my hand and drags me away in the direction of the front hall (gigantic stone cavern with three staircases).

Katherin, shouting after us: Are you leaving me to deal with him on my own?

Tiffy: Bloody hell, woman! Just imagine he's a Tory MP in the seventies, all right?

I don't turn around to see Katherin's reaction, but can hear Rachel's snort of laughter. Tiffy pulls me into ornate nook that looks as if it might once have housed a statue, and kisses me hard on the mouth.

Tiffy: All this staring at you all day. It's unbearable. And I am viciously jealous of everyone else getting to do it too.

Feels like sipping something warm – spreads downwards from my chest, pulls my lips into a smile. Don't know quite what to say, so kiss her instead. Her body presses mine against the cold stone wall, her hands twining around my neck.

Tiffy, against my mouth: Next weekend.

Me: Hmm?

(Am busy kissing.)

Tiffy: It'll be just the two of us. Alone. In our flat. And if anyone interrupts us or drags you off to administer to an eighteen-year-old's scratched finger, I will personally have them executed.

Pauses.

Tiffy: Sorry. This whole castle setting is clearly getting into my head.

Pull back, search her face. Have I not told her? I must have told her.

Tiffy: What? What is it?

Me: Richie's appeal is on Friday. Sorry. I'm staying at Mam's for the weekend afterwards – didn't I tell you?

Feel a familiar fear. This will be the start of an unpleasant conversation – have forgotten to tell her something, am changing her plans . . .

Tiffy: No! Are you serious?

Stomach writhes. Reach to pull her in again, but she bats my hands away, eyes wide.

Tiffy: You didn't tell me! Leon – I didn't know. I'm so sorry, but – Katherin's book launch . . .

I'm confused now. Why is *she* sorry?

Tiffy: I wanted to be there, but it's Katherin's book launch on the Friday. I can't believe this. Will you tell Richie to call when I'm in the flat, so I can apologise properly?

Me: For what?

Tiffy rolls her eyes impatiently.

Tiffy: For not being able to come to his appeal!

Stare at her. Blink a bit. Relax as I realise she is in fact not angry with me.

Me: Never would expect . . .

Tiffy: Are you joking? You didn't think I was going to be there? It's Richie!

Me: You really wanted to come?

Tiffy: Yes, Leon. I really, really wanted to come.

Poke her in the cheek with one finger.

Tiffy, already laughing: Ow! What was that for?

Me: You're real? A real-life human female?

Tiffy: Yes, I'm real, you idiot.

Me: Implausible. How are you so nice, and also very pretty? You're a myth, no? You'll turn into an ogre at stroke of midnight?

Tiffy: Stop it. Bloody hell, you have low standards! Why shouldn't I want to come to your brother's appeal? He's my friend too. I actually spoke to him before I spoke to you, I'll have you know.

Me: I'm glad you didn't meet him first. He is much more attractive than me.

Tiffy wiggles eyebrows.

Tiffy: Is *that* why you didn't mention the appeal date?

Scuff feet. Thought I'd told her. She squeezes my arm.

Tiffy: It's all right, honestly, I'm just teasing.

Think of the months of notes and leftover dinners, the never knowing her. Feels so different now I've met her. Can't believe I wasted all that time – not just those months, but the time before that, the years of dawdling, settling, waiting.

Me: No, I should've told you. We should get better at this. We can't keep relying on snatching days together as and when. Or on colliding by accident.

I pause, testing a thought. Could switch to the occasional day shift? Stay in the flat one night a week? Open my mouth to suggest it, but Tiffy's eyes have gone wide and serious, almost nervous, and I freeze, suddenly sure it's the wrong thing to say. Then, after a moment:

Tiffy, brightly: How about a calendar on the fridge?

Right. That's probably more appropriate – it's early days. Am being far too keen.

Glad I didn't say anything now.

53

Tiffy

I stare up at the very distant, very spiderwebby ceiling. It's absolutely bloody freezing in here, even under a duvet and three blankets, with Rachel's body heat to the left of me like a person-shaped radiator.

Today has been an extremely frustrating day. It's unusual you get to spend an entire eight hours staring at the person you fancy. If we're honest, most of my day has been spent fantasising about all of the other people in this castle being vaporised, leaving just me and Leon, naked (the vaporiser also took our clothes), with many exciting places to have sex in.

I'm still clearly a mess about Justin, and as things progress with Leon I can feel *nice-scary* tilting towards *scary-scary* a little more often. When Leon started talking about making more time for each other, for instance, the panicky trapped feeling tightened right in again. But beneath that, when I'm thinking clearly, I have such a good feeling about Leon. He's where my mind goes when I'm feeling my best. He makes me even more determined to get over what happened with Justin because I don't want to be carrying the weight of that with Leon. I want to be light and footloose and fancy-free. And naked.

'Stop it,' Rachel mumbles into her pillow.

'Stop what?' I hadn't realised she was awake, or I'd have had that whole little thought episode out loud.

'Your sexual frustration is making me tense,' Rachel says, turning over and dragging as much of the duvet as possible with her.

I cling on and yank it back an inch or two. 'I'm not frustrated.'

'Please. I bet you've just been waiting until I go to sleep so you can hump my leg.'

I poke her with a very cold foot. She yelps.

'My sexual frustration cannot be stopping you sleeping,' I say, conceding the point. 'If that was possible, nobody would ever have been able to sleep in Victorian times.'

She turns over to squint at me. 'You're weird,' she says, rolling away again. 'Go sneak out and find your boyfriend.'

'He's not my boyfriend,' I say automatically, the way you learn to from the age of eight.

'Your special friend. Your beau. Your squeeze. Your—'

'I'm going,' I hiss at her, throwing back the duvet.

Hana is gently snoring on the other bed. She actually looks like quite a nice person while she's sleeping, but then it's hard to look bitchy when you're drooling into your pillow.

Leon and I have come up with a plan to see each other tonight. Martin has for some irritating reason moved Leon into a double room, sharing with the cameraman, which means we can't sneak into bed together. But, with Hana and the cameraman fast asleep, there's no reason why we can't slip out and go for a castle adventure. The idea was that we'd each get some rest, and then meet at three in the morning, but I've been too excited to sleep. Still, just-woken-up is nowhere near as good a look as Hollywood would have you believe, so it's probably a good job I've been lying here awake for hours thinking inappropriate thoughts.

I hadn't counted on it being this bloody freezing, though. I'd imagined I'd wear just my underwear and a dressing gown – I brought sexy negligee-style underwear and everything – but right now I'm in fleece pyjama bottoms, woolly socks, and three jumpers, and there's no way I'm taking these off. So I just slick on some lip gloss, give my hair a ruffle, and ease the door open.

It creaks so much it borders on cliché, but Hana doesn't wake. I slip out of the door as soon as it's just about wide enough, and pull it closed behind me, wincing at all the groaning noises.

Leon and I are meeting in the kitchen, because if anyone finds us there we've got a good excuse (given the number of biscuits I consume at work, nobody will have trouble believing that I need a midnight snack). I powerwalk down the carpeted hall, keeping a close eye on the rooms that line the corridor in case anyone else is up and about to spot me.

Nobody. The powerwalking is warming me up a bit, so I take the stairs at a jog too, and by the time I arrive in the kitchen I'm slightly out of breath.

The kitchen is the only bit of the castle that looks loved. It's been redone recently, and, to my absolute delight, there is an enormous Aga at the far end. I plaster my body against it like a girl who's found a former One Direction member in a nightclub and doesn't plan on leaving without him.

'Should I be feeling this jealous?' Leon says from behind me.

I look over my shoulder. He's standing in the doorway, his hair freshly smoothed back, in a loose T-shirt and jogging bottoms.

'If your body-heat is higher than this Aga's temperature, I'm yours,' I tell him, turning to warm my bum and the back of my legs, and to get a better look at him.

He closes the space between us, casual, unhurried. There's this understated confidence to him sometimes – he doesn't show it much, but when he does it's impossibly sexy. He kisses me and I get even warmer.

'Did you have any trouble sneaking out?' I ask, breaking away to push my hair back over my shoulders.

'Larry the cameraman is a very heavy sleeper,' Leon says, finding my mouth again and kissing me slowly.

My heart is already thundering. I feel a little dizzy, as if all the blood that usually hangs around in my head has decided it has other places to be. Our lips barely parting, Leon lifts me up so I'm sitting on the Aga warming plate, and I wrap my legs around him, linking my ankles behind his body. He presses against me.

I become gradually aware of the heat from the Aga working its way through my flannel pyjama bottoms and beginning to scald my bum.

'Ahh. Burny,' I say, pushing forward so Leon takes my weight. He lifts me up, koala-bear style, and moves me to the sideboard instead, his lips slowly beginning to trace patterns all over me – neck and chest, lips again, neck, collarbone, lips. My head is starting to spin; I'm barely thinking. His hands find the narrow opening between my jumpers and pyjama bottoms, and then his hands are on my skin, and barely thinking becomes not thinking at all.

'Is it bad to have sex on surface where other people prepare food?' Leon asks, pulling away, breathless.

'No! It's just . . . clean! Hygienic,' I say, pulling him back to me.

'Good,' he says, and suddenly all my jumpers are off in one go. I'm not cold at all any longer. In fact, I could do with wearing fewer clothes. Why the hell didn't I wear the negligee?

I yank off Leon's T-shirt and tug at the waistband of his jogging bottoms until he slips those off too. As I slide my body up against his he pauses for a moment.

'OK?' he asks hoarsely. I can see the control he's taking to ask the question; I answer with another kiss. 'Yes?' he says, mouth against mine. 'This means OK?'

'Yes. Now stop talking,' I tell him, and he does as he's told.

We're so close. I'm almost naked, he's almost naked, my head is full of Leon. This is it. It's happening. My inner, sexually frustrated Victorian almost weeps with gratitude as Leon pulls me towards him by the hips so I'm pressed up against him, his body back between my legs.

And then, there it is. The remembering.

I stiffen. He doesn't clock it at first, and for three deeply horrible seconds his hands are still moving over my body, his lips still pressed hard against mine. It's very hard to describe this feeling. Panic, perhaps, but I'm completely immobile and feel strangely passive. I'm frozen, trapped, and have the odd sensation that some crucial part of me has detached itself.

Leon's hands slow, coming to a halt on either side of my face. He lifts my head gently to look at him.

'Ah,' he says. He disentangles himself from me just as I begin to shake all over.

I can't seem to get that part of me back. I don't know where this feeling came from – one moment I was about to have the sex I'd been fantasising over all week, and the next I was . . . remembering something. A body that wasn't Leon's, hands that were doing the same thing but I didn't want them there.

'You want space, or a hug?' he asks simply, standing a foot away from me now.

'Hug,' I manage.

He gathers me to him, reaching for the heap of jumpers on the counter as he does so. He drapes one over my shoulder and cuddles me close, my head pressed against his chest. The only giveaway of how frustrated he must be feeling is the thud-thud of his heartbeat in my ear.

'I'm sorry,' I mutter into his chest.

'You never should be that,' he says. 'Not sorry. OK?'

I smile shakily, pressing my lips to his skin. 'OK.'

54

Leon

Am not usually an angry person. Am generally mild-mannered and hard to rile. It's always me who stops Richie fighting (usually on behalf of a woman, who may or may not need any assistance). But now something primal seems to be happening, and it's taking enormous effort to keep my body relaxed and movements gentle. Hostile posture and tenseness will not help Tiffy.

But I want to hurt him. Really. Don't know what he did to Tiffy, what in particular triggered her this time, but whatever it was, it has hurt her so much she's trembling all over like a kitten come in from the cold.

She surfaces, wiping her face.

Tiffy: Sorr— Umm. I mean. Hi.

Me: Hi. You want a tea?

She nods. Don't want to let go of her, but holding on after she's expecting me to is probably a bad plan. Dress again and head to kettle.

Tiffy: That was . . .

Wait. Kettle begins to boil, just a quiet rumble.

Tiffy: That was really horrible. I don't even know what happened.

Me: Was it a new memory? Or something you've already talked through with the counsellor?

She shakes her head, frowning.

Tiffy: It wasn't like a memory, it's not like something came into my mind's eye . . .

Me: More like muscle memory?

She looks up.

Tiffy: Yeah. Exactly.

Pour the teas. Open fridge for milk and pause. It's filled with trays of little pink cupcakes iced with 'F and J'.

Tiffy pads over to join me, sliding an arm around my waist.

Tiffy: Ooh. These must be for the wedding happening after we leave.

Me: How closely do you think they paid attention to the quantity?

Tiffy laughs. Not quite a full laugh, and a little wet with tears, but still good.

Tiffy: Probably very. Although there are *so* many.

Me: Too many. I'd estimate . . . three hundred.

Tiffy: Nobody invites three hundred people to their wedding. Unless they're really famous, or Indian.

Me: Is it a famous Indian person's wedding?

Tiffy: Lordy Lord Illustrator didn't explicitly say so.

Pinch two cupcakes and give one to Tiffy. Her eyes are still a little pink from crying, but she's smiling now, and eats the cupcake in almost one bite. Suspect she needs sugar.

We eat in silence for a while, moving to lean against Aga side by side.

Tiffy: So . . . in your professional opinion . . .

Me: As a palliative care nurse?

Tiffy: As a vaguely medical person . . .

Oh, no. These conversations never go well. People always assume they teach us all the medicine in the world at nursing school, and that we remember it five years later.

Tiffy: Am I going to freak out like this every time we're about to have sex? Because that is literally the most depressing thought ever.

Me, carefully: I suspect not. May just take some time to work out triggers and how to avoid them until you feel safer.

She looks at me sharply.

Tiffy: I'm not . . . I don't want you to think . . . he never, you know. *Hurt* me.

Would like to dispute that. Seems he has hurt her rather a lot. But it's definitely not my place, so I just go and fetch her another cupcake and hold it up for her to bite.

Me: I'm not presuming anything. Just want you to feel better.

Tiffy stares at me, then, from nowhere, pokes me in the cheek.

Me, with a yelp: Hey!

Cheek-poke is a lot more startling than I'd realised when I did it to her earlier.

Tiffy: You're not real, are you? You're implausibly nice.

Me: Am not. I'm a grumpy old man who dislikes most people.

Tiffy: Most?

Me: There are a small number of exceptions.

Tiffy: How do you choose them? The exceptions?

Shrug, uncomfortable.

Tiffy: Really. Seriously. Why me?

Me: Umm. Well. I suppose . . . There are some people I just feel comfortable with. Not many. But you were one before I even met you.

Tiffy looks at me, head tilted, eyes holding my gaze for so long I twist on the spot, itching to drop the subject. Eventually she leans forward and kisses me slowly, tasting of icing.

Tiffy: I'll be worth the wait. You'll see.

As if I'd ever doubted it.

55

Tiffy

I lean back in my desk chair, taking my eyes off the screen. I've been staring at it for way too long – the castle knitwear photos have been picked up on *Daily Mail*'s Femail, and it's *weird*. Katherin is officially a celebrity. I can't believe how quickly this has happened, and also can't stop reading comments from other women about how hot Leon is in those photos. I obviously already know he's hot, but still, it's simultaneously horrible and kind of good to get external validation.

I wonder how he's feeling about it. I'm hoping he's too techno-logically incapable to scroll to the comments section on the *Daily Mail*, because some of the comments are really quite X-rated. There's obviously a few racist ones in there as well, this being a comments section on the Internet, and everything briefly descends into an argument about global warming being a liberalist conspiracy, and before I know it I have circled my way into the plughole of the Internet and wasted half an hour following people's outlandish opinions on whether Trump is a neo-Nazi and whether Leon's ears are too big.

I go to counselling after work. As per usual Lucie sits in borderline uncomfortable silence for a while, and then, seemingly spontan-eously, I start telling her awful, painful stuff I mostly can't even bear to think about. How cleverly Justin made me believe I had a bad memory, so he could always say I'd misremembered things. How brazenly he convinced me I'd thrown a bunch of clothes out when really he'd just been chucking stuff he didn't like me wearing to the back of the wardrobe.

How subtly he turned sex into something I owed him, even when he'd made me so sad I couldn't think straight.

It's all business as usual for Lucie, though. She just nods. Or tilts her head. Or sometimes – in extreme cases, when I've said something out loud that almost physically hurts to utter – she says a supportive 'yes'.

This time she asks me at the end of the session how I think I'm getting on. I start with the usual stuff – 'oh, this has been so great, honestly, thanks so much', like when the hairdresser asks if you like the cut they've just given you. But Lucie just stares at me for a while, so then I think, how actually *am* I getting on? A couple of months ago I couldn't face saying no to Justin taking me out for a drink. I was expending most of my mental energy keeping memories at bay. I wasn't even willing to acknowledge that he'd abused me. And now, here I am, talking to Someone Who isn't Mo about how what happened with Justin wasn't my fault, and actually believing it.

I listen to a lot of Kelly Clarkson on my way home on the tube. Facing my reflection in the glass, I throw my shoulders back and meet my own gaze, just like that first train journey from Justin's place to the flat. Yes, I'm a little teary-eyed from counselling, but this time I'm not wearing sunglasses.

You know what? I am extremely proud of myself.

The question of how Leon feels about the photos in Femail is answered on my return to the flat. He has left this note for me on the fridge:

Didn't cook dinner. Too famous for that now.
(i.e. got Deliveroo to celebrate Katherin's/your success. Delicious Thai food in fridge for you.) x

Well, it seems he's not let it get to his head, so that's something. I stick the Thai food in the microwave, humming 'Stronger (What Doesn't Kill You)', and reach for a pen while it whirs. Leon's working until Wednesday, then off to his mum's; I won't see him in person before Richie's appeal on Friday. He's keeping busy – he's off on his last Johnny White visit tomorrow morning, planning on taking the earliest train he can to Cardiff and getting back in time for a nap before he's back to work. I'd point out that that's not enough sleep for him to function on, but I can tell he's not sleeping well even when he's here, so maybe it's better for him to be out and about. He's finally finished *The Bell Jar*, a sure sign he's awake in the daytime, and seems to be surviving on caffeine mostly – at this point in the month we are not usually running this low on instant coffee.

I keep it brief.

I'm glad you've taken well to your new life of celebrity. I, on the other hand, am now embarrassingly jealous of about a hundred women on the Internet who think you are 'so yummy lol', and have decided I much prefer it when it's just me that gets to stare at you.

I'm crossing my fingers that Johnny White the Eighth is The One! xx

When the reply comes the next evening I can tell Leon's exhausted. It's something about the handwriting – it's looser than usual, like he couldn't muster the energy to hold the pen tight.

Johnny White the Eighth is not our guy. Is actually very unpleasant and homophobic. Also made me eat a lot of out-of-date fig rolls.

Richie says hi. He's OK. Holding up. x

Hmm. Richie may be holding up, but I'm not convinced that Leon is.

56

Leon

Late for work. Talked to Richie for twenty minutes he couldn't really afford about PTSD. It's the first time in a long time that I've talked to Richie about something other than the case, which is strange as appeal is in three days' time. Think Gerty has spoken to him so often he actually wanted a change of topic.

Asked him about restraining orders too. He was clear on the subject: it's for Tiffy to decide. Would be bad idea for me to seem to be imposing decisions on her – I must let her come to that conclusion on her own. Still hate that the ex knows where she lives, but must remember it is not my place to say.

Late late now. Button up shirt on way out of building. I'm an expert at efficient flat departure. It's all in the shaved-off seconds and the foregoing of brinner, which will come to haunt me at 11 p.m. when day nurses have eaten all the biscuits.

Strange man from Flat 5: Leon!

Look up as building door slams shut behind me. It's strange man from Flat 5, the one who (according to Tiffy) does energetic aerobics at 7 a.m. sharp, and accumulates banana crates in his parking space. Surprised to discover he knows my name.

Me: Hi?

Strange man from Flat 5: I never believed you were a nurse!

Me: Right. I'm running late for work, so—

Strange man from Flat 5 waves his mobile phone at me, like I should be able to discern what is on screen.

Strange man, triumphantly: You're a famous person!

Me: Pardon?

Strange man: You're in the *Daily Mail*! Wearing a poncey famous-person jumper!

Me: Poncey is no longer a politically correct term, strange man from Flat 5. Got to go. Enjoy the rest of Femail!

Scarper as quickly as possible. Decide, on reflection, not to pursue life of celebrity.

Mr Prior is awake for long enough to see the photos. He'll drop off again soon, but I know this will amuse him, so make sure to take the opportunity and get pictures up on phone screen.

Hmm. Fourteen-thousand likes on a photo of me staring into distance in a black T-shirt and enormous crocheted scarf. Odd.

Mr Prior: Very dashing, Leon!

Me: Why, thank you.

Mr Prior: Now, am I right that a certain fine young lady persuaded you to humiliate yourself in this fashion?

Me: Eh. Umm. It was Tiffy's idea.

Mr Prior: Ah, the flatmate. And . . . the girlfriend?

Me: No, no, not 'girlfriend'. Not yet.

Mr Prior: No? Last we spoke I got the impression you were rather smitten with each other.

Check Mr Prior's chart, keeping face carefully blank. Deranged liver function tests. Not good. To be expected, but still, not good.

Me: I'm . . . yes. I'm that. Just don't want to rush things. I don't think she does either.

Mr Prior frowns. His little beady eyes almost disappear under the folds of his eyebrows.

Mr Prior: May I offer you some advice, Leon?

I nod.

Mr Prior: Don't let your natural . . . reticence hold you back. Make it clear how you feel about her. After all, you're something of a closed book, Leon.

Me: Closed book?

Notice that Mr Prior's hands tremble as he smooths down the bedspread, and try not to think about prognostics.

Mr Prior: Quiet. Brooding. I'm sure she finds it very attractive, but don't let it be a barrier between you. I left it too long to tell my— I left things too late, and now I wish I'd just said what I wanted when I still could. Think what my life could have been. Not that I'm not happy with my lot, but . . . you do waste an awful lot of time when you're young.

Can't do anything around here without someone imparting wisdom in your direction. But Mr Prior has made me a little nervous. Felt after Wales I shouldn't rush things with Tiffy. But maybe I'm holding back too much. I tend to, apparently. Wish I'd mentioned about changing to day shifts now. Still, I did go to a Welsh castle for her, and pose against windswept tree in large cardigan. Surely that makes my feelings clear?

Richie: You're not a *naturally* open person.

Me: I am! I am . . . I'm forthcoming. Expressive. An open book.

Richie: You're not bad at the old talking-about-feelings with me, but that doesn't count, and it's usually because I do it first. You should take a leaf from my book, bro. I've never had any time for the whole hard-to-get thing. Easy-to-get and put-it-on-the-line has always worked for me.

Feel a bit wrong-footed. Was feeling good about everything with Tiffy, and am anxious now. Shouldn't have told Richie what Mr Prior said – should've known what his opinion would be. Richie was writing love songs to serenade girls in school corridors when he was ten years old.

Me: What am I meant to do, then?

Richie: Fucking hell, man, just tell her you like her and you want to make things official. You clearly do, so it can't be that hard. I have to go. Gerty's got me talking her through the ten minutes after leaving the club *again*, seriously, I'm not sure that woman is human.

Me: That woman is—

Richie: Don't worry, don't worry. I won't hear a word against her. I was *going* to say superhuman.

Me: Good.

Richie: Hot, too.

Me: Don't you even—

Richie belly-laughs. I find myself grinning; I can never resist smiling with him when he laughs like that.

Richie: I'll be good, I'll be good. But if she gets me out of here, I'm buying her dinner. Or asking for her hand in marriage, maybe.

Smile fades a little. I feel a twinge of worry. The appeal is really happening. Two days to go. Haven't even let myself imagine scenario where Richie is found not guilty, but my brain keeps going there against my will, playing out the scene. Bringing him home to sit on Tiffy's paisley beanbag, drink beers, be my little brother again.

Can't find the words for what I want to tell him. Don't get your hopes up? But of course he will – I have too. That's the whole point. So . . . don't let it get to you if it doesn't work? Also ridiculous. No good words for the magnitude of the problem.

Me: See you Friday.

Richie: That's the open book I know and love. See you Friday, bro.

57

Tiffy

It's first thing on Friday. The Day.

Leon is at his mum's place – they're going to court together. Rachel and Mo are at mine. Mo's tagging along to the book launch – given everything I've done for this book, even Martin could not deny me a plus one.

Gerty pops in with Mo when he arrives, for a quick, cursory hug and a very hurried chat about Richie's case. She is already dressed in her ridiculous lawyer wig, as if she's doing an impression of an eighteenth-century painting.

Mo is in his tux, looking adorable. I love it when Mo dresses up smartly. It's like when you see photos of puppies dressed up as humans. He is visibly uncomfortable, and I can tell he's itching to at least take off his shoes, but if he so much as reaches for his shoelaces then Gerty snarls at him and he withdraws, whimpering. When Gerty leaves, he looks visibly relieved.

'Just so you know, Mo and Gerty are totally shagging,' Rachel tells me, passing me my hairbrush.

I stare at her in the mirror. (There are nowhere near enough mirrors in this flat. We should have got ready at Rachel's, which has an entire wall of mirrored cupboards in the bedroom for what I suspect to be sexual reasons, but she refuses to let Gerty in her flat since she made a comment about how messy it was at Rachel's birthday party.)

'Mo and Gerty are *not* shagging,' I say, coming to my senses and snatching the hairbrush. I'm attempting to tame my mane into a sleek up-do from one of our DIY hairstyling books. The author promised me that it was easy, but I've been on step two for fifteen minutes. There are twenty-two steps in total and half an hour left on the clock.

'They are,' Rachel says matter-of-factly. 'You know I can always tell.'

I just about refrain from informing Rachel that Gerty also thinks she can 'always tell' when a friend is sleeping with someone. I don't want this to become a competition, especially as I've still not had sex with Leon.

'They live together,' I say, through a mouthful of hairpins. 'They're more comfortable with each other than they used to be.'

'You only get that comfortable if you get naked together,' Rachel insists.

'That's weird and gross. Anyway, I'm pretty sure Mo is asexual.'

Belatedly, I check that the bathroom door is closed. Mo is in the living room. He has spent the last hour looking either patient or bored, depending on whether he thinks we're looking.

'You *want* to think that, because of the whole he's-like-a-brother-to-you thing. But he's definitely not asexual. He came on to my friend Kelly at a party last summer.'

'I cannot handle these sorts of revelations right now!' I say, spitting out the hairpins. I put them between my teeth way too early. They're for step four, and step three still has me flummoxed.

'Come here,' Rachel says, and I breathe out. Thank God.

'You really left me hanging there,' I tell her, as she takes the hairbrush, smooths out the damage I have done so far, and flicks through the up-do instructions with one hand.

'How else will you ever learn?' she says.

*

It's 10 a.m. It's weird being in formal dress this early in the morning. For some reason I am incredibly paranoid about dripping tea down the front of my fancy new dress, though I'm pretty sure if I were drinking a martini I wouldn't have the same anxieties. It's just weird drinking from a mug while wearing silk.

Rachel has outdone herself – my hair is all smooth and shiny, knotted at the nape of my neck in a series of mysterious swirls just like in the picture. The side-effect, though, is that a copious amount of my chest is on show. When I tried this dress on I had my hair down – I didn't really notice quite how much skin the off-the-shoulder sleeves and structured sweetheart neckline leave exposed. Oh well. This is my night, too – I'm the acquiring editor. I'm perfectly entitled to dress inappropriately.

My alarm beeps to remind me to check in on Katherin. I call her, trying not to notice that she's higher up my most-called list than my own mother.

'Are you ready?' I ask as soon as she picks up.

'Almost!' she trills. 'Just made a quick adjustment to the outfit, and—'

'*What* quick adjustment?' I ask, suspicious.

'Oh, well when I tried it on again I realised how dour and boring this dress that your PR people picked makes me look under the bright lights of the day,' she says, 'so I've tweaked the hemline and the neckline.'

I open my mouth to tell her off, and then close it again. Firstly, the damage is clearly already done – if she's re-hemmed, the dress is unsaveable. And secondly, my risqué dress choice will look much better next to someone else who has also decided to show an unprofessional amount of skin.

'Fine. We'll pick you up at half past.'

'Toodles!' she says, hopefully ironically, though I'm not sure.

I check the time as I hang up. Ten minutes spare. (I had to factor in time for Rachel to get ready, which always takes at least fifty per cent longer than you think it will. She'll blame it on me for making her do my hair, obviously, but it's really because she is the self-proclaimed queen of contouring, and spends at least forty minutes subtly altering the shape of her face before she even gets started on eyes and lips.)

I'm just about to text Leon and see how he is when the flat phone rings.

'What the fuck is that?' shouts Rachel from the bathroom.

'It's our landline!' I yell, already making a dash for the sound (it seems to be coming from the vicinity of the fridge). Dashing is not easy in this outfit – there's a lot of billowing in the skirt region, and at least two risky moments where my bare foot catches in the tulle as I go. I wince as it yanks at my bad ankle. I can walk on it now, but it's not enjoying this running thing. Not that my good ankle likes running either.

'It's your *what*?' Mo asks, sounding amused.

'Our landline,' I repeat, fumbling around with the unbelievably large quantity of things on our kitchen surfaces.

'I'm sorry, you didn't tell me this was the 1990s,' calls Rachel, just as I find the phone.

'Hello?'

'Tiffy?'

I frown. 'Richie? Are you all right?'

'I'll be honest with you, Tiffy,' he says, 'I'm shitting myself. Not literally. Though it might be a matter of time.'

'Whoever it is, I hope they're enjoying the latest Blur CD,' Rachel calls.

'Hang on.' I head for the bedroom and close the door firmly behind me. With difficulty, I rearrange my skirt so that I can perch on the edge of the bed without anything ripping. 'Shouldn't you be, I don't know, in a van or something? How are you calling me? They *have* remembered your court date, right?'

I've heard enough horror stories from Gerty and Leon now to

know that prisoners don't always make it to court when they should, thanks to the various prison-related bureaucracies that are required to overlap in this situation. They moved Richie down to a (even grimmer) London prison a few days ago so he'd be in the area for the appeal, but there's still the journey from the prison to the courthouse. I feel physically sick at the thought of all this preparation going to waste because someone forgot to call someone else about transportation.

'No, no, I've done the van bit,' Richie says. 'Barrel of laughs, let me tell you. Somehow spent five hours in there, though I could have sworn we weren't moving for half of it. No, I'm at the courthouse now, in a holding cell. I'm not really allowed a phone call, but the guard is an Irish lady, and she says I remind her of her son. And that I look terrible. She told me to call my girlfriend, but I don't have one, so I thought I'd call you, since you're Leon's girlfriend and that's close enough. It was that or Rita from school, who I don't think I ever technically broke up with.'

'You're rambling, Richie,' I tell him. 'What's the matter? Is it nerves?'

'"Nerves" makes me sound like I'm an old lady. It's *terror*.'

'That does sound better. More horror movie. Less fainting because your corset is too tight.'

'Exactly.'

'Is Gerty there?'

'I can't see her yet. She's busy doing whatever lawyers do, anyway. I'm on my own now.' His tone is light and self-deprecating, as always, but you don't have to listen hard to hear the tremor in his voice.

'You are *not* on your own,' I tell him firmly. 'You have all of us. And remember – when we first spoke you told me you're coming to terms with being in prison. Well, that's the worst-case scenario here. More of what you have already coped with.'

'What if I vomit in the courtroom?'

'Then someone will clear the room and call a cleaner, and you'll pick up where you left off. It's not exactly going to make the judges think you're an armed robber, is it?'

He gives a strangled version of a chuckle. For a moment there is silence.

'I don't want to let Leon down,' he says. 'He's got his hopes up so high. I don't want— I can't bear to let him down again. Last time was the worst thing. Honestly, it was the worst. Seeing his face.'

'You have never let him down,' I say. My heart is thumping. This is important. 'He knows you didn't do it. The . . . the system let you both down.'

'I should have just taken it. Served my sentence and got out, and let him get on with his life in the meantime. All this – it's only going to make everything worse for him.'

'Leon was going to fight no matter what you did,' I say. 'He was never just going to let his little brother get picked on. If you'd given up, *that* would have hurt him.'

He takes a big, juddering breath, and lets it out again.

'That's good,' I say. 'Breathing. I hear that's a good one for those with delicate nerves. Have you got any smelling salts?'

That gets another chuckle, a little less strangled this time.

'Are you calling me a pussy?' Richie asks.

'I fully believe that you're a very brave man,' I tell him. 'But yes. I'm calling you a pussy. In case that helps you remember how brave you are.'

'Ah, you're a good girl, Tiffy,' Richie says.

'I'm not a dog, Richie. And – now that you're hopefully less green . . . Can we go back to how you just said "Leon's girlfriend"?'

There's a pause.

'Not Leon's girlfriend?' he says.

'Not yet,' I tell him. 'Well, I mean, we've not discussed that. We've only been on a few dates, technically.'

'He's mad about you,' Richie says. 'He might not say it out loud, but . . .'

I feel a twinge of anxiety. I'm crazy about Leon, too. I spend most of my waking hours thinking about him, and a few of the sleeping ones too. But . . . I don't know. The idea of him wanting to be my boyfriend makes me feel so *trapped*.

I adjust my dress, wondering if I'm the one having the problem with corsets and nerves. I really like Leon. This is ridiculous. Objectively, I would like to call him my boyfriend, and introduce him to people as such. That's what you always want when you're crazy about someone. But . . .

What would Lucie say?

Well, she'd probably say nothing, to be honest. She'd just leave me to stew on the fact that this weird fear of getting trapped is almost certainly to do with the fact that I was in a relationship with a man who never really let me go.

'Tiffy?' Richie says. 'I should probably get going.'

'Oh, God, yes,' I say, coming to my senses. I don't know what I'm doing worrying about relationship labels when Richie is about to walk into court. '*Good luck*, Richie. I wish I could be there.'

'Maybe see you on the other side,' he says, voice trembling again. 'And if not – look after Leon.'

This time, the request doesn't sound strange. 'I will,' I tell him. 'I promise.'

58

Leon

Hate this suit. Last wore it for court case number one, and then shoved it in wardrobe at Mam's place, tempted to burn it like it was contaminated. Glad I didn't. Can't afford to keep burning suits every time the legal system fails to deliver justice. This might not be our last appeal.

Mam is weepy and shaking. I try so hard to be strong for her, but can't bear to be in the room with her. Would be easier with any other person, but with Mam, it's awful. I want her to mother me, not the other way around, and it almost makes me angry seeing her like this, even while it makes me sad.

I check my phone.

I've just spoken to Richie – he called here for a bit of a morale boost. He's doing fine. You're all going to be fine, whatever happens. Text me if there's anything I can do. I can always duck out for a phone call. Tiffy xx

I feel warm for a moment, after a morning of sustained cold fear. Remind myself of new resolve to tell Tiffy explicitly how I feel and move things in direction of seriousness, e.g. meeting parents etc.

Mam: Sweetie?

One last look in mirror. Thinner, longer-haired, stretched-out

Richie stares back at me. I can't get him out of my head – I keep remembering how he looked when they read out his sentence, the endless barrage of nonsense about his cold-blooded, calculated crime, how his eyes went wide and blank with fear.

Mam: Leon? Sweetie?

Me: Coming.

Hello again, courtroom.

It's so mundane. Nothing like the wooden seats and vaulted ceilings of American legal dramas – just lots of files on desks, carpet, and tiered benches from which a few bored-looking lawyers and journalists have come to spectate. One of the journalists is trying to find a plug to charge his phone. A law student is inspecting the back of her smoothie bottle.

It's bizarre. Earlier this year, I would have wanted to scream at both of them. *Pay some fucking attention. You're watching someone's life being destroyed.* But it's all part of the peculiar drama of this ritual, and now that we know how to play the game – now that we have a lawyer who knows the rules – the ritual doesn't bother me so much.

A wizened man in a long cloak like a Harry Potter character enters with prison guard and Richie. Richie is not cuffed, which is something. But he looks just as bad as I suspected. He's bulked up in the last few months, exercising again, but with his shoulders slumped the muscle seems to weigh him down. Can barely recognise him as the brother who first walked into court last year, the one with total confidence that if you're innocent you walk out free. The brother who grew up at my shoulder, matching me step for step, always having my back.

Almost can't look at him – it's too painful seeing the fear in his eyes. Somehow, from somewhere, I manage an encouraging smile when he looks at me and Mam. They put him in a glass box and close the door behind him.

We wait. Journalist succeeds at plugging in phone, and continues to scroll through what looks like the Reuters homepage, despite enormous sign forbidding use of mobile phones directly above his head. Smoothie-bottle girl is now pulling loose threads out of fluffy scarf.

Have to keep smiling at Richie. Gerty is here, dressed in that ridiculous outfit, almost indistinguishable from the rest of the lawyers even though I've seen her eating Chinese takeaway in my kitchen. I feel myself bristling just at the sight of her. It's something guttural, instinctive now. Have to remind myself over and over that she's on our team.

Wizened robed man: All rise!

Everyone stands. Three judges file into the room. Is it generalising to point out that literally all of them are white middle-aged men whose shoes look like they are worth more than my mother's car? I try to quell my rising hatred as they settle into their seats. Flick through the paperwork in front of them. Look up, finally, at Gerty and the prosecution barrister. Not one of them looks at my brother.

Judge 1: Shall we begin?

59

Tiffy

Katherin is a tiny, black-clad stick figure on the stage. Behind her, blown up to terrifying proportions, she's repeated in close-up – one screen is just her hands, so viewers can watch how she uses the crochet hook, and the other two focus on her face.

It's amazing. The whole crowd is rapt. We're so overdressed for a daytime event about crochet, but Katherin insisted on the dress code – despite all her anti-bourgeois values, she bloody loves an excuse to wear something fancy. Women in cocktail dresses gaze up at Katherin's enormous face, immortalised on the big screens beneath the vaulted ceiling. Men in tuxedos chuckle warmly at Katherin's witticisms. I even catch one young woman in a satin gown copying the movements of Katherin's hands, though all she's holding is a miniature goat's cheese canapé, no crochet hook in sight.

Despite all of this, all its distracting absurdity, I can't stop thinking about Richie and the way his voice trembled on the phone.

Nobody would notice if I just sneaked out. I might look a little incongruous for the courtroom, but maybe I could head via my flat, and pick up a change of clothes for the taxi ride . . .

God, I can't believe I'm considering paying for a taxi.

'Look!' Rachel hisses suddenly, poking me in the ribs.

'Oww! What?'

'Look! It's Tasha Chai-Latte!'

I follow her pointing finger. A young woman dressed in a subtle lilac cocktail dress has just entered the crowd, a staggeringly attractive boyfriend in tow. An intimidating man in a tux follows the two of them – their bodyguard, presumably.

Rachel's right, it's definitely her. I recognise the chiselled cheekbones from YouTube. Despite myself, I feel my stomach flutter a little – I'm such a sucker for a famous person.

'I can't believe she came!'

'Martin will be ecstatic. Do you think she'll let me take a picture with her?' Rachel asks. Above us, the gigantic Katherins on their screens smile out at the crowd, and her hands hold up a finished square.

'It's the big man in the tux I'd worry about, if I were you.'

'She's filming! Look!'

Tasha Chai-Latte's impossibly handsome boyfriend has pulled a compact, expensive-looking video camera out of his satchel, and is fiddling with the buttons. Tasha checks her hair and make-up, dabbing a finger along her lips.

'Oh my God. She's going to put the event on her YouTube channel. Do you think Katherin will mention you in her thank-you speech? *We'll be famous!*'

'Calm down,' I tell her, exchanging a look with Mo, who is currently working his way through the large pile of canapés he has been hoarding while everyone else is too distracted by crochet to capitalise on the food.

Tasha's boyfriend lifts the camera, training it on Tasha's face. Immediately she is wreathed in smiles, all thought of hair and make-up forgotten.

'Get closer, get closer,' Rachel mutters, shooing Mo in the direction of Tasha. We shuffle along, trying to look nonchalant, until we're just about close enough to hear them.

'. . . amazing lady!' Tasha is saying. 'And isn't this place *beautiful*? Oh my God, you guys, I feel so lucky to be here, and to be able to share it with all of you – live! You know how I feel about supporting real artists, and that's exactly what Katherin is.'

The crowd bursts into applause – Katherin has finished her demonstration. Tasha gives an impatient gesture, telling her boyfriend to do another take. I guess they're warming up for the live stream.

'And now a few thank-yous!' Katherin says from the stage.

'This is it,' Rachel whispers excitedly. 'She'll *definitely* mention you.'

My stomach twists. I'm not sure I want her to mention me – there are a *lot* of people in this room, and an extra few million who will soon be watching via Tasha Chai-Latte's YouTube channel. I adjust my dress, trying to inch it a little higher.

I needn't have worried, though. Katherin starts by thanking her entire network of friends and family, which turns out to be extensive to the point of absurdity (I can't help wondering if she's taking the piss a bit – it would be just like her). The crowd's attention shifts; people begin to move around in search of prosecco and tiny food.

'And finally,' Katherin says grandly, 'there are two people who I just had to save until last.'

Well, that can't be me. It'll be her mum and dad or something. Rachel shoots me a disappointed look, and then returns her attention to Tasha and her boyfriend, who are filming everything with quiet concentration on their faces.

'Two people without whom this book would never have happened,' Katherin goes on. 'These two have worked so hard to make *Crochet Your Way* possible. And, even better than that, they believed in me from the very start – long before I was lucky enough to gather crowds this large for my events.'

Rachel and I turn to stare at one another.

'It won't be me,' Rachel whispers, suddenly looking very nervous. 'She doesn't even remember my name most of the time.'

'Tiffy and Rachel have been editor and designer on my books for the last three years, and they are the reason for my success,' Katherin says grandly. The crowd applauds. 'I cannot thank them enough for making my book the best it can possibly be – and the most beautiful it can possibly be. Rachel! Tiffy! Will you get up here please? I have something for you both.'

We gawp at one another. I think Rachel might be hyperventilating. I have never regretted an outfit choice more than I do now. I have to get up onstage in front of one thousand people, wearing something that only just covers my nipples.

But as we stumble our way to the stage – which really does take quite some time, we weren't very near the front – I can't help noticing Katherin smiling down from her giant screens. In fact, she almost looks a little teary. God. I feel like a bit of a fraud. I mean, I have worked pretty much full-time on Katherin's book for the last few months, but I also complained about it a lot, and didn't actually pay her very much to begin with.

I'm onstage before I've really registered what's happening. Katherin kisses me on the cheek and hands me an enormous bouquet of lilies.

'Thought I'd forgotten you two, didn't you?' she whispers in my ear, with a cheeky smile. 'The fame's not gone quite that far to my head yet.'

The crowd is clapping, and the sound echoes down from the roof until I can't tell where it's coming from. I smile, hoping that sheer willpower will be sufficient adhesive for the top of my dress. The lights are so bright when you're up here – they're like starbursts on the insides of my eyes every time I blink, and everything is either very white and shiny or black and shadowy, like someone's messed with the contrast.

I think that's why I don't really notice the commotion until it reaches the front of the crowd, trembling its way through the throng, sending heads turning and people crying out as they stumble as though they've been pushed. Eventually a figure shoves its way through and vaults on to the stage.

I can't really see properly, eyes burned with all the lights, lily heads bobbing in front of me as I try to get a good hand-hold on the bouquet of flowers and wonder how I'm going to get down off the stage in these shoes without being able to use the handrail.

I recognise the voice, though. And once I've registered that, everything else drops away.

'Can I have the mic?' says Justin, because of course, implausibly, impossibly, the figure pushing his way through the crowd was his. 'I have something I want to say.'

Katherin's passed him the mic before she's even thought about it. She glances at me at the last moment, frowning, but it's already in Justin's hand. That's Justin: he asks, he gets.

He turns to face me.

'Tiffy Moore,' he says, 'look at me.'

He's right – I'm not looking at him. As though he is holding me on strings, my head snaps around and my eyes meet his. There he is. Square jaw, perfectly trimmed beard, strong shoulders beneath a tuxedo jacket. Eyes soft and trained on my face as if I'm the only girl in the room. You can't see a trace of the man I have been talking about in counselling, the one who hurt me. This man is a dream come true.

'Tiffy Moore,' he begins again. Everything feels wrong, as if I've stepped into my *Sliding Doors* alternative world, and suddenly all trace of my other life, the one where I didn't need or want Justin, is threatening to desert me. 'I have been lost without you.'

There's a pause. A lurching, sickening, echoing silence, like the long raw note in your ears when the music stops.

Then Justin drops down on one knee.

All at once I am aware of the crowd's reaction – they coo and *ahh* – and I can see the faces onstage around me, Rachel's twisted in shock,

Katherin's mouth open. I desperately want to run away, though I suspect that even if I could muster the strength, my legs would be too frozen to do everything required of them. It's as if the whole lot of us onstage are performing some sort of tableau.

'Please,' I begin. Why have I started by pleading? I try the sentence again, but he doesn't let me.

'You're the woman I am meant to be with,' he says. His voice is gentle but carries well with the microphone. 'I know that now. I can't believe I ever lost faith in us. You're everything I could possibly want and more.' He tilts his head, a gesture I used to find irresistible. 'I know I don't deserve you, I know you're far too good for me, but . . .'

Something twangs inside me as if it's pulled close to snapping. I remember how Gerty said Justin knows exactly how to play me, and there it is: the Justin who got me in the first place.

'Tiffany Moore,' he says, 'will you marry me?'

There's something about his eyes – it was always his eyes that got me. As the silence stretches taut it seems to tighten around my throat. The feeling that I am in two places at once, that I'm two people at once, is so acute it's almost like being half asleep and tugged between waking and dreaming. Here is Justin, begging for me. The Justin I always wanted. The Justin I had right at the start, who I went through countless rows and break-ups for, the one who I always believed was worth fighting for to get back.

I open my mouth and speak, but without the microphone my voice is lost behind the lilies. Even I can't hear my answer.

'She said yes!' Justin yells, standing up, stretching his arms out wide. 'She said yes!'

The crowd erupts. The noise is too much. The light sears stripes under my eyelids, and Justin is bundling me in, hugging me close, his mouth on my hair, and it doesn't even feel strange, it feels like it always used to – his firm body against mine, the warmth of him, all horribly, perfectly familiar.

60

Leon

Ms Constantine: Mrs Wilson, as our first expert witness, please could you begin by telling the judges what your expertise entails?

Mrs Wilson: I'm a CCTV analyst and enhancer. Have been for fifteen years. I work for the UK's leading CCTV forensics business – it was my team that pulled that enhanced footage together [gestures to screen].

Ms Constantine: Thank you very much, Mrs Wilson. And in your experience of examining CCTV footage, what can you tell us about these two short clips that we have seen today?

Mrs Wilson: Plenty. They're not the same bloke, to start with.

Ms Constantine: Really? You sound absolutely sure of that.

Mrs Wilson: Oh, sure as anything. For starters, look at the colour of the hoodie in the enhanced footage. Only one hoodie is black. You can tell by the shade that it comes out as, see? The black is a denser colour.

Ms Constantine: Can we have images from both up on screen, please? Thank you.

Mrs Wilson: And then look at how they walk! It's a fair imitation, all right, but the first bloke is clearly fu— is clearly drunk, My Lords. Look at how he's zigzagging. Almost walks into the display. Then the next guy walks much straighter and doesn't fumble or anything when he reaches for the knife. Our first bloke nearly dropped the beers!

Ms Constantine: And with the new CCTV footage from outside Aldi, we can see the distinctively . . . zigzagged walk more clearly.

Mrs Wilson: Oh, yeah.

Ms Constantine: And of the group that we see walking by a few moments after the first figure, who we have identified as Mr Twomey . . . would you be able to identify any of those figures as the man with the knife in the off-licence?

Mr Turner, to the judges: My Lords, this is nothing but speculation.

Judge Whaite: No, we'll allow it. Ms Constantine is calling on her witness's expertise.

Ms Constantine: Mrs Wilson, could any of those men have been the man in the off-licence, looking at this footage?

Mrs Wilson: Oh, yeah. Bloke on the far right. His hood is down, and he's not putting on the walk there, but look at how his shoulder drops with each step of his left foot. Look how he rubs his shoulder – the same gesture as the bloke in the off-licence makes before he pulls out the knife.

Mr Turner: We are here to examine an appeal against Mr Twomey's conviction. What is the relevance of implicating an unidentifiable bystander?

Judge Whaite: I see your point, Mr Turner. All right, Ms Constantine – do you have any further questions which are pertinent to the case at hand?

Ms Constantine: None, My Lord. I hope perhaps we can return to this discussion at a later date, should this case be reopened.

Prosecution lawyer, Mr Turner, scoffs into his hand. Gerty turns a freezing cold glare on him. I remember how Mr Turner intimidated Richie at the last trial. Called him a thug, a violent-minded criminal, a child who took whatever he wanted. I watch Mr Turner pale under

Gerty's gaze. To my delight, even robed and wigged, Mr Turner is not immune to the power of Gerty's dirty looks.

I meet Richie's eye, and, for the first time all day, crack a genuine smile.

Step outside in the break and switch on my phone. My heart's not exactly beating faster than usual, just beating . . . louder. Bigger. Everything feels exaggerated: when I buy a coffee, it tastes stronger; when the sky clears, the sun is stark and bright. Can't believe how well it's going in there. Gerty just doesn't stop – every single thing she says is so . . . *conclusive*. The judges keep nodding. The judge never nodded first-time around.

I've imagined this too many times, and now I'm living it. Feels as if I'm inside a daydream.

A few messages from Tiffy. I go to tap out a brief reply, palms sweaty, almost afraid writing it down and sending will jinx it. Wish I could call her. Instead I check Tasha Chai-Latte's Facebook page – Tiffy says she's filming the book launch. There's already a video on her page with thousands of views; looks like it's from the launch, judging by the vaulted ceiling in the holding image.

I watch, settling down on bench outside the court building, ignoring the gaggle of paparazzi waiting there for the chance of shooting someone they might get paid for.

It's Katherin's thank-you speech. I smile as she talks about Tiffy. From what Tiffy says, editors never get much credit, and designers even less – I can see Rachel beaming as she takes the stage with Tiffy.

Camera jolts. Someone pushing through to the front. As he jumps up on to the stage I realise who it is.

Sudden awful, guilt-inducing urge to leave courtroom and go to Islington. Sit forward, staring at the tiny video playing out on my screen.

Video cuts after she's said yes.

Surprising how truly terrible it feels. Perhaps you never know how you feel about someone until they agree to marry someone else.

61

Tiffy

Justin pulls me off the stage to the wings. I go with him, because more than anything else I want the noise and the lights and the crowd to go away, but as soon as we're through the curtain I yank my hand from his grasp. My wrist sings out in pain; he was holding on tightly. We're in a narrow, black-walled space to the side of the stage, which is empty aside from a black-clad man with a walkie-talkie and lots of cables around his feet.

'Tiffy?' Justin says. The vulnerability in his voice is completely contrived, I can tell.

'What the fuck do you . . .' I begin. I'm shaking all over; it's hard to stand, especially in these high heels. 'What was that?'

'What was what?' He reaches for me again.

Rachel bursts through the curtain behind us, kicking off her shoes. 'Tiff— Tiffy!'

I twist towards her as she runs into me, letting her hold me tightly. Justin looks down at us both, eyes narrowed a little – I can see he's calculating something behind those eyes, so I turn my head into the thick mass of Rachel's braids and try very, very hard not to cry.

'Tiffy?' calls someone else. It's Mo. I can't work out where he is.

'Your friends are here to congratulate you,' Justin says benevolently, but his shoulders are stiff and tensed.

'Mo?' I call. He appears from behind Justin, through the curtains that separate us from the main backstage area; his jacket is gone and his hair is mussed as though he's been running.

In a moment, he's at my side. Behind me I can hear Katherin valiantly trying to bring the subject back to *Crochet Your Way* onstage.

Justin watches the three of us. Rachel still has hold of me, and I lean into her as I look up at Justin.

'You know I didn't say yes,' I say flatly.

His eyes widen. 'What do you mean?' he says.

I shake my head. I know what this is – I remember this feeling, the nagging sense of wrongness. 'You can't make me believe something that I know isn't true.'

There's a flicker behind his eyes – maybe he's thinking, *I already have, plenty of times.*

'Not any more,' I say. 'And do you know what it's called, when you do that? It's called gaslighting. It's a form of abuse. Telling me things aren't the way I can see them.'

This knocks him. I'm not sure Rachel or Mo will notice it, but I watch him take the hit. The Tiffy he is familiar with would never have used words like 'gaslighting' and 'abuse'. Seeing him waver sends a rush of fearful excitement through me, like the feeling when you stand close to the edge as the train rushes by.

'You did say yes,' he says. The light from the stage creeps between the curtains behind us, leaving a long stripe of yellow across the shadowy lines of Justin's face. 'I heard you! And . . . you *do* want to marry me, don't you, Tiffy? We belong together.'

He tries to reach for my hand. The whole thing is so obviously a performance. I pull back and, quick as a flash, Rachel reaches out and slaps his outstretched hand away from me.

He doesn't physically react. When he speaks, his voice is light and wounded. 'What was that for?'

'You don't touch her,' Rachel spits at him.

'I think you should leave, Justin,' Mo says.

'What is this all about, Tiffy?' Justin asks me, voice still gentle. 'Are your friends upset with me because we were broken up?' He keeps trying to move closer, just in inches, but Rachel has hold of me tight, and, with Mo at my other shoulder, we're a unit.

'Can I ask you something?' I say suddenly.

'Of course,' Justin says.

The sound guy in black glances at us in irritation. 'You're not meant to stay back here,' he tells us, as the crowd outside bursts into noisy applause.

I ignore him, my eyes on Justin. 'How did you know I'd be here today?'

'What do you mean? This event was advertised all over the place, Tiffy. I could hardly use the Internet and miss it.'

'But how did you know *I* would be here? How did you even know I was working on this book?'

I know I'm right. I can see it in the shiftiness in his eyes. He eases a finger under his collar.

'And how did you know I would be at that book launch in Shoreditch? And how did you know I'd be on that cruise ship?'

He's unsettled; he scoffs, giving me the first unpleasant, disparaging look of the evening. That's more like it – that's the Justin I've begun to remember.

For a moment he's caught in indecision, and then he opts for an easy smile. 'Your mate Martin has been giving me tip-offs,' he says sheepishly, like a naughty boy caught pinching things. Sweet, mischievous, harmless. 'He knew how much I care about you, so he's been helping to get us back together.'

'You're joking,' Rachel blurts. I glance at her; her eyes are flashing and she looks more terrifying than I have ever seen her looking before, which is really saying something.

'How do you even know Martin?' I ask in disbelief.

'Quiet!' the sound guy hisses. We all ignore him.

'We met at your work night out, remember?' Justin says. 'Is this important? Can't we go somewhere quieter, just the two of us, Tiffy?'

I don't remember the work night out. I missed most of them because Justin never liked going, and didn't like me going to them without him.

'I don't want to go anywhere with you, Justin,' I say, taking a deep, shaky breath. 'And I don't want to marry you. I want you to leave me alone.'

I have imagined saying this lots and lots of times. I always thought he'd look wounded, perhaps step back in shock, or raise a hand to his mouth. I imagined him crying and trying to pull me closer; I'd even been afraid he might try to get hold of me physically, and not let go.

But he just looks perplexed. Irritated. Maybe a little pissed off, as if he's been terribly misled somehow, and it's all been rather unfair.

'You don't mean that,' he begins.

'Oh, she does,' says Mo. His voice is pleasant, but very firm.

'She really, really does,' Rachel adds.

'No,' Justin says, shaking his head. 'You're not giving us a chance.'

'A chance?' I almost laugh. 'I went back to you over and over. You've had more chances than I can count. I don't want to see you. Ever again.'

He frowns. 'You said in that bar in Shoreditch that we could talk in a couple of months. I stuck to your rules,' he says, stretching his arms out. 'It's October, isn't it?'

'A lot can change in a couple of months. I've been doing a lot of thinking. A lot of . . . remembering.'

There it is again – a flicker of almost fear behind his eyes. He reaches for me one last time, and this time Rachel slaps him across the face.

'Couldn't have put it better myself,' Mo mutters, and he pulls the two of us further back into the mess of cables and darkness as Justin stumbles backwards, eyes wide with shock.

'You. Out,' the irate sound guy says firmly to Justin, clearly identifying him as the root cause of all the noise. He steps forward, forcing Justin further back.

Steadying himself, Justin holds out a warning hand to the sound guy. He glances over his shoulder to find the exit, and then turns back to find my gaze.

For a moment I lose the sense of Mo and Rachel beside me and the sound guy in here with us. It's just me and Justin's broad, tuxedo-ed body in this cramped, dark space, and I feel desperate, as if I'm running out of air. It's only a second or two, but it's somehow worse than everything that's just happened put together.

Then Justin backs out between the curtains into the backstage area, with a rush of noise, and I melt shakily into Rachel and Mo. He's gone. It's over. But he's left that desperate breathlessness behind him, and as I grasp at Rachel and Mo's arms with clammy fingers I feel a sudden, sickening fear that I won't ever be able to shake him, no matter how many times I see him walk away.

62

Leon

Can't think. Can't anything. Somehow find my feet and get back to the courtroom, but the daydream feeling has morphed into an aura of unreality around everything. Mechanically, I smile at Richie. Notice how bright his eyes are, how hopeful he looks. Fail to feel anything.

It's probably the shock. I'll recover shortly and get my head back into the hearing. I can't believe anything has managed to distract me from this. Feel suddenly furious with Tiffy, choosing today of all days to dump me and go back to Justin, and can't help but think of Mam, how she'd always go back to those men no matter what Richie and I said.

Some part of my brain reminds me Mam didn't *want* to be with those men. She just didn't think she was allowed to be anywhere else. She didn't think she meant anything if she was on her own.

But Tiffy wasn't on her own. She had Mo, Gerty, Rachel. Me.

Richie. Think of Richie. Richie needs me here, and there's no fucking way I'm losing him again. Too.

Gerty is summing up. Just about manage to listen – she's so good you can't help but follow her argument. Then, with peculiar lack of fanfare, it's over. We all stand. Judges leave. Richie is taken back to wherever it was he was brought from, with a wistful backwards glance. We walk through the court building in silence, Gerty tapping away at her phone, Mam cracking her knuckles incessantly.

Mam looks sideways at me as we reach the entranceway.

Mam: Lee? What's wrong?

Then Gerty gives a little gasp. Hand to mouth. Glance over, dull-eyed, and notice that she is watching the video play out on Facebook.

Gerty: Oh my God.

Mam, on alert: What's happened?

Me: Tiffy.

Mam: Your girlfriend? What's she done?

Gerty: She *wouldn't*.

Me: She would. You know people do. Go back. It's hard to leave what you've known. Not her fault. But you know people do.

Gerty's silence says enough. Suddenly more than anything I need to get away from here.

Me: We won't get a verdict over the weekend, will we?

Gerty: No, it'll be next week. I'll call when—

Me: Thanks.

And I'm gone.

Walk and walk. Can't cry, am just dry-throated and aching-eyed. I'm sure that some of this is fear about Richie, but all I can think about is Justin, arms out, yelling 'She said yes' to the whooping crowd.

Play out every scene. The endless notes, Brighton, the night eating tiffin together on the sofa, the trip to Holly's party, kissing against the Aga. My gut twists at the memory of how her body would go cold when she thought of him, but then I harden myself. Don't want to feel sorry for her. For now, just want to feel betrayed.

Can't help it, though. Can't stop thinking of the way her knees would shake.

Ah, there we go. There's the tears. Knew they'd turn up eventually.

63

Tiffy

The smell of lilies is suffocating. Mo's holding the bouquet beside me as we huddle there in the darkness, the blooms pressing close to my dress, staining the fabric with pollen. As I look down at the marks on the silk I notice I'm shaking so much the full skirt of my dress is quivering.

I don't remember exactly what Justin said as he left. In fact, I already feel like I don't remember a lot of the conversation that just happened. Perhaps it was all a surreal daydream, and I'm actually still standing out there in the crowd, wondering if Katherin will mention me in her thank-you speech, and whether those little roll things on that canapé tray are duck or chicken.

'What . . . what if he's still right there?' I whisper to Rachel, pointing towards the black curtains Justin left through.

'Mo, hold this,' Rachel says. I think 'this' is referring to me. She disappears through to the backstage area, while onstage Katherin says goodbye to the audience to resounding applause.

Mo dutifully holds my elbow. 'You're OK,' he whispers. He doesn't say anything else, he just does one of those hug-like sort of silences that I love so much. In the world on the other side of these dark curtains the crowd is still clapping; muffled, here, the sound is like heavy rain on tarmac.

'You really can't be back here,' the sound guy insists in exasperation as Rachel re-enters. He takes a step backwards when she turns to look at him. I don't blame him. Rachel has her battle face on, and she looks bloody terrifying.

Rachel sweeps past him without answering, lifting her skirts to step over the cables. 'No crazy ex in sight,' she tells me, returning to my side.

Katherin bundles in suddenly from the stage; she almost walks into Mo.

'Gosh,' she says, 'that was all rather dramatic, wasn't it?' She pats me in a motherly sort of way. 'Are you all right? I'm assuming that fellow was . . .'

'Tiffy's stalker ex-boyfriend,' Rachel supplies. 'And speaking of stalking – I think we need to have a few words with Martin . . .'

'Not now,' I beg, grabbing hold of Rachel's arm. 'Just stay with me for a minute, all right?'

Her face softens. 'Fine. Permission to hang him by the testicles at some later time?'

'Granted. Also, eww.'

'I can't *believe* he's been telling that . . . that *scumbag* where you are all the time. You should press charges, Tiffy.'

'You should certainly file for a restraining order,' Mo says quietly.

'Against Martin? Might make work awkward,' I say weakly.

Mo just looks at me. 'You know who I meant.'

'Can we leave this . . . dark . . . curtain-room now?' I ask.

'Good idea,' says Katherin. Discreetly, out of Rachel's sight, the sound guy nods and rolls his eyes. 'I'd better go and mingle, but why don't you lot take my limo?'

'I beg your pardon?' Rachel says, staring at her.

Katherin looks sheepish. 'It wasn't *my* idea. The Butterfingers PR team got it for me. It's just sitting outside. You can take it, I can't be seen dead getting driven around in one of those, they'd never let me back into the Old Socialists' Club.'

'Thanks,' Mo says, and I briefly surface from the fog of panic to marvel at the thought that the head of PR voluntarily shelled out for a limousine. She is infamously tight on budget.

'So now we just need to get out. Through the crowd,' Rachel says, her mouth set in a grim line.

'First, though, you need to call the police and report Justin for harassment,' Mo tells me. 'And you need to tell them everything. All the other times, the flowers, Martin . . .'

I let out a half groan, half whimper. Mo rubs my back.

'Tiffy, do it,' Rachel says, handing me her phone.

I move through the throng as though I'm somebody else. People keep patting me on the back and smiling and calling to me. At first I try to tell everyone in turn – 'I didn't say yes, I'm not getting married, he's not my boyfriend' – but either they can't or they don't want to hear me, so as we get closer to the door I stop trying.

Katherin's limo is parked around the corner. It's not just a limo – it's a *stretch* limo. This is ridiculous. The head of PR must be about to ask Katherin to do something very important for very little money.

'Hi, excuse me?' Rachel says to the limo driver through the window, in her best sweet-talking-the-barman voice. 'Katherin said we can have this limo.'

A lengthy conversation ensues. As probably should be the case, the limo driver is not about to just take our word for it that Katherin has let us take the car. After a brief phone call to Katherin herself, and the return of Rachel's battle face, we're in – thank God. I'm shivering like crazy, even with Mo's jacket over my shoulders.

Inside is even more ridiculous than outside. There are long sofas, a small bar, two television screens, and a sound system.

'Fucking hell,' Rachel says. 'This is absurd. You'd think they could pay me more than minimum wage, wouldn't you?'

We sit in silence for a while as the driver pulls away.

'Well,' Rachel goes on, 'I think we can all agree today has taken an unexpected turn.'

For some reason that tips me over the edge. I cry into my hands, leaning my head back on to the plush grey upholstery and letting the sobs rack my body like I'm a little kid. Mo gives my arm a compassionate squeeze.

There's a buzzing noise.

'Everyone all right back there?' calls the driver. 'Sounds like someone's having an asthma attack!'

'Everything's fine!' Rachel calls, as I wail and wheeze, struggling to breathe through the tears. 'My friend has just been cornered by her crazy ex-boyfriend in front of a crowd of a thousand people and manipulated into looking like she would marry him, and now she is having a perfectly natural reaction.'

There's a pause. 'Crikey,' says the driver. 'Tissues are under the bar.'

When I get home I call Leon, but he doesn't pick up. Beneath all the roaring blinding craziness of the day, I'm desperate to know more than he gave me in the last text: *Things going well at court.* How well? Is it over? When will Richie get a verdict?

I so badly want to speak to him. Specifically, I want to cuddle up against his shoulder and breathe in his gorgeous Leon smell and let him stroke the small of my back the way he does and *then* speak to him.

I can't believe this. I can't believe Justin. The fact that he put me in that position, in front of all those people . . . What did he think, that I'd just go along with it because it was what he wanted me to do?

Maybe I would have once, actually. God, that's sickening.

The fact that he reached out to Martin to keep track of me takes the whole thing to a new level of disturbing – all those strange meetings that he made me feel crazy for thinking were anything other than coincidental. All carefully planned and calculated. But what was the *point*? If he wanted me, he had me. I was his – I would have done anything for him. Why did he push me so far, then keep trying to get me to come back? It's just . . . so bizarre. So unnecessarily painful.

Rachel couldn't come back to my flat with us – she's babysitting her niece tonight, going from looking after one crying snotty mess to another – but Mo has promised me he'll stay with me, which is so lovely of him. I feel a bit guilty, because the truth is, right now it's Leon I want.

It almost surprises me how clear that thought is. I want Leon. I need him here with me, nervously fidgeting and lopsidedly smiling and effortlessly making everything feel brighter. After the madness of today, it strikes me with new force that if *nice-scary* is sometimes *scary-scary* as I learn to do this whole relationship thing again, so bloody what? If I give in to that fear, if I let it hold me back with Leon, then Justin really does win.

And Leon is so worth a bit of fear. He's so worth it. I reach for my phone and call him again.

64

Leon

Three missed calls from Tiffy.

Can't talk to her. Don't want to hear her explain herself. I'm still walking, God knows where – maybe around in circles. I do seem to be seeing a lot of very similar Starbucks. It's all poky and Dickensian, this part of London. Cobbles and pollution-stained brick, tiny narrow strips of sky overhead between grimy windows. You don't have to walk far to end up in the shiny, pale blue world of the City, though. Turn a corner and find I'm face to face with myself, mirrored in the glass headquarters of some accountancy firm.

I look terrible. Exhausted and crumpled in this suit – suits have never looked good on me. I should have tried harder to smarten up; might have reflected badly on Richie. Already got Mam to contend with, whose idea of smart is slightly higher heeled knee-high boots.

I pause, surprised by the viciousness of that thought. Cruel and judgemental. I don't like that my head could come up with it. I've come a long way to forgiving Mam – or I thought I had. But right now the very thought of her makes me angry.

I'm just an angry man today. Angry that I would settle for being happy just to have judges listening to my brother's case, when he should never have been led in there by a prison officer in the first place. Angry that I was caught up worrying about showing Tiffy how

I feel, and didn't do it in time, and got outdone by a man who gives her nightmares, but certainly knows his way around a big romantic gesture. Nobody doubts how *Justin* feels now. No danger of that.

I'd really thought she wouldn't go back to him. But then, you always think that, and they always do.

Look down at my phone: Tiffy's name on my screen. She's texted me. I can't bear to open it, but can't handle the temptation, so I turn my phone off.

I think about going home, but home is full of Tiffy's belongings. The smell of her, the clothes I've seen her in, the negative space around her. And eventually she'll come back from the launch – the flat's hers for tonight and the weekend. So that's out. Can sleep at Mam's, obviously, but oddly seem to be just as furious with her as with Tiffy. Besides, can't stand the thought of sleeping in mine and Richie's old room tonight. Can't be where Tiffy is, can't be where Richie isn't.

I have nowhere to go. Nowhere's home. Just keep walking.

This flatshare. I wish I'd never done it. Wish I'd never opened my life up like that and let someone else walk in and fill it up. I was doing fine – safe, managing. Now my flat's not mine, it's *ours*, and when she's gone all I will see is the absence of tiffin and books about bricklayers and that bloody stupid paisley beanbag. It'll be another room full of what's missing. Just what I didn't want.

Maybe I can still save her from a life with him. Yes to a proposal doesn't mean they'll definitely get married, and she could hardly say no, could she, with all those people staring. I feel a dangerous surge of hope, and do my best to quash it. Remind myself that there is no saving of people – people can only save themselves. The best you can do is help when they're ready.

Should eat. Can't remember when I last did. The night before? Already seems like for ever ago. Now that I've realised I'm hungry, my stomach growls.

Swing into Starbucks. Walk past two girls watching Tasha Chai-Latte video of Justin proposing to Tiffy. Drink tea with lots of milk in, eat some sort of overpriced toastie with lots of butter in it, and stare at the wall.

I realise, when barista clearing the table gives me curious, pitying look, that I am crying again. Can't seem to stop, so I don't make myself. Eventually, though, people are noticing, and I want to be moving again, alone.

More walking. These smart shoes are rubbing raw at the skin of my heel. Think longingly of the worn-in shoes I wear at work, the easy way they fit, and within fifteen minutes or so it's clear I'm not just walking now, I'm walking somewhere. There's always room for another nurse in the hospice.

65

Tiffy

Gerty's calling. I pick up, hardly thinking about it – it's reflex.

'Hello?' My voice sounds strangely flat, even to me.

'What the fuck is wrong with you, Tiffany? What the fuck is wrong with you?'

The shock makes me cry again.

'Give me that,' Mo says. I look up at him as he takes the phone off me, and breathe in sharply when I see his expression. He looks really angry. Mo never looks angry. 'What the hell do you think you're doing?' he says into the phone. 'Oh yeah? You watched a video, did you? And it didn't occur to you to ask Tiffy what happened? To give your best friend the benefit of the doubt before you scream down the phone at her?'

My eyes widen. A video? Shit. What video?

And then it dawns on me. Tasha Chai-Latte, filming the whole thing. Martin organised that, presumably, which means Justin would have known about it. No wonder he was so keen to make sure everyone caught my 'reply' to his big question – he needed it for the camera.

Martin also saw me and Leon together in the castle in Wales, right after Justin had had his suspicions raised when he'd dropped around to my flat and found Leon in his towel.

'Mo,' I say urgently. 'Ask Gerty where Leon is.'

*

'Call him again.'

'Tiff, his phone is still off,' Mo says gently.

'Again!' I say, pacing back and forth from the sofa to the kitchen. My heart is beating so hard it feels as if there's something trying to work its way out between my ribs. I can't bear the thought of Leon seeing that video and thinking that I'm engaged to Justin. I can't bear it.

'His phone is still off,' Mo says, my mobile to his ear.

'Try calling from yours. Maybe he's screening my calls. He probably hates me.'

'He won't hate you,' Mo says.

'Gerty did.'

Mo narrows his eyes. 'Gerty has a tendency to be judgemental. She's working on it.'

'Well, Leon doesn't know me well enough to know I'd never do this to him,' I say, twisting my hands together. 'He knows I was really hung up on Justin, he probably just thinks— oh, God.' I'm choking up.

'Whatever he thinks, it's fixable,' Mo assures me. 'We just need to wait until he's ready to talk. He's had a tough day too, going to court with Richie.'

'I know!' I snap at Mo. 'I *know*! You think I don't know how important today was for him?'

Mo doesn't say anything. I wipe my face.

'I'm sorry. I shouldn't snap at you. You've been so great. I'm just angry with myself.'

'Why?' Mo asks.

'Because . . . I bloody well dated him, didn't I?'

'Justin?'

'I'm not saying what happened today was my fault, I know it doesn't work that way, but I can't help but think – if he'd not got to me, if I'd been stronger . . . we'd never have ended up here. I mean, bloody hell. None of your ex-girlfriends try to make you marry them and then use that to break up your current relationship, do they? Not that you have a current relationship, but you know what I mean.'

'Umm,' Mo says.

I look up at him, wiping my eyes again. I'm doing the kind of crying that means your eyes never really get dry, they're just leaking non-stop.

'Don't tell me. You and Gerty.'

'You guessed?' Mo says, looking uncomfortable.

'Rachel did. Her radar is much better than Gerty's, though don't tell – actually, do tell her, who cares about hurting Gerty's feelings?' I say savagely.

'She's calling now,' Mo says, holding out my phone to me.

'I don't want to speak to her.'

'Shall I answer?'

'Do what you like. She's your girlfriend.'

Mo gives me a long look as I sit down on the sofa again with shaking legs. I'm being childish, obviously, but Mo getting together with Gerty at this particular moment feels like he's siding with her. I want Mo on my side. I want to scream at Gerty. She had the chance to tell Leon I would never do something like that to him, that he should check in with me before believing anything, and she didn't.

'She can't find Leon,' Mo tells me after a moment. 'She really wants to speak to you, Tiffy. She wants to apologise.'

I shake my head. I'm not ready to be done feeling angry just because she wants to apologise.

'She's argued for a legal call with Richie when he gets to the prison,' Mo says, after a pause to listen. I can hear Gerty's voice on the other end of the phone, tinny and panicked. 'She says she'll tell him what really happened, so he can use his phone call to try Leon on his mobile – you can call any number on your first-night call. He probably won't be in and processed until late, maybe even tomorrow morning, but it's still our best hope of getting the message out to Leon if he doesn't come home.'

'Tomorrow *morning*?' It's only late afternoon.

Mo looks pained. 'I think it's our best option for now.'

It's ridiculous, really, that a man in prison with only one phone call is a best option for getting hold of someone.

'Leon's phone is off,' I say dully. 'He won't answer.'

'He'll see sense and turn it back on, Tiffy,' Mo says, phone still at his ear. 'He won't want to miss a call from Richie.'

I sit out on the balcony, curled under two blankets. One of them is the Brixton throw that usually lives across our bed – the one Leon tucked me up under that night Justin came round to the flat and threatened him.

I know Leon thinks I've gone back to Justin. I've gone through desperate panic, and now I'm thinking that he should have more fucking faith in me.

Not that I've earned it, I suppose. I *did* go back to Justin, lots of times – I've told Leon that. But . . . I would never have started seeing Leon if I didn't feel this time was different – if I wasn't really ready to leave that part of my life behind me. I was trying so hard. All that time dredging up the worst memories, the endless conversations with Mo, the counselling. I was *trying*. But I guess Leon thought I was just too broken to fix myself.

Gerty rings me every ten minutes or so; I still haven't picked up. Gerty has known me for eight years. If I'm angry with Leon for not having faith in me, and he's known me for less than a year, I am at least eight times angrier with Gerty.

I pick at the sad, yellowing leaves on our one balcony pot plant and very pointedly do not think about the fact that Justin knows where I live. Somehow. Probably Martin – my address is pretty easy to get if you have access to my desk and the payslips that HR drop around.

Fucking hell. I knew I didn't like that man for a reason.

I look down at my phone as it vibrates around and around on our little, rickety outdoor table. The table's surface is covered in bird poo and that thick, sticky dust-grime that covers everything left outdoors for any length of time in London. Gerty's name lights up my phone screen, and with a flash of anger I pick up this time.

'What?' I say.

'I am awful,' Gerty says, talking very fast. 'I can't believe myself. I should never have assumed that you would go back to Justin. I am so, so sorry.'

I pause, taken aback. Gerty and I have fought plenty of times, but she's never said sorry right away like that, unprompted.

'I should have believed you could do it. I *do* believe you can.'

'Do what?' I ask, before I can think of a better, angrier response.

'Get away from Justin.'

'Oh. That.'

'Tiffy, are you all right?' Gerty says.

'Well. Not really,' I say, feeling my bottom lip quivering. I bite down on it hard. 'I don't suppose . . .'

'Richie's not called yet. You know what these things are like, Tiffy, it could be midnight before they even move him from the holding cell to Wandsworth. And the prison's pretty shambolic so I don't want to get your hopes up that they'll even give him his phone call, let alone the legal call I made them promise me. But if I speak to him I'll tell him everything. I'll ask him to speak to Leon.'

I check the time on the screen: it's 8 p.m. now, and I cannot believe how nightmarishly slowly time is passing.

'I am really, really angry with you,' I tell Gerty, because I know I don't sound it. I just sound sad, and tired, and like I want my best friend.

'Absolutely. Me too. Furious. I'm the worst. And Mo isn't talking to me either, if that helps.'

'That doesn't help,' I say reluctantly. 'I don't want you to be a pariah.'

'A what? Is that some kind of dessert?'

'Pariah. Persona non-grata. Outcast.'

'Oh, don't worry, I'm resigned to a life of disgrace. It's all I deserve.'

We sit in companionable silence for a while. I reach around inside to find that enormous pool of Gerty-fuelled rage again, but it seems to have evaporated.

'I really hate Justin,' I say miserably. 'You know I think he did this mostly to break up me and Leon? I don't think he would actually even marry me. He would just leave me again, once he was sure he'd got me back.'

'The man needs castrating,' Gerty says firmly. 'He's done you nothing but harm. I have actively wished him dead on several occasions.'

'Gerty!'

'You didn't have to sit back and watch it happening,' she says. 'Watch him cleaning all the Tiffany-ness out of you. It was sick.'

I fiddle with the Brixton blanket.

'All this mess has made me realise . . . I really like Leon, Gerty. *Really* like him.' I sniff, wiping my eyes. 'I wish he had at least asked me whether I actually said yes. And . . . and . . . even if I *had* . . . I wish that he hadn't just given up.'

'It's been half a day. He's in shock, and drained after the session in court. He's built this day up in his head for months. Justin, as ever, has impeccably dreadful timing. Give it a little time and I hope you'll find Leon un-gives up again.'

I shake my head. 'I don't know. I don't think so.'

'Have faith, Tiffy. After all, isn't that what you're asking from him?'

66

Leon

Move between wards like I'm haunting the place. Should I be able to focus enough to take blood from a vein when even breathing feels like an effort? It's easy, though – blissfully routine. Here's something I can do. Leon, Charge Nurse, quiet but reliable.

Notice after a few hours that I'm circling Coral Ward. Dodging it. Mr Prior's there, dying.

Eventually the junior doctor on shift says a morphine dose on Coral Ward needs countersigning. So. No more hiding. Off I go. White-grey corridors, bare and scratched, and I know every inch of them, maybe better than the walls of my own flat.

Pause. There's a man in a brown suit outside the ward, forearms on knees, staring at the floor. Odd to see someone here at this time of the morning – no visitors on the night shift. He's very old, white-haired. Familiar.

I know that posture: that's the posture of a man Mustering Courage. I've struck that pose enough times outside prison visiting halls to know how it looks.

Takes a little while for it to click – I'm barely thinking, just moving on autopilot. But that white-haired man staring at the floor is Johnny White the Sixth, from Brighton. The thought seems ridiculous. JW the Sixth is a man from my other life. The one full of Tiffy. But here he is, so. Looks like I found Mr Prior's Johnny after all, even if it took him a little while to admit it.

Should feel pleased, but can't.

Look at him. Aged ninety-two, he's tracked Mr Prior down, put his best suit on, travelled all the way up from the coast. All for a man he loved a lifetime ago. He sits there, head bowed like a man in prayer, waiting for the strength to face what he left behind.

Mr Prior has days to live. Hours, possibly. I look at Johnny White and feel it like a punch in the gut. He left it so. Fucking. Late.

Johnny White looks up, sees me. We don't speak. The silence stretches down the corridor between us.

Johnny White: Is he dead?

His voice comes out husky, breaking halfway.

Me: No. You're not too late.

Except he is, really. How much did it hurt to come all this way knowing it was just to say goodbye?

Johnny White: It took me a while to find him. After you visited.

Me: You should have said something.

Johnny White: Yes.

He looks back at the floor. I step forward, bridge the silence, take the seat beside him. We examine the scratched lino side by side. This isn't about me. This isn't my story. But . . . Johnny White on that plastic seat, head bowed, that's what the other side of not-trying looks like.

Johnny White: I don't want to go in there. I was thinking about leaving, when I saw you.

Me: You've made it to here. There's just the doors, now.

He lifts his head as though it's something heavy.

Johnny White: Are you sure he'll want to see me?

Me: He may not be conscious, Mr White. But even so, I have no doubt he'll be happier with you there.

Johnny White stands, brushes down his suit trousers, squares his Hollywood chiselled jaw.

Johnny White: Well. Better late than never.

He doesn't look at me, he just pushes his way through the double doors. I watch them swing behind him.

Left to my own devices, I'm the sort of man who'd never walk through those doors. And where's that ever got anybody?

I get up. Time to move.

Me, to junior doctor: On-call nurse will countersign on the morphine. I'm not on shift.

Junior doctor: I did wonder why you weren't in scrubs. What the hell are you doing here when you're not on the rota? Go home!

Me: Yes. Good idea.

It's two in the morning; London is still and muffled in darkness. Turn on my phone as I jog for the bus, heartbeat thumping high in my throat.

Endless missed calls and messages. I stare at them, startled. Don't know where to start. Don't have to, though, because the phone buzzes into life with an unknown London number almost as soon as I've turned it on.

Me: Hello?

My voice is wobbly.

Richie: Oh, thank fuck for that. The guard is getting really tetchy. I've been ringing you for the past ten minutes. I had to give a long explanation of how this was still my one phone call, because you weren't picking up. We've got about five minutes' credit, by the way.

Me: Are you all right?

Richie: Am *I* all right? I'm fine, you big bellend, other than being mightily pissed off with you – and Gerty.

Me: What?

Richie: Tiffy. She didn't say yes. That mad Justin bloke just answered for her, didn't you notice?

Stop stock still ten yards from bus stop. I . . . can't absorb it. Blink. Swallow. Feel a bit sick.

Richie: Yeah. Gerty rang her and started laying in to her for going back to Justin, then Mo went mental at her. Told her she was a terrible friend for not having enough faith in Tiffy to at least ask the question before assuming she'd gone back to him.

I find my voice.

Me: Is Tiffy all right?

Richie: She'd be a lot better if she could speak to you, man.

Me: I was already on my way, but—

Richie: You were?

Me: Yes. Had a visit from the Ghost of Christmas Future.

Richie, confused: Bit early in the year for that sort of thing, isn't it?

Me: Well. You know what they say. Gets earlier every year.

Lean against the bus shelter. Giddy and sick all at once. What was I *doing*? Coming here, wasting all that time?

Me, belatedly, and with a rush of fear: Is Tiffy safe?

Richie: Justin's still on the loose, if that's what you mean. But her mate Mo is with her, and according to Gerty he reckons Justin won't come back for a while – he'll go nurse his wounds and come up with another plan. He tends to have a plan for everything – that's part of his whole deal, Mo says. You know the prick was using Martin from Tiffy's work to find out information about where Tiffy would be the whole time?

Me: Martin. And . . . oh. Fuck.

Richie: This was all about breaking the two of you up, man. Getting that YouTuber to film it all so you'd see it for sure.

Me: I can't . . . can't believe I just assumed.

Richie: Hey, bro, just go fix it, OK? And tell her about Mam.

Me: Tell her what about Mam?

Richie: I don't need to be a therapist to figure out that you leaving Mam at court with Gerty and not going back to her place had something to do with all this. Look, I get it, man – we both have mummy issues.

Bus approaching.

Me: Not . . . entirely sure how this is relevant?

Richie: Just because Mam always went back to the men who treated her like shit, or found another version of the same guy, that doesn't mean Tiffy's the same.

Me, automatically: It wasn't Mam's fault. She was abused. Manipulated.

Richie: Yeah, yeah, I know, you're always saying that. But it doesn't make it any easier when you're twelve, does it?

Me: You think . . .

Richie: Look, I have to go. But just go tell Tiffy you're sorry, and you fucked up, and you were raised by an abused single mother and basically had to look after your younger brother single-handed. That ought to do it.

Me: That's a bit . . . emotional blackmaily, no? Also, will she enjoy the comparison with my mother?

Richie: Point taken. Fine. You do you. Just sort it, and get her back, because that woman is the best thing that's ever happened to you. All right?

67

Tiffy

We completely forgot about eating, and now it's 2.30 a.m. and I've just remembered to be hungry. Mo has gone out to get takeaway. He's left me on the balcony with a large glass of red wine and an even larger bowl of munchies from the cupboard, which I'm pretty sure were Leon's, but who cares – if he thinks I'd go off and marry someone else, he might as well think I'm a snack thief too.

I'm not sure who I'm angry with any more. I've sat here for so long my legs have cramped up, and I've been through pretty much all the available emotions in that time, and now they're all muddled together in a big ugly soup of misery. The only thing I can think of with any certainty is that I *wish* I had never met Justin.

My phone buzzes.

Leon calling.

I've waited all night to see those words. My stomach drops. Has he spoken to Richie?

'Hello?'

'Hey.' His voice sounds ragged and strangely unfamiliar. It's like the energy has gone out of him.

I wait for him to say something else, staring out at the traffic sliding by below, letting the headlights draw yellow-white streaks on the insides of my eyes.

'I am holding an enormous bunch of flowers,' he says.

I don't say anything.

'I felt like I needed a physical symbol of the enormity of my apology,' Leon goes on. 'But I've realised Justin also left you an enormous bunch of flowers – actually, much nicer, more expensive flowers – so now I'm thinking, flowers, not so good. Then I thought, I'd just come home and tell you in person. But then I realised once I got here that I left my key to the flat at Mam's place because I'm supposed to be staying there tonight. So I'd have to knock on the door, which I thought would probably scare you, since you have an unhinged ex-boyfriend to contend with.'

I watch car after car drive by. That might be the longest I've ever heard Leon speak in one go.

'So where are you now?' I ask eventually.

'Look up. Opposite pavement, by the bakery.'

I see him now. He's silhouetted against the bright yellow light of the bakery's sign, the phone to his ear, his other arm cradling a bouquet of flowers. He's wearing a suit – of course, he won't have changed since court.

'I'm guessing you're feeling very hurt,' he says. His voice is gentle, and it makes me melt.

I'm crying again.

'I am so sorry, Tiffy. I should never have assumed. You needed me today, and I wasn't there for you.'

'I *did* need you,' I sob. 'Mo and Gerty and Rachel are all great and I love them and they have helped so much, but I wanted *you*. You made me feel like it didn't matter that Justin happened. That you cared about me anyway.'

'I do. And it doesn't.' He's crossing the road now, coming over to this side of the pavement. I can make out his face, the smooth, sharp lines of his cheekbones, the soft curve of his lips. He's looking up at me. 'Everyone kept telling me I was going to lose you if I didn't tell you how I feel, and then in comes Justin, king of the romantic gesture . . .'

'Romantic?' I splutter. 'Romantic? And I don't bloody want romantic gestures anyway! Why would I want that? I've had that, and it was shit!'

'I know,' Leon says. 'You're right. I should have known.'

'And I liked that you weren't pushing things – the idea of committing to a serious relationship scares the hell out of me! I mean, look at how hard it was to get *out* of the last one!'

'Oh,' says Leon. 'Yes. That's . . . yes, I see.' He mutters something that sounds like it might be *bloody Richie*.

'I can hear you without the phone now, you know,' I say, raising my voice enough for it to carry over the traffic noise. 'Plus I'm quite enjoying the excuse to shout.'

He hangs up and backs away a little. 'Let's shout, then!' he calls.

I narrow my eyes, and then I pull off all my blankets, put down my wine and munchies, and move to the railings.

'Whoa,' Leon says, voice dropping so I can only just catch the words. 'You look incredible.'

I look down at myself, a little surprised to find I'm still wearing the off-the-shoulder dress from the party. God knows what my hair looks like, and my make-up is definitely at least two inches further down my face than it was this morning, but the dress *is* pretty spectacular.

'Don't be nice!' I shout. 'I want to be angry with you!'

'Yes! Right! Shouting,' Leon calls, tightening his tie and rebuttoning his collar as though he's preparing himself.

'I am never going back to Justin!' I shout, and then, because of how good it feels, I try it again. 'I am never fucking going back to Justin!'

A car alarm goes off somewhere nearby, which I know is coincidental, but still feels pretty good – now all I need is a cat to yowl and a bunch of dustbins to fall over. I take a deep breath and open my mouth to keep yelling, then pause. Leon has a hand up.

'Can I say something?' he calls. 'I mean, shout something?'

A driver slows down as he passes, staring with interest at the pair of us bellowing at one another, two storeys apart. It occurs to me now that Leon has probably never shouted in the street before. I close my mouth, a little taken aback, then nod.

'I fucked up!' Leon yells. He clears his throat and tries a little louder. 'I got scared. I know it's no excuse, but all this is scary for me. The appeal. You, us. I'm not good when things are changing. I get . . .'

He flounders, as if he's run out of words, and something warm gives way in my chest.

'Squirrelly?' I offer.

In the light from the streetlamp I watch his lips move into a lopsided smile.

'Yeah. Good word.' He clears his throat again, moving closer to the balcony. 'Sometimes it feels easier to just be the way I was before you. Safer. But . . . look what you've been able to do. How brave you've been. And that's how I want to be. OK?'

I rest my hands on the railing and look down at him. 'You're doing a lot of talking down there, Leon Twomey,' I call.

'It seems in times of emergency I can be quite verbose!' he yells.

I laugh. 'Don't be doing *too* much changing, now. I like you as you are.'

He grins. He's dishevelled and shabbily handsome in his suit, and suddenly all I want to do is kiss him.

'Well, Tiffy Moore, I like you too.'

'Say again?' I call, cupping a hand around my ear.

'I really, really like you!' he bellows.

A window above me flies open with a clatter. 'Do you *mind*?' shouts the strange man from Flat 5. 'I'm trying to sleep up here! How am I supposed to get up in time to do my antigravity yoga if I'm kept up all night?'

'Antigravity yoga!' I mouth down at Leon, delighted. I've been wondering what he did every morning since the first day I moved in here!

'Don't let the fame go to your head, Leon,' warns the strange man from Flat 5, then he reaches to close the window again.

'Wait!' I call.

He looks down at me. 'Who are you?'

'I'm your other neighbour. Hello!'

'Oh, you're Leon's girlfriend?'

I hesitate, then grin. 'Yes,' I say firmly, and hear a little whoop from street level. 'And I have a question.'

He just stares at me with the air of a man waiting to see what a small child will do next.

'What do you do with all the bananas? You know – the bananas from the empty crates that live in your parking space?'

To my surprise, he breaks into a big, half-toothless smile. He looks quite friendly when he's smiling. 'I distil them! Lovely cider!'

And with that, he slams the window.

Leon and I look at each other and simultaneously burst out into giggles. Before long I am laughing so hard I've started to cry; I'm holding my stomach, ugly-laughing, gasping for breath and screwing my face up hard.

'Antigravity yoga!' I hear Leon whisper, his voice just carrying on a gap in the traffic noise. 'Banana cider!'

'I can't hear you,' I say, but I don't shout for fear of waking the ire of the strange man from Flat 5 again. 'Come closer.'

Leon looks around, and then backs up a few steps.

'Catch!' he calls in a stage whisper, and then he chucks the bouquet up to me. It soars lopsidedly through the air, shedding leaves and the odd chrysanthemum as it goes, but, with a dangerous lunge towards the railings and a squeaky sort of shriek, I manage to catch it.

By the time I've got a good hold on the flowers and laid them on the table, Leon has disappeared. I lean over the edge of the balcony in confusion.

'Where have you gone?' I call.

'Marco!' comes a voice from somewhere nearby.

'Polo?'

'Marco.'

'Polo! This is not helping!'

He's scaling the drainpipe. I burst out laughing again.

'What are you *doing*?'

'Getting closer!'

'I did not have you down as a drainpipe-climbing man,' I say, wincing as he reaches for another handhold and hauls himself up a little higher.

'Me neither,' he says, turning to look at me as he scrabbles about for a spot for his left foot. 'You clearly bring out the best in me.'

He's only a few feet away from me now; the drainpipe passes right up by our balcony, and he can almost reach our railings.

'Hey! Are those my munchies?' he says as he reaches an experimental hand up.

I just give him a look.

'. . . Yeah, fair enough,' he says. 'Give a fella a hand?'

'This is insane,' I tell him, but I move to help anyway.

Carefully, he lets one foot dangle, and then the other, until he's hanging by his hands from our balcony railings.

'Oh my God,' I say. It's almost too terrifying to look at, but I can't look away, specifically because then I won't be paying attention if he lets go, and that idea is much worse than watching him hanging there, scrabbling to find a foothold on the bottom edge of the railings.

He pulls himself up; I give him a hand with the last yank, my hand grasping his as he swings himself over.

'There!' he says, brushing himself down. He pauses, breathless, and looks at me.

'Hi,' I say, suddenly feeling a little shy in my over-the-top dress.

'I'm so sorry,' Leon says, opening his arms for a hug.

I lean into him. His suit smells of autumn, that outdoor-air smell that clings to your hair at this time of year. The rest of him smells of Leon, just the way I want it to, and as he pulls me close I shut my eyes and breathe him in, feeling the solid strength of his body against mine.

Mo appears in the doorway, fish and chips in a plastic *Something Fishy* bag in his hands. I didn't even hear him come in, and I jump a little, but with Leon's arms around me the idea of Justin turning up in the flat doesn't feel nearly so terrifying.

'Ah,' Mo says, seeing the pair of us. 'I'll take my fish and chips elsewhere, shall I?'

68

Leon

Me: It's probably not the right time.

Tiffy: I sincerely hope you're joking.

Me: Not joking, but definitely hoping you'll tell me I'm wrong.

Tiffy: You are wrong. Now is the perfect time. We are alone, in our flat, *together*. It literally does not get better than this.

We stare at each other. She's still wearing that incredible dress. Looks like it would tip off her shoulders to the floor with one tug. I'm desperate to try it. I resist, though – she says she's ready, but it's not been the sort of day for tear-my-clothes-off sex. Slow, lovely, clothes-staying-on-for-tantalisingly-long-time sex, maybe.

Tiffy: Bed?

That voice – exactly like Richie described it. Deep and sexy. Much sexier when it says things like 'bed', too.

We stand at the foot of the bed and turn to face one another again. I lean to take her face between my hands and kiss her. Feel her body melt against mine as we kiss, feel the tension leave her, and pull back to see her eyes have gone fiery behind the blue. The desire is instant, on the moment our lips touch, and it takes enormous effort just to rest my hands on her bare shoulders.

She reaches to loosen my tie and shrug off my jacket. Unbuttons my shirt slowly, kissing me as her fingers move. There's still air between us now, like we're keeping a respectful distance, despite the kissing.

Tiffy turns, holding her hair out of the way so I can unzip her dress. I take her hair into my hands instead, pulling a little as I twist the bunch around my wrist, and she moans. Can't handle that sound. Close that space between us, kissing along her shoulders, up her neck to where her hair meets her skin, pressing as close as I can until she shifts to loosen her own zip.

Tiffy: Leon. Focus. Dress.

I take the zip from between her fingers and pull it down slowly, slower than she wants. She wriggles, impatient. Backs up into me until my legs hit the bed and we're pressed close again, bare skin and silk.

Eventually the dress falls to the floor. It's almost cinematic – a shimmer of silk, then she's there, black underwear and nothing else. She turns in my arms, her eyes still fiery, and I hold her away to look at her.

Tiffy, smiling: You always do that.

Me: Do what?

Tiffy: Look at me like that. When I . . . take something off.

Me: Want to see everything. It's too important for rushing.

Tiffy quirks an eyebrow, unbearably sexy.

Tiffy: No rushing?

She traces her fingers along the top of my boxers. Dips her hand below it, a hair's breadth from where I want her.

Tiffy: You're going to regret saying that, Leon.

I'm already regretting, as soon as she says my name. Her fingers trace across my lower belly, and then, painfully slowly, reach for the buckle of my belt. After she's eased the zip down I step out of my suit trousers and kick off my socks, conscious of how her eyes follow me like a cat's. When I move to pull her close to me again she puts a firm hand on my chest.

Tiffy, throatily: Bed.

That air between us is back for an instant; we move automatically to our old sides of the bed. She's left, I'm right. We watch each other as we slide under the covers.

I lie sideways, looking at her. Her hair spreads across the pillow, and though she's under the duvet I can sense how bare she is, how much of her there is to touch. I place my hand in the space between us. She takes it, bridging the line we'd drawn back in February, and kisses my fingers, then slides them between her lips, and suddenly that space is gone and she's pressed up against me where she should be, skin on skin, not a fraction of an inch between us.

69

'You've seen me naked now. You've had your wicked way with me. And you're *still* looking at me like that.'

His smile drops into that gorgeous lopsided thing, the smile that got me all those weeks ago in Brighton.

'Tiffany Moore,' he says, 'I have every intention of continuing to look at you in this fashion for many moons to come.'

'Many moons!'

He nods solemnly.

'How very charming and ingeniously non-specific of you.'

'Well, something told me a suggestion of long-term commitment might have you running for the hills.'

I think about it, resettling my head against his chest. 'I see your point, but actually, it seems to have just made me feel curiously warm and fuzzy.'

He doesn't say anything, he just kisses the top of my head.

'Also I would not be capable of running non-stop to the nearest hill.'

'Herne Hill, maybe? You could take Herne Hill.'

'Well,' I say, turning on to my front and propping myself up on my elbows, 'I have no interest in running to Herne Hill. I like the many-moons plan. I think it's . . . hey, are you even listening to me?'

'Yes?' Leon tries, lifting his gaze. He smiles. 'Sorry. You have managed to distract me even from yourself.'

'And there was me thinking you were un-distractible.'

He kisses me, his hand moving to stroke rough circles on my breast. 'Sure. Un-distractible,' he says. 'And *you* are . . .'

I already can't think straight. 'Putty in your hands?'

'I was going to say, "excellently easy to distract".'

'I'm playing hard to get this time.'

He does something with his hand that nobody has ever done before. I have no idea what's happening but it seems to involve his thumb, my nipple, and about five thousand prickly hot licks of sensation.

'I'm reminding you of that in ten minutes' time,' Leon says, kissing his way down my neck.

'You're *smug.*'

'I'm happy.'

I pull away to look at him. I realise that my cheeks are starting to hurt, and I think it's genuinely from all the smiling. When I tell Rachel that, I know exactly what she'll do: stick her finger in her mouth and gag. But it's true – despite everything that's happened today, I am sickeningly, dizzyingly happy.

He raises his eyebrows at me. 'No witty comeback?'

I gasp as his fingers shift across my skin, tracing patterns I can't follow.

'I'm just working on one . . . Just give me . . . a minute . . .'

While Leon is in the shower, I write our to-do list for the next day and stick it to the fridge. It reads as follows.

1. *Try very hard not to think about the judges' verdict.*
2. *Get restraining order.*
3. *Talk to Mo and Gerty about, well, Mo and Gerty.*
4. *Buy milk.*

I fidget, waiting for him to appear, and then give up and reach for my phone. I'll just have to listen out for the shower.

'Hello?' comes Gerty's muffled voice down the line.

'Hi!'

'Oh thank God,' Gerty says, and I can almost hear her slumping back against the pillows again. 'You and Leon worked things out?'

'Yeah, we worked things out,' I tell her.

'Oh, and you slept with him?'

I grin. 'Your radar's back on.'

'So I haven't ruined everything?'

'You haven't ruined everything. Although, to be clear, it would have been Justin who ruined everything, not you.'

'God, you are feeling benevolent. Were you safe?'

'Yes, Mother, we were safe. Were you and Mo safe when you made up this morning?' I ask sweetly.

'Don't,' Gerty says. 'It's bad enough me thinking about Mo's penis, you shouldn't have to do it too.'

I laugh. 'Can we have coffee tomorrow, just the three of us? I want to hear about how you got together. Vaguely, and with no penis-related details.'

'And talk about how to get a restraining order?' Gerty suggests.

'Is that Tiffy?' I hear Mo say in the background.

'So sweet that he hears "restraining order" and thinks of me,' I say, heart sinking a little at the change of subject. 'But yeah. We should talk about that.'

'Do you feel safe?'

'Are we back on the contraception subject again?'

'Tiffy.' Gerty has never stood for my arts of deflection. 'Do you feel safe in the flat?'

'With Leon here, yeah.'

'OK. Good. But even so, we need to talk about getting an emergency injunction to cover you before the hearing.'

'An— wait, there's a hearing?'

'Let the poor woman think,' Mo says in the background. 'I'm glad you and Leon are good again, Tiffy!' he calls.

'Thanks, Mo.'

'Have I killed your buzz?' Gerty asks.

'A little. But it's all right. I've still got Rachel to call.'

'Yes, go discuss all the sordid details with Rachel,' Gerty says. 'Coffee tomorrow, text us where and when.'

'See you,' I say, hanging up and pausing to listen.

The shower is *still* on. I call Rachel.

'Sex?' she says when she answers the phone.

I laugh. 'No thanks, I'm taken.'

'I *knew* it! You guys made up?'

'And then some,' I say, in an exaggeratedly sexy sort of way.

'Details! Details!'

'I'll fill you in properly on Monday. But . . . I have discovered that my boobs have been underperforming for my entire adult life.'

'Ah yes,' Rachel says knowledgeably. 'A common problem. You know there are . . .'

'*Shh!*' I hiss. The shower's stopped. 'Got to go!'

'Don't leave me hanging like this! I was going to tell you all about nipples!'

'Leon is going to find it very weird that I have rung around my best friends after sex,' I whisper. 'It's early days. I still have to pretend to be normal.'

'Fine, but I'm scheduling in a two-hour meeting on Monday morning. Subject: Boobs 101.'

I hang up and a moment later Leon wanders in in his towel, hair smoothed back, shoulders gleaming with droplets, and pauses to examine my to-do list.

'Seems manageable,' he says, opening the door and reaching in for the orange juice. 'How're Gerty and Rachel?'

'What?'

He smiles at me over his shoulder. 'Do you want me to get back in? I figured I only needed to allow for two phone calls, since Gerty would be with Mo.'

I feel my cheeks flushing. 'Oh, I, uh . . .'

He leans over, orange juice in hand, and kisses me on the lips. 'Don't worry,' he says. 'I plan on remaining blissfully unaware of how much you overshare with Rachel.'

'When I'm finished filling her in she'll think you're a god amongst men,' I say, relaxing and reaching for the orange juice.

Leon winces. 'Will she be able to look me in the face again?'

'Sure. She'll probably opt for looking somewhere else instead, though.'

70

Leon

The weekend comes and goes in a blur of guilty pleasure. Tiffy barely leaves my arms, except to go for coffee with Gerty and Mo. Was right that we'd have a few triggers to work around; briefly lost her to a bad memory on Saturday morning, but am already learning how to help bring her back again. Is rather satisfying.

She's definitely more nervous about Justin than she's letting on – came up with elaborate heavy-milk-buying ruse to get me to come and meet her at the coffee place and walk her back here. The sooner we can get that restraining order sorted the better. I fixed a chain on the door while she was out, and mended the balcony door, just to be doing something.

Got Monday off, so walk Tiffy to the tube and then cook myself an elaborate fry-up involving black pudding and spinach.

Sitting still alone is not good. Odd – normally I'm all for lonesome sitting. But when Tiffy is out, I feel her absence like a missing tooth.

Eventually, after much pacing and not looking in the direction of my phone, I call my mother.

Mam: Leon? Sweetie? Are you OK?

Me: Hi, Mam. I'm fine. Sorry for walking out like that on Friday.

Mam: It's OK. We were all upset, and what with your new girlfriend marrying that other guy . . . Oh, Lee, you must be heartbroken!

Ah, of course – who would have filled Mam in?

Me: It was a misunderstanding. Tiffy has a, uh, bad-news sort of ex-boyfriend. That was him. She didn't actually say yes to marrying him, he just tried to force her into it.

Dramatic, soap-opera style gasp down the phone. I try very hard not to find it annoying.

Mam: Poor little thing!

Me: Yes, well, she's doing fine.

Mam: Have you gone after him?

Me: After him?

Mam: The ex! After what he's done to your Tiffy!

Me: . . . what are you suggesting, Mam?

I decide not to give her time to answer.

Me: We're looking into getting a restraining order.

Mam: Oh, sure, those are great.

Awkward pause. Why do I find these conversations so difficult?

Mam: Leon.

Wait. Fidget. Look at the floor.

Mam: Leon, I'm sure your Tiffy's nothing like me.

Me: What?

Mam: You were always a sweetheart about it, not like Richie with all his screaming and running off and all, but I know you hated the men I dated. I mean, I hated them too, but you hated them right from the start. I know I set a . . . I know I set a terrible example.

I feel deeply, profoundly uncomfortable.

Me: Mam, it's fine.

Mam: I really am getting sorted now, Lee.

Me: I know. And it wasn't your fault.

Mam: You know, I think I nearly believe that?

Pause. Think.

I nearly believe that too. Who'd have thought – you say something true enough times, you try hard enough, and maybe it sinks in.

Me: Love you, Mam.

Mam: Oh, sweetheart. I love you too. And we'll get our Richie back, and we'll look after him, won't we, like we always have?

Me: Exactly. Like always.

It's *still* Monday. Monday is interminable. I hate days off – what do people do on days off? I just keep thinking appeal, hospice, Justin, appeal, hospice, Justin. Even warm fuzzy Tiffy thoughts are struggling to keep me afloat now.

Me: Hi, Gerty, it's Leon.

Gerty: Leon, there is no news. The judges have not called us back for a verdict. If the judges call us back for a verdict, I will call you, and then you will know about it. You do not need to call me to check in.

Me: Right. Sure. Sorry.

Gerty, relenting: I suspect it will be tomorrow.

Me: Tomorrow.

Gerty: It's like today, but plus one.

Me: Today plus one. Yes.

Gerty: Don't you have a hobby or something?

Me: Not really. Sort of just work all the time, generally.

Gerty: Well, you live with Tiffy. There will be no shortage of hobby-related reading material. Go read a book about crochet or building things out of cardboard or whatever.

Me: Thanks, Gerty.

Gerty: You're welcome. And stop calling me, I am very busy.

She hangs up. It's still a little unnerving when she does that, no matter how many times you've endured it.

71

Tiffy

I can't believe Martin had the guts to come in to work. I always had him down as a coward, but actually, of the two of us, I seem the most nervous about facing him. It's like . . . talking to Justin by proxy. Which is frankly terrifying, no matter how much I tell Leon I'm feeling fine. Martin, on the other hand, is swanning about as usual, gloating about the success story of the party. I guess he probably doesn't know I know yet.

He's yet to mention the proposal, I notice. Nobody in the office has. Rachel put out the memo that I wasn't actually engaged, which has at least saved me a morning of warding off congratulations.

Rachel [10:06]: I could just walk over, kick him in the balls, and we'd be done with it.

Tiffany [10:07]: Tempting.

Tiffany [10:10]: I don't know why I'm being such a wuss. I had this conversation totally planned out in my head yesterday. Seriously, I had some *great* one-line putdowns cued up. And now they've just gone, and I feel a bit freaked out.

Rachel [10:11]: What would Someone Who Isn't Mo say, do you reckon?

Tiffany [10:14]: Lucie? She'd tell me it's natural to be freaked out after what happened on Friday, I guess. And that talking to Martin feels a bit like confronting Justin.

Rachel [10:15]: Right, I can see that, except . . . Martin is Martin. Weedy, petty, malicious Martin. Who kicks my chair and undermines you in meetings and kisses the head of PR's arse like it's Megan Fox's face.

Tiffany [10:16]: You're right. How can I possibly be afraid of Martin?

Rachel [10:17]: Want me to come with you?

Tiffany [10:19]: Is it pathetic if I say yes?

Rachel [10:20] It would make my day.

Tiffany [10:21]: Then yes. Please.

We wait until the morning team meeting is over. I grit my teeth through all the congratulations Martin gets for the party. A few curious glances are shot in my direction, but it's glossed over. I flush with shame anyway. I hate that everyone in this room knows that I have ex-boyfriend drama. I bet they're all concocting their own outlandish reasons why I am no longer engaged, and not one of them has come up with the truth.

Rachel grabs my hand and squeezes it tightly, then gives me a little shove in Martin's direction as he gathers up his notebook and papers.

'Martin, can we have a word?' I say.

'Not a great time, Tiffy,' he says, with the air of a very important person who rarely has time for spontaneous meetings.

'Martin, mate, either you step into this meeting room with us or we adopt *my* plan, which was kicking you in the balls right now in front of everyone,' Rachel says.

A flash of fear crosses his face, and my anxiety evaporates. Look at him. He suspects we know now, so he's back-peddling. Suddenly I can't wait to hear what crap he comes up with.

Rachel herds him into the only free meeting room with a

door and clicks it shut behind us. She leans back against it, arms folded.

'What's this about?' Martin asks.

'Why don't you hazard a guess, Martin?' I say. My voice comes out surprisingly light and pleasant.

'I really have no idea,' he blusters. 'Is there a problem?'

'If there is, how long will it be before Justin is informed of it?' I ask.

Martin meets my gaze. He looks like a cornered cat.

'I don't know what you . . .' he tries.

'Justin told me. He's fickle like that.'

Martin sags. 'Look, I was trying to help you out,' he says. 'He got in touch about our flat back in February, saying he was helping you look for a place, and made a deal with us so we could offer you our spare room for five hundred a month.'

Back in *February*? Bloody hell.

'How did he even know who you were?'

'We've been friends on Facebook for ages. I think he added me when you guys first got serious – at the time I figured he was checking out the guys you work with, you know, the protective type. But I posted the ad about the flat on there and that's how he got in touch.'

'How much did he offer you?'

'He said he'd pay the difference,' Martin says. 'Hana and I thought it was sweet of him.'

'Oh, that's Justin,' I say through gritted teeth.

'And then when you didn't take the room, he seemed so down. We'd got chatting when he popped around to discuss the arrangement, and then he asked if I could drop him a line every now and again, just letting him know how you are and what you're up to so he doesn't worry.'

'And that didn't strike you as, I don't know, *creepy*?' Rachel asks.

'No!' Martin shakes his head. 'It didn't seem creepy. And he wasn't paying me or anything – the only time I took money from him was to get Tasha Chai-Latte to come and film, OK?'

'You took *money* from him for stalking Tiffy?' Rachel says, visibly swelling with rage.

Martin cringes.

'Hang on.' I hold my hands up. 'Go back to the start. He asked you to let him know where I was every now and then. So that's how he knew I'd be at that book launch in Shoreditch, and how he knew I'd be on the cruise ship?'

'I suppose so,' Martin says. He shifts back and forth on his feet like a child who needs the toilet, and I find myself starting to feel a little sorry for him, which I immediately quash because the only thing getting me through this conversation is rage.

'And the trip to Wales for the shoot?' I say.

Martin visibly starts to sweat. 'I, ah, he rang me about that one after I texted him to say where you'd be . . .'

I twitch. It's so creepy I want to go and shower immediately.

'. . . and he asked about the guy you'd be bringing to help out with the modelling. I gave him the physical description you'd given me. He went all quiet, and sounded really upset. He told me how much he still loved you, and how he knew this guy and he was going to ruin everything . . .'

'So you spent the whole weekend running interference.'

'I thought I was helping!'

'Well, you sucked at it anyway, because we sneaked off and made out in the kitchen at three in the morning so HA!' I say.

'In danger of losing the higher ground, there, Tiffy,' Rachel says.

'Right, right. So, you debriefed Justin when we got back?'

'Yeah. He wasn't that happy with how I'd handled things. Suddenly I felt really bad, you know? I hadn't done enough.'

'Oh, this man is *good*,' Rachel says under her breath.

'Anyway, then he wanted to plan this big proposal. It was all very romantic.'

'Especially the part where he paid you to get Tasha Chai-Latte to film it,' I say.

'He said he wanted the whole world to see it!' Martin protests.

'He wanted *Leon* to see it. How much did that even cost? I should have known it couldn't have come out of the book's budget.'

'Fifteen thousand,' Martin says sheepishly. 'And two for me for organising.'

'Seventeen thousand pounds?!' Rachel shrieks. 'My God!'

'And a bit leftover, so I got Katherin that limo, in case it would persuade her to do that interview with Piers Morgan. I just . . . figured Justin must really love you,' Martin says.

'No, you didn't,' I tell him flatly. 'You didn't really care. You just wanted Justin to like you. He has that effect on a lot of people. Has he contacted you since he proposed to me?'

Martin shakes his head, looking nervous. 'I figured from the way you left the party that it hadn't exactly gone as he'd hoped. Do you think he'll be mad at me?'

'Do I think . . .' I take a deep breath. 'Martin. I do not care if Justin is mad at you. Soon, I will be taking Justin to court for harassment or stalking, once my lawyer has got around to figuring out which of those she likes better.'

Martin goes even paler than he usually is, which is saying something. I'm surprised I can't see the whiteboard through him.

'So you'd be prepared to testify?' I say briskly.

'What? No!'

'Why not?'

'Well, it's . . . this would be *very* embarrassing for me, and this is a really important time at work—'

'You are a very weak man, Martin,' I tell him.

He blinks. His lip shakes a little. 'I'll think about it,' he says eventually.

'Good. See you in court, Martin.'

I sweep out of the room with Rachel in tow, and as I head to my desk I feel exhilarated. Particularly as Rachel is quietly but unmistakably humming 'Eye of the Tiger' as we walk through the office.

The world seems like a slightly brighter place after the Martin showdown. I sit up taller and decide I'm not ashamed about what happened at the party. So my ex-boyfriend proposed to me and I said no – so what? Nothing wrong with that. In fact, Ruby gives me a silent high-five on my way to the bathroom mid-afternoon, and with Rachel sending me girl-power songs every fifteen minutes I start to feel quite . . . empowered about it all.

It takes enormous effort to concentrate on work, but in the end I manage it: I am researching a new trend in cupcake icing when I get the call. Almost instantly, I realise that I will always remember this website about icing-bag nozzles. It's that kind of call.

'Tiffy?' says Leon.

'Yeah?'

'Tiffy . . .'

'Leon, are you OK?' My heart is pounding.

'He's out.'

'He's . . .'

'Richie.'

'Oh my God. Say it again.'

'Richie is out. Not guilty.'

I let out a shriek that sends every single person in the office staring my way. I make a face and cover the phone for a moment.

'Friend won the lottery!' I mouth to Francine, the nearest nosy person, and let her trundle off to spread that particular piece of news. If I don't nip this in the bud they'll all think I'm engaged again.

'Leon, I don't even . . . I really thought it would be tomorrow!'

'So did I. So did Gerty.'

'So . . . is he just . . . out? In the world? God, I can't imagine Richie out in the world! What does he even look like, by the way?'

Leon laughs, and the sound makes my stomach flip. 'He'll be at our place tonight. You can finally meet him.'

'This is unbelievable.'

'I know. I can't actually . . . I keep thinking it's a dream.'

'I don't even know what to say. Where are you now?' I ask, bouncing in my chair.

'I'm at work.'

'Didn't you have the day off?'

'Didn't know what to do with myself. You want to come down here after you finish? No worries if it's too out of your way, I'll be home by seven, I just thought—'

'I'll be there at half five.'

'Actually, I should come meet you . . .'

'I can do it on my own. Really – I've had a good day, I can do it. See you at half five!'

72

Leon

Drift around wards, checking charts, giving fluids. Speak to patients and amaze myself by managing to sound normal and to talk about something other than the fact that my brother is finally coming home.

Home.

Richie is coming home.

Keep rearing away from the thought, the way I always had to – my mind pastes Richie back into my life, and then it jumps away as if it's touched something hot, because I'd never let myself finish that thought. It was too painful. Too hopeful.

Except now it's real. Will be real, in just a few hours' time.

He'll meet Tiffy. They'll talk just like they do on the phone only face to face, on my sofa. It's literally too good to be true. Until you remember that he should never have been in jail in the first place, of course, but even that thought can't kill the euphoria.

I'm in the hospice kitchen making tea when I hear my name, on repeat, very loudly and getting louder all the time.

Tiffy: Leon! Leon! Leon!

I turn around just in time. She piles into me, rain-wet hair, pink cheeks, big smile.

Me: Whoa!

Tiffy, very close to my ear: Leon Leon Leon!

Me: Ouch?

Tiffy: Sorry. Sorry. I just . . .

Me: Are you *crying*?

Tiffy: What? No.

Me: You are. You are incredible.

She blinks at me, surprised, eyes bright with happy tears.

Me: You've never even met Richie.

She links arms with me and spins me back to the kettle just as it boils.

Tiffy: Well, I've met *you*, and Richie's your little brother.

Me: Just to warn you, he's not that little.

Tiffy reaches for the mug cupboard and pulls out two, then rifles through the teabags and pours the kettle as if she's been in and out of this kitchen for years.

Tiffy: And anyway, I feel like I know Richie. We've talked tons of times. You don't have to meet face to face to know someone.

Me: Speaking of . . .

Tiffy: Where are we going?

Me: Just come on. I want to show you something.

Tiffy: Teas! Teas!

I pause and wait as she adds milk painstakingly slowly. She shoots a cheeky little glance over her shoulder; I immediately want to undress her.

Me: Are we ready?

Tiffy: OK. We're ready.

She hands me a mug and I take it, and the hand that offered it too. Almost everyone we pass along the corridor says, 'Oh, hi, Tiffy!' or 'You must be Tiffy!' or 'Oh my God Leon really *does* have a girlfriend!' but I am in too good a mood to find it annoying.

Tug Tiffy back as she goes to open the door to Coral Ward.

Me: Wait, just look through the window.

We both lean in.

Johnny White hasn't left his side since the weekend. Mr Prior is asleep, but still his papery, sun-blotched hand rests in Johnny White's palm. They've had three whole days together – more than JW could have hoped for.

Always worth walking through those doors.

Tiffy: Johnny White the Sixth was the real Johnny White? Is this literally the best day ever? Has there been some sort of announcement issued? An elixir in everyone's breakfast? A golden ticket in the cereal box?

I kiss her firmly on the mouth. Behind us, one of the junior doctors says to another junior doctor, 'Amazing – I always assumed Leon didn't like anyone who didn't have a terminal illness!'

Me: I think it's just a good day, Tiffy.

Tiffy: Well, I guess we are all overdue one.

73

Tiffy

'OK, how do I look?'

'Relax,' Leon says, lying back on the bed, one arm behind his head. 'Richie already loves you.'

'I'm meeting a member of your family!' I protest. 'I want to look good. I want to look . . . smart and beautiful and witty, and maybe to channel a bit of Sookie in the earlier series of *Gilmore Girls*?'

'I have no idea what you're talking about.'

I huff. 'Fine. Mo!'

'Yeah?' Mo calls from the living room.

'Can you tell me if this outfit makes me look cool and sophisticated or tired and mumsy, please?'

'If you're asking the question, lose the outfit,' Gerty calls.

I roll my eyes. 'I didn't ask you! You don't like any of my clothes anyway!'

'That's not true, I like some of them. Just not in the combinations you choose to adopt.'

'You look perfect,' Leon says, smiling up at me. His whole face looks different today, like someone flicked a switch back there that I didn't even know about, and now everything is brighter.

'No, Gerty's right,' I say, shrugging out of the wrap dress and reaching for my favourite green skinny jeans and a loose-knit jumper. 'I'm trying too hard.'

'You're trying just the right amount,' Leon tells me as I hop on one leg, pulling up the jeans.

'Is there any statement I could say this evening that you wouldn't automatically agree with?'

He narrows his eyes. 'A conundrum,' he says. 'The answer is no, but saying that would mean I'd contradict myself.'

'He agrees with everything I say, and he's so clever, too!' I crawl across the bed to straddle him and kiss him, letting my body melt against his. When I pull back to put my top on, he protests, holding me close, and I smile, swatting his hands. 'This outfit even you must admit is not appropriate,' I point out.

The buzzer for the building door goes off three times, and Leon jumps up so quickly that I'm almost thrown off the bed.

'Sorry!' he calls over his shoulder as he heads to the door. I hear Mo or Gerty lift the receiver to let Richie up into the building.

My stomach flips as I yank on the knitted jumper and run my fingers through my hair. I wait to hear Richie's voice at our front door, hanging back to give him and Leon the moment they've been waiting for.

Instead, I hear Justin.

'I want to talk to you,' he says.

'Oh. Hello, Justin,' Leon says.

At this point, I notice that I'm already hugging my arms close to myself and tucking my body in against the wardrobe so nobody who leans in to check the flat will see me in the bedroom doorway, and I suddenly feel like screaming. He does not get to come here and do this to me. I want him *gone*, really gone, not just out of my life, but out of my head as well. I am done with cowering behind doors and feeling frightened.

Well, I'm not, obviously, because you don't get over shit like this that quickly, but temporarily I am done with it and I'm going to make the most of this current wave of crazy angry confidence. I round the corner.

Justin is squared up in the doorway, broad, muscled and visibly angry.

'Justin,' I say, moving to stand beside Leon until I'm only a few feet from Justin. I rest a hand on the door, ready to slam it closed.

'I'm here to talk to Leon,' Justin says shortly. He doesn't even look at me.

I recoil despite myself, my confidence instantly drained.

'If you're thinking of proposing to me too, the answer's no,' Leon says pleasantly. Justin's hands bunch into fists at the joke; he starts forward, body coiled, eyes flashing. I flinch.

'Watch that foot, Justin,' says Gerty sharply from behind me. 'If it gets any closer to being inside this flat, your lawyer will have a lot more to talk to me about.'

I watch the thought hit Justin, see him re-evaluate. 'I don't remember your friends being this interfering when we were together, Tiffy.' He snarls the words, and my heart thunders in my chest. I think he's drunk. That is not good.

'Oh, we wanted to be,' Mo says.

I take a deep, shaky breath. 'Leaving me was the best thing you ever did for me, Justin,' I say, doing my best to stand as squarely as he is on the other side of the threshold. 'We're done. That's it. Leave me alone.'

'We're not done,' he says impatiently.

'I'm getting a restraining order,' I choke out before he can say anything else.

'No you're not,' Justin scoffs. 'Come on, Tiffy. Stop being such a child.'

I slam the door in his face so hard everyone jumps, including me.

'Fuck!' Justin yells from the other side of the door, and then there's the sound of a fist being rammed into the door and the handle rattles hard.

I let out a little whimper despite myself, backing away. I can't believe I just slammed the door in Justin's face.

'Police,' Leon mouths at us.

Gerty flicks on her phone and dials the number, reaching with her other hand to clasp my fingers tightly. Mo is at my side in moments, standing at my shoulder as I watch Leon slip the new chain across and lean his weight against the door.

'This is so fucking crazy,' I say weakly. 'I can't believe this is happening.'

'Let me *in*!' Justin roars from the other side of the door.

'Police,' Gerty says into the phone.

Justin hammers with both fists on the door, and I think of how he pressed his finger against the buzzer all those weeks ago, how he wouldn't let up until Leon opened the door. I swallow. Each bang seems louder than the last, until I feel like they're right in my ears. My eyes are wet with tears; Gerty and Mo are all but holding me up. So much for being done with feeling frightened. As Justin roars and rages on the other side of the door, I watch Leon, face drawn and serious, as he looks around for other ways to barricade us in. To my left, Gerty answers questions on the phone.

And then, suddenly, all the madness and noise stops. Leon gives us a questioning look, then checks the handle – the door is still locked.

'Why's he stopped?' I ask, gripping Gerty's hand so tightly I can see my fingers going white.

'He's stopped banging on the door,' Gerty says into the phone. I hear a tinny voice respond. 'She says he may be trying to find a way to break down the door. We should move into another room. Step away from the door, Leon.'

'Wait,' Leon whispers, leaning to listen to what's going on outside in the corridor.

His face breaks into a grim smile. He gestures for all of us to come closer; tentative, with shaking knees, I let Mo lead me to the door. Gerty stays back, speaking quietly into her phone.

'You'd love prison, Justin,' says a warm voice on the other side of the door, with an unmistakable accent. 'Really. Loads of guys like you there.'

'Richie!' I whisper. 'But – he mustn't . . .' We've just got Richie *out* of prison. A fight with Justin will not end well for Richie, even if in the short term it means getting him out of the building.

'Good point,' Leon says, eyes widening. He reaches to unlock the door, and I notice his hands are shaking slightly too. From the sounds of their voices Richie seems close to the door, and Justin further away, towards the stairs, but still. I scrub my eyes fiercely. I don't want Justin to know what he does to me. I don't want to give him that power.

Justin makes a rush for us as Leon swings the door open, but Richie pushes him nonchalantly, and Justin stumbles into the wall, swearing, as Richie steps inside and Leon pulls the door closed quickly behind him. It's over in a couple of seconds; I barely have time to process the look on Justin's face as he lunged towards me, desperate to force his way in through the door. What's *happened* to him? He was never like this. Never violent. His anger was always tightly controlled; his punishments were clever and cruel. This is messy and desperate.

'Nice bloke, your ex,' Richie says to me with a wink. 'Serious case of the red mist going on out there. He's going to regret punching the door so much in the morning, I can tell you that.' He chucks a spare set of keys down on the sideboard – that must've been how he got inside the building without buzzing.

I blink a few times and take a proper look at him. No wonder Justin went quiet when Richie turned up in the corridor. He is *enormous*. Six foot four at least, and the kind of muscular that only happens when you've got nothing to do with your time except exercise. His black hair is buzzed short, and there are strings of tattoos down his forearms and one curling up his neck, peeking up under the collar of his court shirt – along with a cord necklace, which I'd bet matches Leon's one. He has the same thoughtful, deep-brown eyes as Leon, too, though they're a little more mischievous-looking.

'The police will be here in ten minutes,' Gerty says calmly. 'Hello, Richie. How are you?'

'Devastated to discover you have a boyfriend,' Richie says, clapping Mo on the shoulder with a grin. I could swear Mo sinks an inch or so deeper into the carpet. 'I owe you a dinner out!'

'Oh, don't let me stop you,' Mo says hastily.

Richie hugs Leon so hard I can hear their bodies colliding. 'Don't worry about that prick outside,' he says to both of us as he pulls back. Through the door, Justin throws something; whatever it is smashes against the wall and I wince bodily. I'm shaking all over – I have been since I first heard his voice – but Richie just gives me a friendly unquestioning smile, and it's like an echo of Leon's lopsided grin – a warm smile, the sort that makes you instantly feel more comfortable. 'Pleasure to meet you in the flesh, Tiffy,' he says. 'And thank you for looking after my brother.'

'I'm not sure this counts,' I manage, pointing to the door as it shakes in the frame.

Richie waves a hand. 'Honestly. If he gets in here, he'll have to deal with me and Leon – and . . . sorry, man, we've not been introduced.'

'Mo,' Mo says, looking very much like the sort of man who sits in a chair and talks for a living, and has suddenly stumbled upon a scenario where this might put him at a disadvantage.

'And me and Tiffy,' Gerty says sharply. 'What is this, medieval times? I bet I'm better at punching people than Leon.'

'Let me the fuck *in*!' Justin roars through the door.

'He's drunk, too,' Richie says cheerfully, and then he lifts our armchair and shuffles us out of the way so he can dump it in front of the door. 'There. No use us hanging about in here now, is there? Lee, balcony still where it used to be?'

'Umm, yeah,' Leon begins, looking slightly shell-shocked. He's moved around to take Mo's place beside me, and I lean into his hand as he strokes my back, letting that sensation pull me together again. Every time Justin yells or thumps the door I flinch, but now that Richie is here weightlifting furniture, and Leon has his arm around me, the flinching is no longer accompanied by totally blinding fear and panic. Which is nice.

Richie ushers us all out on to the balcony and shuts the glass door behind us. We barely fit; Gerty curls into Mo in one corner, and I fit myself in front of Leon in the other, leaving Richie most of the space, which is exactly what he needs. He breathes in and out deeply, beaming at the view from the balcony.

'London!' he says, spreading his arms out wide. 'I've missed this. Look at it!'

Behind, back in the flat, the door thuds over and over again. Leon pulls me tightly against him, burying his face in my hair and breathing warm, calming breaths against my neck.

'And we even get a great vantage point for when the police turn up,' Richie tells us, turning to wink at me. 'Didn't think I'd be seeing them again so soon, I have to say.'

'Sorry,' I say, miserable.

'Don't be,' Richie says firmly, in the same moment that Leon shakes his head into my hair, and Mo says, 'Don't apologise, Tiffy.' Even Gerty rolls her eyes in an affectionate sort of way.

I look around at them all, huddled out on the balcony with me. It helps – only a little, but I don't think anything could help more than a little right now. I close my eyes and lean into Leon, concentrating on my breathing the way Lucie told me to, and try to imagine that the banging noise is just that – a noise and nothing more. It'll stop eventually. Breathing deeply, Leon's arms around me, I feel a new sort of certainty settle. Even Justin cannot last for ever.

74

Leon

The police take Justin away. He's basically foaming at the mouth.
One look at him and you can see what's happened: a man who has
always had control has lost it. But, as Gerty points out, this will at
least make the restraining order more straightforward.

We inspect the door. He's dented the wood with kicking, and
chipped off chunks of paint with his fists. There's blood too. Tiffy
turns her head aside as she sees it. I wonder what it can possibly feel
like, seeing that, after everything she's been through. Knowing that
she loved this man, and that he loved her, in his way.

Thank God for Richie. The man radiates joy tonight. As Richie
launches into yet another story about the lengths 'Bozo' would go to
for first dibs on the weights machine, I watch the colour come back
into Tiffy's cheeks, her shoulders lift, her lips slide into a smile. Better.
I'm relaxing too, with each sign of improvement. I couldn't bear to
see her that way, jumping, crying, afraid. Even watching Justin carted
away by a police officer wasn't enough to ease the rage.

But now, three hours post-police drama, we're scattered around
the living room just like I imagined it. If you squinted, you'd hardly
even notice that the evening I've been looking forward to for the last
year was briefly interrupted by an irate man attempting to break and
enter. Tiffy and I have taken the beanbag. Gerty has pride of place

on the sofa, leaning up against Mo. Richie is ruling the room from the armchair, which hasn't quite returned to its usual place since it was used to blockade the door, so now just sits somewhere between the hall and the living room.

Richie: I called it. Just saying.

Gerty: When, though? Because I called it too, but I don't believe you could have called it right from the—

Richie: From the moment Leon told me he was getting some woman in to sleep in his bed when he wasn't there.

Gerty: Not possible.

Richie, expansively: Come on! You can't share a bed and not share anything else, if you know what I'm saying.

Gerty: What about Kay?

Richie waves a hand dismissively.

Richie: Eh. Kay.

Tiffy: Come on now—

Richie: Oh, she was sweet enough, but she was never right for Leon.

Me, to Gerty and Mo: What *did* you think at the start?

Tiffy: Oh, God, don't ask them that.

Gerty, promptly: We thought it was a dreadful idea.

Mo: Bear in mind you could have been anyone.

Gerty: You could have been a disgusting pervert, for instance.

Richie roars with laughter and reaches for another beer. He has not had a drink in eleven months. I consider telling him that his tolerance will not be what it once was, and then contemplate how Richie will react to this suggestion (almost certainly drinking more to prove me wrong) and decide not to bother.

Mo: We even tried to give Tiffy money so she wouldn't do it—

Gerty: Which she said no to, obviously—

Mo: And then it became clear that this was part of getting away from Justin, and we just had to let her do it her own way.

Richie: And you didn't see it coming? Tiffy and Leon?

Mo: No. To be honest, I didn't think Tiffy would have been ready for a guy like Leon yet.

Me: What sort of guy is that?

Richie: Fiendishly handsome?

Me: Gangly? Big-eared?

Tiffy, wryly: He means a non-psychotic guy.

Mo: Well, yes. It takes a long time to escape from relationships like that—

Gerty, briskly: No Justin-talk.

Mo: Sorry. I was just trying to say how well Tiffy did. How hard it must have been for her to break out of that before it became a pattern.

Richie and I exchange glances. I think of Mam.

Gerty rolls her eyes.

Gerty: Honestly. Dating a counsellor is dreadful, by the way. This man has no concept of light-heartedness.

Tiffy: And you do?

Gerty pokes Tiffy with one foot in response.

Tiffy, grabbing the foot and pulling: Anyway, this is really what we want to hear about. You never did fill me in properly about you and Mo! How? When? Excluding penis-related details, as discussed.

Richie: Eh?

Me: Just go with it. It's best to let the in-jokes wash over you. Eventually they start to make some sort of sense.

Tiffy: Just wait until you meet Rachel. Queen of the inappropriate in-joke.

Richie: Sounds like my kind of girl.

Tiffy looks thoughtful at this, and I raise my eyebrows warningly at her. Bad idea to match-make Richie. As much as I love my brother, he does tend to break hearts.

Me: Go on, Mo, Gerty?

Mo, to Gerty: You tell it.

Tiffy: No, no, Gerty's version will sound like something she'd read out in court – Mo, give us the romantic version of events, please.

Mo gives a sidelong look at Gerty to see how cross that's made her; thankfully she's three glasses of wine in, and has just settled for glaring at Tiffy.

Mo: Well, it started when we moved in together.

Gerty: Although Mo was in love with me for ages before that, apparently.

Mo shoots her a mildly irritated look.

Mo: And Gerty has liked me for over a year, she said.

Gerty: In confidence!

Tiffy makes an impatient noise in the back of her throat.

Tiffy: And you're all loved-up? Sleeping in the same bed and all that?

There is a shifty sort of silence; Mo looks at his feet, uncomfortable. Tiffy smiles up at Gerty, reaching to squeeze her hand.

Richie: Well. Looks like I need to find myself a flatmate, don't I?

SEPTEMBER

Two years later

EPILOGUE

Tiffy

There's a note on the door of the flat when I get home from work. This isn't unusual per se, but as a rule Leon and I try to confine our notes to the inside of our home. You know, so as not to advertise our peculiarities to the neighbours.

Warning: imminent romantic gesture.
   (Be assured, it is very low-budget.)

I snort with laughter and turn the key in the door. The flat looks the same as ever: cluttered, multi-coloured, and just like home. It's only when I go to chuck my bag down in the spot by the door that I see the next note on the wall there.

Step one: dress for adventure. Please assemble outfit from wardrobe.

I stare at the note, bemused. This is eccentric even by Leon's standards. I shrug off my coat and scarf and leave them on the back of the sofa. (It's a sofa-bed these days, which only just fits in our living room even once we sacrificed the telly, but no place will be home unless there's a bed for Richie to stay in.)

On the inside of the wardrobe door, the note is folded over and stuck with Sellotape. On the outside, it reads:

Are you wearing something Tiffy-ish yet?

I mean, I am, but it's a work outfit so there's more of a nod to normality than usual (i.e. I've tried to make sure at least two items are not direct opposites on a colour wheel). I riffle through the wardrobe looking for something suitably 'adventurous', whatever that means.

I pause on the blue and white dress I bought a couple of years back. The one Leon calls my Famous Five dress. It's a little impractical for a cold day, but with my thick grey tights and the yellow mac from Help the Aged . . .

Once dressed, I unstick the note from the wardrobe door and read the message inside.

Hello again. Bet you look beautiful.
You need to collect a few more things before you set off adventuring, if you don't mind. The first is in the spot where we first met. (Don't worry. It's waterproof.)

I grin and head off to the bathroom, moving more quickly now. What exactly is Leon up to here? Where am I supposed to be going? Now I've got my adventuring dress on, the end-of-day work slump has lifted – probably Leon knew I'd feel better with something colourful on – and a fizzing giddy feeling is growing in my stomach.

There's an envelope hanging from the showerhead, carefully and very thoroughly wrapped in clingfilm. On the outside of it is a Post-it note.

Don't read me yet, please.
The next thing you need is in the spot where we first kissed. (Well, not

exact spot as sofa has changed. But please overlook this for the sake of the romantic gesture.)

It's another envelope, tucked between the sofa cushions. This one reads *open me*, so I do as I'm told. Inside there is a train ticket from London to Brighton. I frown, completely flummoxed. Why Brighton? We've not been since before we were together, back when we were looking for Johnny White.

The note behind the ticket reads:

The last thing you need is with Bobby for safekeeping. He's expecting you.

Bobby is the man we once knew as Strange Man in Flat 5. He's a firm friend now, and has thankfully realised you cannot make cider from a banana and moved on to more conventional apple cider. It is very tasty and invariably gives me an extremely bad hangover.

I take the stairs two at a time and knock on his door, shifting impatiently from one foot to the other.

He answers in his favourite tracksuit bottoms (I sewed the hole up for him last year. It was getting indecent. I patched it up with a few inches of pink gingham I had lying about, though, so he definitely doesn't look *less* strange).

'Tiffany!' he says, then shuffles off immediately, leaving me in the doorway. I crane my neck. Eventually he re-emerges holding a small cardboard box with a Post-it note stuck to it. 'There you are!' he says, and beams. 'Off you go!'

'Thanks?' I say, examining the box.

Once you get to Brighton, head to the beach by the pier. You'll know the spot when you see it.

*

It's the most excruciating train journey I've ever taken. I'm itching with curiosity. I can hardly sit still. By the time I get to Brighton it's dark, but it's easy to find my way to the seafront; I walk so fast towards the pier that I'm almost jogging, which is something I only do in extreme circumstances, so I really must be excited.

I see what Leon means as soon as I get there. I couldn't miss the spot.

There's an armchair on the pebbles, thirty yards or so from the sea. It's covered in multi-coloured blankets and strewn around it amongst the rocks there are dozens of tealights.

I cover my mouth. My heart's thumping triple-speed. As I make my way over, stumbling on the pebbles, I look around for Leon, but there's no sign of him – the whole beach is deserted.

The note on the chair is weighed down with a large shell.

Sit, wrap up warm, and open the envelope when you're ready. Then the box.

I rip off the clingfilm and tear the envelope open as soon as I'm sitting down. To my surprise it's in Gerty's handwriting.

Dear Tiffy,

Leon has enlisted me and Mo to help with this madcap scheme because he says you value our opinions. I suspect it is actually because he is a little afraid and doesn't want to do this on his own. I won't hold that against him, though. A bit of humility is good in a man.

Tiffany, we have never seen you as happy as you are now. That came from you – you built that happiness for yourself. But there is no shame in saying that Leon helped.

We love him, Tiffy. He is good for you in the way that only a very good man could be.

It's your decision, of course, but he wanted you to know: he has our blessing.

Mo and Gerty x

P.S. He asked me to say that he didn't ask your father's permission, on account of that being 'a bit archaic and patriarchal', but he feels 'fairly confident Brian is on board'.

I laugh shakily, wiping the tears from my cheeks. My dad *adores* Leon. He's been calling him 'son' in embarrassing social situations for at least a year.

My hands tremble as I reach for the cardboard box. The Sellotape takes an agonisingly long time to work loose, but when I manage to get the lid off I start crying in earnest.

There's a ring inside, nestled in a bundle of rainbow-coloured tissue paper. It's beautiful: vintage, a little wonky, with an oval amber stone in its centre.

And there's one last note.

Tiffany Rose Moore of Flat 3, Madeira House, Stockwell,
Would you like to be my wife?

Take some time to think about it. If you want to see me, I'm at the Bunny Hop Inn, room 6.

I love you x

When I can, when my shoulders have stopped shaking from happy-crying and I've wiped my eyes and blown my nose, I head back up the beach to the warm light of the Bunny Hop Inn.

He's waiting for me on the bed in room 6, sitting cross-legged, fidgeting. He's nervous.

I take him at a flying leap. He lets out a happy sort of *oof* as I roll him back on to the bed.

'Yes?' he asks after a moment, pushing back my hair so he can look at my face.

'Leon Twomey,' I say, 'only you could find a method of proposing that means you don't actually have to be there.' I kiss him hard. 'Yes. Absolutely definitely yes.'

'Sure?' he asks, pulling back to look at me properly.

'I'm sure.'

'Really?'

'Really really.'

'It's not too much?'

'Bloody hell, Leon!' I say, exasperated. I look around and reach for the hotel stationery on the bedside table.

YES. I would love to marry you.

Now it's written down it is unequivocal and probably binding in a court of law although check with Gerty because I literally just made that up right now. xx

I wave the note under his nose so he gets the gist, then tuck it in the pocket of his shirt. He pulls me in and presses his lips to the crown of my head. I can feel that he's doing one of those lopsided smiles, and it all seems too good, as if we can't possibly deserve it, as if we're taking too much happiness and not leaving enough for everyone else.

'This is the bit where we turn on the telly and a nuclear war has started,' I say, twisting to lie down next to him.

He smiles. 'I don't think so. Doesn't work that way. Sometimes the happy thing just happens.'

'Look at you, with all the sunny optimism! That's usually my jam, not yours.'

'Not sure what's brought it on. Recent betrothal? Bright future? Love-of-life in arms? Hard to say.'

I chuckle, nuzzling into his chest, breathing him in. 'You smell like home,' I tell him after a moment.

'You *are* home,' he says simply. 'The bed, the flat . . .'

He pauses, the way he always does when he's looking for enough words for something big.

'It was never home until you were there, Tiffy.'

ACKNOWLEDGEMENTS

My first thank you goes to the incredible Tanera Simons, who gave Tiffy and Leon a shot before anybody else, and then kickstarted the craziest, most wonderful time in my life. The next thanks go to Mary Darby, Emma Winter, Kristina Egan and Sheila David for everything they've done to take *The Flatshare* out into the world. I am so lucky to have found a home at Darley Anderson Agency.

You might not believe it after reading about Martin and Hana, but in reality the publishing industry is full of truly wonderful people – and the bunch who've brought *The Flatshare* into the world are particularly incredible. To Emily Yau and Christine Kopprasch, my amazing editors at Quercus and Flatiron, thank you for making this an infinitely better book with your edits, and for the countless other things you've done to make *The Flatshare* the best it can be. Thank you to Jon Butler, Cassie Browne, Bethan Ferguson, Hannah Robinson, Hannah Winter, Charlotte Webb, Rita Winter, and all the other lovely Quercus people who have done so much to make this book a reality. And thank you to my wonderful international publishers for believing in Tiffy and Leon so early and making this experience even more of a dream.

My next thank yous go to: Libby, for being my muse; Nups, for being my rock, battling toilet mushrooms with me, and telling me (very emphatically) that this book was The One; and Pooja, for being a wonderful, generous friend and giving so much time and expertise. Thank you to Gabby, Helen, Gary, Holly and Rhys for the early reads, the bright ideas and the messy nights at Adventure Bar, and to Rebecca Lewis-Oakes, for giving me a good talking-to when I was too scared to send out queries. Sorry for keeping the name Justin, Rebecca!

To my wonderful family, and the fabulous Hodgson family too, thank you for always being there for me, and for getting so excited about all things Flatshare. Mum and Dad, thank you for your endless support and for filling my life with love and books. And Tom, thank you for your help with the details. I love you and think of you every day.

To Sam. This is the hardest part, because I feel just like Leon – I can't find the words for something this big. Thank you for your patience, your kindness, your puppy-like enthusiasm for everything life brings, and thank you for reading and laughing when it mattered most. This book is dedicated to you, but really it's not just for you, it's because of you, too.

Finally, a huge thank you to every reader who picked up this book, and to every bookseller who helped make that moment happen. I'm so grateful and honoured you did.

Read on for an exclusive extract of the heart-warming
new novel by Beth O'Leary,

THE
SWITCH

1

Leena

'I think we should swap,' I tell Bee, bobbing up into a half-squat so I can talk to her over my computer screen. 'I'm bricking it. You should do the start and I'll do the end and that way by the time it gets to me I'll be less, you know . . .' I wave my hands to convey my mental state.

'You'll be less jazz hands?' Bee says, tilting her head to the side.

'Come on. Please.'

'Leena. My dear friend. My guiding light. My favourite pain in the ass. You are much better than I am at starting presentations and we are not switching the order of things now, ten minutes before our key client stakeholder update, just like we didn't switch at the last programme board, or the one before that, or the one before that, because that would be madness and quite frankly I haven't a bloody clue what's on the opening slides.'

I sag back into my chair. 'Right. Yes.' I bob up again. 'Only this time I am *really* feeling–'

'Mmm,' Bee says, not looking up from her screen. 'Absolutely. Worst ever. Shaking, sweaty palms, the lot. Only as soon as you get in there you'll be as charming and brilliant as you always are and nobody will notice a thing.'

'But what if I . . .'

'You won't.'

'Bee, I really think—'

'I know you do.'

'But this time—'

'Only eight minutes to go, Leena. Try that breathing thing.'

'What breathing thing?'

Bee pauses. 'You know. Breathing?'

'Oh, just normal breathing? I thought you meant some kind of meditative technique.'

She snorts at that. There's a pause. 'You've coped with way worse than this hundreds of times over, Leena,' she says.

I wince, cupping my coffee mug between my palms. The fear sits in the hollow at the base of my ribs, so real it feels almost physical – a stone, a knot, something you could cut out with a knife.

'I know,' I say. 'I know I have.'

'You just need to get your mojo back,' Bee tells me. 'And the only way to do that is to stay in the ring. OK? Come on. You are Leena Cotton, youngest senior consultant in the business, Selmount Consulting's one-to-watch 2020. And . . .' she lowers her voice, 'soon – one day – co-director of our own business. Yes?'

Yes. Only I don't *feel* like that Leena Cotton.

Bee's watching me now, her pencilled brows drawn tight with concern. I close my eyes and try to will the fear away, and for a moment it works: I feel a flicker of the person I was a year and a half ago, the person who would have flown through a presentation like this without letting it touch her.

'You ready, Bee, Leena?' the CEO's assistant calls as he makes his way across the Upgo office floor.

I stand and my head lurches; a wave of nausea hits. I grab the edge of the desk. Shit. *This* is new.

'You OK?' Bee whispers.

I swallow and press my hands into the desk until my wrists start to ache. For a moment I don't think I can do it – I just don't have it in me, God, I'm so *tired* – but then, at last, the grit kicks in.

'Absolutely,' I say. 'Let's do this.'

Half an hour has passed. That's not an especially long time, really. You can't watch a whole episode of *Buffy* in that time, or . . . or bake a large potato. But you *can* totally destroy your career.

I've been so afraid this was coming. For over a year now I've been fumbling my way through work, making absent-minded slip-ups and oversights, the sort of stuff I just don't *do*. It's like since Carla died I've switched my writing hand, and suddenly I'm doing everything with my left, not my right. But I've been trying so hard and I've been pushing through and I really thought I was getting there.

Evidently not.

I honestly thought I was going to die in that meeting. I've had a panic attack once before, when I was at university, but it wasn't as bad as this one. I have never felt so far out of my own control. It was like the fear got loose: it wasn't a tight knot any more, it had tendrils, and they were tightening at my wrists and ankles and clawing at my throat. My heart was beating so fast – faster and faster – until it didn't feel like part of my body any longer, it felt like a vicious thrashing little bird trapped against my ribcage.

Getting *one* of the revenue numbers wrong would have been forgivable. But once that happened the nausea came, and I got another wrong, and another, and then my breathing started coming too fast and my brain was filled with . . . not fog, more like bright, bright light. Too bright to see anything by.

So when Bee stepped in and said *allow me to*–

Then when someone else said *come on this is laughable*–

And when the CEO of Upgo Finance said *I think we've seen enough here don't you*–

I was already gone. Doubled over, gasping, quite sure I was about to die.

'You're OK,' Bee's saying now, her hands gripping mine tightly. We're tucked away in one of the phone-call booths in the corner of the Upgo offices; Bee led me here, still hyperventilating, sweating through my shirt. 'I've got you. You're OK.'

Each breath is coming in a jagged gasp. 'I just lost Selmount the Upgo contract, didn't I?' I manage.

'Rebecca's on a call with the CEO now. I'm sure it'll be fine. Come on, just breathe.'

'Leena?' someone calls. 'Leena, are you all right?'

I keep my eyes closed. Maybe, if I stay like this, that will not be the voice of my boss's assistant.

'Leena? It's Ceci, Rebecca's assistant?'

Gah. How did she *get* here so fast? The Upgo offices are at least a twenty-minute tube ride from Selmount headquarters.

'Oh, Leena, what a mess!' Ceci says. She joins us in the booth and rubs my shoulder in nagging circles. 'You poor little thing. That's right, cry it out.'

I'm not crying, actually. I breathe out slowly and look at Ceci, who is wearing a couture dress and a particularly gleeful smile, and remind myself for the hundredth time how important it is to support other women in business. I really, fully believe that. It's a code I live by, and it's how I plan to make it to the top.

But women are still, you know, people. And some people are just awful.

'What can we do you for, Ceci?' Bee asks, through gritted teeth.

'Rebecca sent me to check you're all right,' she says. 'You know. After your . . .' She waggles her fingers. 'Your *little wobble*.' Her iPhone buzzes. 'Oh! There's an email from her now.'

Bee and I wait, shoulders tensed. Ceci reads the email inhumanely slowly.

'Well?' Bee says.

'Hmm?' says Ceci.

'Rebecca. What did she say? Has she . . . Did I lose us the contract?' I manage.

Ceci tilts her head, eyes still on her phone. We wait. I can feel the tide of panic waiting too, ready to drag me back under.

'Rebecca's sorted it – isn't she a marvel? They're retaining Selmount on this project and have been *very* understanding, considering,' Ceci says eventually, with a little smile. 'She wants to see you now, so you'd better hotfoot it back over to the office, don't you think?'

'Where?' I manage. 'Where does she want to meet me?'

'Hmm? Oh, Room 5c, in HR.'

Of course. Where else would she go to fire me?

Rebecca and I are sitting opposite each other. Judy from HR is beside her. I am not taking it as a good sign that Judy is on her side of the table, not mine.

Rebecca pushes her hair back from her face and looks at me with pained sympathy, which can only be a very bad sign. This is Rebecca, queen of tough love, master of the mid-meeting put-down. She once told me that expecting the impossible is the only real route to the best results.

Basically, if she's being nice to me, that means she's given up.

'Leena,' Rebecca begins. 'Are you all right?'

'Yes, of course, I'm absolutely fine,' I say. 'Please, Rebecca, let me explain. What happened in that meeting was . . .' I trail off, because Rebecca is waving her hand and frowning.

'Look, Leena, I know you play the part very well, and God knows I love you for it.' She glances at Judy. 'I mean, Selmount values your . . . gritty, can-do attitude. But let's cut the crap. You look fuck-ing terrible.'

Judy coughs quietly.

'That is, we wonder if you are a little run-down,' Rebecca says, without missing a beat. 'We've just checked your records – do you know when you last took a holiday?'

'Is that a . . . trick question?'

'Yes, yes it is, Leena, because for the last year you have not taken *any annual leave.*' Rebecca glares at Judy. 'Something which, by the way, should not be possible.'

'I told you,' Judy hisses, 'I don't know how she slipped through the net!'

I know how I slipped through the net. Human Resources talk the talk about making sure staff take their allotted annual leave, but all they actually do is send you an email twice a year telling you how many days you have left and saying something encouraging about 'wellness' and 'our holistic approach' and 'taking things offline to maximise your potential'.

'Really, Rebecca, I'm absolutely fine. I'm very sorry that my – that I disrupted the meeting this morning, but if you'll let me . . .'

More frowning and hand-waving.

'Leena, I'm sorry. I know it's been an impossibly tough time for you. This project is an incredibly high-stress one, and I've been feeling for a while that we didn't do right by you when we staffed you on it. I know I'm usually taking the piss when I say this sort of thing, but your well-being genuinely matters to me, all right? So I've talked to the partners, and we're taking you off the Upgo project.'

I shiver all of a sudden, a ridiculous, over-the-top shake, my body reminding me that I am still not in control. I open my mouth to speak, but Rebecca gets there first.

'And we've decided not to staff you on any projects for the next two months,' she goes on. 'Treat it as a sabbatical. Two months' holiday. You are not allowed back in Selmount headquarters until you are rested and relaxed and look less like someone who's spent a year in a war zone. OK?'

'That's not necessary,' I say. 'Rebecca, please. Give me a chance to prove that I—'

'This is a fucking gift, Leena,' Rebecca says with exasperation. 'Paid leave! Two months!'

'I don't want it. I want to work.'

'*Really?* Because your face is saying you want to *sleep*. Do you think I don't know you've been working until two in the morning every day this week?'

'I'm sorry. I know I should be able to keep to regular working hours – there have just been a few—'

'I'm not criticising you for how you manage your workload, I'm asking *when you ever bloody rest*, woman.'

Judy lets out a little string of quiet coughs at that. Rebecca shoots her an irritated look.

'A week,' I say desperately. 'I'll take a week off, get some rest, then when I come back I'll—'

'Two. Months. Off. That's it. This isn't a negotiation, Leena. You need this. Don't make me set HR on you to prove it.' This is said with a dismissive head-jerk in Judy's direction. Judy draws her chin in as though someone's clapped loudly in her face, perhaps, or flicked her on the forehead.

I can feel my breathing speeding up again. Yes, I've been struggling a little, but I can't take two months off. I can't. Selmount is all about reputation – if I step out of the game for eight whole weeks after that Upgo meeting, I'll be a laughing stock.

'Nothing is going to change in eight weeks,' Rebecca tells me. 'OK? We'll still be here when you get back. And you'll still be Leena Cotton, youngest senior, hardest worker, smartest cookie.' Rebecca looks at me intently. 'We all need a break sometimes. Even you.'

I walk out of the meeting feeling sick. I thought they'd try to fire me – I had all these lines prepared about unfair dismissal. But . . . a sabbatical?

'Well?' Bee says, appearing so close in front of me I have to stumble to a stop. 'I was lurking,' she explains. 'What did Rebecca say?'

'She said I . . . have to go on holiday.'

Bee blinks at me for a moment. 'Let's take an early lunch.'

As we dodge tourists and businessmen on our way down Commercial Street, my phone rings in my hand. I look at the screen and falter, almost running into a man with an e-cig hanging out of his mouth like a pipe.

Bee glances at the phone screen over my shoulder. 'You don't have to answer right now. You can let it ring out.'

My finger hovers over the green icon on the screen. I bash shoulders with a passing man in a suit; he tuts as I go buffeting across the pavement, and Bee has to steady me.

'What would you tell me to do if I was in this position right now?' Bee tries.

I answer the call. Bee sighs and pulls open the door to Watson's Café, our usual haunt for the rare, special occasions when we leave the Selmount offices for a meal.

'Hi, Mum,' I say.

'Leena, hi!'

I wince. She's all breezy and faux casual, like she's practised the greeting before making the call.

'I want to talk to you about hypnotherapy,' she says.

I sit down opposite Bee. 'What?'

'Hypnotherapy,' Mum repeats, with slightly less confidence this time. 'Have you heard of it? There's someone who does it over in Leeds, and I think it could be really good for us, Leena, and I thought perhaps we could go together, next time you're up visiting?'

'I don't need hypnotherapy, Mum.'

'It's not hypnotising people like Derren Brown does or anything, it's . . .'

'I don't need hypnotherapy, Mum.' It comes out sharply; I can hear her smarting in the silence that follows. I close my eyes, steadying my breathing again. 'You're welcome to try it, but I'm fine.'

'I just think – maybe, maybe it'd be good for us to do something together, not necessarily therapy, but . . .'

I notice she's dropped the 'hypno'. I smooth back my hair, the familiar stiff stickiness of hairspray under my fingers, and avoid Bee's gaze across the table.

'I think we should try talking maybe somewhere where . . . hurtful things can't be said. Positive dialogue only.'

Behind the conversation I can feel the presence of Mum's latest self-help book. It's in the careful use of the passive voice, the measured tone, the *positive dialogue* and *hurtful things*. But when it makes me waver, when it makes me want to say, *Yes, Mum, whatever would make you feel better*, I think of the choice my mother helped Carla to make. How she let my sister choose to end treatment, to – to give up.

I'm not sure even the Derren Brown kind of hypnotherapy could help me deal with that.

'I'll think about it,' I say. 'Goodbye, Mum.'

'Bye, Leena.'

Bee watches me across the table, letting me regroup. 'OK?' she says eventually. Bee's been on the Upgo project with me for the last year – she's seen me through every day since Carla died. She knows as much about my relationship with my mum as my boyfriend does, if not more – I only get to see Ethan at the weekends and the odd midweek evening if we can both get away from work on time, whereas Bee and I are together about sixteen hours a day.

I rub my eyes hard; my hands come away grainy with mascara. I must look an absolute state. 'You were right. I shouldn't have taken the call. I handled that all wrong.'

'Sounded like you did pretty well to me,' Bee says.

'Please, talk to me about something else. Something that isn't my family. Or work. Or anything else similarly disastrous. Tell me about your date last night.'

'If you want non-disastrous, you're going to need to pick another topic,' Bee says, settling back in her chair.

'Oh no, not good?' I ask.

I'm blinking back tears, but Bee kindly ploughs on, pretending not to notice.

'Nope. Odious. I knew it was a no as soon as he leaned in to kiss me on the cheek and all I could smell was the foisty, mouldy man-towel he must've used to wash his face.'

That works – it's gross enough to startle me back to the present. 'Eww,' I say.

'He had this massive globule of sleepy dust in the corner of his eye too. Like eye snot.'

'Oh, Bee . . .' I'm trying to find the right way to tell her to stop giving up on people so quickly, but my powers of pep-talking seem to have deserted me, and in any case, that towel thing really is quite disgusting.

'I am on the brink of giving up and facing an eternity as a single mother,' Bee says, trying to catch the waiter's eye. 'I've come to the decision that dating is genuinely worse than loneliness. At least when you're alone there's no hope, right?'

'No hope?'

'Yeah. No hope. Lovely. We all know where we stand – alone, as we entered the world, so we shall leave it, et cetera, et cetera . . . Whereas dating, dating is *full* of hope. In fact, dating is really one long, painful exercise in discovering how disappointing other humans are. Every time you start to believe you've found a good, kind man . . .' She wiggles her fingers. 'Out come the mummy issues and the fragile egos and the weird cheese fetishes.'

The waiter finally looks our way. 'The usual?' he calls across the café.

'Yup! Extra syrup on her pancakes,' Bee calls back, pointing at me.

'Did you say *cheese* fetishes?' I ask.

'Let's just say I've seen some photos that've really put me off brie.'

'Brie?' I say, horrified. 'But – oh, God, brie is so delicious! How could anyone corrupt brie?'

Bee pats my hand. 'I suspect you'll never have to find out, my friend. In fact, yes, if I'm supposed to be cheering you up, why aren't we talking about *your* ever-so-perfect love life? Surely the countdown's on for Ethan to pop the question.' She catches my expression. 'No? Don't want to talk about that either?'

'I've just got . . .' I flap my hand, eyes pricking again. 'A big wave of the horror. Oh, God. Oh God, oh God.'

'Which life crisis are you oh-godding about, just so I know?' Bee asks.

'Work.' I press my knuckles against my eyes until it hurts. 'I can't believe they're not staffing me for two whole months. It's like a . . . like a mini firing.'

'Actually,' Bee says, and her tone makes me move my hands and open my eyes, 'it's a two-month holiday.'

'Yes, but . . .'

'Leena, I love you, and I know you've got a lot of shit going on right now, but please try to see that this could be a good thing? Because it's going to be quite hard to continue loving you if you're going to spend the next eight weeks complaining about getting two months' paid leave.'

'Oh, I . . .'

'You could go to Bali! Or explore the Amazon rainforest! Or sail around the world!' She raises her eyebrows. 'Do you know what I'd give to have that kind of freedom?'

I swallow. 'Yes. Right. Sorry, Bee.'

'You're all right. I know this is about more than time off work for you. Just spare a thought for those of us who spend our allotted holiday at dinosaur museums full of nine-year-olds, yeah?'

I breathe in and out slowly, trying to let that sink in. 'Thank you,' I say, as the waiter approaches our table. 'I needed to hear that.'

Bee smiles at me, then looks down at her plate. 'You know,' she says casually, 'you *could* use the time off to get back to our business plan.'

I wince. Bee and I have been planning on setting up our own consultancy firm for a couple of years – we were almost ready to go when Carla got sick. Now, things have kind of . . . stalled a little.

'Yes!' I say, as cheerily as I can manage. 'Absolutely.'

Bee raises an eyebrow. I sag.

'I'm so sorry, Bee. I want to, I really do, it just feels . . . impossible, now. How are we going to launch our own business when I'm finding it so hard just holding down my job at Selmount?'

Bee chews a mouthful of pancake and looks thoughtful. 'OK,' she says. 'Your confidence has taken a hit lately, I get it. I can wait. But even if you don't use this time to work on the business plan, you should use it to work on *you*. My Leena Cotton doesn't talk about "holding down a job" like that's the best she can do, and she definitely doesn't use the word "impossible". And I want my Leena Cotton back. So,' she points her fork at me, 'you've got two months to find her for me.'

'And how am I doing that?'

Bee shrugs. '"Finding yourself" isn't really my forte. I'm just doing strategy here – you're on deliverables.'

That gets a laugh out of me. 'Thank you, Bee,' I say suddenly, reaching to clutch her hand. 'You're so great. Really. You're phenomenal.'

'Mmm, well. Tell that to the single men of London, my friend,' she says, giving my hand a pat and then picking up her fork again.

2

Eileen

It's been four lovely long months since my husband made off with the instructor from our dance class, and until this very moment I haven't missed him once.

I stare at the jar on the sideboard with my eyes narrowed. My wrist is still singing with pain from a quarter of an hour trying to wrench off the lid, but I'm not giving up. Some women live alone all their lives and *they* eat food out of jars.

I give the jar a good glare and myself a good talking-to. I am a seventy-nine-year-old woman. I have given birth. I have chained myself to a bulldozer to save a forest. I have stood up to Betsy about the new parking rules on Lower Lane.

I can open this wretched jar of pasta sauce.

Dec eyes me from the windowsill as I rummage through the drawer of kitchen implements in search of something that'll do the job of my increasingly useless fingers.

'You think I'm a daft old woman, don't you?' I say to the cat.

Dec swishes his tail. It's a sardonic swish. *All humans are daft*, that swish says. *You should take a leaf out of my book. I have my jars opened for me.*

'Well, just be grateful your tea for tonight is in a pouch,' I tell him, waggling a spaghetti spoon his way. I don't even like cats. It was Wade's idea to get kittens last year, but he lost interest in Ant and Dec when he found Miss Cha-Cha-Cha and decided that Hamleigh was too small for him, and that only old people keep cats. *You can keep them both*, he said, with an air of great magnanimity. *They suit your lifestyle better.*

Smug sod. He's older than me, anyway – eighty-one come September. And as for my lifestyle ... Well. Just you wait and see, Wade Cotton. Just you bloody wait and see.

'Things are going to be changing around here, Declan,' I tell the cat, my fingers closing around the bread knife in the back of the drawer. Dec gives a slow, unimpressed blink, then his eyes widen and he swishes out of the window as I lift the knife with both hands to stab the lid of the jar. I let out a little *ha!* as I pierce it; it takes me a few stabs, like an amateur murderer in an Agatha Christie play, but this time when I twist the lid it turns easily. I hum to myself as I triumphantly empty the contents into the pan.

There. Once the sauce has warmed through and the pasta's cooked, I settle back down at the dining-room table with my tea and examine my list.

Basil Wallingham

Pros:
- Lives just down the road – not far to walk
- Own teeth
- Still got enough oomph in him to chase squirrels off birdfeeders

Cons:
- Tremendous bore
- Always wearing tweed
- Might well be a fascist

Mr Rogers

Pros:

- Only 67
- Full head of hair (very impressive)
- Dances like Pasha off of *Strictly* (even more impressive)
- Polite to everyone, even Basil (most impressive of all)

Cons:

- Highly religious man. *Very* pious. Likely to be dull in bed?
- Only visits Hamleigh once a month
- Shown no signs of interest in anyone except Jesus

Dr Piotr Nowak

Pros:

- Polish. How exciting!
- Doctor. Useful for ailments
- Very interesting to talk to and exceptional at Scrabble

Cons:

- Rather too young for me (59)
- Almost certainly still in love with ex-wife
- Looks a bit like Wade (not his fault but off-putting)

I chew slowly and pick up my pen. I've been ignoring this thought all day, but ... I really ought to list *all* the unattached gentlemen of the right age. After all, I've put Basil on there, haven't I?

Arnold Macintyre

Pros:

- Lives next door
- Appropriate age (72)

Cons:

- Odious human being
- Poisoned my rabbit (as yet unproven, granted, but I know he did)
- Cut back my tree full of birds' nests
- Sucks all joy from the world
- Probably feasts on kittens for breakfast
- Likely descended from ogres
- Hates me almost as much as I hate him

I cross out *likely descended from ogres* after a moment, because I ought not to bring his parents into it – they might have been perfectly nice for all I know. But I'm leaving the part about kittens.

There. A complete list. I tilt my head, but it looks just as bleak from that angle as it does straight on. I have to face the truth: pickings are very slim in Hamleigh-in-Harksdale, population one hundred and sixty-eight. If I want to find love at this stage of my life, I need to be looking further afield. Over to Tauntingham, for instance. There's at least two hundred people in Tauntingham, and it's only thirty minutes on the bus.

The telephone rings; I get to the living room just in time.

'Hello?'

'Grandma? It's Leena.'

I beam. 'Hold on, let me get myself sat down.'

I settle back into my favourite armchair, the green one with the rose pattern. This phone call is the best part of any day. Even when it was bitterly sad, when all we talked about was Carla's death – or anything but that, because that felt too painful – even then, these calls with Leena kept me going.

'How are you, love?' I ask Leena.

'I'm fine, how are you?'

I narrow my eyes. 'You're not fine.'

'I know, it just came out, sorry. Like when someone sneezes and you say "bless you".' I hear her swallow. 'Grandma, I had this – I had a panic attack at work. They've sent me off on a two-month sabbatical.'

'Oh, Leena!' I press my hand to my heart. 'But it's no bad thing that you're getting some time off,' I say quickly. 'A little break from it all will do you good.'

'They're side-lining me. I've been off my game, Grandma.'

'Well, that's understandable, given . . .'

'No,' she says, and her voice catches, 'it's not. God, I – I promised Carla, I told her I wouldn't let it hold me back, losing her, and she always said – she said she was so proud, but now I've . . .'

She's crying. My hand grips at my cardigan, like Ant or Dec's paws when they're sitting in my lap. Even as a child, Leena hardly ever cried. Not like Carla. When Carla was upset, she would throw her arms in the air, the very picture of misery, like a melodramatic actress in a play – it was hard not to laugh. But Leena would just frown and dip her head, looking up at you reproachfully through those long, dark eyelashes.

'Come on, love. Carla would have wanted you to take holidays,' I tell her.

'I know I should be thinking of it as a holiday, but I can't. It's just . . . I hate that I messed up.' This is muffled, as if she's speaking into her hands.

I take off my glasses and rub the bridge of my nose. 'You didn't *mess up*, love. You're stressed, that's what it is. Why don't you come up and stay this weekend? Everything looks better over a mug of hot chocolate, and we can talk properly, and you can have a little break from it all, up here in Hamleigh . . .'

There's a long silence.

'You haven't been to visit for an awfully long time,' I say tentatively.

'I know. I'm really sorry, Grandma.'

'Oh, that's all right. You came up when Wade left, I was ever so grateful for that. And I'm very lucky to have a granddaughter who calls me so often.'

'But I know chatting over the phone isn't the same. And it's not that I . . . You know I really would love to see you.'

No mention of her mother. Before Carla's death, Leena would have come up to see Marian once a month at least. When will this end, this miserable feud between them? I'm so careful never to mention it – I don't want to interfere, it's not my place. But . . .

'Did your mother call you?'

Another long silence. 'Yes.'

'About . . .' What was it she'd settled on in the end? 'Hyper-therapy?'

'Hypnotherapy.'

'Ah, yes.'

Leena says nothing. She's so *steely*, our Leena. How will the two of them ever get through this when they're both so bloody stubborn?

'Right. I'll stay out of it,' I say into the silence.

'I'm sorry, Grandma. I know it's hard for you.'

'No, no, don't worry about me. But will you think about coming up here at the weekend? It's hard to help from so far away, love.'

I hear her sniff. 'Do you know what, Grandma, I will come. I've been meaning to, and – and I really would love to see you.'

'There!' I beam. 'It'll be lovely. I'll make you one of your favourites for tea and clue you in on all the village gossip. Roland's on a diet, you know. And Betsy tried to dye her hair, but it went wrong, and I had to drive her to the hairdresser's with a tea towel on her head.'

Leena snorts with laughter. 'Thanks, Grandma,' she says after a moment. 'You always know how to make me feel better.'

'That's what Eileens do,' I say. 'They look after each other.' I used to say that to her as a child – Leena's full name is Eileen too. Marian named her after me when we all thought I was dying after a bad bout of pneumonia back in the early nineties; when we realised I wasn't at death's door after all it got very confusing, and so Leena became Leena.

'Love you, Grandma,' she says.

'You too, love.'

After she hangs up the telephone, I realise I've not told her about my new project. I wince. I promised myself I would tell her the next time she called. It's not that I'm embarrassed to be looking for love, exactly. But young people tend to find old people wanting to fall in love rather funny. Not unkindly, just without thinking, the way you laugh at children behaving like grown-ups, or husbands trying to do the weekly shop.

I make my way back to the dining room and, when I get there, I look down at my sad little list of eligible Hamleigh men. It all feels rather small now. My thoughts are full of Carla. I try to think of other things – Basil's tweed jackets, Piotr's ex-wife – but it's no use, so I settle down and let myself remember.

I think of Carla as a little girl, with a mass of curls and scuffed knees, clutching her sister's hand. I think of her as the young woman in a washed-out Greenpeace T-shirt, too thin, but grinning, full of fire. And then I think of the Carla who lay in Marian's front room. Gaunt and drawn and fighting the cancer with all she had left.

I shouldn't paint her that way, as if she looked weak – she was still so Carla, still fiery. Even on Leena's last visit, just days before she died, Carla would take no nonsense from her big sister.

She was in her special hospital bed, brought into Marian's living room one evening by a group of gentle NHS staff, who put it up with astonishing efficiency and cleared out before I could make them so much as a cup of tea. Marian and I were standing in the doorway. Leena was beside the bed, in the armchair we'd moved there once and never shifted back. The living room didn't centre around the television any more, but around that bed, with its magnolia-cream bars on each side of the mattress, and that grey remote control, always lost under the blankets, for adjusting the bed's height and shifting Carla when she wanted to sit up.

'You're incredible,' Leena was telling her sister, her eyes bright with tears. 'I think you're – you're incredible, and so brave, and . . .'

Carla reached out, faster than I'd thought she could, now, and poked her sister in the arm.

'Stop it. You'd never say that sort of thing if I wasn't dying,' she said. Even with her voice thin and dry, you could hear the humour. 'You're way nicer to me these days. It's weird. I miss you telling me off for wasting my life away.'

Leena winced. 'I didn't . . .'

'Leena, it's fine, I'm teasing.'

Leena shifted uncomfortably in the armchair, and Carla raised her eyes upwards, as if to say, *Oh, for heaven's sake*. I'd grown used to her face without eyebrows by then, but I remember how strange it had looked at first – stranger, in some ways, than the loss of her long brown curls.

'Fine, fine. I'll be serious,' she said.

She glanced at me and Marian, and then reached for Leena's hand, her fingers too pale against Leena's tanned skin.

'All right? Serious face on.' Carla closed her eyes for a moment. 'There is some stuff I've wanted to say, you know. Serious stuff.' She opened her eyes then, fixing her gaze on Leena. 'You remember when we went camping together that summer when you were back from uni, and you told me how you thought management consultancy was the way to change the world, and I laughed? And then we argued about capitalism?'

'I remember,' Leena said.

'I shouldn't have laughed.' Carla swallowed; pain touched her features, a tightening around the eyes, a quiver of her dry lips. 'I should have listened and told you I was proud. You're shaping the world, in a way - you're making it better, and the world needs people like you. I want you to kick out all the stuffy old men and I want you to run the show. Launch that business. Help people. And promise me you won't let losing me hold you back.'

Leena was crying, then, her shoulders hunched and shaking. Carla shook her head.

'Leena, stop it, would you? Jesus, this is what comes of being serious! Do I have to poke you again?'

'No,' Leena said, laughing through her tears. 'No, please don't. It actually kind of hurt.'

'Well. Just know that any time you let an opportunity slip, any time you wonder if you can really do it, any time you think about giving up on *anything* that you want . . . I'll be poking you from the afterlife.'

And that was Carla Cotton for you.

She was fierce, and she was silly, and she knew we couldn't manage without her.

3

Leena

I wake up at six twenty-two, twenty-two minutes after my usual alarm, and sit bolt upright with a gasp. I think the reason I'm freaked out is the strange silence, the absence of my phone alarm's horrendous cheery beeping. It takes me a while to remember that I'm not late – I do not have to get up and go to the office. I am actually not *allowed* to go back to the office.

I slump back against the pillow as the horror and the shame resettle. I slept terribly, stuck in a loop of remembering that meeting, never less than half-awake, and then, when I did fall asleep, I dreamt of Carla, one of the last nights I spent at Mum's house, how I'd crawled into the bed and held Carla against me, her frail body tucked to mine like a child's. She'd elbowed me off, after a bit. *Stop getting the pillow all wet*, she'd told me, but then she'd kissed me on the cheek and sent me off to make midnight hot chocolate, and we'd talked for a while, giggling in the dark like we were kids again.

I haven't dreamt of Carla for a good few months. Now, awake, reliving that dream, I miss my sister so much I cry out with a little, strangled *Oh God*, remembering the gutting sucker-punches of grief that floored me in those first few months, feeling them again for a heart-splitting instant and wondering how I survived that time at all.

This is bad. I need to move. A run. That'll sort me out. I throw on the Lululemon leggings Ethan got me for my birthday, and an old T-shirt, and head out the door. I run through the streets of Shoreditch until dark bricks and street art give way to the repurposed warehouses of Clerkenwell, the shuttered bars and restaurants on Upper Street, the leafy affluence of Islington, until I'm dripping with sweat and all I can think about is the inch of pavement in my eyeline. The next step, next step, next step.

When I get back, Martha's in the kitchen, attempting to wedge her very pregnant body into one of the ridiculous art deco breakfast stools she chose for the flat. Her dark-brown hair is in pigtails; Martha always looks young, she's got one of those faces, but add the pigtails and she looks like she should not legally be bearing a child.

I offer her an arm to lean on as she clambers up, but she waves me away.

'That's a very lovely gesture,' she says, 'but you are far too sweaty to be touching other people, my sweet.'

I wipe my face with the bottom of my T-shirt and head to the sink for a glass of water. 'We need proper chairs,' I tell her over my shoulder.

'No we do not! These are *perfect*,' Martha tells me, wriggling backwards to try to fit her bottom into the seat.

I roll my eyes.

Martha is a high-end interior designer. The work is flashy, exhausting and irregular; her clients are nightmarishly picky, always ringing her out-of-hours to have lengthy breakdowns about curtain fabrics. But the upside is that she gets discount on designer furniture, and she has dotted our flat with an assortment of very stylish things that either serve no purpose – the W-shaped vase on the windowsill, the cast-iron lamp that barely emits the faintest glow when turned on – or actively don't fulfil their intended function: the breakfast stools you can hardly sit on, the coffee table with the convex surface.

Still, it seems to make her happy, and I'm so rarely in the flat it doesn't bother me much. I should never have let Martha talk me into renting this place with her, really, but the novelty of living in an old printworks was too good to resist when I was new to London. Now this is just a very expensive space in which I can collapse into bed, and I don't notice that what we're doing is, apparently, 'artisan warehouse living'. When Martha leaves I really should talk to Fitz about the two of us moving somewhere more reasonable. Aside from the weird old cat lady next door, everyone who lives in this building seems to have a hipster beard or a start-up; I'm not sure Shoreditch is where we belong.

'You manage to speak to Yaz last night?' I ask, getting myself another glass of water.

Yaz is Martha's girlfriend, currently touring a play out in America for six months. Yaz and Martha's relationship causes me high levels of vicarious stress. Everything seems to involve incredibly complex logistics. They're always in different time zones and sending one another important documents transatlantically and making crucial life decisions on WhatsApp calls with really patchy signal. This current situation is an excellent example of their style: Yaz will be returning in eight weeks' time, taking possession of a house (which has yet to be bought) and moving her pregnant girlfriend into it before the baby is scheduled to come a few days later. I'm sweating again just thinking about it all.

'Yeah, Yaz is good,' Martha says, idly rubbing her bump. 'Talking at four hundred miles an hour about Chekhov and baseball games. You know, Yaz-like.' Her fond smile stretches as she yawns expansively. 'She's getting skinny, though. She needs a good meal.'

I suppress a smile. Martha may not be a mother yet, but she's been mothering everyone within reach for as long as I've known her. Feeding people up is one of her favourite forms of benevolent attack. She also keeps insisting on bringing friends from her Pilates class around for tea in the blatant hope that they might make an honest man of Fitz, our other flatmate.

Speaking of Fitz – I check the time on my fitbit. He's on his fourth new job of the year; he really shouldn't be late for this one.

'Is Fitz up yet?' I ask.

He wanders in on cue, pushing up his collar to put on a tie. As per usual, his facial hair looks like it was cut against a ruler – I've lived with him for three years and am still no closer to understanding how he achieves this. Fitz always looks so misleadingly *together*. His life is in a permanent state of disarray, but his socks are always perfectly ironed. (In his defence, they *are* always on show – he wears his trousers an inch too short – and they are more interesting than the average person's socks. He has one pair covered in a SpongeBob SquarePants motif, another speckled like a Van Gogh painting, and his favourite pair are his 'political socks', which say 'Brexit is bollocks' around the ankle.)

'I'm up. Question is, why are *you* up, holidayer?' Fitz asks, finishing off knotting his skinny tie.

'Oh, Leena,' Martha says. 'I'm sorry, I'd totally forgotten you weren't going to work this morning.' Her eyes are wide with sympathy. 'How're you feeling?'

'Miserable,' I confess. 'And then angry with myself for being miserable, because who feels miserable when they've been given a paid two-month holiday? But I keep reliving the moment in that meeting. Then all I want to do is curl up in the foetal position.'

'The foetal position is not as static as people think,' Martha says, grimacing and rubbing the side of her belly. 'But yeah, that's totally natural, sweetheart. You need to rest – that's what your body is telling you. And you need to forgive yourself. You just made a little mistake.'

'Leena's never made one of those before,' Fitz says, heading for the smoothie maker. 'Give her time to adjust.'

I scowl. 'I've made mistakes.'

'Oh, please, Little Miss Perfect. Name one,' Fitz says, winking over his shoulder.

Martha clocks my irritated expression and reaches to give my arm a squeeze, then remembers how sweaty I am and pats me gently on the shoulder instead.

'Do you have plans for your weekend?' she asks me.

'I'm going up to Hamleigh, actually,' I say, glancing at my phone. I'm expecting a text from Ethan – he had to work late last night, but I'm hoping he's free this evening. I need one of his hugs, the really gorgeous long ones where I tuck my face into his neck and he wraps me right up.

'Yeah?' Fitz says, making a face. 'Going back up north to see your mum – *that's* what you want to do right now?'

'Fitz!' Martha chides. 'I think that's a great idea, Leena. Seeing your granny will make you feel so much better, and you don't have to spend any time with your mum if you don't feel ready. Is Ethan going with you?'

'Probably not – he's on that project in Swindon. The delivery deadline's next Thursday – he's in the office all hours.'

Fitz gives the smoothie machine a rather pointed whir at that. He doesn't need to say anything: I know he thinks Ethan and I don't prioritise each other enough. It's true we don't see each other as much as we'd like to – we may work for the same company, but we're always staffed on different projects, usually in different godforsaken industrial parks. But that's part of why Ethan is so amazing. He gets how important work is. When Carla died and I was struggling so much to stay afloat, it was Ethan who kept me focused on my job, reminding me what I loved about it, pushing me to keep moving forward so I didn't have the chance to sink.

Only now I don't have any work to keep me going, not for the next eight weeks. Two enormous months gape ahead of me, unfilled. As I think of all those hours of stillness and quiet and time to think, the bottom seems to drop out of my stomach. I need a purpose, a project, *something*. If I don't keep moving those waters will close over my head, and the very thought of that makes my skin prickle with panic.

I check the time on my phone. Ethan's over an hour and a half late – he probably got cornered by a partner as he was leaving work. I've been cleaning the flat all afternoon, and finished up in time for his arrival, but now an extra two hours have passed, during which I've been pulling out furniture and dusting chair legs and doing the sort of excessive cleaning that gets you a spot on a Channel Four documentary.

When I finally hear his key in the door I wriggle my way out from underneath the sofa and brush down my gigantic cleaning-day sweatshirt. It's a *Buffy* one: the front is a big picture of her face, doing her best kick-ass expression. (Most of my clothes that aren't suits are gigantic nerdy jumpers. I may not have much time to indulge in cult telly shows these days, but I can still show my loyalties – and frankly it's the only kind of fashion I consider worth spending money on.)

Ethan does a dramatic gasp as he enters the room, spinning on his heels at the transformation. It *does* look great. We keep the place fairly tidy anyway, but now it's sparkling.

'I should've known you couldn't even manage one day off without some sort of frenzied activity,' Ethan says, swooping in to kiss me. He smells of rich, citrussy cologne and his nose is cold from the chilly March rain. 'The place looks great. Fancy doing mine next?'

I swat him on the arm and he laughs, tossing his dark hair back from his forehead with his trademark lopsided flick. He bends down and kisses me again, and I feel a flash of envy as I sense how buzzed he is from work. I miss that feeling.

'Sorry I'm late,' he says, moving away and heading for the kitchen. 'Li took me aside to talk through the R&D numbers for the Webster review and you know what he's like, can't take a hint for love nor money. How are you holding up, angel?' he calls over his shoulder.

My stomach twists. *How are you holding up, angel?* Ethan used to say that to me on the phone each night, when Carla was barely holding on; he'd say it on my doorstep, turning up just when I needed him, with a bottle of wine and a hug; he said it as I wobbled my way to the front at Carla's funeral, gripping his hand so tightly it must have hurt. I couldn't have got through it all without him. I'm not sure how you can ever be grateful enough for someone leading you through the darkest time in your life.

'I'm . . . OK,' I say.

Ethan comes back in, his socked feet looking a little incongruous with his business suit. 'I think this is a good thing,' he says, 'the time off.'

'You do?' I ask, sinking down on the sofa. He settles in beside me, pulling my legs over his.

'Absolutely. And you can keep your hand in anyway – you're always welcome to chip in on my projects, you know that, and I can drop in with Rebecca how much you're helping me out, so she knows you're not losing your edge while you're away.'

I sit up a little straighter. 'Really?'

'Of course.' He kisses me. 'You know I've got your back.'

I shift so I can look at him properly: his fine, expressive mouth, that silky dark hair, the little string of freckles above his high cheek-bones. He's so beautiful, and he's here, right now, when I need him most. I am beyond lucky to have found this man.

He leans to the side to grab his laptop bag, slung down by the sofa arm. 'Want to run through tomorrow's slide deck with me? For the Webster review?'

I hesitate, but he's already flicking the laptop open, settling it across my legs, and so I lean back and listen as he starts talking, and I realise he's right – this is helping. Like this, with Ethan, hearing his soft, low voice talk revenue and projections, I almost feel like myself.